A *Regency* Collection

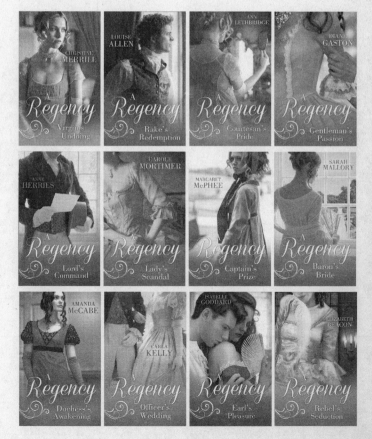

CHRISTINE MERRILL — A Regency: Virgin's Undoing

LOUISE ALLEN — A Regency: Rake's Redemption

ANN LETHBRIDGE — A Regency: Courtesan's Pride

DIANE GASTON — A Regency: Gentleman's Passion

ANNE HERRIES — A Regency: Lord's Command

CAROLE MORTIMER — A Regency: Lady's Scandal

MARGARET McPHEE — A Regency: Captain's Prize

SARAH MALLORY — A Regency: Baron's Bride

AMANDA McCABE — A Regency: Duchess's Awakening

CARLA KELLY — A Regency: Officer's Wedding

ISABELLE GODDARD — A Regency: Earl's Pleasure

ELIZABETH BEACON — A Regency: Rebel's Seduction

A
Regency
Virgin's
Undoing

CHRISTINE MERRILL

MILLS & BOON

Published in Great Britain 2015
by Mills & Boon, an imprint of Harlequin (UK) Limited,
Eton House, 18-24 Paradise Road, Richmond, Surrey, TW9 1SR

ISBN: 978-0-263-91564-8

052-0815

Printed and bound
by CPI Group (UK) Ltd, Croydon, CR0 4YY

Lady Drusilla's Road to Ruin

CHRISTINE MERRILL

Christine Merrill lives on a farm in Wisconsin, USA, with her husband, two sons and too many pets—all of whom would like her to get off the computer so they can check their e-mail. She has worked by turns in theatre costuming, where she was paid to play with period ballgowns, and as a librarian, where she spent the day surrounded by books. Writing historical romance combines her love of good stories and fancy dress with her ability to stare out of the window and make stuff up.

Chapter One

John Hendricks took a sip from his flask and leaned back into his corner of the northbound mail coach, stretching his legs in an effort to take up as much space as he could before another passenger encroached on his person. After the week he'd had, he was in no mood or condition to be packed cheek to jowl with strangers.

Mr Hendricks, if there is something else you have to say on your hopes for my future, know that I decided on the matter from the first moment I laid eyes on Adrian Longesley. Nothing said by another is likely to change me on the subject.

The words were still ringing in his ears, three days later. And with each repetition of them the heat of his embarrassment flared anew. The woman was married, for God's sake, and above his station. She'd made her uninterest in him plain enough. If he'd suffered in silence, as he had for three years, he could have kept his job and his pride. Instead, he'd been so obvious in his infatuation that he'd forced her to speak the truth aloud.

He took another swig from the flask. If the blush on his cheeks was visible in the darkness, better to let the others think it was from drunkenness and not the shame of unrequited love.

Adrian had known all along, of course. And would have allowed him to continue as a part of the household, if he'd not made such an ass of himself. But once it was out in the open, there was nothing to do but give up his position and slink away from London.

John's feelings for his old friend rose in a tangle of jealousy, pity and embarrassment at his own behaviour. Despite all that had happened, he liked and respected Adrian, and had enjoyed working for him. But what did it say of his own character that he'd even consider stealing the wife of a man who would need her support and unwavering love as the last of his vision faded?

And how foolish did it make him to think that Emily would leave a blind earl for an unacknowledged natural son? He might have been an equal to Lord Folbroke in looks and temperament, but he had no rank, no fortune. And though his sight was better than Adrian's, he could hardly call it perfect.

John slipped the flask into his pocket and removed his spectacles to give them a vigorous wipe. There was not a woman alive who would leave her husband for a man whose only asset was marginally better vision.

He stared sullenly through the cleared lenses at the two people on the seat opposite as though daring them to comment about his earlier drinking. When he had bought the ticket, he'd had some hazy idea that travelling to Scotland would be like venturing into the wilderness. It would be a place to heal the soul and the nerves in quiet and solitude. He had not allowed for the fact that, to arrive at this hermit's paradise, he would be crammed into a small enclosure with the very humanity he despised. They had been rattling about the interior of the conveyance like three beans in a bottle for hours already. He felt the impact of each bump and rut in his bones, his teeth and his aching brain. The swaying of the coach was made even worse by the gusting winds and the rain that hammered the sides and tried to creep in at the poorly sealed window on his right, wetting the sleeve of his coat when he tried to relax against the curtain.

He thought of the coaching schedule, forgotten in his pocket. It was over thirty hours to Edinburgh and he suspected that, with the wet roads and the gathering darkness, it would take even longer than normal. Not that it mattered to him. He was his own man now, with no schedule to keep.

He wished that the thought cheered him. Thank God that he was still half-drunk. When the last effects of the alcohol had gone from his system, they would be replaced by the panic of a man who had destroyed his old life.

Hung over was no way to start a new one. But when he'd gone to the Swan with Two Necks, trying to buy a ticket out of London, he had been several gins past the point of making that decision and would now have to live with the consequences.

'Beastly weather we are having.' The man across from him seemed to think that stating the obvious was a witty opening gambit.

John ignored him. He'd been forced to leave London because he had said far too much to his employer. That did not mean he wished to blurt every thought to strangers.

The woman that shared the coach with them seemed to have similar sentiments. At the sound of the man's voice, her skirts rustled and she clutched the book of sermons she had been reading, bringing it closer to her face to catch the flickering light of the reading lamp in her corner.

John saw her give the slightest flinch as the other man turned his attention to her. 'Travelling alone, miss?'

She looked up long enough to give the man next to her the frosty glare of someone who did not answer to those to whom she had not been properly introduced. Then she returned to her book.

But the man who addressed her was undeterred. 'Because I would be happy to escort you to your destination.' Although there was plenty of room in the body of the coach, he'd made a point of choosing the seat next to the young lady and tended to use each swerve and jostle as an excuse to crowd her. Now, he was definitely leering.

John had a moment's concern that she might be naïve enough to accept the man's offer out of hand. Then he dismissed it as none of his business.

Her skirts gave another rustle as she drew them tightly to her legs, as though trying to shrink herself enough to minimise contact with the stranger. But that would be near to impossible, for she was of an uncommon height. She did not seem to realise that the movement of the cloth over her legs outlined areas of her body that the man accosting her found most interesting.

As did John, come to that. They were long legs, to match the length of her body. If they matched the small amount of ankle he glimpsed beneath her skirts, they were well shaped. A pity the girl was so Friday-faced. If she'd smiled, she might have been quite pretty.

Though her expression hinted that she was travelling to a funeral, her clothing did not. Bright colours suited her fair skin and the deep blue of her gown made her brown eyes seem even darker. The fabric was expensive, but the cut was conservative, as though she renounced fashion when it impinged on movement or modesty. Her long, black hair was dressed severely away from her face and hidden under a poke bonnet.

If John had to guess, he'd have said *spinster*. Clearly, this was a girl with money, but no prospects. It was a very unusual combination, for the former often created the latter. But reading sermons in public hinted at a moral propriety that would make her unpleasant company, should she deign to open her mouth.

Her dark eyes caught his, just for a moment. In the dim light they seemed to glitter sharp and dark, like the eyes of a hawk.

Do something.

Had she spoken? Or had he just imagined the words, planted firmly in his brain? Surely, if they had come from her, there would have been some softness in them, some urgent courtesy in their appeal to a stranger for help. The command was an invention of his own drunken mind.

'It is quite lonely,' the other man announced, 'to travel without a companion of some kind.'

A merchant, thought John, for he could not seem to resist speculating about the other passengers. And a prosperous one as well. The man could afford his extra weight, for the fabric of the vest stretched across the bulging stomach was a fine brocade. But his head seemed to be outgrowing his hair, which struggled to conceal an expanding forehead that the man now mopped in the early summer heat. He spoke again, addressing the girl, who had not responded to his earlier comment.

'Is there someone waiting to join you at the next stop?' He was eyeing her carefully to see if there was some small acknowledgement that she was not as alone as she appeared.

John looked as well and saw no such response. The mystery deepened.

Her eyes flicked to him again, and then away, sharp and quick as a knife cut.

Well?

Well, indeed. The only advantage of being a gentleman of leisure was that he did not have to be at the beck and call of anyone. Not even young ladies with large dark eyes and forbidding expressions. It was ungentlemanly of him, but so be it. If nothing else, the last few weeks should have taught him not to become embroiled in the schemes of beautiful women who, in the end, would offer nothing more than dismissive thanks as they rushed past him to the object of their desire.

Very deliberately, he yawned and closed his eyes, pretending to sleep. Then he opened them just enough so that he could continue to watch his companions.

There was a flash of lightning, followed close by a crack of thunder loud enough to make the other man jump in his seat. But the woman was unmoved and the cold white light threw the annoyance on her features into sudden sharp relief.

Do you mean to allow this?

When John did not respond, she turned to look at the man next to her. The merchant was impervious to whatever messages she was sending or he'd have turned to dust in his seat before speaking again. This time, he was louder, as though he thought she might not have heard him before. 'I said, is there someone to greet you at your destination?' John watched the flicker of truth on the face of the girl that admitted she had no one.

Their companion saw it as well. 'I noticed, at the last stop, that you did not eat. If you lack funds, you needn't fear. The Cap and Bells does a fine joint. I would be only too happy to share my portion with you. And perhaps a brandy and hot water, to keep away the chill.'

Then he'd offer to share his room as well, John had no doubt. The fine example of London citizenry across the coach from him was on the make for a bedmate. Without someone to aid her, the man would grow more predatory the farther they got from town.

John offered a silent plea to the sense of duty that

pushed him to become involved in the business of others, begging it to lie still, just this one time.

Without warning, the girl announced, 'I am not alone. I am travelling with my brother.' And then she kicked John smartly in the ankle.

It was rather like a nightmare he'd once had, of being an actor forced on stage in a play that he had not learned. The girl opposite him seemed to think him obliged to rescue her, though she had no way of knowing whether his intentions were any more gentlemanly then their companion's.

Very well, then. And be damned to his own sense of honour for participating in this farce. He gave a garumphing, snuffling cough, as someone awakening after a long sleep, opened his eyes with a start and shouted, 'What is it? What? Have we arrived already?' He looked straight into the eyes of the girl across from him, shocked at the feeling of sudden connection between them, as though she could manage to relay the whole of her situation with just a glance. Then he stared at the man beside them, as though just noticing him. 'Is this man bothering you, dear heart?'

'I most certainly am not,' the other man replied. 'And I doubt that you know any more of this girl than I do, for you have been travelling with us for some time and have said not a word to her.'

'I did not feel the need to speak to someone I have known since birth,' John said with some asperity.

'And you—' the man glared at the girl '—I'll wager you do not even know this man's name.'

Come on, he thought, in her general direction. *Choose anything and I will answer to it.*

'It is John,' she said.

He tried to contain his surprise, for she had chosen the single most common name in the world. There was something disappointing about the fact that it fit him so well. He glared at the insolent cit. 'And if I were to give you leave, you would call her Miss Hendricks. But I do not. My dear?' He held out a hand to her, and when she took it without hesitation, he pulled her across the body of the carriage into the seat beside him.

The carriage gave a sudden jolt and she landed half in his lap. The sudden contact was most pleasant, and, for a second, his thoughts were in no way filial. But not a hint of answering blush tinted her pale skin and she grabbed the strap beside the door and sorted herself into the seat between him and the opposite window without further assistance.

To hide his momentary confusion, he removed his spectacles and wiped the lenses on the corner of his handkerchief. When he replaced them, he could see that the woman next to him was bristling in outrage. But she was directing it at the other passenger, glaring in triumph across the coach at her adversary.

You are beautiful when you are angry. It was a foolish sentiment, even when true. Knowing the trouble that they could cause, what sane man wanted to make a woman angry? But in her case, there was a strength and energy in her that was accented by her indignation. John had a moment's desire to reach out and touch her, running a hand lightly over her back as one might, when soothing the feathers of a flustered falcon.

'My apologies,' the man muttered, giving John a wary look. 'If that was the way of it, you'd have best spoken sooner.'

'Or you could have found your manners before speaking at all,' John said back, annoyed at the cheek of the man and at himself for his foolish thoughts. Then he settled back into his seat, pretending to doze again.

Beside him, the woman removed a small watch from her reticule, and looked uneasily from it to the shadows of the landscape passing by their window. In the flashes of lightning, he saw violent movement, as though the trees and hedges were being whipped about by the wind. The swaying of the coach increased. Though it was barely midnight, it appeared that their journey was about to take an unfortunate turn.

Chapter Two

The rain had been falling steadily for hours, and Drusilla Rudney fought the desire to remove the coaching schedule from her reticule to try to catch a glimpse of the stops in the guttering lamplight. They had been forced on several occasions already to get out of the coach and walk in the pouring rain as the horses navigated difficult stretches of wet road. That last time, as they'd stumbled in the dark and the gale, she had managed to raise her head to look and she'd seen the difficulty the coachman had in controlling the frightened animals, who rolled their eyes behind their blinders, trying to watch the storm. But he had managed to calm them again and shouted to the passengers to hurry and take their seats so that they could start again. And now the three of them sat, damp and unhappy in their clothes, waiting for the next stop and hoping that there would be enough time for a hot drink.

Since the fat man who had bothered her could not

manage to keep quiet, he had speculated briefly with the other man about the likelihood of a delay. But her pretend brother had said not a word to her since pulling her down to sit beside him.

She remembered the way the fat man beside her had pressed his leg against her skirts, and then imagined how much worse it might have got, had Mr Hendricks not intervened. She had never been this far from home without some kind of chaperon. And although she had known the risks to her reputation, she had not thought that they might involve actual harm to her person. Leaving in haste had been foolish. But common sense had been overcome by her fears for Priscilla. Even now, her sister might be experiencing similar dangers.

She did her best to disguise the involuntary shudder that had passed through her at the thought, hoping that the two men would think it a reaction to sitting in rain-dampened clothing. It would be unwise to reveal her fear in front of a man who had already showed himself willing to prey upon a vulnerable woman. She glared at the merchant across the coach.

She should consider herself lucky that all men were not like him. If they were forced to spend a few hours at the next coaching inn, she would try to pull Mr Hendricks aside and thank him for his aid. Maybe she could even explain some portion of her story, although there was nothing about him that made her think he wished to know her reasons for travelling alone. He had been rather slow to take an interest when she'd needed his help. But now that he had given it, she wished to know if she could call on him again.

She'd heard the slur in his speech when he'd bought his ticket. But his tone had been mild enough. And the spectacles he wore gave a scholarly cast to his features. She'd decided he was a man of letters, perhaps studying for holy orders. Although he was clearly lost to drink, there was something in his face and his mannerisms that made him seem kind and trustworthy. Thus, he would be easily manipulated, even by one as inexperienced with men as she. Of course, Priscilla would have had the man dancing like a puppet by now. But Dru had assumed that his sense of chivalry would bring him promptly to heel in defence of any lady. Instead, it had taken an actual, physical goad.

Of course, now that she could see him from close up, there was a touch of the disapproving schoolmaster about the set of his mouth. She wondered if he thought her fast for travelling alone. Not that he had any right to cast aspersions. When he had first entered the carriage, he had brought with him a cloud of gin and had fallen rather heavily into his seat as though his legs would be taking him no farther for quite some time. But he had been nipping regularly from his flask and had refilled it with brandy at the last stop.

She held the book of sermons before her, wondering if he was more in need of it than she. If he was a clergyman of some kind as she'd suspected, then he had best see to his own weaknesses before correcting others. He had fallen in with her lie quickly enough, when he could just as easily have defended her with the truth. A liar and a drunkard, then. But compared to the coarseness of the other man, he seemed quite harmless.

Yet when she'd almost fallen to the floor of the coach, his response had proved that his reflexes were excellent and his arm strong. He had sorted her back into the other seat as though she weighed nothing. And the thighs on which she'd accidently sat had been hard from riding.

It was a conundrum. She'd have expected him to forgo the saddle for a pony cart, as would befit someone of his nature. The physical prowess he seemed to possess was wasted on a man of letters. And there was something about his eyes, when he had removed his glasses in that moment when he'd cleaned them. The clarity of the colour in them was quite handsome. They were a strange, light brown that shimmered protean gold in the lamplight. They were the eyes of a man who had seen much, balked at little and feared nothing.

But the man of action she'd imagined, who would ride like a centaur and fight like a demon, was just a trick of the light. He was gone with the return of the spectacles, leaving a drunken cleric in the seat beside her.

At the next inn, the guard shouted for them to leave the vehicle. And they alighted, meaning to stretch their legs and twist the kinks from their backs, only to step down ankle deep into the puddles in the courtyard. The wings of the inn sheltered them from the worst of the wind, but gusts of it still tore at their clothes, making the short scurry to the front door a difficult trip. But her unwilling protector raised his topcoat over their heads to offer some shelter from the worst of it and shepherded her quickly into the public room. In the doorway behind them, the driver was deep in conversation with the inn-keeper. When she glanced out of the window, the team was being unhitched from the coach and led away, but there were no replacements stamping eagerly on the flags, waiting to be harnessed.

'What—?' she said to the man who might be called Hendricks.

He held up a hand to silence her, clearly eavesdrop-ping on the conversation of the guard with some other drivers who were gathered at a table by the bar. Then he turned to her. 'It is too bad to go on. I might have known, for it has been growing worse by the hour. Our driver fears that there may be downed trees ahead of us, and does not want to come upon them in darkness. If the mail gets through at all, I am afraid it will be without us, at least until the morning. We will set out again, at first light, if the storm has abated.'

'That cannot be,' she said firmly, even though she recognised the futility of it.

He gave her a disgusted look. 'Unless you have some arcane power that allows you to change the weather, you are stuck here, as we all are.'

Glancing around the room, she could see that the place was crowded even though the hour was late, for many other coaches on the road had used this town as safe haven. She scanned the faces for the only two she wished to find. But they were not there, probably farther up the road, clear of the storm and still travelling north. 'Never mind a little rain. I must get to Gretna Green before—' Then she shut her mouth again, not wanting to reveal too much of the truth.

He gave her an odd look and said, very clearly 'Nonsense, Sister. You are going to Edinburgh.' He glanced at the fat merchant who had bothered her, then gave her a significant look. 'With me.'

'Not on this coach we are not,' she answered. 'If you notice, we are in Newport, headed for Manchester. If you wish to travel to Scotland on this route, a more logical destination would be Dumfries.'

The man next to her narrowed his eyes and pulled the coaching schedule out of his pocket, paging hurriedly through it. Then he cursed softly, turned and threw the thing out the door and into the rain, glaring at her, as though geography were somehow her fault. 'Dumfries it is then.'

'You do not care about your destination?'

'There are many reasons to go to Scotland,' he said cryptically. 'And for some of them, one destination is as good as the next. But in my experience, there can be only one reason that a young lady would be rushing to such a rakehell destination as Gretna.' He looked at her sharply, the schoolmaster expression returning. 'And what kind of brother would I be, if I encouraged that?'

True enough. She knew from experience that when one's sister had chosen to rush off for the border, one must do their best to put a stop to it. And to share as little of the story as possible with curious strangers. So she looked at the man beside her, doing her best at an expression of wide-eyed innocence. 'Do we have family in Dumfries, Brother?' she asked. 'For suddenly I cannot seem to recall.'

He gave a snort of derision at her inept play-acting and said, 'No family at all. That is why I chose it. But perhaps I am wrong. I did not know until today that I had a sister.'

'And you took that well enough,' she said, unwilling to offer further thanks, lest they be overheard. 'In case anyone enquires, would it be too much trouble for you to have a sick aunt in Dumfries?'

'I suppose not.' He gestured to a table at the fireside. 'As long as you do not mind sitting in comfort, while we have the chance, instead of hanging about in the doorway.'

When she hesitated, she noticed that behind his lenses, there was a twinkle in his eyes that might almost have been amusement. 'It is marginally closer to Scotland on the other side of the room,' he said, as though that would be enough to pacify her. After he had seated her, he procured a dinner for her, adding, in a perfectly reasonable voice, that there was no reason not to take nourishment while they had the chance.

There was one perfectly good reason, she thought to herself. The contents of her purse would not stand for many stops such as this. She thought of Priss, halfway to Gretna by now, and carrying her allowance for the month, because, as the note had said, she had *greater need of it than you, Silly.*

Without thinking, she sighed aloud and then came back to herself, relieved that her new, false sibling had gone back across the room to get himself a tankard of ale. Now that she could compare him to other men, she found him taller than she had estimated, but powerfully built. The timidity of his demeanour did not carry to his body when in motion, nor did the liquor he'd drunk seem to affect him. There was strength and surety in his gait, as though a change in circumstances did not bother him a bit. He navigated easily back to her through the crowded room without spilling a drop of his drink, then slid easily on to the chair on the other side of the small table they shared.

She looked at him apprehensively and wet her lips. And then she stared down into the plate that had been placed before her, as though she had not used his absence to make a detailed examination of his person. She really had no reason to be so curious. While she might tell herself that it was a natural wariness on her part, and an attempt to guard herself against possible dishonour, she was the one who had come on this journey alone and then sought the protection of this stranger, based on necessity and assumptions of good character.

She took the first bite of dinner though she had no appetite for it, and found it plain fare, but good. She vowed that she would finish it all, hungry or no, for who knew when she might eat again? As long as he showed no signs of troubling her as the other man had, she would allow Mr Hendricks to pay as well. If he complained, she would inform him that she had not requested to be fed and that it was sinful to waste the food.

But the man across the table from her was not eating, simply staring back at her, waiting. 'Well?' he said at last, arms folded in front of him. He was looking rather like a schoolmaster again, ready to administer punishment once a confession was gained. 'Do not think you can sit with me, well out of earshot of our companion, and give nothing in return.'

She swallowed. 'Thank you for coming to my aid, when we were in the coach.'

'You left me little choice in the matter,' he said with reproof, shifting his leg as though his ankle still pained him from the kick. 'But even without your request for help, I could not very well sit silent and let the man accost you for the whole of the journey. It was an unpleasant enough ride.' He glanced around him at the rain streaking the window of the inn. 'And not likely to become more pleasant in the immediate future.'

That was good, for it sounded almost as though he would have helped her without her asking. That made him better than the other man in the carriage who would surely have pressed any advantage he had gained over her from her lie. 'I am sorry that circumstances forced me to trouble you, Mr...' And now she would see if he had given the correct name before.

'Hendricks,' he supplied. 'Just as I said in the coach. And you guessed my given name correctly. While I do not overly object to the loan of mine, I suspect you have a surname of your own.' He stared at her, waiting.

Should she tell him the truth? If the whole point of this journey was to avoid embarrassment to the family, it did no good to go trumpeting the story to near strangers.

'Come now,' he said, adjusting the fold of his arms.

'Surely you can be more open with me. We are kin, after all.' He leaned forwards on the table, so that their heads were close together and he could whisper the next words. 'Or how else do we explain our proximity?'

The obvious reason, she supposed. On this route, anyone seeing a couple in a tête-à-tête would think them eloping for Scotland, just as Priscilla had done. She took a breath, wondering if she should she tell him of her father's title, and then decided against it. 'I am Lady Drusilla Rudney.' Then, hoping there would be a way to gloss over the rest of it, she fluttered her eyelashes at him and attempted a smile. 'But to my friends, I am Silly.'

And then, she waited for one of the obvious responses.

I expect you are.

Did they give you cause to be?

Apparently, Mr Hendricks had no sense of humour. 'An unfortunate family nickname, I assume.' And one he would not be using, judging by the pained look in his eye. 'And given to you by the Duke of Benbridge, who is your uncle. No…your father.'

He'd read her as easily as the sermon book in her pocket. She must learn to be quicker or he'd have all the facts out of her, before long. 'Actually, it was my sister who gave me the name. A difficulty in pronunciation, when we were children…' Her explanation trailed off. It surprised her, for rarely did conversation with a stranger leave her at a loss for words.

'Well then, Lady Drusilla, what brings you to be travelling alone? You can afford a maid, or some sort of companion. And to travel in the family carriage, instead of stuck in the mail coach with the likes of me.'

'It is a matter of some delicacy and I do not wish to share the details.'

'If you are going to Gretna, then you are clearly eloping, travelling alone so that your father does not discover you. Little else is needed to tell the tale, other than to ascertain the name of the man involved.'

'I beg your pardon,' she said sharply, insulted that he would think her so foolish. 'I am not eloping. And how dare you think such a thing.'

'Then, what are you doing?' he shot back, just as quickly. The alcohol had not dulled his wits a bit, and the speed of his questioning left her with her mouth hanging open, ready to announce the truth to a room full of strangers.

She took a breath to regain her calm. 'I wish to go to Gretna and stop an elopement,' she whispered urgently. 'And I do not want anyone to know. Once my end has been achieved, there must be no hint of gossip. Not a breath of scandal. No evidence that the trip was ever made.'

Mr Hendricks paused as though considering her story. Then he said, 'You realise, of course, that the trip may be futile.'

'And why would you think that?' Other than that it was probably true. But it was better to appear obtuse in the face of probable defeat, than to be talked into giving up.

He tried again in a much gentler tone. 'Should the couple involved be determined, they will not listen to you. And if they had much of a start on you, they are miles ahead already.'

'Quite possibly,' she agreed.

'The honour of the girl in question is most assuredly breached.'

'That does not matter in the least.' After a day and a night with her lover, allowing the wedding to occur would be the logical solution. But if Priss disgraced herself by marrying Gervaise, she disgraced the family as well. And Dru would get the blame for it, for it had been her job to chaperon the girl and prevent such foolishness. Father would announce that, no matter how unlikely it might be that his awkward daughter Silly could find a man to haul her to Gretna, he was unwilling to risk a second embarrassment. There would be no Season, no suitors and no inevitable proposal. She would spend the rest of her life in penance for Priss's mistake, on the unfashionable edge of society, with the wallflowers and the spinsters.

Was it so very selfish if, just this once, she ignored what was right for Priscilla and looked to her own future? 'I will not let him marry her.' If she had to, she would grab Priss from the very blacksmith's stone and push Gervaise under a dray horse. But there would be no wedding. Dru narrowed her eyes and glared at Mr Hendricks.

He glared back at her, his patience for her wearing thin. 'By travelling alone and in secret, you have compromised your reputation, and are just as likely to end in the soup as the couple you seek to stop.'

'With the need for speed and secrecy, there was little

else I could do.' The Benbridge carriage was already tearing up the road between London and the Scottish border, and Priss had left her barely enough to buy a ticket on the mail coach, much less rent a post-chaise. But the scandal of it would work to her advantage in one way: in comparison with Priss's elopement, a solo journey by her ape-leading older sister would hardly raise an eyebrow.

Mr Hendricks saw her dark expression and amended, 'Perhaps you will be fortunate. The rain that traps us might trap them as well.'

This was hardly good news. Until now, she had been imagining her sister and Gervaise travelling night and day in a mad rush to reach their destination. But if they were held up in an inn somewhere, the chance for recognition and disgrace multiplied by a thousandfold. And in the time they spent alone together, unchaperoned…

She decided firmly that she would not think about the details of that at all. There was nothing she could do about the truth of that, especially if she was already too late. She gave her new brother a look that told him his opinions were unwelcome and said, 'Knowing Mr Gervaise as I do, they are likely to dawdle, for he will not wish to spoil his tailoring in the rain.'

'You do not know the man as well as you think if he has taken some other girl to Scotland.' Mr Hendricks's gaze was direct, and surprisingly clear, as though he were trying to impart some bit of important information. But what it might be was lost upon her.

'It does not matter that I do not know his character. It only matters that I know his destination. He is going to Gretna. We had an understanding.' She had paid him well enough to leave Priss alone. He had taken her money, then he had taken her sister as well. And she was not exactly sure how, but when she found him, she would make him suffer for tricking her and dishonouring the family. She glared at the man across the table. 'The marriage must not occur.'

Mr Hendricks was watching her uneasily, as though he did not quite know what to make of such illogical stubbornness. In the end, he seemed to decide that the best response was none at all, and focused his attention upon his meal, offering no further words of advice or censure.

But watching his enthusiasm for the food, she could not contain a comment of her own. 'After the amount you have been drinking, it is a wonder you can eat at all.'

He glanced up at her, and said, around another bite of meat, 'If you are shocked by it, then you had best stick to your sermons, little sister. What you have seen me drink is nothing, compared to what I imbibed before.'

'That is hardly a point of pride,' she said with a sniff.

'Nor is it any of your business,' he added, taking a large drink of ale. He thought for a moment, and then said, 'Although if it hadn't been for my level of inebriation, I might be riding, right now, in the coach that I intended to take, and not have collapsed into the first one I found. With an excess of blue ruin, I have found my long-lost sister.' He toasted her with his tankard. 'Fate works in mysterious ways.'

'Do you often drink so much that you cannot tell

one route from another?' For though he was somewhat rumpled now, when she looked closely at him, she doubted that the behaviour was habitual.

He stared down into his glass, as though wishing it would refill itself. 'My life, of late, has taken an unusual turn.' Then he looked at her, thoughtfully. 'It involves a woman. Given the circumstances, an excessive amount of alcohol and impromptu coach travel made perfect sense.'

'And is this woman in Edinburgh?' she asked, remembering his original destination.

'She is in London. My plan was to take a coach to Orkney.'

'You cannot take a coach to an island,' she said, as patiently as possible.

'I planned to ride as far as John O' Groats and then walk the rest of the way.' The glint in his eyes was feverish, and a little mad. 'The woman in question was married. And not interested in me.' The sentences fell from his mouth, flat and heavy, like pig-iron bars.

For a moment, Drusilla considered offering her sympathy. Though he was inebriated, Mr Hendricks had come to her aid, and gone so far as to buy the food she was eating. But the recent changes in her own life had put her quite out of charity with young lovers, either star-crossed or triumphant. 'If your goal is no more specific than that, you might just as well drown yourself by the Hebrides. Once we reach Scotland, they will be closer.'

'Thank you for your kind words of advice, Sister.'

He gave her a strange, direct look, as though he were equally tired of the likes of her.

They would have fallen into silence again had not the innkeeper appeared at their table, followed close behind by the fat merchant, who was shifting eagerly from foot to foot as though he had heard some bit of gossip that he could not wait to share. 'It has been decided that the coach will not continue until morning, if then,' he said, with a satisfied smile.

'I am aware of that,' Mr Hendricks said. His eyes never left hers, as though he thought it possible to ignore the other man out of existence.

'I assume you will be seeking accommodations?' the innkeeper added.

'Obviously.'

'Then there is a small problem,' the innkeeper responded. 'There are three of you, and I have but two rooms left.'

From behind him, the merchant gave an inappropriate giggle, although why he found the prospect of further discomfort to be amusing, she could not imagine.

The innkeeper continued. 'One of the rooms will go to the lady, of course. But you gentlemen must work out between you what is to be done with the remaining space. You can share the other bed, or draw lots for it. The loser can take his chances in the parlour, once the bar is closed. But you had best decide quickly, or I shall give the space to someone else. I suspect we will be seeing more like you with coaches stalled here, or turning back because of the rain.'

'And I see that as no problem at all,' the merchant

responded before Hendricks could speak. 'My companions are brother and sister. Since they are such close family, a single room will suffice for them and I will take the other.' He shot her a leer, as though pleased to have caught her in her own trap, and waited for her to admit the truth.

'That will be all right, I am sure,' Mr Hendricks answered before she could so much as gather her breath. She wanted to argue that it would most certainly *not* be all right. She was the Duke of Benbridge's daughter and had no intention of sharing a room with any stranger, much less a strange man.

But there was something calming about the tone of Mr Hendricks's voice, like a hand resting on her shoulder.

It will be all right. Although why she was certain of that, she could not say.

In her silence, he continued as though he was accustomed to speaking for her, and it mattered not, one way or the other whether or not she was in his bed. 'Drusilla shall have the mattress, of course. But if you could spare another blanket for me, I would be most grateful.'

The merchant looked vaguely disappointed, like a dog that had not managed to flush a bird. Then he turned his scrutiny on her, waiting for the weak link to break and the truth to come tumbling out of her.

She stared back at him, showing what she hoped was the correct amount of annoyance at having her plans changed by nature and an overfull inn, but without the outrage that she should be feeling.

Beside her, Mr Hendricks was haggling with the hosteller, who allowed that there might be enough bedding. But there would, of course, be an extra charge for it. Apparently it was at least twice the rate that Mr Hendricks found appropriate.

As the innkeeper argued about supply and demand and reminded her *faux* sibling that the same blanket could be let at triple the price to the next passenger who would be forced to sleep on the floor, the sounds of the room seemed to diminish. All Drusilla heard was the sound of imaginary coins clinking from her reticule into the hand of the innkeeper. She had taken all the loose money she could find when setting out after Priss, without picking the pockets of the servants or going to her father and explaining the predicament. There had been scant little available. She suspected Priss had seen to that, specifically to prevent her following.

When Dru had counted her funds, it had seemed enough to mount a rescue. There was enough for the ticket, her food and perhaps one stop along the way. But she had not allowed for tipping the guard, emergencies, or the exorbitant rates that she might find in places where travellers were at the mercy of innkeepers and would pay what the market might bear. At this rate, she would be penniless by tomorrow's lunch. She would be forced to turn back and admit everything to Father, or to put herself at the mercy of strangers and hope for the best.

She glanced at Mr Hendricks, who was still arguing with the innkeeper. 'I will do without the blanket. But for that price, I expect we will have space to continue this meal in our room. Give us the larger of the two, and send the bags up so that we might be comfortable. Drusilla?' His tone was that of an older brother, used to controlling his family.

But the sound of her own name, said in that smooth male voice, and without any polite preamble or foolish nicknames, made her skin prickle. 'Yes, John,' she answered, ducking her head in submission and grabbing her plate to follow him.

Chapter Three

When the door of the room closed behind them, Mr Hendricks released a string of curses directed at no one in particular. And although she should have been shocked, Drusilla had to admit that they effectively described her own feelings on the latest turn of events. He turned to glare at her. 'Do not think to complain about what has occurred, for it is completely your own fault. If you had not forced me to lie for you, you would have the room to yourself.'

'And at the prices they are charging, I would not have been able to pay for it,' she responded, just as cross.

'You are a duke's daughter. And you do not have enough blunt in your pocket to stay in an inn?' He laughed. 'Call the innkeeper back, mention your father's name and not only will he extend you credit, he will turn out one of the other guests so that we may have two beds and a private sitting room, instead of this squalid hole he has given us.'

'If I wished to bandy my father's name in every inn between here and Gretna, I would be travelling escorted in a private carriage. And you would be sleeping on the floor of the taproom.' She narrowed her eyes. 'Where you belong.'

Her unwilling companion bowed in response. 'Thank you so much for you kind opinion of me, Lady Drusilla. It is particularly welcome coming from one who cannot pay for her own bed.'

Though she was used to being the brunt of sarcasm at home, somehow it hurt more coming from Mr Hendricks. And she had brought it upon herself by taunting him.

But before she could apologise, he continued. 'I suppose the next thing you will do is request that I loan you sufficient to cover your dinner, the room and tomorrow's breakfast as well.' When she did not correct him, he laughed bitterly. 'Why am I not surprised at this? Is it not typical that a member of your class should be relying on me, yet again, to rescue them from their own folly at the expense of my own needs?' He was gesticulating wildly now, pacing the little space available in their room. 'Mr Hendricks, write my letters for me. Mr Hendricks, rent me a room. Mr Hendricks, lie to my wife. Not a word of this to my husband, Hendricks. As if I have no other goal in life than to run hither and yon, propping up the outlandish falsehoods of people too foolish to predict their outcome.' He stopped suddenly, as though just noticing that he was speaking the words aloud. Then he dropped his hands to his sides and examined her closely. 'You are not about to cry, are you?'

'Certainly not.' She reached up and touched her own cheek to make sure. She was not normally given to bouts of tears, but it would be most embarrassing to succumb without warning.

'That is good,' he said. 'I am not normally so transparent in my feelings. But it has been a trying week. And as you pointed out earlier, I am somewhat the worse for drink and ranting about things that are no fault of yours.'

'But you are right in your displeasure,' she allowed. 'It was unfair of me to request your help in a situation you had no part in creating.'

He sat down next to her suddenly. 'I almost wish you were crying. I'd have been much more able to resist you had that been the case.'

Resist me? She had hardly brought the force of her personality to bear on the man, other than the kick on the ankle. And although she was often described by men as formidable, it was usually said in a tone of annoyance, or occasionally awe. Though it meant nearly the same, it felt much nicer to be irresistible.

He looked at her thoughtfully, pushing his spectacles up the bridge of his nose as though trying to get a clear view of the situation before speaking again. Then he said, 'Leaving London with no chaperon and no money was very foolish of you. But since I was equally foolish to leave the city drunk and on the wrong coach, I have no right to upbraid you.'

Comparing the two situations, she could hardly call

them equal. His was probably the worse. But he was the one with the fatter purse and she was in no position to make enemies. 'Thank you,' she said as mildly as possible.

He frowned for a moment, as though trying to remember something, then added, 'Did I mention earlier that I am currently without a position?'

'No, you did not.' Although why it should matter, she had no idea.

'Then, my lady, I see a solution to both our problems.' His previous insolence evaporated in a single sentence. In its place was a natural deference, with no hint of the obsequious servility she'd seen in some servants. 'I have some experience in dealing with situations rather like yours. Until several days ago, I was personal secretary to the Earl of Folbroke.'

That would explain it, then. He wasn't a preacher or a teacher. He had been a confidential employee of a peer. 'And under what circumstances did you leave this position?' she asked, trying to decide where the conversation was likely to lead them.

'Nothing that would prevent him from giving a positive reference, were he here now.'

Drusilla was glad he was not. The room was hardly big enough for the two of them, without adding former employers into the mix.

'I have letters to that effect,' Mr Hendricks said.

'Which are?'

'In London.'

'I see.'

He removed his spectacles to polish them before

continuing. 'But that job gave me experience in dealing with the sort of delicate situations that sometimes occur in families such as yours.'

Utterly mad ones, you mean. The way he'd been raving before, she was sure that he had interesting stories to tell, were he the sort of man to share confidences about his employers. Which he was not.

'Handling matters with discretion is a personal strong point of mine,' he confirmed, as though reading her mind. 'And if you could ensure me of repayment when we return to London, a bit more for my troubles, and perhaps a letter of reference?'

'More than that. My father will write the letter himself. And he will see to it that you are generously rewarded at the end of the affair.'

Behind his glasses, Mr Hendricks's amber eyes glittered. References from an earl were no small thing. But if he could win the favour of a duke, he would be seen as nearly invaluable by his next employer.

'The Duke of Benbridge will be most grateful to hear that the matter was handled with discretion.' After he got used to the idea, at any rate.

'He will not mind that you are travelling alone?' Hendricks asked, searching for a flaw in her story.

Her father would be livid when he learned that Priss had run, and even angrier to know that Dru had not caught her before she'd left the house. In comparison to that, travelling alone or hiring a stranger would be as nothing. 'He will not be happy,' she admitted. 'But it is not as if I am the one eloping with Mr Gervaise. I am trying to prevent his elopement…with another.' If it was possible, she would keep Priss out of the story a while longer. If Hendricks knew of her father, then it was possible he'd heard gossip of Benbridge's wilful younger daughter and would realise that the girl might need to be dragged kicking and screaming back home. 'Just a trip to Scotland and back. It will be very little trouble at all.' At least Drusilla meant to be no trouble. Her sister was likely to be trouble enough for two people. 'Once I find the couple, I will be able to handle the rest of it. But if you could clear the way for me, paying bills, handling luggage and protecting me from men such as our companion?'

'And keep my mouth shut at the end of it?' For a moment, the candid Mr Hendricks had returned and was grinning at her.

She returned a small, polite smile. 'Precisely.'

'Very well, then. I am at your disposal.' He offered his hand to her. She accepted it and was given a manly shake. His palm was warm and dry against hers and the feeling of carefully contained power in his arm gave her a strange feeling in the pit of her stomach.

When he released her hand, he had an odd look on his face, as though he'd felt something as well. Perhaps it had to do with the quality of the cooking, for they had shared the same food.

And now they shared a room.

Her stomach gave the same little flip. It was probably nothing more than nerves. Because Mr Hendricks showed no signs of quitting the place and leaving her in privacy. To speed him on his way, she asked, 'And this evening?' She glanced around the room, and then significantly at the door. 'Where do you intend to sleep?'

'Right here, of course.'

'You most certainly will not—'

He cut her off before she could object and the firmness returned to his voice. 'There was nothing in the agreement we have made that would lead me to believe I must sleep in the stable.'

'Nor was there anything about it that implied that I wish to share a room with you.'

'The implication was tacit,' he said. 'If not, you could have announced in the tavern that our relationship was an illusion.'

'I never expected things to progress as quickly as they did,' she said. 'Nor did I expect you to be stubborn on the point.'

'I see,' he said. 'You think my wishing to sleep in a bed when one presents itself is a sign of stubbornness and not common sense.'

'I expect you to behave as a gentleman,' she said. 'And as one who is in my employ.'

'It is late. And it is not in my ability to aid you until the morning,' he said. 'My service to you will begin at first light. I expect, at that time, that I will need all my wits to keep ahead of you. And for that, I will need adequate sleep. If you were seeking a dogsbody who would lie in the hall just to ensure your modesty, then you must seek him elsewhere. In my last position, I was treated almost as a member of the family and well paid.'

'And yet you left it,' she pointed out and saw the tiny twitch of his eye at her reminder.

'But even dead drunk, I had the sense to leave London with enough money for accommodations,' he countered. 'You did not. I have paid for this room and mean to stay in it.' He smiled benevolently. 'Since you are my employer, I will hardly deny you the space, if you wish to remain with me.'

Perfectly true and annoyingly rational. 'Then it is I who must sleep in the stable,' she said, doing her best to look pathetic and elicit his sympathy.

'Or on the floor,' he offered. 'Although it does not look very comfortable. Or you can take your half of the mattress, if you will leave me in peace.'

'If I leave *you* in peace?' she said, outraged.

'I have no intention of accosting you in the night, nor do I mean to tell anyone of the close quarters,' he said. 'I know my own nature and feel quite able to resist your charms.'

'Thank you,' she said, a little annoyed that at the first sign of conflict she had gone back to being her easily resistible self.

He glanced at her, as though speculating. 'But I cannot vouch for your motives. In our first meeting, you were the aggressor. For all I know, you are the sort of woman who forces herself on to unwary travellers and robs them of their purses, or murders them in their beds.'

'How dare you.'

Then she saw the twinkle in his eye. 'I am properly convinced. Only a lady of the bluest blood can raise that level of outrage over so small a jest. Your honour is safe from me. And as for my honour?' He shrugged.

'I doubt you would know what to do with it, should you find it.' He sat down on the edge of the bed and pulled off his boots, then stripped off his coat and waistcoat and loosened his cravat.

There was no reason that his words should hurt her, for they were true. They were not even an insult. No decent girl should have any idea how to approach a strange man in her bed. But she hated to be reminded of her ignorance and to feel that he was amusing himself with her *naïveté*. But it was late and she was tired, and could think of no alternative sleeping arrangements if he was unwilling to move. She stared at the bed, then at him. 'If it is only for the few hours until dawn, I think I can manage to control myself.'

'Unless you are driven wild by the appearance of a man's bare feet,' he said, not bothering a glance in her direction. 'I will retain my shirt in deference to your modesty. But I mean to remove my socks and dry them by the fire.'

'Is there any reason that I would be inflamed at the sight of them?' she asked, suddenly rather curious. For other than in paintings, she could not remember ever seeing any male feet.

'None that I know of. But if you wish, you may assure yourself that they are not cloven hooves.' He pulled back the covers and she caught a glimpse of them as he rolled easily into his side of the bed. They were quite ordinary, although there was something distinctly masculine about the size.

But being able to travel with dry toes tomorrow would be rather pleasant. So she went to her side of the bed, with her back to him, and as discretely as possible removed her boots, undid her garters and rolled her own stockings down.

Then she glanced at the bed again, trying not to look at the body already in it. To lie down beside it would be more than a careless disregard for modesty. But she was very tired, and there might not be another chance to sleep in a bed, not even part of one, between here and the end of her journey. 'I have, in the past, been forced to share a mattress with my sister. That did not upset my sleep.' But Mr Hendricks seemed much larger than Priscilla. And he was occupying slightly more than half of the available space. She wondered, uneasily, how much room she was likely to need.

He rolled so that he could look at her again as she arranged her stockings next to his. His eyes flicked briefly to her feet, bare on the cold floor of the inn, and then just as quickly back to her face. He gave her a strange, tight smile. 'But I am not really your brother.' Then he removed his spectacles, folded them and placed them on a stool next to the bed. 'We will manage the best we can.' He rolled so that his back was to her again. 'When you are ready to retire, please extinguish the candle.'

Once she was sure that his eyes were truly closed, Dru dropped the front of her gown and loosened the stays built into it to make sleeping a little easier. She feared that the shortness of breath she was experiencing was more the sign of rising panic. She was not even a day from home, but it was farther than she had ever travelled without escort. And on the very first night, she had fallen into what the map maker might label *terra incognita*, a place where the rules as she understood them did not apply. She was in bed with a strange man and both of them were barefoot. Although no governess had lectured her on this particular circumstance, she was sure that the forecast would have been dire.

She suspected that Priss would have managed the situation much better, for the girl had been so unwilling to follow the dictates of convention that she would not feel their absence.

But Dru missed them sorely. She must hope that the man she had hired to aid her was as honest and dependable as he managed to look, in some lights at least. Once he was rested and sober, and wearing his spectacles again, everything would be all right. She remembered the flash of gold in his eyes, after he'd removed his glasses, but just before he'd closed them. Strange, deep, unfathomable eyes. Eyes that had been places and seen things. And they had been looking at her.

'Here there be dragons,' she whispered, blew out the candle and lay down beside him.

From somewhere on the other side of the mattress, she heard a groan, and the muttered, 'I will slay them in the morning.' And then, there was nothing but silence.

Chapter Four

When she woke the next morning, she was stiff with discomfort and not all the pain she felt could be blamed on the stress of travelling. She had slept with her arms folded tightly across her chest, fearing that the least movement would rouse her companion.

But he had not seemed at all bothered by her presence. His even snoring was a demonstration of that. It had roused her several times during the night. Of course, he was quiet enough now that it was almost light and time to be getting up again. She grumbled to herself at the unfairness of it, tossing to lie on her other side.

He was silent because he was awake. Only inches from her nose he lay facing her, watching.

And why she had thought him a parson on the previous day she had no idea. So close like this, his eyes were reminiscent of some great cat. His body reminded her of that as well, for there was a stillness in it now that

did not seem so much immobility, as the gathering of
energy that came, right before the pounce.

And that attention was focused on her. Like a rabbit,
she responded to it by freezing. Unable to turn away
from him, she lay there, paralysed, waiting for the eventual assault, yet was unable to fear it. While she'd not
thought further than the desperate effort to save her
sister's reputation, she'd put her own honour at stake.
And that particular commodity was so shelf worn as
to be practically useless. While it was foolish to put it
at risk, she sometimes wondered if anyone even cared
that she possessed it.

But in this moment, she was sure that Mr Hendricks
had noticed, was giving the matter some thought and
would divest her of it with efficiency and discretion,
should she ask him to.

Then the man next to her sat up, yawned, stretched
and reached for his glasses. He put them on; when he
looked at her again, it was as if the great cat she feared
was safely encased behind a thick, protective window. It
watched her for a moment, then lost interest, retreating
slowly back into its cage and out of sight, leaving the
somewhat owlish parson she had noted on the previous
day.

'You slept well, I trust?' he asked.

'As well as can be expected,' she admitted.

'Very good.' He swung his legs out of the bed and
to the floor, reaching for his socks and boots. 'I will
leave you to prepare yourself for the day, and will be
returning in...' he reached for his watch and checked

the time '…approximately fifteen minutes. Will that be sufficient?'

'Certainly. I will go down to the common room for breakfast, so that you will know when the room is empty.'

He nodded, then left her.

In his place was a strange feeling, almost of bereavement. It was hardly appropriate. She had only just met the man and should be relieved that he was allowing her some privacy so that she could have a wash. And she had best get about it, for she was willing to wager that when he'd said fifteen minutes, he had meant exactly that and would be measuring it on a watch that was both properly maintained and more than usually accurate. He would be an efficient task master, well aware of the schedule and the need to adhere to it, if she wished to reach her goal.

She should be pleased. Had this not been exactly what she needed? But as she sat up and reached for her valise and prepared to refresh herself, she sighed.

Less than an hour later, they were side by side again in the carriage and travelling north. The man who had bothered her yesterday was there again today, watching her closely from the other seat. He eyed Mr Hendricks as well, as though looking for some resemblance between them or some sign that the night had been spent in more than sleep.

Mr Hendricks noticed it as well and gave the man a dark look. 'I trust *you* slept well, sir.'

Drusilla smiled to herself as the man coloured from guilt.

'I expect the day's travel to be equally uncomfortable,' he said, this time to Dru. 'The driver was in the parlour when I took my breakfast; he has got word that the roads grow more difficult the farther north we travel. They may become impassable.'

'I prefer not to invoke disaster by discussing it,' she said uneasily.

Mr Hendricks shrugged. 'It is better to be prepared against the eventuality of it. Then one can posit likely alternatives, should the worst occur and the coach fail us. Now, if you will forgive me, Sister, I mean to rest. It was a beastly night and I got little sleep.' He glared at the man opposite them, making it clear who was to blame for his bad humour.

The merchant answered with a similar glare, as though to say, even if they were siblings, he did not care.

'But if you need anything, my dear, do not hesitate to wake me.' Although he said it mildly, there was an underlying tone of menace in the words. Yesterday's troubles would not be repeated. If her harasser gave so much as a glance in her direction, he would pay dearly for it. Then Mr Hendricks closed his eyes and tipped his hat forwards to shield his face as he napped.

Drusilla reached for the book in her reticule and tried to hide the strange thrill that it gave her to be protected. When Priss was in attendance, Dru's life was largely without such courtesies. If required to, the men who flocked around her sister might come to her aid, but it would be done as an afterthought, in an effort to curry favour with the daughter that actually interested them.

Of course, Mr Hendricks was doing so because she had agreed to pay him—and he was worth every penny. At each change of horses, he was up and out the door in one smooth movement, even if the coach was not fully stopped. It was strange to think of his movements as graceful, but there was a kind of economy to them that rivalled anything Mr Gervaise could demonstrate on the dance floor. And the sun glinting off his short blond hair was every bit as attractive as Gervaise's dark handsomeness.

He would ignore the coachman's cautions to 'Have a care!' and the shouts from the guard that there would be no time for passengers to alight, then go straight to the innkeeper. She could watch from the window as he described their quarry in succinct terms: a tall dark man, nattily dressed, travelling with a petite blonde in a black carriage with a crest upon the door. He would take in the innkeeper's response, toss the man a coin for his troubles and be back in his seat before the horses were fully harnessed.

He was organised, efficient, left nothing to chance and seemed totally focused on her comfort. He would adjust curtains to make sure her seat was shaded from the sun, but not too gloomy to read. He got her food and refreshments almost before she could request them.

If she was the sort of woman prone to flights of fancy, she would come to enjoy it all a bit too much and imagine that it was anything other than a job to him.

A particularly vicious bump sent her sliding across

the seat into him. Without waking, he reached out an arm to steady her.

To maintain their fictional relationship, she tried to take the sudden contact without flinching, but his hand on her arm was strangely unsettling. And for that, she had only herself to blame. She had been too much out of the society, if she could not even manage to accept a little help without reading things into it. Though it was hardly gentlemanly to touch a lady without permission, he could not very well let her slide off the seat.

Yet this felt like somewhat more. Almost as if he had been her brother, or a very close friend, and cared what happened to her, even without opening his eyes.

Because you employ him, said a voice in her head that was as cold and rational as her father would have been. *It is in his best interest to keep you intact, if he wishes the favour of the Duke of Benbridge.*

But more than that, his touch had been innocent, yet strangely familiar. Sure of itself. And sure of her. It had made her want to reach out and clasp his hand in thanks.

She took a firmer grip on the binding of her book, to make sure that the temptation was not acted upon.

It appeared, as they travelled, that Mr Hendricks would be proven right about the difficulties that lay before them. The carriage had been slowing for the better part of the morning, and Mr Hendricks had removed his watch from his pocket on several occasions, glancing at the time, comparing it to the schedule and making little tutting noises of disapproval. When she raised a questioning eyebrow, he said, 'The recent rains have spoiled the roads. I doubt we will be able to go much farther today.'

'Oh dear.' There was little more to be said, other than to voice her disappointment. It was not as if arguing with Mr Hendricks would change the quality of the road, after all.

Half an hour later, the coach gave a final lurch and ground to a stop in the mud. The drivers called to the passengers to exit and for any men strong enough to assist in pushing.

As Mr Hendricks shrugged out of his coat and rolled up his sleeves, Drusilla looked in dismay at the puddle in front of the door. As she started down the steps, her companion held up a hand to stay her. 'Allow me.' Then he hopped lightly to the ground, and held out his arms to her.

'You cannot mean to carry me,' she said, taking a half-step back.

'Why not?'

'I am too heavy for you.'

He gave her an odd look. 'I hardly think it will be a problem. Now hurry. My feet are getting wet.'

Gingerly, she sat on the edge and lowered herself towards him. Then he took her in his arms, turned and walked a little way up the hill to a dry place. He proved himself right, for he carried her easily. His body was warm against hers; suddenly and unreasonably, she regretted that she had not lain closer to him in the night. It felt delightful to have his arms about her and she allowed her own arms to creep about his neck, pretending it was only to aid in balance and had nothing to do with the desire to touch him.

Too soon he arrived at the safe place and set her down on the ground. 'Wait for me here, Sister.'

Was the last word a reminder of her role? she wondered. As he laboured behind the coach, she could not manage to think of him thus. His broad shoulders strained, outlining themselves against the linen of his shirt. She could see muscle, bone and sinew in the strength of his arms and his legs as well, his lower anatomy well defined by the tightness of his mud-splattered trousers.

It made her feel strange, rather like she had first thing in the morning, when he had been staring at her. She put a hand to her forehead, wondering if she had taken ill, and then let it fall to her side in defeat. It was getting harder and harder to pretend that her reactions to Mr Hendricks were related to heat or indigestion. It excited her to have his attention, if she fluttered at every glance and touch.

Perhaps her sister's foolishness was contagious. She was normally far too sensible to be looking at a man and thinking the things she was. More importantly, she should not be looking at this particular man. She had hired him, for heaven's sake. He was her inferior. Not a suitor. Not a lover. Not even a friend. It was no different than Priscilla and her dancing master.

Except in one thing. Mr Hendricks had shown no interest in seducing her. Last night, with the candour brought on by too much alcohol, he had admitted that his heart was already bruised. He had been eager to withdraw from civilisation, particularly the company of women. If he had even the slightest idea what was going on in her head, he would depart from her at the first opportunity, leaving her to face this calamity alone.

As if to punish her for her lapse, the horses gave a tug and the body of the coach overbalanced still further. And then, with a horrible splintering, the mired wheel gave way. She covered her eyes with her hands, wishing she could reject the reality of the destroyed transport and the attractiveness of her companion. It was all ruined, as was her Priss.

And she could not help but think that it was all her fault. If she had behaved with more foresight while they were still in London, been more strict... Or perhaps less so... If she had been a better example, or listened with more compassion to her sister's problems...then Priss would not have run away. And she would not be sitting beside a broken coach, staring at a man's shoulders and thinking nonsense.

She felt the shadow of him cross her face, before he spoke. 'Well, then. That's done for.'

'It's over.' Because it was. She could not walk to Scotland. By the time they could find another carriage, the couple would be even farther ahead of them. She might as well adjust to the idea of Mr Gervaise for a brother-in-law, and a father so angry that she would never see polite society again, lest she follow the path of her younger sister and humiliate him.

He gave a short laugh. 'Then you will be glad that

I am here. For while the coach is done, the journey is hardly over. If you wish to continue, that is.'

'Continue? Of course.' Her eyes flew to the coach. 'Can they get us a post-chaise?'

'They'll do it for two passengers, but not for three.'

'There are only two of us,' she said.

Mr Hendricks cocked his head in the direction of their companion who was leaning against the broken axle. 'After the way we have treated him, it is unlikely that he will yield his place to us. And do not think for a moment that you will change partners as though you were waltzing at Almack's and go on with him instead,' Hendricks said firmly. 'I hesitate to think what might happen to you if he gets you alone.'

A variety of responses occurred to her. She should have told him that she was not that foolish, that he had no right to talk to her in that tone. Instead, she announced, 'I have never been waltzing at Almack's, and, if I had, I certainly would not leave you in the middle of a dance.' It was true. She had procured the vouchers with Priss in mind. She had not needed Father to tell her that the girl would not show to best advantage if both of them were on the floor. But it made her look like a looby to announce the fact now. It was bad enough to be thought foolish, but worse to be seen as exactly what she was: a wallflower spinster, too busy watching over the virtue of others to get the benefit of a Season.

Mr Hendricks was staring at her as though she has sprouted feathers. 'Go and speak to the driver. See what else can be done,' she commanded in her most aristo-cratic tone. 'I wish to be in Scotland before tomorrow,

Hendricks. There is no time to waste.' He did not need to be told his job. She hated people who solved their problems by tongue-lashing the nearest servant, but at least it made him turn from her so she could no longer see his look of pity.

He came back a short time later, holding out a hand to her as though there was nothing strange between them. 'The coachman tells me that southbound drivers claim it is this bad and worse for quite some way. Not fit for coach or wagon even if we could get one. But two horses, keeping to dry ground and travelling cross country, will have more success. I've bribed the driver to give us the wheelers and let us go on alone.'

'You want us to continue on horseback?' As though that was not obvious, without her chattering like a parrot at the poor man.

He answered with a nod; if he thought her dull witted, he was kind enough to ignore it. He produced a compass from his pocket, glancing up at the sun for confirmation. 'We will travel north and hope for drier roads when we reach Lancashire.' Then, as though remembering that it was not he who led, said, 'Does this meet with your approval, my lady?'

She blinked, wondering if she would have managed to snatch victory from the jaws of defeat in such a handy way had she not found him. 'I think I am most fortunate to have taken you on, Mr Hendricks.'

'Thank you, Lady Drusilla.'

Chapter Five

Thank you, Lady Drusilla. As you please, my lady. Even as John walked back to help unhitch the horses from the coach, the voice in his head mocked him. In taking this trip, hadn't he been planning to get out from under the thumbs of attractive and unattainable women? He'd only just got clear of Emily. And now, this.

When he'd realised that there was no space at the inn, he should have offered to pig up with the cit instead of carrying the farce any further. But he'd been drunk and querulous and the man annoyed him more than the girl.

Of course, it had been fortunate that he'd got time alone with Lady Drusilla Rudney and found a way to make himself invaluable. The Duke of Benbridge was terribly high in the instep; a letter of thanks from him would be a welcome addition to his references. But there would be no glowing recommendations if he was caught playing chamber games with the duke's lovely daughter.

Only moments after he'd accepted her offer of employment, he'd got a look at those shapely calves bared as the stockings came off and begun to regret the whole plan. When he'd managed to sleep, he'd dreamt of her. And he'd woken with a morning's desire, hurrying from the room before she could notice and enquire.

He had avoided her at breakfast, drinking strong black coffee to dull the after-effects of the gin and keeping busy with the plans for their departure. Then he had taken his place beside her to prevent the other man from encroaching upon her space. The carriage rocked her against his body in a way that would have been pleasant had not his role as her brother prevented any enjoyment. To curb the effect her nearness had on his nerves and body, he'd been forced to close his eyes and sink into the headache still plaguing him.

It disgusted him that his resolve to forswear all women and live in solitude had not even lasted as long as his inebriation. But he could hardly be blamed; the cit in the carriage had been panting after her as well and he had not been forced to share a bed with her. Lady Drusilla was a damned attractive woman, but seemed unaware of the effect she had on the men around her, wandering about alone and putting her virtue at risk. Any feelings John had for her were not a symptom of fickleness. They were proof that he was male.

But when she'd said she had an 'understanding' with the gentleman they were chasing, his first thought had been, *At least you are not yet married.* As if that would matter. Even if she was unattached, she was a duke's daughter and he was the bastard of who knew who.

Of course, she had said her Gervaise was a plain mister and not the Marquis of Gretna Green. It seemed that if the lady's heart was engaged, a title was not required. And John knew himself to be a better man in one respect. No matter what the circumstances of his birth, at least he was not the sort who made promises to one lady and ran for the border with another.

He had half a mind to thrash sense into this Gervaise fellow for running off on her. Though Lady Dru's tongue was sharp, she deserved better. That John would find himself rushing her north and into the arms of such a lacklustre lover was an even sharper irony. It was too like the part he'd played in the reconciliation of Emily and her husband.

He'd told himself often enough that his own parentage was not a reflection of his worth as a man. But when given a chance to test the theory, society always proved the opposite. And if Lady Dru was eager enough for her Mr Gervaise to set off cross country without a feather to fly on, hoping to win him back, then she would not be interested in some itinerant gentleman she met in the coach, even if that man was unwise enough to take a fancy to her.

Which he did not mean to do. John thought of a certain amiable widow who lived near the Folbroke country estate. It had been some months since his last visit to her. The extended period of celibacy must be addling his brain. Though he never seemed to be the target of it, the haze of feminine lust around his recent employers had raised something in him that was nothing more than envy disguised as infatuation and a desire to take care of natural and unmet needs.

When the carriage had got stuck, as he'd known it would, it had been almost a relief to exercise some of demons from his brain with pushing on the thing. Of course, to do it he had taken his employer in his arms and taken her to high ground, which had only made things worse. She was curvy under the simple gown she wore. And she had clung to his neck as though she'd enjoyed it, her red lips parted in surprise at how easily he'd carried her. He'd set her down quickly, out of the mud, before she could notice her lapse and his impropriety. If she spotted it, she would scold him for it, putting up barriers of rank and bad temper that were not the least bit threatening, once one knew her.

Strangely, he felt he did know her. Perhaps he was reading too much into the intent way she looked at him, or how easy it had been to talk to her on the previous evening, when they had been alone and no one could hear.

Then there had been that moment of awkwardness she'd displayed earlier, when she'd said she had not danced at Almack's. She must have meant that she had no permission to waltz and that she would not have been so rude as to slight any partner. For a moment, it had almost sounded as though she was woefully inexperienced in the arts of society and had some personal reason not to give him up when he'd held her.

He shook his head. He was dreaming again. If he was fortunate, at the end of the journey he would find a

Scottish widow sympathetic to his plight, and he would regain his equilibrium.

As he led the horses back to Lady Dru, he put on his most proper and deferential air, getting clear in his own mind the distance between them and the relationship they must have: respectful courtesy on his part and complete indifference on hers.

She looked dubiously at the horses, which were probably not the fine bloods to which she was accustomed.

'You have experience enough to ride, do you not?' he asked.

'Yes,' she answered, although her tone did not make her sound the least bit sure. 'But I did not pack a habit.'

He almost sighed in relief to hear the sort of clothes-obsessed response he'd expected from a smart young lady of the *ton*, foolish and easily dismissed. 'There is no place to change into it, even if you had it.' He gave her an encouraging smile. 'In any case, there will not be room enough to take much luggage. You will have to make do with a single bag; the rest will travel north to meet you when you reach your destination.'

'I do not have more than that now,' she said, glaring at him again. 'I left in rather a hurry and am not such a great ninny that I wasted what time I had in packing band boxes.'

Damn. 'Of course, my lady.'

Then she whispered more urgently, 'But, Mr Hendricks, there is a problem. This saddle is...wrong.'

'You are referring to the lack of a side saddle?' he asked. 'Coach horses are not generally equipped for a lady's Sunday ride. These are accustomed to having a postillion, so at least we will not have to worry about being thrown into the dirt. But I cannot promise more than that.'

Such an enormous beast would frighten a normal woman to tears, but his employer was staring at the horse with a raised chin and a dark look. Then she stared back at the saddle with apprehension. 'But what am I to do?'

There, at last, he saw the frightened girl under the iron façade. Perhaps this trip was not as easy as she made it out to be. He tried to hide his smile at the well-bred delicacy that thought spreading her legs was more risky than breaking her neck on a coach horse. 'You must weigh your desire for further rapid progress against the need to retain your modesty in the wilds of the country, where no one will see you.' He hoped she would take the more sensible choice, but knew that she would not.

'I cannot ride astride,' she said, finally, 'but I must continue north.'

'Then you can balance on your hip as best you can with no pommel to hold on to. Or we can use one horse for the luggage and you may ride with me.' It would be faster than walking the horses so that she did not slip from the saddle, but it would mean that he would have to hold her close as they travelled, which would be awkward in ways she could not possibly imagine.

She stared back at him, brow smooth, eyes cool, chin raised and lips narrowed. 'It cannot be helped, I suppose.' The expression put him firmly in his place, assuring him that the ride would not be a pleasant one for either of them.

And yet… He thought for a moment that he saw a fluttering in the pulse of her neck and a nervous swallow. And the faintest of pink flushes to her cheek. Then it was gone.

He cursed his wayward imagination and mounted the larger of the two horses, then offered her a hand up. To assure her, he said, 'Let us go a short way and see how we manage. You need have no concern for your safety, for I am an excellent horseman.'

'I know you will not let me fall,' she said. Her confidence in his abilities would have pleased him had it not been delivered in a testy voice, as though she'd just as soon be dropped upon her head than share his saddle. But she sat before him comfortably enough, posture good, and an arm about his waist with a grip that was firm and not the least bit missish.

It took only a few miles for him to begin wishing she'd taken the other choice. It was nice to ride with her—far too nice. She fit easily into the space before him, her soft hip pressed into his thigh as though it belonged there. As he spurred the horse, wisps of her fine black hair escaped from her bonnet and whipped in the breeze, teasing the skin of his cheeks. It was a tickling sweetness, bringing with it a whiff of cologne that made him want to lean forwards and bury his face in the side of her throat. He had to work to stifle the urge to loosen the bonnet and free the rest of it to let it stream in the wind.

He wished he was in a position to make conversation with her, for it might have helped to pass the time and occupy his mind in anything other than the scent of her hair.

'Who are you?' The words came from her suddenly, with no preamble. And then she stopped herself, probably shocked at sounding ridiculous, nonsensical and, worst of all, rude.

But she was unaware of what a blessed relief it was to him.

'I am John Hendricks, as I have already told you. I worked for the Earl of Folbroke as a personal secretary.'

She relaxed a little as though she'd been bracing for some sort of harsh retort. It made him wonder at the sort of conversation she was accustomed to, if a simple question was not met with a polite answer.

'But I think that is not what you are asking me,' he said. 'I would be happy to answer you in detail, if you would clarify your meaning.'

'How did you come to be who you are? Who are your people? Where did you come from?' And again he felt her tense, as though she were expecting ridicule. It made him want to reach out and offer physical comfort of some kind—a touch on the shoulder, a word in her ear urging her to relax in his company. Or, worse yet, to ask similar questions of her. He must remember that conversation between them, given his position and hers, was a one-sided affair at best. A desire to know his personal history did not demonstrate a desire to share hers.

He answered carefully, giving just the information

required. 'I was born in London, though I spent very little time there. My mother died when I was quite young; there is not much I can tell you of her, other than that she was beautiful. But that is what all children say of their mothers and so it hardly signifies.'

And that had been enough to loosen her tongue and relax her rigid posture. 'I suppose you are right, Mr Hendricks. I would say the same of my departed mother. Beautiful and happy.'

'Mine was sad.' He reflected for a moment, surprised that her questions had raised a fresh feeling of loss for something that had happened so long ago. 'I was sent away to school when she died. To Eton and then to Cambridge. There was never any question of how it would be paid for. But around the time of the death of Duke of Summersly, I received a nice settlement. I think that tells us both all we need to know about the identity of my father.'

'A bastard son of a duke?' Again she had blurted the words in a way that was the height of bad manners. He could almost hear her mouth snap shut.

'Of him, or some member of that family. While he did not acknowledge me in life, I cannot really complain about the way I was treated.' At least, he had no right to. 'I was a natural student and quite happy at all the schools I attended. I cannot say the same of my fellows. I took great pleasure in besting them when I could, at lessons or at games. It proved...' and then he remembered his audience and shut his own mouth.

'That it is not always one's parentage that proves one's abilities,' she finished for him, unbothered by the idea. Of course, she had no reason to feel threatened by it. She was a symbol of the rank he'd been denied; nothing he could say would change her status in society. 'And when you were finished with your education?' she prompted.

'I used the money I was given to buy a commission and did quite handsomely for myself as a soldier. I was aide-de-camp to the Earl of Folbroke. We were friends as well as comrades. When he returned home, I followed and took a position in his household.'

'And you might have been equals…'

'Or perhaps his superior,' he added calmly, 'had I been born on the right side of the blanket.' He waited for her chilly response and the inevitable withdrawal. Their circumstances were unusual and some curiosity was natural. But a well-bred young lady would not stoop to befriend a by-blow.

Instead, she continued as though she found nothing particularly unusual about his past. 'I enjoyed my schooling as well. There is a great comfort to be found in books.'

And why did you need comforting, I wonder? The woman was a curiosity.

'But in such places as I was sent, most of the time is spent ensuring that young ladies are properly prepared to take their roles as wives and mothers, and are assets to the households of their intended husbands.'

Which made them sound little better than servants. Perhaps they had more in common then he'd thought.

She sighed. 'When Mother died, it was agreed,

amongst us, that it would be for the best that I come home from school and see to things.'

Liar. Her father had commanded it, he was sure. He risked a question. 'And what sorts of things needed seeing to?'

'Once we were out of mourning, my younger sister, Priscilla, was ready to make her come out. And it has been decided that I must be her guard, until she finds a husband. The stronger must protect the weaker, after all.'

'And you are the stronger,' he said, softly.

Her eyes narrowed. 'I am. In mind and in body. I am older and wiser, as well. And with no mother to advise or protect her, someone must care for Priscilla.' There had been the faintest, most fleeting hint of a something on her face as she had said it, as though she remembered a time not so long ago when she had not thought that way at all. But her father had called her home. And like an obedient daughter, she had come and done exactly as she was told, putting all of her own dreams aside for the good of her sister. More than her mother had died on that day, John was sure of it, but Lady Dru had convinced herself otherwise.

Out of the blue, she added, 'Priscilla is the prettier of the two of us, and with the extra attention she receives from so many gentlemen, there is an increased risk.'

'Prettier than you?'

For a moment, her frown faded into a look of surprise, softening her features into a dark attractiveness that quickened his pulse. 'Of course. She is of a more appropriate height, delicate of frame, fair of hair, pale of skin.'

And that explained why she would run to Scotland after a man who no longer wanted her. If she thought this Mr Gervaise was her only opportunity, if their understanding was that he would wait until she felt free to marry, she would be loathe to let him go.

It pained him to see such hesitance in one who was normally so sure of herself. Would it do any harm to give her some assurance on her looks? For it was clear that no one else, not even the errant Gervaise, had done so. 'There is nothing inappropriate about your height,' he said. 'It suits you. And your frame suits your height. In my experience, delicacy is as likely to go hand in hand with sickness as it is with beauty. A lack of frailty on your part is hardly an imperfection.'

She was blinking at him again, as though she could not quite understand what it was that he meant. But it had brought a faint flush to her pale cheeks that made her all the more attractive, so he dared and went on, 'Your colouring might not be the same as your sister's, but it is most fetching. I am sure the two of you, when side by side, are an attractive counterpoint to each other.' Now he was wishing he had a hand free to adjust his spectacles so that he might get a better look at her face before continuing. 'That is only my opinion, of course. But there is nothing unusual about my tastes and assessment of feminine beauty. There are men who prefer the fair sex to be fair. And there are an equal number that enjoy raven hair and large dark eyes.' At the moment, he fell too much in the latter category to say more.

In fact, he had said too much already. He checked his watch. They were making good time, now that they could leave the roads as needed. He gave his passenger a brief warning and took the horses up a steep embankment, in an effort to find higher ground for them.

And since he'd put his hand on her waist to steady her, it had seemed only natural to leave it there and enjoy the warmth of her ribs. It was a shame that she did not see beauty when she looked into the mirror, for he found nothing wrong with her. Perhaps she was tall for a woman, but there was nothing in the least masculine about the rest of her. He spread his fingers to span as much of her as he could, easing her body back against him.

She responded by nestling closer. She relaxed against him, almost as if it required conscious effort to depend on the strength of another.

And he wanted to be her strength. In the years he had worked for Folbroke and doted on the man's wife, she had never once shown an interest in his past. They had been friends, of course, but not particularly close.

But in less than a day together, Lady Drusilla Rudney had ferreted out the truth of his birth and forged a connection between them. This trip was not the only time she'd felt alone. He could see it in her guarded eyes, in the way she held herself, carefully self-contained at all times, and the way she was leaning into him, unguarded and fragile.

Because of that fragility, he was a danger to her.

Though his mind might want to reach out and comfort, his body felt the flesh-and-blood woman beside him and wanted a much more earthy connection. The movement of the horse shifted her against him and he had idle thoughts of stretching his fingers upwards to graze the bottoms of her breasts. And each change in gait raised a fresh fantasy as she rocked against him. Walking brought to mind a languid afternoon of love making. A canter made him think of a quick coupling and fear of discovery. And as he nudged them to a full gallop, he thought of a night of wild, uncontrolled, vigorous…

'Mr Hendricks!'

Chapter Six

He pulled on the reins, bringing the horse up short, suddenly afraid that she had guessed the contents of his mind or felt his obvious physical response. 'My lady?'

He glanced around him, checking his surroundings, his watch and his compass, and comparing the results to the last mile marker he had seen to pretend that their progress had been the only thing on his mind.

'Could we stop to rest? I think—'

'An excellent idea.' He practically leapt from the horse, helping her down and stepping quickly away from her. 'The stand of trees over there looks quite inviting.' He waited for the rebuke that must be coming. There should be shock and outrage, or at least some sign that she feared to be near him.

Instead, she was biting her lip as though unsure what to say or do next. Then she gave a hesitant nod and half-muttered, 'Perhaps that is it. I need to rest.'

He let out a sigh of relief. She did not seem to be worrying about him at all. 'Was the ride tiring for you?' He offered her an arm to help her over the uneven ground as they walked the horses towards a stream by the grove.

She gave an uneasy laugh. 'I fear I do not make the best passenger. I could not seem to sit still.' There was a gruffness about her words, as though they were more denial than total innocence. But the look in her eyes was confusion, and perhaps embarrassment. It seemed he was not the only one affected by their nearness.

'It did not bother me overly,' he said, for it hardly seemed fair to call such pleasant sensations an annoyance.

'All the same, I do not think I wish to ride that way any longer. Is there no other way?' She was looking at him, vulnerable and desperate, trusting that he would understand and help her. And though he wanted nothing more than to tumble her in the grass, or sweep her into his arms and back into the saddle, he knew that he would not.

He stared at her, wondering if he dared suggest what he was thinking. 'There is a way that we can make better progress, if you are willing to take certain risks.'

'Anything,' she said eagerly, then looked at him, trying to appraise his plan and regain some of her old composure. 'Well, nearly anything. What do you suggest, Mr Hendricks?'

He went to the other horse and pulled down his bag, removing the clothing he had stashed there. He held them out to her. 'Leather riding breeches, Lady Drusilla. And I have a spare shirt as well. If you were dressed in a less feminine way, you could ride astride with more comfort.'

'Men's clothing?' she said, clearly appalled. 'You expect me to wear breeches?'

'From a distance, you would be mistaken for a boy. It would lessen the risk of someone recognising you as the Duke of Benbridge's daughter.'

'But it is very improper. I do not think I could...'

'They will fit,' he assured her. 'While you appear to be...' He cleared his throat, trying not to comment on the shape of her, which was as far from a man's as he could imagine. 'Well, at least we are of a similar height and, in most ways, I am larger than you. If we can cobble together a disguise out of spare clothing from my pack, it would do quite well for you.'

She touched the clothes gently and he noticed how fine her hand looked, lying against the leather. 'Would it add so much to the speed of our progress?'

'You will find that men's clothing is much less restrictive for trips like this. We will be able to move more quickly and will stop before returning to populated areas, to allow you to change into something more appropriate to your gender.'

'And no one would ever know?' she asked hopefully.

'I will certainly tell no one,' he said. 'It is much better, is it not, that Lady Drusilla not be seen travelling alone with a strange man?'

She gave a little shiver at the thought. He did not know whether to be angry or flattered by it, for at least it proved that she recognised him as a threat and not some neutered tool. 'That is probably true. If the story of this trip gets out, I have already done great harm to my reputation. Can the addition of breeches make it worse?'

He smiled encouragingly. 'Very well, then. Take these and step behind the trees to change. If you run into difficulties…' He thought of her half-dressed body and realised that there was not a damned thing he dared to do for her. 'Make a brave attempt.'

He waited where he was as she took the proffered clothing and concealed herself. To prevent temptation, he turned his back on the scene as well, so that he would not catch even a glimpse of bare skin through the sparse leaves.

Or, worse yet, he might catch himself straining to see something. Though he had managed to keep his eyes respectfully averted for most of last night, after the ride they'd just shared, his will was not so strong.

He heard her return a short time later and turned to find her standing with hands spread before her, in a gesture that sought approval. 'Is this all right?'

'Yes,' he responded, trying to modulate his own voice and looking hurriedly away. 'Yes. That will be quite satisfactory.'

Dear God.

When he'd made the suggestion, he had not given two thoughts to it. They were his own clothes, after all. He had seen them before.

But never like this. The shirt was full, and covered her to the throat, obscuring the curves underneath it with billows of fabric. But it was far too thin. The dark peaks of her breasts were displayed plain for anyone

who wished to look. The tender budding tips jutted
against the cloth. And his eyes strained to see, like
dogs at the end of a lead. He forced them back to her
face, and stripped off his topcoat and handed it to her.
'Perhaps this will help.'

It did not. Not really. Her legs still protruded from the
tails of the coat and the shapeliness of her calves was
not obscured through the heavy stockings. The leather
of the breeches pulled tight against her thighs and her
nicely rounded bottom. The buff colour looked almost
like bare skin. And it all seemed to settle into that final
crease at the top of her legs, drawing his gaze to a place
that he should never look, but that he very much wanted
to admire. They were alone, far from interruption, and
only a few buttons separated him from paradise.

He turned away from her, busying himself with
the harnessing of the horses, trying not to notice the
increasing tightness in his own trousers, then pulled
his glasses off, folded them and tucked them into the
pocket of his coat.

'Mr Hendricks,' she said, 'will you not need those
to see what you are doing?'

'Resting my eyes for a moment,' he assured her. 'It
has been a long day, has it not?' He turned back to the
horse and raised the stirrups as though this were the
only thing on his mind. 'You must manage in your own
boots, I'm afraid. Even if I had spares to offer, mine
would fall off your feet.'

Such dainty little feet.

He rummaged in his pack for a soft hat. 'Here. Put
this over your hair.'

She smiled at him in approval and pulled it into place. 'It is a relief to know that you do not expect me to cut it. There are some things I would not do in the name of disguise.'

'No. Never.' He hoped that his sigh had not been too obvious to her. But he'd have as soon asked her to cut off her arm as lose that glorious dark hair. He imagined it, down, smooth and thick in his hands. Then he did his best to imagine anything else. For a moment, he tried to think of Emily, who had occupied so much of his thoughts only two days ago. Her hair had been shorter and blond. It was strange how quickly a thing that had seemed so important to him, had faded so quickly from memory.

The same would likely be true of Lady Drusilla, once he was out of her sphere of influence. It must be, or it would drive him mad. When he glanced back at her, looking into her eyes this time, he could see that she would not. Or almost see, at any rate. For the blurring of his vision without the spectacles made her face soft, more childlike, her eyes large and bewildered, and her mouth rounded into a soft red bow. This was how she would look when he made love to her.

Which he would never do, he reminded himself. He had no right to even think such things about her. The list of reasons against it was almost too long to count.

'It is time we were going again,' he said, staring up at the sun. 'I do not mean to stop until dark. Then we will return to the main road, find an inn and enquire about your friend.'

He went to her and offered her a leg up into the

saddle of the big horse. For a moment, her foot rested in the cradle of his hands, and his face was far too near to her leg. He felt light headed with the desire to press his lips against the place he could reach. Then it was over and she was mounted, the horse dancing until she took control of the reins.

He looked up critically. 'You are sure that you will be all right with this?'

She straightened, stiffened and seemed to grow braver with each passing moment, though her eyes widened at the feel of the horse between her legs. 'It will be fine, because it must be so. And you are right. I can tell already that it is easier to ride when one can control the beast under one and not perch on it like a decoration.' She glared down at him, eyebrows and chin raised. 'And if you ever tell anyone I said that, I shall sack you immediately.'

'Yes, my lady,' he responded, with a small bow, dropping with difficulty back into the role of servant.

He rearranged the luggage and mounted his own horse. Then he pointed her in the right direction and allowed her to set the pace, for he did not wish to push her beyond her capacities.

He watched her ride. For someone with little experience, she had a good seat and showed no signs of fearing the animal he had given her. That was fortunate; he had no wish to end the day tearing across the open country after a runaway stallion, trying to save her from a fall. She chose a gait that was not too arduous on horse or rider, but still gained them time over the unreliable coach. It was hard not to admire her almost masculine single-mindedness in pursuit of a goal.

From his position behind her, he could admire her body as well. Now that the coat hid her form, there was really nothing to see. But his imagination was good, as was his memory. At some point, they would have to stop. And he would sleep in the stable before sharing another bed with her, lest he forget himself again.

Chapter Seven

Mr Hendricks pulled up beside her, and signalled her to slow her horse to a walk. 'We shall be stopping soon,' he said, checking his watch against the position of the sun. 'While it might be possible to travel farther, we must change horses to keep this pace. We could take a room—' He corrected himself '—rooms. And get some dinner.'

'Or we can hire fresh mounts and continue for a few more hours,' she said.

'You are not tired?'

'Not if there is a chance that we are gaining on them.' They'd had no information since the stop this morning. And she must hope that the speed they were moving had closed the distance.

'And you are comfortable as you are attired?' He looked doubtfully at her borrowed costume.

'I am accustomed to it,' she said, not wishing to commit herself. It was strangely freeing to go without skirts, as long as she did not think of how it must look. She could bend low over the horse's neck and gallop if she wished, unencumbered by petticoats, not worrying about the set of her hat or the attractive arrangement of the garments. And while she felt the stretching of unused muscles, it was not so much painful as troubling. There was a guilty pleasure in it that would not be repeated. And she wished to prolong that a few more hours, if she could.

'Very well, then. We will stop at the next inn, and I will check for your wayward carriage and hire us some new steeds. You...' He looked her up and down before speaking again. 'You had best remain in the courtyard. Keep your coat buttoned and your hat pulled low. Speak to no one and do not wander off.' He looked at her again as though he expected to see something he had not noticed before. 'I am sorry to say it, my lady, but you do not make a very convincing man.'

And then he laughed, a kind of choking snort as though his proper demeanour had failed him.

'Is there something amusing that I am not aware of?' she said in a voice that should have frozen him to silence.

He was still chuckling slightly. 'You seemed most unhappy with a statement that, in any other context, would have been good news. Just now, you were glaring into the air as though you had wished to hear you wore it better. I found the juxtaposition funny.'

'I do not like to be reminded that I am unable to perform a role to the satisfaction of others.' She'd had enough of that at home to last a lifetime.

'It is no fault of yours, I assure you,' he said. 'Perhaps a less attractive woman might have managed it.' He laughed again.

'Please do not joke with me about my appearance,' she snapped. 'If you thought that I was angling for a compliment, I assure you, that was not the case.

'I am not laughing at your appearance,' he said in the same mild patient tone he'd used to coax her into wearing his clothes, but stifling a smile. 'Only at the way you frowned again upon being told that you were attractive.'

'Because it is nonsense,' she said. 'Fine words meant to flatter me into a better humour.'

'Give me more credit than that, Lady Drusilla. I have not been in your employ for long, but I am smart enough to realise that it would take more than flattery to put you in a good humour.' Before she could reprimand him, he shot her another sidelong glance, then turned his attention to the road. 'This is what comes from reading sermons,' he muttered. 'You think too much. If I wished to flatter you, I would have mentioned your pleasant features and your beautiful dark hair. Both comments would have been true. But they would have nothing to do with your inability to disguise such an obviously female body in masculine clothing with any degree of success. And now, if you tell me that the Lord has given it to you, and you deserve no credit for it, then I will take that little book of sermons from your pocket and throw it into the next stream.'

To put an end to the conversation, he gave his beast

a gentle kick in the sides and was off at such a pace that she had to struggle to follow him.

He needn't have bothered. Any retorts she had for him had flown quite out of her head. Left in their place was a swirl of words: attractive, pleasant, beautiful and, best of all, obviously female. Somewhere in the midst of it, he had commented on her bad humour. But she was hardly bothered by a comment on something which was seen as a universal truth by those close to her.

And he had laughed, not exactly at her, but in her direction, as though her temper amused more than it upset him. The negatives he'd thrown into the last inter-change were like salt in a pudding, serving to emphasise the sweetness and bring out the subtle flavours of the rest.

And he had threatened to throw her sermon book into the river. Taken as a whole, she could not decide if she wanted to stammer a blushing thank you, or ring a peal over him. But the last statement could not be allowed to stand.

She spurred her horse to draw even with him. 'I would not care if you did throw the sermons in a stream,' she said, a little breathless from the ride. 'It is not as if they are my exclusive reading.'

'You brought other books with you?'

'Not on this journey, no.'

His features had returned to mild-mannered passiv-ity, as though he had collected enough evidence for a decision, but saw no reason to comment on it.

'Perhaps it was because I thought that the couple I was searching for needed a reminder of their duty.'

'So you sought to give a sermon and not to read one?' It was an innocent observation. But it made her feel horribly priggish, not at all like the beautiful hoyden of a moment ago.

'We cannot always have what we want,' she said firmly. 'Where would the world be if everyone went haring off after their desires, eloping to Scotland on the least provocation?'

'Where indeed?'

'It would be chaos,' she said, sounding depressingly like the voice of her father.

'And you are sure you wish to stop this particular elopement,' he said carefully. 'If we are lucky, we might catch up with your friends tonight. Or perhaps tomorrow. But sometimes, when people are in love and intent upon their goal, they cannot be turned from it. If you stop them now, they will find another way.'

'If they run again, I will chase them again,' she said, feeling as stiff and flat as her sermon book. 'I do not mean to give them any choice in the matter. This marriage cannot take place. It simply cannot.' She was already near to on the shelf. With a scandal in the family, her own reputation would be in tatters. Her father would be livid at Priscilla and in no mood to launch the other daughter: the one who had failed to protect his favourite.

The man beside her sighed. 'Very well, then. If you are resolute, I load my pistols and prepare myself for the inevitable.'

'The inevitable?'

'To haul the loving couple back across the border by force, if necessary.'

'You would do that?'

'If you wished me to.'

And now she was the one smiling at incongruity. He had replaced his spectacles since their last stop and the sun glinted off his lenses, causing him to squint slightly. He hardly looked the type to resort to physical violence. 'If you will remember our conversation last evening, I requested discretion.'

'The sound of a single shot will not carry all the way to London,' he replied. 'And from what I understand of females, a wound in a non-vital spot is often deemed quite romantic.'

'It is not my goal to make Mr Gervaise even more attractive to the opposite gender.'

'Perhaps not, then.' He thought again. 'Maybe I should punch him. A broken nose will solve the problem of his good looks quite nicely, I am sure.'

The idea did have appeal. As did dragging Priscilla back to London by the hair. But it would only make her run away again. And the last thing she needed to risk was engendering sympathy for the villain who had taken her away. 'No, as I said, discretion is the watchword.' She glanced at him again. 'But thank you for the offer.'

He ducked his head. 'At your service, Lady Drusilla.'

Of course. That was all it had been. She had employed him to solve the problem and he had offered suggestions. The protectiveness that she was sure she'd heard were imaginings on her part. Nothing more than that.

She sighed. For a moment, it had felt quite nice to think that there was a man on the planet who could be moved to brutal overreaction in defence of her.

They kept the pace until they arrived at the next inn, and Mr Hendricks left her standing by a wall in the courtyard, out of the way of departing coaches, as he went to see about the horses and make enquiries about recent guests. While she waited, she did as he'd suggested and buttoned the coat, pulling his hat low over her eyes and thrusting her hands into her pockets in a way that she hoped looked insolent and unwelcoming.

But she could tell from the looks she got from the stable hands that they saw easily through her disguise. She shrank back into Mr Hendricks's overcoat, vowing that whatever might happen between here and Scotland, she would not be out of his sight for another moment. He had been right. There was no way that she would be taken for a male. She did not want to think about what the clothes might be exposing to view. Even hidden in the coat, she was exposing so much of her legs that she might as well be standing naked in the courtyard.

But despite her fears, the boys' attitudes were not so much menacing as amused. She could hear the muttered conversation between them, as they came for the horses and brought out the fresh pair. One was guessing it was an elopement. The other disagreed. The gentleman seemed more interested in who had gone before than who might come from behind. It must be some sort of bet or a strange prank.

The first insisted that the man was too old to be just down from Oxford. And the woman was too fine to be the sort of woman who would don breeches for the amusement of the lads. Only love made people act as cork-brained as this. It was an elopement for sure. He'd bet a penny on it.

Drusilla tried not to smile. There was some comfort in knowing that though she did not look like a boy, neither did everyone mistake her for a whore. But the idea that she might be thought the one eloping?

What a wonderful thought that was. For a moment, she imagined herself as being that sort of girl. Just once, she wished to be the one racing for the border with a laughing lover as the hue and cry was raised after her. And chaperons all over London would shake their heads and murmur to their charges about the bad end one was likely to come to, if one behaved like the notorious Silly Rudney.

Mr Hendricks was in the doorway, haggling back and forth with the innkeeper, struggling to pull coins from his pockets and muttering to himself. Then he walked back to her through the busy coach yard, dipping his head low to speak in confidence to her. 'Are you still carrying your reticule?'

She nodded.

'Please give it to me.'

She produced the blue silk bag from the pocket of her man's coat and was certain she heard laughter from the boys who had been watching her. It became even louder as they saw Mr Hendricks rooting through the contents for the sad collection of coins remaining there, swearing at the little money in his hand. Then he thrust the purse back to her and stalked away.

One stable boy passed a penny to the other, agreeing that only a man in love could be brought so low, and Dru cringed in embarrassment for her companion. And the boys glanced in the direction of the doorway to the inn, then looked hurriedly away.

There was a young lady, standing alone beside a stack of bandboxes, waving a handkerchief in the hopes of receiving aid. The burden was light and would have been no trouble for boys strong enough to handle cart horses. But when Dru got a better look at the identity of the girl, she disappeared into Mr Hendricks's coat, sympathising with the sudden deafness of the stable hands.

Priss's friend, Charlotte Deveral, was not someone she might wish to meet under the best circumstances. The girl was too young and pretty to be a harridan, but it was only a matter of time. If her disposition was as Dru remembered, she was most likely in a temper over nothing. And she would take it out on a tardy servant, or any lad who left a smudge on a package while trying to earn a penny or two.

'Boy!' Char's voice was sharp and ugly. 'Boy!' And then she muttered an aside to her paid companion. But it was a theatrical *sotto voce*, meant to embarrass the targets of her wrath. 'These country clods are all either deaf or stupid. One must shout to make them understand. I say! Boy!'

For a moment, Dru was reminded of her own tone as she ordered Mr Hendricks about. Did it sound like that to him? she wondered. She felt suddenly ashamed of herself and more than a little embarrassed for Char, who was making a spectacle of herself with all the shouting and flapping of linen.

'Boy, I am talking to you.'

And it was then that it occurred to Dru that there was no one else near and that Char was addressing her. 'Eh?' She managed a deep masculine grunt, and thrust her hands even deeper into her pockets, as though she did not care a bit for what some London piece might think of her.

'Help me with these packages. My coachman is nowhere to be found.' And another aside, loud enough so the stable boys might hear, 'And the rest of the staff here are useless.'

Dru touched the brim of her hat in what she hoped was a respectfully masculine way, managing to pull it even lower over her face as she did so. Then she sauntered towards Charlotte.

She heard one of the stable boys snicker.

But Charlotte noticed nothing unusual about the 'boy' she'd called to aid her, looking right through Dru and refusing to recognise someone she had seen dozens of times before. Of course, a lad in an inn yard was so far beneath her that he might as well have been an ant upon the ground. What reason would she have to assume he was no lad at all? And he was not nearly as important as the bandboxes, to which Char gave her full attention. 'Help me place my packages in the carriage.'

'Miss,' Dru said with false respect, bowing low to take them from the ground at Char's feet.

'The correct form of address is my lady.'

The devil it was. The Deveral family was gentle enough, but there was not a title in it. And though Charlotte had her hopes, she would be settling for a plain Mister at the end of the season. But Dru could not exactly announce a fact that she should be in total ignorance of. 'My lady,' she corrected herself and bowed deeper.

And heard another snicker from the boys behind her.

She went around to the back of the carriage and clambered into the basket, securing the packages with the rest of the luggage and, quite by accident, placing Char's bonnet where it might be crushed at the next stretch of rough road. Then she helped Char and her chaperon into their seats as the groom who should be doing the job appeared from the taproom, too late to be of help to anyone.

As Drusilla closed the door and withdrew, Char gave an insolent toss of her head and said, 'For your trouble.' And then she pulled a coin from her purse and made as if to hand it out of the window. But she realised at the last moment that she had no wish to touch a filthy stranger and dropped it in the direction of Dru's hand.

Before she could snatch it from the air, the shilling hit the cobbles and rolled into the muck.

Dru stared down at it in disgust. Under normal circumstances, she would not have noticed the loss of it. But things were far from normal and she was still far from Scotland. She stooped and grabbed, trying to ignore the dirt clinging to her fingers. To add insult to injury, the Deveral carriage had started on its way. Before she could step clear, the wheels and hooves sent up a fine spray of mud that struck her cheek.

To make her humiliation complete, Mr Hendricks appeared with two fresh horses, just in time for a view of the tableau: Lady Drusilla Rudney, muck spattered and scrambling for coins, to the great amusement of ladies and stable boys alike. She could expect no more fine words about her obvious feminine beauty now that he'd seen her debased, dismissed as something less than human by a woman of her own kind. Even worse, she had disobeyed him by talking to Char at all. She waited for a stern lecture on speaking to strangers and the need for secrecy. Or, worse yet, laughter.

Instead, he said nothing, offering her his handkerchief to wipe off the mud. Then he spoke as though he had seen nothing unusual. 'The news is both good and bad, I'm afraid. The couple you seek were here just this morning.'

She hurriedly wiped her face, clinging to this one small success. 'How many hours ago?'

'Four, perhaps. Maybe less. They stayed for luncheon, before starting out again. They seemed in no hurry, wherever it was they were going.'

'So we are gaining on them.' Dru smiled in satisfaction. 'They were a day ahead when I started off. If they continue to dawdle, then we are likely to catch them before they reach the border.'

'If that is still what you wish,' Hendricks replied. 'We are at the end of our funds, I am afraid.'

'I thought you had ample money to help me,' she said, feeling even worse than before. If she'd taken the man's last groat to catch her sister, she could hardly fault him if they failed.

'I thought I had sufficient funds as well,' he said. 'But now that I have brought us to the middle of nowhere, I find that my purse is still in my pocket, but its contents are gone.' His brows knit and the darkness of his expression was truly fearsome. She braced herself, ready to bear the brunt of the inevitable tirade.

Instead, he turned it inwards upon himself. 'I have only myself to blame for our circumstances. Like a fool, I left my coat behind in the mail coach, as I helped to push. And that grudge-bearing, bacon-fed cit went through my pockets and helped himself to it. Now I am reduced to picking through a lady's reticule and letting you grovel for pennies in a coach yard.' He looked to her again, obviously pained by the confession. 'I am sorry, Lady Drusilla. I have failed you.'

She felt a rush of sympathy. After all he had done to get her this far, she was amazed that he would think so harshly of himself. 'You most certainly have not failed me,' she said. 'We have simply hit another difficulty and must take the time to examine our options. What do you suggest?'

'As I see it, we have two alternatives. We return to the place we left and find the man responsible.'

'And what good would that do us? He would likely deny that he had taken anything.'

'At first, perhaps. But all the same, I would give him a thrashing that would shake the coins from his pockets.' His cold smile and the glint in his eye said that the experience would be the most emotionally satisfying option and the one he favoured.

'Mr Hendricks!' Drusilla said sharply. 'Attend, please. To return to find the thief would put my goal quite out of reach. If I have come this far, I do not wish to turn back without some satisfaction. Is there no other way to get to Scotland?'

Now, he was staring at her in silence, as though she were a piece in the puzzle that he could not quite seem to make fit. He did not immediately answer and she repeated, 'Mr Hendricks?'

'I am thinking,' he said, a little too sharply for a servant, and then corrected his tone before responding. 'There is another way, if you are dead set on continuing. We will press northwards as we have been doing and ride this change of horses to the end. We will be forced to sleep rough. We will take the shilling in your hand to buy some bread and cheese for our supper. But after that, we will have to beg or steal what we need for sustenance.' He looked heartily sorry that he could not do better. 'I fear it is not what you are accustomed to. But the only other alternative I can offer is to admit defeat and appeal to your father for help.'

'And that is precisely what I will not do.' She stood straight again, remembering that she was the daughter of a duke and not some slouching farm boy. Then she wiped the muddy coin and handed it back to Hendricks along with his handkerchief. 'Take this and buy us some dinner, so that we might set off again.' She glanced up the road at the dust of the retreating carriage, focusing all her anger and frustration on it, longing for revenge. And then an idea occurred to her. 'And if you hurry I think there is a way that we might solve all our problems, given a little darkness and a little luck.'

Chapter Eight

'This is mad, you know.' Mr Hendricks spoke in the same soft voice he used on those times when he managed to remember that she employed him.

'You have told me that on several occasions already.'

'I did not think one more would make a difference,' he said, with a sigh. 'But if there was even the smallest chance, then I had to try. When I suggested we steal to survive, this was not at all what I was intending. I meant that we would take only what was necessary. A loaf from a farmer's window sill, perhaps.'

'Which would leave the poor family there with nothing to eat,' she said. 'Does it not diminish the hurt to all concerned if we steal from someone who lives a life of excess?'

'Perhaps that is true, in theory. But you are not discussing some distant and romantic utopia. You are asking me to rob a coach on a modern highway. I believe, my lady, that you have confused me with some idealised combination of Robin Hood and Dick Turpin.'

'Just as you have confused me with a character in a Drury Lane comedy,' she snapped back, 'and persuaded me to traipse halfway across England in your cast-off clothing.' His tone annoyed her, for it was no longer mild subservience. There was a distinct air of derision. And it was just another example of the way those around her had no trouble leading her into jeopardy with their outrageous plans, then resisting when she offered an equally outrageous plan of her own.

'If you mean to rob every farm between here and Scotland, we will never reach our destination. Rather than stealing one loaf at a time, we could take a single purse from someone who can afford a closed carriage and have more than enough gold to finish the trip. In the eyes of the Lord, the latter is far worse.'

'It is to be my misfortune that you were reading the story of the widow's mite,' he said. 'I should have taken that book from you when I had a chance.'

'If you had, my opinion now would be the same,' she snapped back. 'I have no desire to spend a week sleeping in barns and munching on stolen bread and green apples.' Although, were she honest, the prospect of being forced to sleep in the wilderness, huddled against Mr Hendricks for warmth, had a certain appeal to her.

'I am sorry, my lady, if all that I can offer you is not to your liking.' There was a surprising bitterness in the way he said her title, as though it were caught in his teeth.

'And I am sorry if you do not like the position you

have been engaged to perform.' She gave him her cruellest smile and let the words be an equally bitter reminder for him, as well as herself, that her present condition was nothing more than a colossal inconvenience.

'Begging your pardon, my lady.' He offered a false bow and tugged his forelock. 'I will not forget my place again.'

The soft blond hair falling in his eye gave her the sudden and inappropriate impulse to smooth it back with her fingers. She ignored it and said, 'Your apology is accepted. Now, about the matter of the coach robbery...'

'Which I cannot in any way condone.'

She huffed in disgust. 'Your weak resolve had been duly noted. And I dismiss it. The occupants of the vehicle we will be stopping are unworthy of your sympathy. Char Deveral is a pampered, foolish girl of carefully cultivated prettiness, who would leave a full purse on the ground rather than soil her hands picking it out of the mud.'

Or a coin from a coach yard. The incident still stung, even now that her hands were clean. She had made Mr Hendricks ride the next miles hard and well off the road, until her anger had abated. But at least she was sure they had passed the carriage and could lie in wait for it.

And now, even if she did not get to Priscilla in time, she would have her revenge for that muddy coin and for a host of other small tricks and social slights delivered over the years by Char and her friends. She smiled at the prospect. 'I know her type well. They are always talking behind their hands at those not of their set, laughing at their own empty jokes, and despite all the warnings of those who know better, running off with men who are little better than servants, heedless of what it might to their reputations, leaving the more rational members of their family to rescue them from their own foolishness, causing no end of misery...'

Now she had gone totally off her track and could tell by the look in his eye that he thought her even madder than before. He broke into her tirade. 'It is not the character of your potential victims that concerns me, Lady Drusilla. Or their tendency to fraternise with men who are beneath them. It is the result of our likely capture.'

She waved away his objections. 'If we are caught, then I shall tell everyone who I am and that you are my servant, forced into the actions by my misguided desire for adventure.'

He held his hand heavenwards as though to summon the angels to witness what he was forced to endure. 'And I suppose, when they ignore you, and I am hanged for highway robbery, it will be a consolation to know that it was not really my fault.'

'Nonsense,' she insisted. 'My father has bought justice to a halt for my sister more often than you can imagine. If this time the felonious prank perpetrated was the fault of Silly Rudney instead of his darling Priss, he will be annoyed with me, but will not hesitate. While the world has heard of no such actions on my part, a single mistake of mine can hardly compare to the sum total of the rest of my family.'

Mr Hendricks swore aloud, not caring that she heard

the words, and said, in a more moderate tone, 'The upper classes are all quite mad. For a time I had hoped that you were proving to be otherwise. But you are blessed with a stubbornness that is well outside the bounds of sanity and a single-mindedness that could wear reason down to a nub.'

So, she had lost the good opinion of the man who sat beside her. 'At least I am consistent, Mr Hendricks.'

'You are that, my lady.'

Then she tried something that had not occurred to her before and dipped her head slightly, doing her best at a shy smile, as her sister would have done when trying to charm a man. She looked up at him through her long dark lashes. 'I am sorry to have been such a bother. You have done your best to keep me safe and I have much to be grateful for. If you can help me in this one last thing, I will see to it that you are properly rewarded for the inconvenience of it.'

He laughed. 'So it has come to this, has it? You mean to use your wiles on me, now that all else has failed?' There was a strange pause before his response, as he stared boldly back at her in challenge. 'And how might you reward me, if I risk my neck for you?' His voice was not mild at all, but hoarse, deep and strangely thick. She could feel the answering thickness in her blood as her pulse slowed.

She swallowed, wondering what she had meant to tell him. Some part of her mind was sure that her sister would have offered a single kiss as though it had some material value, but she doubted the currency of her inexperienced lips was of comparable worth. Nor could she inform him that, should they manage to find Priscilla, she could procure that kiss for him from her sister.

Then a thought occurred to her. She could tell him to take what he liked for a reward. Then *he* would kiss *her.* And though it would seem like a forfeit, only she would know that she had been rewarded twice.

But now that she needed it most, her nerve failed her. 'My father will pay you double whatever you intended to receive from this escapade. What else could I possibly mean?'

He shook his head in amazement. 'I cannot imagine. Double the pay it is, then. And enough money to replace what was stolen from me?'

'Of course.'

'Then for you, I shall turn highwayman, my Lady Dru.'

His anger with her must have dissipated, for the way he'd shortened her name had none of the frustrated affection that she felt when someone called her Silly. This made her feel odd. She tingled, almost as though he had reached out and touched her cheek to show her that they were friends again, and she needn't worry.

He stared down the road. The sun was near to dipping behind the horizon; with each moment, it became more difficult to make out details of their surroundings. But from just behind the last hill she could hear the sound of horses, and the jingling of harnesses growing louder as they drew near.

Mr Hendricks removed his spectacles and tucked them into the pocket of his coat.

'Do you not need them to see what you are about to do?' she asked.

He shook his head. 'Sometimes it is better not to see. It will be easier to do something as foolish as we are doing tonight without a clear view of it.' Then he reached behind him to the bag that was strapped to the back of his saddle and removed a pair of pistols and two black neckcloths. He tossed a cloth to her, and then carefully handed her one of the guns. 'Pull the cravat up and over your face,' he cautioned. 'Stay well out of the way, up on this hill with the setting sun to your back. You will seem much more intimidating if they do not have a clear view of you. And keep the pistol pointed up and over the heads of the drivers.'

'It is not loaded.' She said, trying not to sound relieved, for he had not troubled with ball and powder for her gun as he had with his own.

'But they do not need to know that and I do not mean you to shoot. Just hold it as if it is properly ready. They will have no idea, unless you do something that might cause them to fire at you and do not respond.' Then he looked at her seriously. 'And if they do, if there is any trouble at all, then you will turn and ride away, do you understand?'

'But that will leave you here alone.' At last, she saw the truth of the risk she had forced him to take. The empty gun trembled in her hand.

His face was dark, as threatening as one would expect from someone desperate enough to rob a coach. But it was with concern for her, not anger. 'If there is gunplay, it is no place for a lady to be, much less a lady disguised that might be treated with as little care as one might treat another man. If there is a problem, you will leave me to my fate.'

'I am your employer and I ordered you to this.' If he was hurt, it would be her fault. The thought almost choked her with anxiety.

'You have not answered me,' he said firmly. 'I brook no discussion of this, nor will I waste time listening to any suggestions you might give me. Swear that you will do as I say, or I will not proceed. And hurry, for there is not much time.' Without his glasses, there was no mildness in him at all. And the way he was staring at her made her feel small, easily managed.

It made her wish that there would be cause for him to look at her like that again. Perhaps in a situation where she had not put his life in jeopardy. For if he did, she would respond to any command he might give. She stifled a sigh and said, 'As you wish.'

'Very good. The coach is almost here and we have no more time to argue.' He pointed to a spot well up the hill from the road. 'Wait for me there. The height will appear to give you a good shooting position and will make retaliation difficult. You will be perfectly safe, as long as you do what I say.'

He pulled his own dark scarf over his face, and she masked herself as well. There was nothing attractive about highway robbery. Or, at least, there should not have been. But the way he sat atop his horse, and the sight of him with nothing but those strange amber eyes visible above the scarf, was quite dashing.

It was incongruous with the look of quiet competence

that she had come to expect when seeing Mr Hendricks. The man before her now was the very devil on horseback. His thighs were muscular, the dark coat stretched over broad shoulders and a shock of blond hair crept out from beneath the low brim of his hat. And, once again, her body tingled in the unexpected way it had when she had first sat upon the horse with him. He had been so strong, when he'd helped her easily in and out of the saddle. Now she wondered how those strong hands would feel if they lingered on her body.

They waited in silence, as the carriage approached. Suddenly, it was too late to lay a hand on his arm, or call out a warning to stay him. He was thundering down the road into the path of it, causing the driver to pull up and the horses to shy.

'Stand and deliver!' Mr Hendricks's voice echoed off the surrounding hills, and his horse reared as he fired a single shot into the air. But he kept his seat as though there were nothing in it, waving the driver and groom to the ground with his pistol.

And she would do everything she could to help him, even if it meant doing nothing at all. She kept her horse still and the pistol steady, held high so that the coachmen below her could see it.

They got down from their seats and made no effort to defend the family they served. Having met the inhabitants of the carriage, Dru could guess why. There was little to recommend Char that would give one the desire to risk life and limb.

Mr Hendricks was down from his horse in a trice, waving the coachmen to the side of the road and directing them to lie upon their bellies and out of the way, gesturing up at her to show them it would go harsh with them should they try anything. When he was sure that they would do as directed, he strode up to the carriage and opened the door.

Charlotte gave a ladylike shriek from inside. 'My jewels!'

Hendricks gave a slight bow and a tip of his hat, then said in a plummy voice, 'I would not, for all the world, threaten your lovely person, nor steal the baubles from your beautiful throat.' Under his mask, she was sure he was smiling. 'I seek the money in your purse and mean to take only as much as I need.' He held open the door, then held out his hand for her reticule.

And the foolish girl leaned so far forwards, trying to get a good look at the man in the road, that she tumbled out into his arms.

From Dru's position, it was the most contrived thing she had ever seen in her life. Char's shameless behaviour very nearly made her forget the two men she was supposed to be watching. But when she looked back at them, they showed no signs of rising and seemed more interested in a flask they were passing back and forth between them, than in regaining the pistols resting on the seat of the carriage.

Mr Hendricks caught Charlotte easily before she hit the ground. Then he said, in a voice deeper than usual, 'You needn't fear, my lady. Your person and your jewels are perfectly safe. Though indeed, now that I see you, they are hardly necessary to enhance your beauty.'

Dru's eyes narrowed. For while she had no wish to

see Mr Hendricks shoot Char, Priss's friend was doing it much too brown. The girl reached to open the reticule, pretended to fumble, dropping her purse in the dust of the road. Then she began to sag.

Hendricks rescued the money and tightened his grip on the girl fainting in his arms. Dru could remember how nice those arms felt when they had been around her body. But he'd never had cause to hold her as tightly as this. And he never would, if the only way to accomplish it was to fake a swoon.

Charlotte gave a weak laugh. 'I fear I am close to overcome.' She put her hands upon his bicep, so she could feel the muscle there. 'You are very strong.' She tipped her head back in an obvious invitation. 'And I am quite defenceless.'

'Are you, now?' She could tell, even from this distance, that Hendricks was responding favourably to the shameless play-acting. And it irked her to see the trick she'd tried on him played better by one who had no responsibilities to prevent her from feigning helplessness when it suited her.

In the carriage, Char's chaperon gave a warning tutting noise, but did little more than fan herself and watch eagerly. In Dru's opinion, the woman did far too little to put a stop to her charge's behaviour, even when there was not a pistol drawn.

Hendricks had pulled the coin purse from inside the bag and was feeling the weight of it in his hand. 'This will do nicely, I think. I will not take from your companion. If she has any money, she will need it more than you.' He glanced over his shoulder, gauged the distance and tossed the purse expertly up to Dru, who loosed the strings and counted the substantial curl of notes inside.

'If there is anything else you want sir, you are welcome to it. As long as you spare my life and my necklace.'

She'd said nothing of her innocence, Dru noted. And now Char was batting her eyelashes as though she had cinders in her eyes.

Mr Hendricks gave a little laugh and reached to undo the bottom of his mask. 'Then you shall sacrifice a kiss, my dear, and I will go on my way.' And then he put his lips upon hers. It was hard for Dru to see past the edge of the mask and the red haze forming in her own eyes. But it appeared that he had opened her mouth. His mouth was open as well. There was much movement and what looked like mutual chewing.

The coachmen were nudging each other and chuckling where they lay on the ground. The rate of the chaperon's fan increased, as though she was about to overheat in the closed carriage.

Now Char was making little noises in the back of her throat that sounded suspiciously like moans of pleasure. Her body trembled and her hands clutched urgently at Mr Hendricks's coat, as though she wished to crawl inside it with him.

And Dru felt sick, wishing that she could call the last few moments back and beg bread from farm wives as he'd first suggested. Her petty desire to take revenge on Charlotte might have gained them the money needed to finish the trip, but it had earned Charlotte a conquest.

And Char had got *her* kiss. If she had only chosen the

right words a few moments ago, she would be the one bent over Mr Hendricks's arm. It would be her mouth he'd opened. And she would be the one shuddering in ecstasy and hanging from his lapels.

Instead, she had offered him money.

Dru stared down at the purse. Then she pocketed the bills, which were more than enough to get them to Scotland and back, and let the little bag drop again to the ground. She gave her horse a little kick that caused him to shift uneasily and stamp the thing into the mud at his feet.

When she looked back to the road again, Mr Hendricks was setting Char back upon her feet to more ineffectual noises from the companion. Dru could see the look of dazed happiness on the face of her sister's friend.

She felt the strange, hot feeling again, in her cheeks and lower. Her throat felt flushed; the fabric of her shirt seemed to chafe at her breasts. And in the tight confining cases of leather there was a spot between her legs that seemed to pulse and burn and make her want to leap from the horse and rip the breeches from her body.

Now Mr Hendricks had secured his mask again and was helping Charlotte back into the coach. Then he ran to his horse, springing easily into the seat as though invigorated by the robbery. He tipped his hat again. 'Thank you, my lady.' And then, another tip of the hat for the chaperon. 'Apologies, ma'am.'

The casual courtesy annoyed her almost as much as the kiss had. How many times had she experienced that polite, dismissive attention from an attractive man, only to have him turn back to Priss?

'And now, I must be going.' Mr Hendricks looked back to the coachmen. 'See to your mistress, gentlemen. And if you are smart, you'll take your time about it.' Then he spurred his horse up the hill towards her, and they were off, into the open country, far away from the road.

They rode for some time without stopping; she ripped off her mask when he did and followed him without question. But her mind was seething and her body still in turmoil. If there was such a thing as a chaperon's corner for highwaymen, she had been left there tonight, holding an empty gun instead of her knitting. As usual, the real excitement was occurring close enough to be seen. And, as usual, no one had wanted her participation.

Mr Hendricks pulled up suddenly in the shelter of a copse of trees. Then he reached into his pocket and retrieved his glasses, looking through them and polishing the lenses. Without her having to ask, he supplied, 'I stayed not far from here, while growing up. There is no reason to ride blind. But it was pleasant to learn that I still know the roads well enough for pranks such as this.' He adjusted the spectacles and gave her a dark look. 'Not that I mean to pull any more of them.' Then he held out his hand for the money and counted it.

'And no more robberies should be necessary. This is enough that we might hire a carriage for the remainder of the journey. Once we reach Lancaster you may put on skirts again and travel properly, as a lady.'

As though that would matter to him, for she doubted he thought any more of her than he had of the unfortunate young lady fanning herself in Char's carriage. 'I do not have to put on skirts again, if it is more convenient to proceed as we have been.'

'I should think you'd be happy for the chance to ride in comfort. We can resume a normal rate of travel, rather than tearing across country, higgledy-piggledy.' He looked off in the direction of the northern horizon. 'Although we will keep it up for some time yet. There is a short cut I know that will bring us out on the road far away from the carriage we have just visited and closer to the one you seek.' He glanced back at her, taking in her unusual costume. 'The night is clear and I do not expect pursuit. We shall stay as we are and sleep under the stars. But tomorrow, it would be better that you were a woman again and I take back my hat and coat.'

'If I were a woman?' This was even worse than being ignored. It seemed she had lost her gender altogether, with a simple change of clothes.

'If you were dressed as one,' he corrected. 'Of course, I know you are a woman.' He laughed in a funny, awkward way that did not match his earlier self-assurance.

'Do you really?' Suddenly it was very important that he say it aloud.

'And my employer as well,' he added quickly. And this was worse than neutering her. She might as well have been another species. But to choose now, of all times, to remind her of the distance between them was particularly cruel. 'If I am so far above you,' she snapped, 'then I am surprised that you think yourself entitled to choose my attire.'

A difference in their stations had not mattered a bit when he had been kissing Char. And the fact that she employed him did not mean that she was without feeling. She had a good mind to show him…to prove to him…to make him see…

Something. It was as if there was a word on the tip of her tongue that she could not quite remember. But she was sure that, whatever she meant to say, it was a uniquely female thing that everyone had learned but she. And if she'd asked Char or Priss what it was, they'd have looked knowingly one to another and then laughed at her.

She was tired of sitting in the corner while others danced, and even more tired of watching others being kissed in the moonlight. And beyond everything else, she was tired of Mr John Hendricks looking through her and holding another woman in his arms.

He was looking at her, aghast, and she wondered if some portion of her thoughts could be read on her face. Then he said in a mild, servile voice, 'I only meant that if any are searching for two daring highwaymen, they will not recognise them in us, should you choose to don a dress.'

It was so perfectly rational, and had so little to do with her femininity or his awareness of it, that she felt a complete fool. So she pulled herself together, gathered what little respect she had left, and answered just as reasonably, 'You are probably right. It is time to put this foolishness aside and behave properly.'

But her heart said something far different. Before the night was over, she would teach the man beside her that she would not be overlooked.

Chapter Nine

For their evening resting place, John chose a field that was at least a mile from the highway and every bit as remote as he could have hoped. There were trees for shelter, a nearby stream and not even a house in the distance. And there was a haystack with a single, rather uninterested cow munching upon it. He jumped down from his horse, feeling well satisfied with the night's doings.

Although it had been the height of foolishness to take to highway robbery, it had been strangely exhilarating. Rather like being back in the army where every moment might mean one's death. He had acquitted himself well and survived the incident with an intact skin and a purse in his pocket.

And Lady Drusilla was safe as well. And a living example of why men should not take foolish risks for the glory of it. There were far better ways to expend energy waiting at home in England for those lucky men who could win them.

Not that he was the man for the lovely Drusilla. But the little fool in the carriage would have tumbled for him, easy enough, had he coaxed her. Kissing her had done nothing to ease his desire for dark eyes and luscious red lips. But it was an assurance that he was not the eunuch that his position required him to be. 'We will stop here,' he said.

'And sleep in a haystack?'

'You will find it a more comfortable bed than the ground is likely to be,' he assured her. His employer was out of sorts with him again and had been behaving more curiously than usual since the robbery. He had assumed that she would have some reaction to her participation in the robbery. But he had assumed that it would be fear, or perhaps excitement. He had not been prepared for annoyance.

Although it took some experience to gather what behaviour was unusual for the Lady Drusilla. The girl was a genuine eccentric. She rode like a man when the situation required it, miles at a time and without complaint. Where another woman might have held even an unloaded pistol with shaking hand, she'd played her part like a veteran of the road. And she'd snatched the booty from the air as he'd tossed it to her as though they were true partners and the action was old hand.

But now her silence had a prickly quality to it. And it seemed to stem not from the hay in front of them, but his earlier suggestion that she would be able to hire a post-chaise and travel in skirts like a normal lady of the *ton*, sleeping in inns and ordering him about in front of the coachman. After the day's easy camaraderie, the change in her grated on his nerves. 'Well?' he asked.

She frowned at him in the moonlight, the pucker of her mouth deeper than usual. He tried not to be flustered by it. But he could hardly look elsewhere because of what he had come to term in his mind 'the issue of the breeches'. While it was difficult to look at her face and not think of kissing her, it was even more difficult to deal with the thoughts that arose when he looked anywhere else.

'What do you mean by that?' she demanded.

'You are cross with me, though I have done just as you asked. I wish to know the reason for it. I can hardly remedy the problem if you do not state clearly what it is.'

'There is nothing,' she said, removing her hat and giving an imperious toss of her head meant to put him in his place.

'There damn well is,' he snapped back, looking at the cascade of shining black hair and forgetting his place yet again. After what they had just been through together, it irked him that she felt the need to play high and mighty.

'It is nothing important,' she corrected.

'If it is important to you, then it is important to me as well. Now tell me what is bothering you.'

She bit her lip in the way that she had when she feared she was revealing a weakness, as though she were accustomed to having any such used against her.

'I am tired, is all. And my muscles are sore from too much riding.'

'You have not been eating or sleeping properly and you are stiff from exertion. And not accustomed to riding astride.' She did look tired, swaying a little as she dropped to the ground beside her horse. It made him want to take her in his arms to soothe her, stroking her hair as one might a sleepy child.

Then she squirmed. 'I think I am not accustomed to these breeches.'

Nor was he accustomed to seeing her in them. And his thoughts changed instantly from innocence to hunger. 'I trust that they are not too uncomfortable.'

'It is not that.' She shifted again, but made no effort to explain.

'All the more reason you should return to your own clothing tomorrow,' he prodded. 'If mine is so disturbing, I should think you'd be happy to be rid of it.'

And that was badly phrased. It made him imagine her without any clothes at all. He stepped closer until she was so close that he had no choice but to look into her eyes. If she released his gaze, he'd not have been able to take his eyes from the place where her legs met, imagining the hot wetness of it, wanting to touch, to smell, to taste.

It was absolutely the last thing he should be thinking. And nothing like the chaste devotion he'd felt for Emily Folbroke. This was an all-consuming lust.

And Dru was looking back at him with eyes fixed and yet unfocused, the pupils large in the thin dark irises. But the firm set of her lips had a slight curve to it, as though she was daring him to reveal his feelings.

And he wondered—could it be that the tight clothing was arousing her? Perhaps she had learned more from her wayward lover than she'd let on. While it was flattering to imagine that she wanted him, it was far more likely that what she was experiencing was little more than a passing urge.

If so, there was no real harm in indulging it. A slight bruising of his pride, perhaps, when she cast him off in the morning. But it was better than feeling unmanned and invisible as he rode at her side.

As an experiment, he smiled at her in a way intended to charm.

In response, she bit her lip again, as though plumping it before a kiss.

And so he gave her permission to reveal herself. 'We have not really been speaking of doffing a disguise, have we?'

'We have not.' The words were half-statement, half-question, as though she was aware of what they did not mean, but was unsure of what they did.

He took a step closer. 'Or whether my clothing is an ill fit. Which it is not, if you were wondering.'

'It is not uncomfortable. But it is very improper.' She'd said it with a half-smile, as though telling him a secret.

'The impropriety is probably what makes it so damned fetching.' He waited for the firm snap of her disapproval at his impertinence and a return to the cold and aloof woman who had been ordering him around Britain.

Instead, there was only a slight gasp and the whispered words, 'You have been admiring me?'

'Any sane man would. And I could recommend something that might ease your distress, if you are feeling unsettled. Do you wish me to be of assistance?'

'In what way?' Perhaps she was not as experienced as he suspected. There was no trace of guile in the question, or any sense that she was trying to shift the responsibility for what was about to happen.

Which was why he ought to turn away, and do nothing at all. If she was unaware of the truth, it was not his job to change that fact.

But he could not help himself. After the adventures they'd had together, he was as restless as she was. There might never be a night when she was less of a lady, and he more of a rogue. The distance between them had shrunk until it hardly seemed to matter. For better or worse, he would take advantage of the opportunity and touch the woman who had been driving him mad, almost from the first. He put a hand on her shoulder.

And she did not pull away.

So he said in a voice that was low and full of seduction, 'Sometimes, after a long ride, it helps to massage the stiff muscles, to return the natural ebb and flow of the blood.'

'I see,' she said, though clearly she did not, for she added, 'Like currying the horses.'

'Yes. Rather.' He was thrown momentarily off his stride.

'And you would do that for me.'

He regained his balance and lowered his voice again. 'If you wished.' Again, he waited for the outraged dismissal.

And again it did not come. Instead, she said, very softly, 'Perhaps you could demonstrate.'

So he stepped behind her, letting his fingers caress her shoulders as he moved, and eased the heavy coat from her body. He began, very innocently, by rubbing her neck and shoulders, stroking his hands down her back. She wore nothing beneath the shirt, having discarded her stays with her dress. It allowed him to enjoy the delicious feel of firm, smooth flesh under the linen, and the way the knots in her muscles seemed to melt at his touch.

It would be wrong of him to do more than this. And it was not as if he could pretend there was mutual seduction in play. Despite her forward nature, Lady Drusilla was considerably more innocent than the girl in the carriage had been. But he told himself that he was performing a service. She was tense and tired, and would sleep better after his ministrations.

She swayed against him; he heard her sigh and imagined her lips parted for a kiss.

So he put his arms around her waist and laid his cheek against her hair. No point in pretending that he was soothing her aching back. He was holding her for his own enjoyment, his lips resting an inch from the skin of her throat.

She did not move or tense, but stayed comfortably

in his grip. And then, suddenly, she spoke, blunt and alert. 'Why did you kiss Charlotte?'

He started, but did not release her. It had not occurred to him that she had seen the kiss. But she could not have missed it. He just had not thought it would bother her.

And this sounded almost like jealousy. It was really quite flattering and a very good sign that further action on his part would be welcomed. So he pretended for a moment that he had room in his head for thoughts about the silly chit in the carriage they'd robbed. 'I knew she would be much less likely to send the law after us if I left her in a good humour. And she seemed to wish me to kiss her, did she not? When a woman makes such an effort to fall all over a man, it is cruel not to oblige her with a kiss.'

'So you knew she was shamming her faint?'

'Of course.' *But what are you are fishing for, in asking me these questions?* Dru was naïve, of course. But surprisingly savvy, when she had a need to be. There must be a purpose to this. And her movements against his body seemed almost an invitation. If she wanted to be aroused by a detailed description of the event, he was happy to oblige her.

'The kiss was pleasant for me as well,' he admitted. Then he could not resist goading her. 'Your friend is a very pretty girl, is she not?'

'I suppose.' He could feel Dru's shoulders tighten, as though he had struck her. 'And she is not my friend,' she added. Then she lifted her head again, rubbing her hair against his cheek as a cat might rub against its owner. 'I expect she will tell everyone who will listen that she was forced into submission by a wicked stranger, while revelling in the details of the experience.'

He felt his body tighten in response to her words and wondered how much of the discomfort she was feeling had to do with the sight of that kiss, and the hunger it had raised in her. 'Well, I expect that a well-bred young girl would find it an unusual and exciting thing to be kissed by a highwayman.'

Dru made a sound of displeasure and he imagined the bow of her lips, moist and waiting for him. 'She is not so young, come to that. She has been out for two years, already. Nor do I find her particularly well-bred. She really is the most appalling gossip.'

'And not too innocent,' he supplied, slipping his hands around her waist. 'It was quite clear to me, as I kissed her, that she knew exactly what to do with herself, from previous experience.'

'What do you mean?' she asked.

So she wanted the details, did she? He smiled and obliged her, shifting his lips so they touched her ear. 'She pressed close against me as I held her, to make sure that I could feel her breasts against my own body. She opened her mouth at the first touch of my lips, and took my tongue into it as though she could not get enough of me.'

Under his hands, he could feel the slight hitch in her breath as she listened. It had nothing to do with hisses of disapproval, and everything to do with salacious curiosity.

'But she is a blonde. And fair-haired women are not

to my taste.' And he stroked up over her ribs and took her breasts in his hands.

She started. 'That is not the area which was affected by riding.'

He stilled, but did not remove them. 'One cannot treat one area of the body without seeing to the others, any more than one grooms just one leg of a horse.' It was a most unromantic analogy, but she was not a particularly romantic female.

Her shoulders pressed into his chest and then relaxed. 'I suppose that makes sense.'

'You will find it quite satisfying, I promise.'

'Well, then,' she said again, 'carry on with your story.'

'Of course, Lady Drusilla.' He stopped to wet his lips, allowing the tip of his tongue to accidentally stroke the shell of her ear and felt her hips settle against his in reward. She could feel him now, he was sure, for she was pressing herself against the growing desire he had for her. But she did not pull away from him, so he continued their game. 'I meant to be gentle with her. Just a light touch of the lips and then I would be gone. But when a woman is willing, it is hard to resist.'

And the woman in his arms was giving her evidence of that, right enough. Her hands reached behind her to steady herself and gripped his thighs, sending another surge of desire through him.

'So I held her firmly and thrust my tongue deep into her mouth over and over, until she was quite weak with it.'

And it had felt nothing like this. Drusilla was heavy

in his hands, warm and round, and he thanked God to his very soul for the wonder of her, massaging gently, and then more vigorously until the nipples stood out hard against his palms. He pinched them easily between his fingers and felt her gasp in pleasure at his touch.

'Oh.' The word was little better than a moan, as she writhed against his body, and a cue that he must stop before things got out of hand.

'Are you feeling better?' he asked.

'Somewhat.' Her head was lolling back, now, against his shoulder. 'But I do not wish you to stop, just yet.' She turned enough so he could see her eyes half-closed in the moonlight and her lips relaxed and parted. 'It was very wrong of Char to behave in that way,' she said, pursing her lips and wetting them with her tongue.

He threw caution to the winds. 'Perhaps you had best show me how a proper girl ought to react,' he offered.

'I do not know—if that is wise…' she said, slowly and deliberately, as though she had over-imbibed and were trying to remember why it was that she should not agree. But even as she said it, she turned in his arms and lifted her face for a kiss.

'For the purposes of edification, if nothing else,' he whispered, and gathered her close to him, one hand around her waist, the other sinking his fingers into her hair. It was heavy, as he'd imagined it to be, still smelling faintly of soap, even after three days on the road. Her lips, when he touched them, were perfect. As soft and full as her breasts and with that same pucker to them.

If he stopped to look at them, they might seem to

be set in disapproval. But on closer inspection, they were open slightly, ready and waiting, as the other girl's had been. More hopeful than demanding, his Drusilla wanted a kiss as much as he longed to give her one.

And so he did, brushing her lips with his, and then licking deep into her mouth, settling there, as though he had a right to possess her. In response, her hands came up to touch his shoulders and she brought her body close to his, brushing her breasts against his chest as though she was not sure that she was doing it correctly.

He struggled to hold himself still, to allow her to grow used to the feeling of his mouth on hers. And to enjoy the feel of her kissing him back: the gentle touch of her tongue on his and the soft movements of her lips as they parted with his, to touch the line of his jaw.

When they reached his ear, she whispered, 'You make me feel most unusual, Mr Hendricks.'

He could feel, in her sweet and uneven breaths against his hair, that she desired him, just as he did her. 'The way you feel is the most natural thing in the world and nothing to be concerned about.'

'The fact that something is natural does not mean there is no cause for concern,' she said.

'Very logical of you, Lady Drusilla,' he answered and laughed to himself that she would even try to think at a moment like this. But it was very her, and very appealing, and it only made him want to touch her all the more. 'Does it frighten you?'

He had found his question aright if he wanted to urge more passion from her—he ought to know by now that there was nothing that frightened this woman. At least nothing that she might admit to. 'Certainly not. I only wonder if it is a wise course of action.'

'Probably not,' he admitted.

'But it is…' she wet her lips and touched them to his earlobe '…quite pleasant. And I suppose, as long as we are still standing and not lying down together…'

'Which we will not,' he assured her.

'And we are both fully dressed…'

'Which we will remain,' he added, swearing to himself that it was true and realising that she must understand very little of what he could accomplish without breaking either of her restrictions.

'Then it cannot be so very bad.' She then smiled against his skin.

'That is good. For I am not ready to let you go.' He kissed her again, dragging his lips along the curve of her jaw, to her throat and shoulder, and back up again, until his lips were resting beside her ear and he could whisper back to her, 'May I touch you again?'

'Please do.'

Then he let his hands go where they wished, exploring every inch of her that he could reach. Firm breasts. Tiny waist. Flat belly. He let his thumb sink into the dent that was her navel and imagined joining with her. Round bottom. Soft lush thighs. He pushed his hand between them and imagined those thighs wrapped around his waist. Then he cupped her womanhood, pressing his palm upwards, squeezing it possessively, feeling the heat of her in his hand and envisioning how she would look if he undid the drop of his breeches. 'Does this do anything to ease your suffering?' For it was increasing his, sure enough.

He waited for her to struggle free of his grasp, but instead her hands reached out to grasp his biceps to steady herself and she pushed back against his palm, groaning at the increased sensation. 'That is the spot, exactly,' she said, clearly amazed that he had guessed. And then added, 'Perhaps, a little less gently.'

'Very well, Lady Drusilla.' He looked into her eyes and smiled, then allowed himself the freedom to stroke more vigorously, imagining the flesh heating and growing damp at his touch. She closed her eyes. But her lashes still fluttered, as though she could not control them, and her neck arched ever so slightly as she caught her lower lip in her teeth. 'More?' he asked, leaning close and letting his breath caress her skin.

But she was quite beyond speech at this point, lost in the beginnings of a wordless response to his touch. She gave the barest nod of encouragement. In a few more strokes of his hand, her lips were trembling, open, moist and perfect. And so he kissed her roughly, pulling her body to meet his, safely separated by their clothing as he thrust himself against her and imagined being inside her, surrounded by her, consumed.

Her tongue came to life, darting against his in frenzy as her hands tightened on his arms. He was desperately hard and more than half-wishing that he had not started a game that could not end in his own satisfaction, but equally happy to have his supposed employer gasping into his mouth and pressing her sex eagerly against his as though she could not get enough of him. And he felt the moment that she lost the last of her control and came for him, breaking the kiss in a desperate bid for air as her back arched and her body went limp, swooning in his arms.

He held her like that for a moment, almost lifeless. And he brushed the hair from her eyes and thought, *I did this to you. And it was the first time.* 'Dru,' he said softly, loving the sound of the word.

She took a great, smiling, shuddering breath.

Then she realised how she had behaved and was shaking off the near-swoon and pushing away from him, brushing hands down to straighten the skirts that she was not wearing, trying to pull together the injured dignity of Lady Drusilla Rudney and pretend that she was still in charge. 'What was that?' The words were said with a stern frown as though her own physical response to his touch was somehow a trick that had been played upon her.

He gave her a benign smile. 'That was a perfectly normal, physical reaction.'

'To your kiss?'

'I suspect it had more to do with the way the breeches were fitting, and my—' he glanced down and then quickly back up at her outraged face '—ministrations in that area. You will find you feel much more relaxed, now that the moment has passed. And you can just as easily perform the actions yourself, should you feel the need again.'

'Certainly not.'

'Or I will continue to help you, if you wish.' He smiled, thinking that it was unlikely anyone would give him a reference should they find out what had happened and deciding that he did not care one whit who her father was, or what it might do to his career. He would not take back a moment of what had gone on between them.

'You know that is not what I meant at all,' she snapped. 'I would prefer not to feel this way. Certainly not ever again.'

The thought that she would not want to experience unbridled response was disheartening. But by the look in her angry eyes, Lady Drusilla had no real complaints with the way he performed his duties. There was a softness in them that she was trying very hard to hide from him.

'I feel unsettled. Even, after…the improper thing you just did to me.' Then she added in a whisper, 'It is as if I have forgotten to finish a task. And I do not know, for the life of me, what it is.'

If he was not careful, he would have those breeches off her and lay her down in the grass right now to help her remember. He was a careless fool and this had been a mistake. A horrible lapse of judgement. It was the first step on a journey that he would never be allowed to take.

He caught her warm brown eyes with his gaze and held them. 'I am afraid you are quite as finished as I can allow you to be, Lady Dru. Pleasurable though it would be, I do not dare show you the rest. I apologise for my behaviour,' he said, taking the burden of the indiscretion upon himself. 'It will not happen again and we need never speak of it. We will treat it as if it never occurred, if you wish.'

He was backing away from her now and it felt as if he were backing away from the act itself. *Do not make me go.*

'Thank you,' she said, her voice brittle.

'I had best see to the horses. And you…can take this to prepare a bed.' He tossed her a blanket from his pack. 'You will find the hay is quite comfortable. And I will just… The horses…' And he turned from her, stumbling towards the horses and wading into the icy cold stream.

Chapter Ten

It will not happen again.

That was rather a shame, she thought, as Dru gathered the blanket to her body and went to shoo the cow from the hay. The less sensible part of her wanted to demand an immediate repeat of the experience.

All she had wanted was a kiss. And she had assumed that, if she allowed him, that was all he would take, as he had with Char. But she had underestimated Mr Hendricks, just as she had from the first. Things had got quite out of hand. And while he had claimed that what he was doing was meant for edification and was merely meant to assist her in being comfortable, she suspected that there was much more to it than he had let on.

But she was not likely to know what had occurred without further experimentation and questioning of the man. What had happened was so pleasant that she was quite sure it must be unusual, unhealthy or improper.

She sighed. Many things that were pleasant seemed to fall into those categories.

But, if this was what came of wearing trousers, then it explained much of what she had heard of men and their insatiable desires. There had been nothing in Mr Hendricks's other behaviour that had made her think of a man crazed by lust. But her governesses had assured her that all men became so on the least provocation.

Of course, they had been quite sketchy on the details of what such a mania might entail. But she was sure that there would be some obvious sign of it. In any case, she doubted that she was the sort of female that would engender such emotions. Especially not attired in muddied breeches and smelling slightly of horse.

Still, it would be nice to know. And to imagine what it would be like to drive Mr Hendricks mad. Because, if there was an answering madness, she suspected that she might be experiencing some of the symptoms. It was probably all the fault of the breeches.

The idea that they would be sleeping side by side again tonight made her... She shook her head in disgust. It made her want to giggle. To simper, just as girls did in the retiring room after having had a waltz with a particularly handsome gentleman. There was nothing about the current situation that should be so amusing. Or even give rise to the sort of nervous tittering that other girls engaged in.

Sleeping beside him was a necessary evil of the trip, a way to share warmth without laying a fire. Or at least it had been, until he had touched her. Her body resonated like rung crystal. And it proved that, no matter what she had feared, he did not think of her as genderless. He knew she was a woman and had apparently given the matter some thought. The look in his eyes had been confident, knowing and faintly amused. It had been there in the kiss as well, as though he had known what to expect from her mouth and her body. He had seen potential in her and had sought to develop it.

After, he had looked as she had felt: utterly confused. As he had promised, she was relaxed, more sure of herself and her surroundings. But he looked tense. Nervous. Unable to meet her eyes. And she had ruined everything by being harsh with him, scolding and pretending that she had not wanted exactly what he'd given her.

And then he had hurried away from her with muttered excuses about seeing to the horses. If she did not change her tone with him, it was unlikely that he would share the blanket with her at all tonight. He would go to sleep beside his horse and she would sleep alone.

Tomorrow, they would ride on, she would find Priss and they would take her back to London. She would explain to her father what had occurred and Mr Hendricks's part in it. Omitting certain details, of course. He would be paid and she would see to it that he received a polite but vague letter of thanks and recommendation for his help in handling a delicate matter with utmost discretion.

Then he would go. And she would never see him again. All the anxiety of the previous days came flooding back to her at once. What was she to do without him?

The same things she had always done, of course. She would manage herself and those around her. She would raise her chin, standing firm in the face of all the nonsense her family was capable of, and put up with her father's endless disapproval. She would put her needs to one side in the vain hope that, some day, things would be settled and she would have time for herself.

For the first time since childhood, she wanted to stamp her foot and cry. Sometimes, she worried that there would never be more to her life than what she already had, an endless string of duties and loneliness. In the moment she had kicked the strange man seated across the carriage from her, the burden of responsibility had been lifted. Now she did not want to take it back. It would be even more difficult to return home, knowing that there was a wonderful world of experience that she had sampled just one small corner of.

She wanted him to come back, so she could put her arms around his neck and pull him down into the haystack. Then she would demand that he tell her everything. He must teach her to touch him in the way he had touched her, right to the very soul, until he was lying beside her, as happy and sated as she felt.

She wanted him to assure her that there was more between them as well, that it didn't have to end in a week, with a discreet thank you and a return to their normal stations.

She bundled the blanket in her arms and set off towards the trees to find him. 'Mr Hendricks!'

He was leaning against a tree, eyes closed and at peace, almost as if he meant to sleep standing up. But when he realised she was near, he started in panic, glancing around himself as though he thought to run. 'Lady Drusilla.'

'Mr Hendricks,' she said, more gently. 'I wish to retire. Will you be joining me on the haystack this evening?' It sounded ridiculously formal. But what else did one say, at a moment like this?

But it must have been right. When she caught his eyes, he smiled. No. Not a smile. He grinned. It was insolent and inappropriate.

Without even thinking, she grinned back at him, then they both looked hurriedly away. She straightened her clothing; he polished his spectacles.

And then he said, 'I do not think it wise that I join you, after what just occurred. That is, if you do not wish…'

'I do not wish to be cold or alone, either,' she said firmly. 'And in the hay, there are likely to be…other residents. Vermin, perhaps, or adders.'

'And that frightens you?'

Of course it didn't. It would be unpleasant, of course, but it was foolish to worry about things that were so small. But for once, she managed to answer correctly. 'Yes, the very idea terrifies me.'

He let out a bark of laughter to show that he did not believe her in the least, then he stood up and took the blanket from her. 'Of course I shall share a haystack with you, Lady Drusilla. I would not dream of leaving you, a frail female, alone and afraid.' They walked back to the hay and he took the blanket from her, spreading it out to make a kind of nest for them. Then he climbed up and helped her up beside him. And added, more quietly, 'At the very least, I will come to see what you look like when frightened. In my experience, it must be a rare thing.'

'Not really,' she admitted. 'But I have found there is little point in displaying such emotions. Fear is invariably used against one by those who sense it. In the end, one is worse off than before.'

He made a noise, low in his throat, like a beast growling at an intruder, then he pulled her to him, so that she could form herself around the bumps and hollows of his body. They were as close as pieces of a puzzle. 'You need have no fear of showing your true colours to me, Dru. You are safe, as are your secrets.'

She felt something deep inside of her relax, as though she'd kept a spring coiled tight and just now released it. Had she really been frightened, all this time? 'Mr Hendricks,' she said, testing her newfound bravery.

'Yes, my lady?' If he was trying to go back to the way it had been before, when he was nothing more than a solicitous servant, he was not quite succeeding. Though his words seemed innocent enough, there was an added depth to them, as though he meant something quite different.

'If I had not hired you...' she wet her lips '...would you still have helped me? I know I trapped you into accompanying me, at least a little way. But there was no real need. Even from the first, you could have exposed the lie.'

'Of course I would have helped you. While the offer of remuneration was certainly welcome, I could not have left a woman in need.' He smiled. 'And while you might not like to admit it, you had need of me.'

'Oh.' As always, her voice sounded gruffer than she wished. And the tone, which Priss would have called her schoolmistress voice, hid the little stab of joy she felt.

Then she stifled it. Of course he would have helped her. He was a gentleman, after all—not rich or titled like her father. But in the sense that he had proper manners, and respect for the fairer sex.

As though he had guessed her next question, he said, 'If you are now thinking that I would have treated any woman I found just the same, then the answer is, no, I would not. I would never have abandoned a lady in distress. And once my services were engaged, I was bound to do as you wished. But there are some things that cannot be commanded, by manners or money. Robbing a coach, for instance. It would take an exceptionally persuasive woman to achieve that.'

She took a deep breath and said, 'And what happened after?'

'That was something I did by choice, not out of a sense of obligation to anyone.' He tipped his head to the side and looked at her. 'While I might kiss some women on a whim, it is unusual to be so moved by the presence of another that I lose all common sense. Nor do I usually take to…grooming horses…to keep the incident from getting totally out of control.'

She stifled another sudden smile, glad that it was dark and he was close by. He seemed to understand her, and she would not be required to explain herself. For she hardly knew where to begin.

His arm draped easily over her side now, holding her with more tenderness than passion. 'What happened was not about money, or duty. It was something very special; I doubt it would have happened had you been here with another, or had I. Do you understand?'

She gave a slight nod; they were so close that he must feel the motion of it against his shoulder.

'And you do not have to be worry that it will go any further. You are safe with me, just as you were before.'

Safe. Then clearly he knew less about the situation than she did. For there had been nothing safe between them from the first moment they had been alone together. But the lack of safety bothered her less than her reaction to it. She had never felt so alive and so strangely happy.

From now on, when she looked at Mr Hendricks with one eye she could still find the quiet, responsible man in spectacles that would follow her instructions to a T. But with the other, she saw a highway robber, a devil-may-care rogue, up for any challenge, who might help a lady politely down from a coach only as an excuse to urge her to impropriety. And instead of giving him the disapproving sermon he deserved, her heart fluttered with excitement.

'I wish to ask you a question as well.'

She knew the sort of questions that a gentleman should ask, once they had behaved as Mr Hendricks had with her. He meant to offer. She was sure of it. And if he did, she would say yes to him. It would be quite impossible, for her father would never permit them to be together. But no matter what happened when they returned to London, tonight she would tell him the truth of her feelings. 'After the last few days, I think you are entitled to any answers you wish,' she said, trying to sound soft and approachable.

'After all that has happened, are you still intent on going to Scotland to find and retrieve your friend?'

She tried to hide her disappointment. Though her goal was the most important thing, she did not really wish to speak of it now. 'Yes. I am not bothered in the least by the difficulties we have had. And we do seem to be gaining on them, do we not? This stop is not putting us too far behind?' If dallying in the arms of Mr Hendricks had lost her a sister, it would be difficult to forgive herself. But was it so wrong to wish for just a small share of what Priss took for granted?

'I suspect we shall be quite close behind them, once we take to the main road again,' he assured her. 'But you understand that this means they have not been hurrying towards their goal. They have not hesitated to take meals together where people can see them. And they spend their nights at an inn and not on the road.'

She had known, of course. But she had not wished to think about it.

'The lady involved is hopelessly compromised. A gentleman would have only one honourable course of action towards her. And was I not pledged to aid you in stopping the marriage, I would feel honour-bound to make him go through with it for the sake of the girl.'

'I understand.' She put her hands between them, flat

on his chest to feel the beat of his heart. It was steady and true and a great comfort. 'But you will help me, just as you promised? Because they cannot marry. I will not allow it.'

His body stiffened under her hands and he let out his breath in a slow exhalation, as though he had kept it in check to hear her words. When he spoke, his voice was placid. 'Of course, my lady. If you truly wish it, it will be so.'

He sounded like her servant again. She had done something wrong, or failed some test. But she had no idea what the mistake might have been.

'Tell me about this Mr Gervaise that we are seeking.' And he had changed again. This time, it was his voice that was gruff, like the growling of a dog when meeting a rival. The sheer masculinity of it made the hair on the back of her neck prickle.

She thought for a moment, searching for a way to answer the question without revealing too many of the details of Priss's embarrassing flight from home. 'Mr Gervaise is a most pleasant gentleman,' she said. And then added, 'I believe he is a French viscount.' That was most likely a complete invention. For all she knew Gerard Gervaise had been born plain Gerry Jarvis.

Mr Hendricks grunted in disgust.

'He ran from France when Boney came to power,' she assured him, fearing that he thought that her family was consorting with the enemy.

'How very tragic for him,' Hendricks allowed in a flat voice. 'And yet it is romantic in just the way that ladies appreciate. They think a French title is better than none at all. He is wealthy as well, I suppose?'

'A man of independent means,' she hedged. For wasn't his temporary employment a form of independence? Mr Hendricks was similarly self-reliant, now that she thought of it.

The independent man next to her grunted again. 'And I'll wager he is handsome as well.'

'Very.' That at least she could answer with sincerity. 'He is a little taller than you, well formed and with clear dark eyes and features that manage to be both strong and fine. He is quite charming as well. And an excellent dancer.' Of course, his profession required that of him. But his looks and manners were an asset. Taking it all into account, she could not blame her impressionable sister for running away with him.

'And the woman he is with?'

'Of no consequence,' she said hurriedly. The last person she wished to discuss, when a man was holding her in his arms, was her prettier and more charming sister. He would see her soon enough and note the differences between them. If her luck continued as it had so far, his attention to her would evaporate like a morning mist in the face of the sunny blonde delicacy that was Priss.

'I would find it difficult to live with myself if our actions in parting them caused her hardship or disgrace.'

'Do not worry about her,' Dru added hurriedly. 'I will see to it that she is back in the fold of her family by the end of the week.' With the doors and windows locked to prevent any more nonsense. 'If we manage to keep the trip a secret, her honour will be untouched.' Because appearance was all. 'And after?'

'After?' Mr Hendricks said dully, as though he had not thought that there would be an end to the trip.

'Your plans, as I remember them, were somewhat vague when we met.' Perhaps a nudge would be all it took to remind him that there was a woman in his arms.

'That is a kind way to describe my situation,' he replied. 'I was drunk and broken hearted. And ready to throw myself into the North Sea.'

'And how are you now?' she asked, hopefully.

'Sober. But otherwise unchanged.'

She had forgotten the story he'd told her the first night, dismissing his past as unimportant, since it did not concern the trip. 'When we met, you said that you were avoiding the company of a lady...'

'I had the misfortune to fall in love with her,' he finished. 'But I did not tell you that she was the wife of my employer.'

'Lady Folbroke?' Though she could not remember meeting the Earl, she had met Emily Longesley at a rout, during one of the countess's rare appearances in London. She had been as beautiful as Priss, and with a lively wit that held the attention of every man in the room. She had been friendly and welcoming, even to a spinster elder sister, urging her away from the chaperons' corner to sit with one of Priss's beaus. The prospect that her Mr Hendricks might, even now, be comparing her with such a nonpareil made her want to sink beneath the hay in embarrassment.

'She and her husband were estranged for much of the last three years. I spent most of my time relaying information between the two. I grew to be quite smitten with her.'

'And I suppose she is very unhappy in her marriage,' she said, wanting to think the best of the situation.

'Not particularly. If you are spinning wild fancies about an evil husband and a beautiful countess in need of rescue, do not bother yourself.' His arm tightened about her for a moment, as though drawing strength before remembering something painful. 'While Emily was certainly beautiful enough to be such a heroine, her husband was equally handsome and vastly superior to me in wealth and position. He was also a man I counted as a friend.'

'Then she was unfaithful to him,' Drusilla supplied. 'And led you astray.'

'On the contrary. Even when they were apart, she doted on him. She had no interest in me whatsoever, and made the fact quite plain.'

'How very cruel.'

'Cruelty is a kindness, when the object is being as obtuse as I was. It had reached the point where the parties involved could no longer ignore my feelings. I revealed myself not in some sort of dramatic and romantic declaration, but in a few and fumbling words that were unwelcome and ill received.'

Dru wound her arms around him and pressed her face into his shirt front. She felt his embarrassment as if it were her own: a replay of a dozen days, where some chance word revealed her feelings to those around her, only to find them unwelcome.

In return, he gave her an awkward pat on the back. 'Adrian was very understanding about the whole thing. Emily would have looked the other way as well. But I was too embarrassed to remain in the house. I quit my position that same day. Then I packed my bag, drank myself into oblivion and took a seat in the wrong coach.'

'How awful for you,' she managed. And for her as well, if his actions tonight were an attempt to forget another.

'Not so very bad, I think.' He gave her a kind smile. 'Travelling with you has taken my mind off my troubles.'

So that was all she had been to him: a temporary diversion. 'I am glad to be of help,' she said, closing her eyes tight and burrowing into his coat.

'Emily was delightful company and we worked well together. I have many fond memories of time spent with her and the dreams I had when I thought there might be hope for me.'

'I can see where you would be tempted, if you worked in close proximity with her. She is quite lovely.' *Please, do not tell me about her and all the ways she is unlike me.* 'But in the end, I think you made a sensible choice in leaving,' she said, wanting the conversation to end.

There was a pause and he brought a hand up to stroke her hair. 'I just wanted you to know that the revelation of my infatuation with Lady Folbroke, and my behaviour when you met me, were out of character for me. I can always be counted on to do the sensible thing in the end, Lady Drusilla. Some of us are cursed with a natural stability.'

'Lucky for the rest of the world that we are,' she said.

'But even the most sensible of us are not immune to love.'

'You make it sound rather like influenza.'

He laughed again. 'It is like a sickness, in a way.'

And you have given it to me. How could he lie beside her and have no idea what she felt for him, or what his philosophical musing was doing to her?

He went on as though it were nothing. 'I pined over Emily for several years in silence. But recently, being forced to see the hopelessness of it…' His hands on her stilled again. 'In telling you this, I meant to dissuade you from your cause and show you the hopelessness of reasoning with people who love. But it seems, Lady Drusilla, that you have persuaded me. It is not that I do not believe in constancy of affection. While I was caught up in them, I would have sworn that my feelings for Emily were everlasting. They are fading, after only a few days. If the union you seek to dissolve is of such a transient nature, then perhaps you will have more success than I first thought.'

'I am glad you think so. It is good to have hope.' *In something, at least.*

'I think so as well. If I land on my feet after this, I mean to take my recent behaviour as a sign and find a wife, if only to clear the nonsense from my head.' He did not sound terribly enthused about it. But she understood the need to have some plan to anchor his future to. Marriage was certainly better than throwing himself into the sea.

He laughed. 'Of course, the girls that I have the right to court would bore me to tears.'

'And what sort of women might they be?' she pressed, almost afraid of the answer.

'Women with parents who are not bothered that my own father will not claim me,' he said. 'And I should learn to accept that fact as well. When I was enamoured of the countess, it was not just her husband that was the problem. I tend to overreach myself. It is the height of foolishness on my part. I will not allow myself to make that mistake again, I assure you.' He pulled away from her and looked into her eyes with his serious amber ones. 'It is time I learned my place and to be content in it.'

He traced the curve of his bottom lip as though the touch were a farewell kiss. Then he pulled his coat up to cover them both and pulled her close, offering his arm for a pillow. 'And now we should rest. If we get an early start, we will steal a march on your escaping lovers and have them before luncheon.'

Chapter Eleven

Damn it. Damn it. Damn it.

The curses in John's mind rung in time to the strike of the horse's hooves. Dru had lain in his arms all night and he had slept not a wink. And the sweet torment of loving Emily was nothing, compared to what he was experiencing now.

He'd lulled her, and touched her, and brought her to climax. Then she'd spurned him. And five minutes later, she'd lured him back to bed, so she could tell him that she had no intention of giving up the trumped-up French noble she was chasing after.

He gave a snort of disgust. It was just as likely that, if he gave the man a firm shaking, he'd turn out to be an English nobody putting on a fine accent and a tight coat to get on the right side of the ladies. When they caught up to the beggar today, he'd have to put up with his Dru fawning all over the man and holding the handkerchief while some other poor chit wept her eyes out.

And she was not *his Dru* at all, he reminded himself firmly. She was Lady Drusilla Rudney. He should call her by her title as often as he could, to re-establish the distance between them. Seeing a woman's legs did not entitle him to an intimate acquaintance.

Although grabbing her between those legs should have. Apparently, the peerage, when one got them alone in the dark, was a different sort of animal entirely. She had awoken the next morning showing no sign that the previous day had affected her at all. She'd combed the straw from her hair, splashed a bit of water in her face and declared herself ready to travel. And it had all been done without so much as a 'Good morning, John'.

It had been Mr Hendricks this and Mr Hendricks that since the first night. And 'a little farther before we stop, Mr Hendricks' all this morning. Of course, now that he thought of it, she had never used his first name at all. That should have been a warning to him.

He had learned nothing at all by his experience. He had given a fine speech to her last night about knowing his place, and not repeating past mistakes. But it was all lies. In less than a week, he had transferred the affection he had felt for Emily to the next inappropriate female.

Of course, Dru was as unlike Emily as it was possible to be. Dark where Emily was pale. Cool where she had been warm, awkward where she had been graceful. And interested in him in a very personal way. She had shown more than a passionate response to his touches. She had been curious about him, sympathetic, and desired to be reassured that he would be well, even after they'd parted.

She cared.

Or she had last night. This morning, she seemed to have forgotten what had gone on between them and to be utterly indifferent to his presence. She was back to stalking the unfortunate Gervaise like she had ice in her veins.

And it was likely his own fault. If he had wanted more from her, then he should have declared his interest and not made a dramatic show of setting her free. He could have spared them both the pretty words about not overreaching and his plans to stick to his own class in the future. If she'd felt any lasting affection for him, he had crushed it with his reminders of the unbreachable distance between and his decisions to set up housekeeping on the other side of it.

This morning he should not be encouraging her to pursue a man who did not deserve her. When they'd come to an inn, he'd hopped off his horse and raced inside to hear that the elegant black carriage they were seeking was just ahead of them. After that, he'd persuaded her it was time to cast off his clothes and dress like a lady again before they came to another inn, reminding her that she did not want to catch up with the man looking like she'd spent two days in a haystack with him.

She had taken her bag down from her horse, stepped behind a hedge beside the road and he had stood guard, back politely turned so that he would not catch a glimpse of his employer's delectable flesh. She'd reappeared a short time later in a travelling gown of deep green, braiding her long black hair so that she could pin it up under her bonnet.

He reached out and plucked another bit of hay from it, then stepped a respectful distance away.

She gave him a curt thank you, then said, without much confidence, 'Is the rest of me all right? It has been so long since I've seen a mirror.'

'Very fetching, Lady Drusilla. But straighten the bow on your bonnet. To the left. Just so.' And when he was sure she was occupied with her ribbon, he tucked the hay into his pocket as a keepsake.

He'd helped her up on his horse to ride the last few miles to the inn where they would hire a carriage; he had tried not to think of the extremely sensible drop-front gowns she favoured. He'd enough experience with women to know that they were a boon to mankind. Without even undoing a button, he could slip a hand inside her bodice and bid her a proper goodbye.

Then he had reminded himself that the fact they were alone did not give him the right to take liberties. She was young, although she pretended that she was not. And a virgin, even though she was not as innocent as when he'd found her. She was not married, but she might as well have been. She had given her heart elsewhere.

Take it back. He could rein in the horse and tell her how he felt, pull her to the ground and prove to her that there was no need to chase an unwilling man all the way to Scotland, when there was one right beside her who would stick like a burr if she gave him a chance. *Take her heart back and keep it for yourself.*

And do what with her? Shout, 'I love you. It has only

been three days. And I am not worthy. But I am falling in love with you.'

Marry me.

He wished he could think of a way to make it all more palatable. They were well suited in temperament, used to being the ones pushed to the side and left to clean up the messes of others. That alone should have gained some sympathy from her. He understood her in a way that no other man could. He would make her happy, as she would him.

If he'd had savings, or family, or even a position… but no. Employment was likely to make it worse. 'Come away with me, my darling, to my tiny room in Cheapside and live as a clerk's wife.' He winced at the banality of it. Perhaps he could beg his way back to Folbroke. They would probably allow him to bring a wife into the household, relieved that he would no longer be sniffing after the countess.

But what kind of future might that be for Dru? Not at all what she'd been raised to expect from marriage. She was trained to navigate flawlessly in society and control a large household staff while her husband made laws and collected rents gained from the labour of others. She would be equal in birth to his employers. Yet, because of him, she would always be set aside. There was no hope for them at all. No place for him in her life, other than as a lackey. And no place in his world that she could possibly want.

So he did nothing. She sat primly in front of him on the saddle and he touched her no more than was necessary, riding as quickly as he could for the next inn.

* * *

When they arrived, John dropped to the ground and steeled nerves that had been worn to tissue since he'd received that fateful kick on the ankle. Then he held out his arms and Dru slid from the horse and down his body to the ground. It would have been better to let her stumble than to ever touch her again. But touching her was far too nice and he was running out of reasons to do it.

And he'd sworn as her breasts grazed his chest that the nipples tightened to demonstrate their awareness of him, even though their owner did not. There was nothing in those huge dark eyes to indicate any arousal at all. Only a deeper furrowing of her brow, and a slight tightening of her lush lips. She probably thought it was a grimace of disapproval, but it only made them seem more kissable.

'What are we to do now?'

'You may wait in the parlour, my lady. Take refreshment. Relax and let me see to all. I will ask about the ones you seek and hire a post-chaise and driver.'

As he escorted her into a room already crowded with waiting travellers, he could see the wistful gratitude in her eyes at the thought of a soft chair and a cool drink. It made him wish that he'd had a right to put that small smile upon her face by offering something other than such a mundane service. Then he pushed the thought away, led her to her seat and went about his business, as he was paid to do it.

The hostler informed him that Mr Gervaise and his 'sister' had indeed stayed the previous night in his best room. The innkeeper gave a disapproving shake of his head that said that the girl was clearly no one's sister, but that it was no business of his. The couple had argued endlessly, much to the annoyance of the other guests. The gentleman had ended the night shut out from his bed and asleep in a chair by the parlour fire. The girl had been slow in rising, and there had been much more fighting and slamming of doors to get her out of her bed and back into the carriage. But at last, they had gone, travelling northwards little more than an hour before.

If the couple was the sort to dally, which it was obvious they were, then they might be found at the next stop, or perhaps the one after. John could feel the eagerness to be done, like an itch that must be scratched. They would catch up before they reached Scotland. Lady Drusilla would have her Frenchman back and they would tack a plaster on the wounded honour of the other girl. There would be much weeping all around; John would be left to nod sympathetically, get the coach turned around and get everyone back to London before their absences were noted.

It would be over. And he could pocket his earnings, open his flask and return to his original plan to drown his broken heart. But as God was his witness, he would ride on top with the driver before getting back in a closed carriage to sit opposite Dru and her lover. There was a limit to the extent his gentlemanly manners would carry him and he expected to reach it well before nightfall.

A short time later, after a visit to the stables, he was back before his lady to explain why everything could not be accomplished as promised.

'If there is no chaise to let us, then get the innkeeper to give us more horses,' she said. 'I will don trousers again, and we can bump along as we have been.'

John shook his head. 'I have seen the poor nags in the stable, and I doubt they will take us one mile, much less ten. All the beasts with any spirit are saved for harness, and the best of them are hitched to the Reliant, the coach that runs regularly on this stretch of road. It is waiting in the courtyard now.'

'Then buy us two tickets for the stage.' She gave him a stubborn smile as though wondering why he had not suggested the obvious solution.

'It is full up,' he said with equal mulishness. 'And delayed to boot. The passengers surround you now. It seems the driver imbibed too deeply last night and has his head stuck in a slop bucket. He is in no condition to drive anyone anywhere, and unlikely to be so for several hours.'

Dru's eyes narrowed, clearly looking for someone to blame. 'You are telling me they are nearly in our grasp, we have money in our pocket and yet they will escape us?'

He gritted his teeth. All he had to say was 'yes', and offer an apology. The man she loved would slip through her fingers and over the border with another girl, leaving Drusilla angry, but free.

But free for what? There was no chance that he would have her. None at all. He would only be leaving her free for some other man. And if he was unfortunate, she would compliment his efforts to her father and he could stay on in the household to watch her marry another.

'No,' he said. 'This is not the end, unless you wish it to be. How strong are your nerves?'

She smiled at him; there was the playful spark in her eyes that made his heart tighten. 'You ought to know the answer to that by now.'

'Then keep the innkeeper occupied, while I ready the horses. We will steal the coach.'

For a moment, he had surprised her. 'You cannot mean it.'

'You did not baulk at highway robbery when I begged you to reconsider. Do not tell me you are having second thoughts about a life of crime, just as I develop a taste for it.'

'But who shall drive?'

He smiled at her and was pleased to see a flush on her cheeks and a slight dip of her head, as though she did not want to show him the excitement that was written plain on her face. 'Just do as I say.'

Chapter Twelve

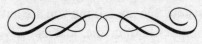

Dru kept one eye on the innkeeper, and circulated amongst the passengers, whispering that if they were up for an adventure and could get to their seats, the coach would be leaving directly. One by one they escaped into the courtyard; she watched Mr Hendricks slipping pound notes to the stable hands to keep them quiet, carefully checking harnesses and blinders, examining wheels and making sure that all was at the ready. Then he hopped up into the driver's seat without letting go of the ribbons. He took up the whip and waited.

She ran for the carriage and he whistled to her, offering a hand to swing her up into the seat beside him. He gave a quick snap of the reins—they were on their way.

They were gaining speed, heading for the end of the stones and the beginning of the open road. Behind them, the coachman came roaring out of the taproom, and she turned to see the man shaking a fist and swearing.

'May I suggest you cover your ears, Lady Drusilla?

I fear the man behind us does not realise there is a lady present. And head down, please.' He reached over and forced her to duck as they went under the stone arch that marked the edge of the coach yard, then released her, letting her spring erect again like a bent reed.

She looked behind her at the rapidly disappearing inn, then in front of her, then at him again. 'You drive four in hand?' she said, unable to contain a gasp of feminine admiration that would have done Priss proud.

'When I was a wag at Cambridge, I was considered the best of my lot at foolish stunts like this,' he answered calmly, keeping an eye on the horses. 'It will be more work for you than riding, but far more comfortable. And if you do as I say, we shall make quite good time. I expect we will find your friend within the hour. Then we shall see if Mr Gervaise is quite the man you remember him to be.'

That was an odd remark. She remembered Gervaise to be pretty, but soft and useless. She doubted he had changed a bit in three days. She glanced again at the man next to her, as he gave a smart crack of the whip to speed the horses. She sighed happily. Gervaise certainly would not have been able to drive himself to Scotland. She dared not tell her sister how they'd made the last leg of the journey. A man that could handle the ribbons as her Mr Hendricks was doing could likely dance as well. And manage an elopement without getting caught. When Priss learned of that, poor Gervaise would be out on the street and Hendricks would be left fighting to save his honour.

He cracked the whip over the horses' heads again,

and said, 'Keep your reticule handy, my lady, for there are likely to be tollgates. It is up to you to pay, and to keep a watch on the passengers, while I manage the team. And if you can learn to blow the horn to warn oncoming traffic, as well? I think you will make an admirable guard.'

The wind was buffeting her bonnet, so she removed it and placed it behind her feet, letting the breeze blow the pins from her hair. The sun was touching her cheeks and there was a strong and handsome man at her side. It was bittersweet to think it was almost at an end. But the moment was glorious. So she smiled, and persuaded herself that it was a lark he'd arranged, just to amuse her. 'Mr Hendricks, is there anything that you cannot do?'

'It is a wonder what can be accomplished, if one only tries,' he said, as modestly as possible. 'And being born with fewer opportunities gives one reason to dare.'

As he stared down the road, his spectacles slipped down the bridge of his nose. And without another thought, she reached out a finger and adjusted them for him. Then she blurted the truth.

'I beg your pardon?' he said, tipping his head to the side to better catch the words.

'It was nothing important,' she said hurriedly. 'I was wondering how fast we were going.'

As they took the next turn in the road, the carriage rocked dramatically to the side, and he slipped his arm around her waist for a moment to keep her from sliding off the seat. Behind him, she could hear the angry mutters of the passengers, and offered a silent prayer that they would arrive in one piece and hear no complaints about the inexperience of the driver.

'We are going as fast as we are able and somewhat faster than the coachman would have gone. At least eleven miles an hour, I think. But do not worry, I will have us there safely.'

Dru gave him a satisfied nod, and turned her attention to learning the coach horn, afraid that she would speak again, where the road was quiet and he might hear the truth.

I love you.

She might have managed to turn the words into a statement of respect for his abilities, which were prodigious. But more likely she'd have clung to him like a foolish girl, and said it again with the sort of sheep-eyed expression that made her near to nauseous when she saw it on others. Now, at least, she could understand the reason for it and the idea that it really was possible to fall in a swoon of rapture, as she nearly had in the hayfield. She was in love with Mr Hendricks. And when he left her, she would weep as loudly as any girl in London.

They took another turn and she grabbed for his coat tails with one hand and raised the carriage horn to her lips with the other. The best she could manage was a gooselike squawk and not the sprightly tunes that some guards could play. But if there were obstructions in the way, it was better to give them some sort of warning and she must do her best.

Of course, puckering her lips on the mouthpiece

made her think of kissing. And kissing would, now and for ever, make her think of Mr Hendricks.

In response to her grab for him, he caught her waist again and held her until danger was past. It was so like him that it made her want to cry in frustration. If he had not been there, every step of the way, smoothing her path, seeing to her comfort and making her happy, she would not be thinking such foolish thoughts now.

And none of it had meant anything to him. He was an employee. A servant. He had been doing his job. Her father would pay him, he would leave and that would be the end of it. Unless, of course, she went to her father and insisted that he be kept on in some permanent way, so that she could have his company whenever she liked.

Although what he would do, she had no idea. Father already had clerks and secretaries and stewards enough. And she could not exactly ask for a manservant of her own.

But he had assured her that what had happened last night had not been part of the position. It was instead the thing which they were both trying very hard not to speak of.

She was trying, at least. There was no indication in Mr Hendricks's usually tranquil demeanour that it required any effort on his part at all. Even if she could convince Father to hire him, she could not keep him like a pet. He would have duties to perform. She would wander about the house, mooning after the man, hoping to catch sight of him, just as she would have cautioned Priss not to have done. And Mr Hendricks would continue to politely ignore it.

And when he found the wife he claimed to be seeking, a girl of modest expectations with a father who valued good sense over parentage, it would break her heart.

Hendricks nudged her; she let go with another feeble blast on the horn and dropped the required coins to the toll keeper. Then he gave a nod in the direction of a building on the horizon. 'There is your inn. And still twenty miles to Scotland.' He was pulling up on the reins and the carriage was slowing marginally.

'Well done, Mr Hendricks.' She put a hand on his arm and felt the muscles. They did not seem to strain to control the horses, but they were taut with the effort. Such strong arms, but gentle as they held her. She took a breath and let her hand drop away, pointing towards the courtyard, as though she still cared. 'There is the carriage, plain and black, with a crest on the door. And there is our livery.'

'Your livery?' He'd tensed on the reins in a way that made the horses start and the carriage jolted at the sudden slowing of the pace.

'Yes,' she said, lifting her chin as though the truth was a small omission that should have been obvious to him. 'It is my family's carriage that we have been seeking.'

'And you could not have mentioned this before?' he said. 'For when I asked about it, in all the inns between here and London, another detail would have been a welcome aid.'

'I did not want to run the risk of someone identifying

the crest,' she replied. 'The fewer people that realise the identity of the couple, the better.'

'But, apparently, I could not be trusted with the information.' There was definitely reproof in his voice.

'A few days' acquaintance is hardly a reason to take someone totally into confidence,' she said.

'Of course not. What reason would I have to expect such intimacy? My lady.' Her title was added as an ice-cold afterthought, to make it plain that she had been badly mistaken if she thought him unmoved by recent events.

He cracked the whip for emphasis. 'Now do you mean to tell me, before we arrive, how Mr Gervaise came to be riding in your father's carriage? Or is it to be a surprise? Speak quickly, for we are almost in the courtyard.'

He was right. There was no reason to keep the secret any longer, for he would know the answer the moment they saw Priss. 'Mr Gervaise is riding in my father's carriage, because he has eloped with my sister, Priscilla.'

The horses broke their gait and a cry of complaint went up from the passengers. And then, all was right again, and they were slowing to an orderly stop in front of the inn. 'Speak to your coachman, to make sure he does not leave. He is your servant and will do your bidding, just as I have. And then, tend to your sister. I will speak to your precious Mr Gervaise.' And before she could say another word to him, he was out of the seat, handing the ribbons to the stable boy and stalking towards the door of the inn.

Chapter Thirteen

John pushed through the doors and into the taproom, in no mood to explain the stolen carriage to the stable hands, or to share one more word with the woman in the driver's seat. She had dragged him all this way, never mentioning the coat of arms on the carriage, or the fact that this meeting was nothing more than a sibling squabble over the same man. If she'd kept those secrets, then what else did he not know?

Although, knowing Dru as he did, he could not see that a battle between the sisters would be a fair fight. Young Priscilla had been wise to run, for her elder sister had to be the stronger-willed of the two. If she had wanted Mr Gervaise, the other girl would have no chance at him, had she stayed in London.

He scanned the occupants of the room quickly. Seeing no one, he asked the innkeeper about the couple attached to the carriage in the yard. He was directed to a private sitting room. He pushed through the door without a second word.

On a banquette near the windows sat the young couple, the plates on the table before them pushed to one side and their heads close together in some sort of heated conversation. The man looked up suddenly at his arrival, guilty, and quite aware of how this must look.

The girl looked strangely triumphant. As John watched, her arms twined about the elbow of the man at her side as though she wished to make clear their relationship.

Of course, it might just have been to hold her escort in his seat. The infamous Mr Gervaise was half out of his chair and leaning towards the door before the girl could pull him down again.

'Mr Gervaise, I presume? And Lady Priscilla?' He offered a bow to Dru's sister, and turned his attention to the man involved, watching the fellow's Adam's apple bobbing in his throat as his hand reached for the ale in front of him. There was none of the outrage at an interruption that he'd have expected from a peer, or the bluster of a soldier. Only a man who was thin but well built, hands neatly manicured and soft, with a coat cut tight to his body, of good quality but perhaps a little too flash to be tasteful.

A dancing master?

John looked at the pathetic excuse for a Lothario before him, sure of the truth. Then he turned to the girl clinging to him like a damp handkerchief. She was nothing at all like his Dru. Priscilla was petite and insubstantial, with an excess of strawberry blonde hair and bright blue-green eyes. But those eyes had a mutinous light in them that put him in mind of his own lover's iron will as it might look if disguised with candy floss and ribbons. It was the sort of combination that could turn a man inside out, if he was not prepared for it.

But then he remembered that recent events were proving that Dru's character was not as he'd expected either. John had imagined a young lord for her, being forced into a marriage by her father. His breeding would be excellent, but his character weak. He'd have bolted with Dru's rival for the border, rather than wed the formidable lady he'd won. Or perhaps Gervaise was a rake whose house and title would more than make up for his disgraceful behaviour.

But of all the men he'd pictured, there had never been a doubt that the gentleman would be worthy. When Dru went to him, John would know that blood had bested him again. He could step quietly to the side, because it was best for her.

But a dancing master? Was the girl mad? Or as foolish as the rest of her kind, and willing to throw aside her honour for an elopement with a dandified nothing?

'Well, man? Are you going to stand there all day or explain yourself? What is the meaning of this intrusion?' Gervaise's French accent was as atrocious as he knew it would be.

'It is not I who must explain myself, Gervaise. I am not trying to steal over the border with the Duke of Benbridge's daughter.' The whole thing would drive the duke to fury, once he heard of it. He would have stopped it long before now, had he known a tenth of what was going on.

Priscilla gave her fiancé a slap on the arm. 'Do not be an idiot, Gerard. He is from Father, aren't you, sir?' She looked up at John with eyes as blue and liquid as a mountain lake. 'Is Papa here? Has he come for me?'

Gervaise turned in a panic to the window behind him, searching the courtyard.

'My name is John Hendricks,' he said with a polite bow to Lady Priscilla. 'I am in the employ of your sister, Lady Drusilla.'

Though Priscilla drooped in disappointment, the man beside her looked even more frightened at the mention of the sister. 'Silly sent you here?'

'Lady Drusilla did not send me,' he said, eyeing the man with contempt. 'She engaged me to accompany her.'

'She is here, as well?' Lady Priscilla slumped in her chair and put a hand to her temple. 'That will not do at all. Take her away immediately. Send for my father. I wish to go home.'

'Now, sweetness,' Gervaise said, petting her arm, 'we are very nearly to Gretna Green.'

'You are yet in England, Gervaise. And no marriage has yet taken place.'

'But it will once we cross the border,' he said with an arched brow. 'Just as Priss wished it to.'

'I wished no such thing, you great oaf,' the girl said, slapping at Gervaise again.

John held a hand out to the girl. 'If I might suggest

that you go to your sister, my lady, I will take care of everything.' He shot Gervaise a warning look.

Gervaise ignored him, turning to the girl. 'It was not as if I forced you into the carriage. You arranged for the transport yourself. It was your idea from start to finish, and I will tell your shrew of a sister the whole truth, when next I see her.'

'I never wished to marry you, Gerard. Only to elope.' Having spent his life dealing with her kind, it was just the sort of nonsensical statement that John expected to hear from a young lady of quality. He took a breath before another wave of foolishness grabbed him and sucked him under the impending tide.

'The one leads to the other, Priss,' Gervaise explained. 'As I told you before, when a girl runs off with a man and behaves in a certain way, it gives that man certain expectations—'

'You worthless bounder!' John slammed his fist down upon the table, trying not to imagine what liberties the cad had taken with either of the daughters to get them into such a state over him. 'Lady Priscilla, I must insist that you come away so that I might deal with this…thing.' He gestured to Gervaise.

'I have no idea who you are, sir. But I am not moving an inch until Father arrives.'

'He is not coming, Priss, though you sit here 'til doomsday.' Dru stood in the doorway, arms folded.

Priss looked at her desperately. 'But if I go home now, you will ruin everything for me.'

'And if I allow you to stay, you will ruin everything

for me. Now come to the carriage. We are leaving immediately.'

'You may do as you please. But I am not going anywhere.' The younger girl rushed past her, towards the hall. 'I am going to my room and I do not wish to be disturbed.'

'We do not have rooms here, Priss,' Gervaise called after her.

'Then I will take one,' Priss announced.

'And I am putting you in it and locking the door,' Dru muttered. Then she turned to the dancing master. 'But first, I shall deal with you, Gerard.'

'You most certainly will not,' John said. God help him, he would not see one sister dislodged from the clutches of this parasite, only to have the other take her place.

'This is none of your concern, Mr Hendricks,' she snapped.

'I beg to differ.'

She turned her anger from Gervaise to him, furious that he had disobeyed. 'While I employ you, it is not your decision to make. If you will excuse us, I wish to speak to Mr Gervaise alone.'

'Then I resign,' he barked back. 'Now that I have seen the whole of it, the chances of my winning your father's favour are all but moot should I continue to follow the mad orders that you have been giving me. You will not spend a moment unchaperoned in the company of this louse. In fact, you will spend no time with him at all. You will go immediately to tend to your weeping sister and give me no further trouble. And once you are gone, I will deal with Mr Gervaise. Now, go!'

He waited for the angry outburst, the shower of tears, or even the worthless Gervaise rising to her defence. But all he received was a muttered, 'Discretion, Mr Hendricks…' as though it were the only thing that mattered.

'Oh, I shall be discreet, my lady. Have no fear of that.' But what he would not be was the poor fool who watched the woman he loved clinging to a primping caper merchant all the way back to London. Or, worse yet, a witness as she dragged him to the anvil. He removed his glasses so that they would not be damaged.

'Now, sir,' Gervaise said with a nervous laugh, staring at the retreating back of Drusilla. 'You seem to be suffering under a misapprehension.' Then he looked back to Hendricks. 'Lady Priscilla was quite insistent that we make this trip. I meant no disrespect to her, for I hold the girl in high esteem.'

'Do not think you can shift the blame to an innocent girl, you muckworm!' Hendricks spat.

'There can be no sin in love, Mr Hendricks. No sense of blame in following one's heart.' Gervaise said it with such convincing piety that it was no wonder the girls had been swayed. 'And I would do anything to get the lovely Priscilla out from under the thumb of the Lady Drusilla. She has the eyes of a hawk and the tongue of a viper. And she would not let me alone.'

After three days in her company, John might have felt some small bit of sympathy for his rival, had he not just then imagined the pair on the dance floor, Gervaise's oily good looks a good match for the pale skin of his travelling companion.

'Now she has caught up to you. And she has brought me as well.' John flexed his arms. 'And I will make you wish you'd never met either of them.'

'I can wish that without your help, Hendricks,' Gervaise said, shaking his head. 'You must have sussed out the truth of it by now. Both the hot and eager Priscilla and her silly spinster of a sister are totally mad, and in need of a hearty prigging to set their wits to right.'

For a moment, John saw nothing but red. When he came back to himself, his hands were on the man's throat, dragging him towards the door.

'What…what…what…?' Gervaise was flopping in his hands like a fish on a boat dock.

'For talking in such a way about a lady, I would meet you on the field of honour. But it is clear that you have none. And so I think a good thrashing is in order.'

The man under his hands gave out a small sound that was rather like 'Akkk'. Hendricks loosened his grip, pushing Gervaise ahead of him through the taproom and out into the courtyard of the inn.

'This will do, I think. Unless you have a better choice. Boy,' he called to a stable hand, 'hold my coat.' He released Gervaise, so that he could remove it.

His rival rubbed his windpipe and uprighted himself, brushing at his garments as though it were possible to gather his dignity. 'I have no intention of fighting you.'

'Then I fear you shall be soundly beaten,' Hendricks said reasonably and raised his fists.

'Very well, then. But be warned. Mr Jackson says I

am quite handy with my fives,' Gervaise announced, raising his bony fists and giving them a threatening rattle.

'It is a pity that he is not here to see how you acquit yourself,' said Hendricks, and punched him in the nose.

Gervaise let out a yowl of pain and cupped his face in his hands. 'You hit me.'

'Perhaps you do not understand the principles behind the art you practise,' Hendricks responded. 'Now come back here, for I mean to hit you again.'

'Help!' cried Gervaise, his eyes watering in outrage and pain and peeping between the spread fingers of the hands that guarded his nose.

'Oh, for God's sake,' Hendricks muttered, almost embarrassed to be harassing the man.

And then he thought of Dru, and decided that perhaps he was not embarrassed after all. 'Stop squalling, Gervaise, and take your medicine.'

'I will not.' The man rubbed his nose. 'If I do, you will only hit me again.'

'You dishonoured the ladies.' Hendricks said, as reasonably as possible. 'You did not think your behaviour would have no repercussions. And I called you a louse. A muckworm. A prancing dunghill,' he added for good measure, trying to reason the man into defending his honour.

Gervaise picked himself up, shook the dust from his coat and shrugged. *'Cherchez la femme.'*

Hendricks knocked him down again and glared at the coward lying at his feet. 'Did I not tell you not to blame what has happened on the ladies involved?'

Gervaise shrugged again, from his place on the ground. 'Miss Priscilla wished to escape the restrictive confines that her father and sister had set for her. Since I was tired of wooing her in secret, I was happy to aid her.' He gave John a significant glance. 'One would think, after all this time without a chaperon, that it might be better for a gentleman to wish us well, and escort us to Scotland. There he could witness that the job is done properly.

Hendricks debated the honour of kicking a man when he was down, decided against it and hauled Gervaise to his feet. 'I have heard from the lady's own lips that she does not wish to go. Her sister is equally insistent that no marriage take place.'

Gervaise produced a handkerchief and tended to the blood leaking from his nose. 'Then it seems that I should be owed something for my silence. And the damage to my person and my coat, as well.' He looked sadly at his tailoring, then in accusation at John.

'I suppose you expect it from me.'

'You are here as Lord Benbridge's agent, aren't you?'

'Actually, I am not,' Hendricks admitted. 'At the moment, I am without employment of any kind and acting according to my own desires. And I have decided, Mr Gervaise, that I do not like you.'

He caught the man by the lapels and gave a twist and a lift that put Gervaise up his toes and flailing his arms, complete with torn sleeve and bloody handkerchief.

Then he continued in a voice, low and full of menace. 'I do not care what happened between you and either of the ladies. Nor do I mean to buy your silence. I have found, Mr Gervaise, that when dealing with a certain type of person there are more effective and inexpensive ways to ensure a permanent and total silence.'

'You would not...'

'You would be surprised, sir, just what I am capable of, if it concerns the welfare of Lady Drusilla. Or her sister,' he added, trying to be less transparent. 'But I can assure you, if you ever return to London, and if I ever hear so much as a word of scandal about either of the Rudney sisters, I will find you and make an end to you.' He glanced at the stable boy. 'Young man, get me the coach ticket from the breast pocket of my coat.'

The boy brought him the ticket and he released Gervaise and forced the thing into his hand. 'I suggest, Mr Gervaise, that you go north. For your health. I hear that Orkney is lovely this time of year.'

Gervaise looked puzzled. 'But the Orkneys are on the other coast. With this ticket it would make far more sense—'

'Never mind!' John spun away and snatched the coat from the hands of the shocked stable boy. Then he turned to the Benbridge servants, who had been observing the scene without comment. 'Take this refuse and his baggage away. Anywhere he likes as long as you drop him on a north-bound coach route. Return in the morning for the ladies. They shall be ready to depart after breakfast.'

Then he returned to the inn to deal with Dru.

Chapter Fourteen

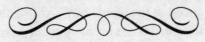

Dru paced the confines of the little room she had taken to freshen herself and await the return of Mr Hendricks. There was no point in trying to talk to Priss, for the girl was as good as her word. She had shut herself up in the largest room that the innkeeper could offer and was deep in the throes of a tantrum that would last the better part of the day. It would go on even longer if Dru indulged it by giving it any attention.

That left her alone and with time enough to worry. Through the door, Priss had sobbed something about Gervaise having a pistol. Dru could not know if it was an attempt by her sister to make her departure look more coerced than simply willful. But if it was true, then surely Mr Hendricks deserved a warning that the man he faced might be armed.

When she had announced she was going down to ascertain the direction of things, Priss had roused sufficiently to open the door and offer to join her. She was eager to see the duel being fought in her honour. Dru had renewed hectoring the girl until she was sure that the tears were flowing properly again, then made them all the worse by pointing out that no man would fight for a woman with a red nose and streaming eyes. With that, she was sure she would see no more of her sister until morning.

It would have been much worse had they not rescued Priss before she got to the border. But the idea that Mr Hendricks might come to harm through any of it was quite the worst thing she could imagine. She would never forgive herself if Gervaise managed to do him an injury.

She had told him as they travelled that a physical altercation was hardly necessary. Silence and discretion were key. If he had allowed her to deal with Gervaise as she had wanted, she could have arranged a settlement and sent him on his way without a scene. She had never intended that, when the moment came, Mr Hendricks would have to fight her battles for her, with fist or weapon.

That was foolishness, when all it would take to dislodge Gervaise was money. If it even took that. After a few days alone with Priss, it was quite possible that he'd grown bloated with the contact like a tick and was ready to drop off on his own.

But judging by how angry he had looked in the dining room, the non-violent solution did not seem to be enough to satisfy Mr Hendricks. Perhaps a few days in her company had driven him mad. He had been as inflammatory as possible until enough insults had been exchanged to make a duel inevitable. And before the end of it, he had quit her service, giving her no authority to stop him.

Mr Hendricks was strong and resourceful in his own way, of course. He hardly seemed the sort that would resort to such extremes when he had sufficient brains to find another solution. But it seemed when a girl like Priss was involved, men did not use their brains to lead their actions. Now he was likely to come to a bad end, brawling with a stranger.

She thought of the Countess of Folbroke, who, had she been more charitably disposed to poor John, might have saved him from this fate. Although the woman could hardly cuckold her husband as a matter of gratitude, surely there must have been some way to release him gently, instead of discarding him as though he were nothing.

As Dru had. She wished she could call back the last three days, and start again, to be kinder to him. And to give him some small clue how she felt. Or at least to be sure that he would not go to his grave angry with her.

The door burst suddenly open and Hendricks strode through, alone, slamming it behind him.

'You are safe?' Without another thought she threw herself at him, clinging to his arm, weak with relief. She patted his body and stroked his arms and chest, but could find no wounds or marks upon it, no evidence of the duel that Priss had envisioned.

He glared down at her, but did not shake her off. 'Of course I am. Not that you have any reason to thank yourself for it. After two years in Portugal, I have more than enough battle seasoning to take on a dancing master.' The words came out of him in a sneer, as though it were something he did not want to think, much less speak aloud.

'And Gervaise?'

John gave her a grim smile. 'Is gone, with his pretty nose broken, just as I promised you.'

'But the scandal…'

'There will be none. Wherever the coach takes him, it will not be London.' He shook her from his arm and grabbed his cravat, tearing it from his throat and dashing it to the ground. 'And why young ladies are fascinated with the likes of him, I have really no idea. I should think, if you had any sense at all, you would not bother to cross the street to see to his safety. But to come all the way to Scotland…'

'It would be very distressing, should he come to harm,' she assured him. 'Priss is already distraught. And I did not give you leave to fight the man.'

'Give me leave?' He tossed the coat he was holding over the chair nearest the bed. 'As you remember, Lady Drusilla, I left your employ before putting up my fists.'

'And if the altercation had led to his demise…?'

His eyes narrowed. 'Then it would have served the three of you right. If I had had any idea that such a man was to be the reason for your journey, I would have denied you on the first night.'

'Well, I am thankful that you did not know,' she said, lifting her chin a fraction. 'If you felt so strongly about this, but thought so little of me, then you needn't have risked yourself in confronting him.'

'Oh, ho, ho!' John reached to undo the buttons of his vest. 'Now we have the truth of it. You chose me as your aide in this because you did not think me man enough to stand against him. Did you expect me to stand by, polishing my spectacles as he insulted you, awaiting my dismissal?' The vest was open now and he removed it and tossed it uncaring after his coat, only to miss the chair and send it slithering to the floor.

'That is terribly unfair of you,' she said, retrieving his vest and placing it properly on the chair so that it would not wrinkle. And then she stopped to look at it, puzzled. It was barely supper time, and there was no reason for them to be changing for bed.

Nor was this his room. It was hers and there was no reason to share it. They had money enough to stay properly separated and she had reserved a place for him just down the hall. He must leave this room immediately. At least, after he had put his coat on again. She had her honour to think of, although why she had not thought of it before, she was not sure.

She turned back to him to demand an explanation. And he stood before her, shirt open and showing more bare male skin than she had ever seen in her life.

He went on, heedless of her stare. 'You were the one who was unfair, my Lady Drusilla. You expected me to sleep by your side like some kind of damned monk, so that you could stop this foolish marriage. You sneered at your friend for throwing herself at men beneath her class—'

'Actually she was Priss's friend, and it was not her...' she interjected, trying to tear her eyes away from his body.

But there was no indication that Mr Hendricks had

heard her. 'Then you expect me to clear the field for you, so you can throw yourself on that primped-up popinjay.'

'Clear the field for me? Now just a minute, Mr Hendricks.'

'Not another minute longer.' He took a menacing step towards her, looming in the confines of the little room, making her feel small and helpless. 'If you think I will stand idly by while you make the same mistake as your foolish sister, you are sorely mistaken. I have thwarted one elopement and can just as easily thwart another.'

'My sister is not foolish,' she insisted. Priss was exceptionally so, but that did not give Hendricks the right to comment on it.

Then she realised that he was removing his glasses, folding them with a snap and setting them upon the table, staring at her with those angry amber eyes.

She looked back into them and what she saw frightened her; she could not seem to look away from it, it was terrifying, yet intriguing, wild and unstoppable. She took another step back and felt herself bumping into the edge of the bed.

Then he smiled and it was hard and predatory. And if she was to be totally honest, quite exciting. 'I mean, my dear Dru, that you have dragged me half the length of Britain on a fool's errand, treating me like nothing more than a sexless lackey. And now it is time for you to pay the piper. Run to tend the wounds of your dancing master, if you must. But you will do it when I am through with you, and not a moment before.'

'Me?'

And he was on her, like a wolf in a sheep's fold.

There was a moment, before his lips touched hers, where she had time to suspect that he had misunderstood her motives. She had no intention of going after Gervaise, and owed Hendricks a 'thank you' for his swift handling of the situation. But it did seem that he had got confused about her reasons for the trip.

Then his tongue was in her mouth and she could hardly breathe, let alone think. When she could manage to gather her thoughts, she suspected that the last thing she wanted was to mention Priss and run the risk of receiving a polite apology and the sight of the door closing behind a retreating John Hendricks.

What had she done to imply he was sexless? she wondered. Did he not remember how she had swooned under his hand, that day in the hayfield? And now he was likely to do the same thing to her with a kiss. But there was nothing educational about it. This was to be a final test that assumed she had a complete knowledge of the subject. He was demanding that she prove competence, before moving on to the next lesson. His hand was on her jaw, opening her to him, stroking her throat as his tongue took hers, rhythmically, deeply, over and over.

He was here. He had not left her. She had been so afraid that she would never see him again. With relief, she let him master her.

But it seemed that the kiss was not enough. His hand went lower, reaching between them to undo the drop front of her gown, and he thrust his hand inside of it. When his fingers brushed against her nipples where they peeked out from the lacings that held them, she let out a little squeak of shock, and he pulled away from her to look into her eyes.

'Now you mean to be the prim-and-proper miss again? As though you have no idea what you do to a man, with those big brown eyes and that delicious body? Your tricks will not work with me any longer.'

'What I do?' She was doing nothing. It was he who was driving her to madness. His fingers that were raking lightly along her skin, tormenting her, and outlining her nipples through the fabric of her shift. And now they were untying the ribbon at the neck until it gaped low to expose them. She felt cold and hot at the same time; her knees went weak as he pushed her backward to sit on the mattress. Then he stripped his shirt over his head and bent over her, cupping the back of her neck to push her face into his bare skin until she could feel one of the tiny buds on his chest pressed tight against her closed lips.

It was insanity. She wanted to open her mouth and take him in. She knew she shouldn't, but she did, licking eagerly at what he offered.

Above her, and against her, she could hear the low rumbling of his voice. 'Perhaps you thought it a grand romantic adventure to dangle me on a string while running to meet your lover. But damn it, Dru, a man can only take so much. And I have taken all that I can, and then more.' Then he was pushing her away, on to her back, dragging her up onto the bed and lying on top of her, taking her mouth with slow deep penetrations of his tongue as his hands untied her stays and pushed her bodice and shift to her waist until he could cup her naked breasts in his palms.

It had been good in the hayfield, daring and dangerous. But that was nothing compared to this. She had not been able to see his eyes as he'd touched her then—the bottomless smoky gold of them that seemed to trap her look of pleasure and give it back to her. And she had not seen the smile on his face as he watched her.

Her breasts felt so swollen that they almost hurt. And yet he continued to touch them and lowered his face slowly as though he meant to kiss them. 'Please,' she begged.

And he laughed at her. He took them into his mouth, each in turn, sucking upon them to give her relief. She relaxed back into the pillows, letting him take what he wanted. But it seemed that this was but a calm before a storm. The tension was growing in her again, as it had in the hayfield.

He paused again and climbed up on the bed to straddle her, 'Now, I will take the one thing I truly want from you in payment for this trip. Unfasten my trousers, Lady Drusilla. You know well enough how they come undone.'

And she almost obeyed him without thinking, before sanity returned. 'I mustn't.'

He caught her hand, running his fingers lightly across the knuckles of it, and said, 'I do not mean to give you a choice.' Then he pinned it to her side and stooped to kiss his way down her chest, and settled on her breast again.

She had no choice. She did not have to worry about

her father's anger, or her sister's welfare, or what tomorrow might bring for any of them. For a little time at least, John Hendricks was in complete control and demanding that he be allowed to pleasure her. And if he did not stop what he was doing this instant, she would scream with delight.

Then someone might come and discover them. If nothing else, the beating of her heart would draw them, for it must be so loud that the whole inn could hear it. So she bit her lip to turn the cry of shock into a throaty moan and did her best to slow her pulse to something not quite so deafening.

The cries that she could not manage to stifle were little more than a series of gasps, as the strange rippling inside of her grew, crested and faded. She let out a final sigh of relief that it had passed and they were undisturbed. For a moment, until he was through with her, she was the centre of a man's universe, and she did not want to yield the stage to an outraged knock upon the door.

He released her hand and gave a final lick of her nipple before letting it slip from his mouth. And when he looked up at her, he smiled.

It was a wicked smile that hinted of things to come. Delicious punishments. Wonderful tortures that would leave her helpless with satisfaction. She felt as though some part of her was going to burst like a grape and imagined him licking away the juice of it, staring at her with those strange golden eyes, and running his tongue over his teeth as he smiled.

And before he had even touched her, the trembling

was beginning inside of her again. One of his hands was on her skirt now, lifting the hem until she lay exposed to his gaze. He stared, eyes hooded, intent. And then he trailed a finger up her stocking and higher, settling near the place he had touched her when they had stopped to rest.

And just as it had been with her breast, it was different when he was touching her bare skin. She had not imagined those sensations to be muted, but clearly they were. Now his fingers had the freedom to slide along the most sensitive places of her body, which felt wet and swollen. And suddenly, they speared into her, and the shock of it made her almost rise off the bed.

She struggled for a moment, unsure what was happening. But he held her with his gaze and his fingers pushed harder, deeper, faster.

And as though to prove to her mind how well he knew her, her body crested quickly and then relaxed, legs falling open of their own volition, and her back arched to offer herself to him as his mouth returned to her breasts.

And the spiral began again. She could feel herself slipping away, just as the sensations were blending, fusing, growing and there was a final touch, which was somehow both hard and gentle, and then her soul seemed to leave her body, helpless and shaking on the bed.

Then he rose to straddle her again and removed his fingers, making her moan in disappointment. Again, he smiled his knowing smile and said, 'Now do as I asked.' And he gathered her hands and gave them an encouraging squeeze before placing them on the waistband of his trousers.

With a shudder of suppressed excitement, she undid the buttons until the drop front fell away. Then he pressed his manhood against the palm of her hand and leaned forwards to ring her throat with short eager kisses, as though he meant to eat her. He was rubbing himself gently against her fingers and he seemed to grow larger and harder with each touch. It did not feel as she'd expected it to, warm and heavy and alive.

Nor did she feel as she'd expected, frightened and vulnerable. She felt as she had when he'd finished with her out in the field, strange, tingly and wet. She had not known what was happening then. But as she looked at him now, and thought of what his fingers had been doing, she began to imagine something they might try that would feel even better. In fact, she was convinced that if he did not attempt it on his own, she would have to shock him by suggesting it.

Then she remembered that he was giving her no choice, so she smiled, spread her legs and waited.

And he must have known she was ready, for he pulled away from her and rose so that he could remove his boots and push his trousers down, off, out of the way. He stood above her for a moment, naked and magnificent, staring down at her in her tangle of rumpled bed linens and half-removed clothing as though he owned her, body and soul.

And it occurred to her again, in a quiet, distant way, that this was just the sort of situation that she'd meant to rescue Priss from. And that it was quite possible, if she'd felt as Dru did now, that Priss had not wanted to be saved.

Then his hands were on her ankles, spreading them even wider. He lay down on top of her and his weight was on her, between her, and then in her. And there was a sudden thrust. And pain. And he whispered, 'And now, you are mine.'

I am yours. Whatever became of her, it did not matter any more. In this instant, she belonged to someone and felt safer than she ever had before.

He was lying very still on top of her and she wondered if this was all. She had lost her maidenhead. It had not hurt as much as she had expected. Nor did it feel as good as she'd hoped, compared to what had come before. But the pain was fading, and his lips were on her shoulder, brushing back and forth ever so gently as though to soothe her. 'Lady Drusilla,' he crooned. 'My Lady Drusilla. You feel wonderful.'

And then he was moving again, very slowly. It made her gasp, for it was new and strange, and he was right. It felt wonderful. And she could feel herself beginning to tingle again. 'Mr Hendricks,' she said, a little breathlessly.

He laughed. 'Please, darling. Call me John.'

'John,' she said, trying to sound more confident than she felt. And then, 'Oh. John.' For he was rubbing relentlessly against a most sensitive place in her body, and it was all beginning again.

She reached for him, putting her hands on his shoulders, trying to remain steady. They were warm and smooth; she could not seem to stop touching him once she had started, roaming over his back and his arms and settling upon his bottom to find the rock-hard muscles that drove his thrusts.

In response, he bit her shoulder, just hard enough so that she arched her back and gasped. And when her hips rose to meet him he thrust harder, holding her as she did him, squeezing her from behind and locking her against him.

She should beg him to stop. Hadn't she heard that, even when things had progressed to this point, there was a way to stop that would minimise the possibility of a child? But instead she held him tighter and moved with him. And in opposition, as though she was only playing at escape so that she could come rushing back to meet him with equal force.

But Mr Hendricks showed no sign of slowing. 'John,' she said. And then, again, 'John.' What he was doing felt achingly good, and even better when she tightened the muscles of her body and spoke his name. With each flash of desire, she felt a little more control slipping away, and the madness that she had felt before was beginning to take her again.

Only this time it was better. His groans answered hers, and when she began to move against him, he answered with even more force. Then they both were lost in a hot wet rush of feeling and she thought she called his name, one last time, but she was not sure. She could think of nothing but the helpless, blissful feeling of being with him, under him, and around him.

He went limp against her for a moment, as though there was no strength left in him. But when she tried to struggle out from beneath him, he came to life again and rolled with her farther on to the bed, wrapping his arms around her and stroking her skin until the trembling grew in her muscles again, and then slowly subsided.

And as sanity returned, she realised that she was making sport with a strange man on the way to Scotland. If they had crossed the border, would this have made them married? she wondered. Perhaps it was the act that made the union, not the other way around.

'Drusilla?' The man with her sounded quite dispassionate again. Which was strange for one whose body was still... She flexed the muscles where they were still joined and realised that there was no situation of etiquette that covered just what it was she was supposed to do in this situation.

'Mr Hendricks,' she said at last, 'I think that was probably very unwise of us. Of you,' she corrected, for now that she thought of it, she had not encouraged the beginning, much as she might have enjoyed the end. 'And I think you should probably—'

'What?' he asked. He began to move his thumb over a spot very near the place they were joined. 'What do you wish me to do?'

She had meant to say, 'Leave here immediately.' But perhaps his leavetaking could be postponed for a few moments at least, until he finished what he was doing to her, which was making her body tighten on his.

He smiled against her skin as he kissed her. 'Because I think, for a time, I will decide what it is that I should do. And I mean to make it so you will never think of another man, ever again.' He had begun to move in her again, and his other hand cupped her from behind, lifting her hips to his. 'And I think I shall make you call me John, again.'

She drew her knees up until she could cradle his body with them, wondering, as his hands stroked her legs, lifting them even higher to rest on his shoulders as the shudders began to rack her body again, whether it was possible to be ruined more than once.

Chapter Fifteen

When John woke in the morning, he rolled over and reached without thinking for the woman at his side. The empty space beside him came as a shock; he groped blindly in the pillows for a moment, as though there were a way for her to have got lost in the narrow and uncomfortable bed on which he had slept.

Consciousness returned. After a few moments of waking clarity, he remembered. This was his room, not hers. He had left her only a few hours ago, when the horizon was lightening with the dawn, sneaking back down the hall to the room she had got for him so that he was not seen leaving hers in the morning. He had fallen into his own bed exhausted, to catch a few hours' sleep so that he might pretend to rise refreshed.

But with waking had come the beginnings of dread. The activities of the previous night had been earthshakingly wonderful. And when he had left her, she had been smiling in her sleep. But he would be lying to call them consensual. She had known nothing of lovemaking when he'd met her, only three days ago. She had been a proper, sermon-reading young lady and well on the way to becoming a spinster. And he was sure the kisses he had given her, only yesterday, were the first she had ever received.

He had worked to break down her defences, weaken her resistance and destroy her virtue. Of course, the idea of such a woman remaining unmarried and untouched was so wrong as to be almost criminal. If there was nothing in her sermon book about the need for fruitful multiplication, then its lessons were incomplete and she was in need of other reading material.

But that had given him no right to push his way into her room and have his way with her. He was little better than Gervaise if he tricked the girl out of her maidenhead with no promise of a future. Today, he owed her an apology and an offer.

But until it was too late to take them back, he would have no real evidence to assure him that his words would be well received. She was a duke's daughter and he was someone's unclaimed natural son. In the cold light of morning, she could be screaming for her father, who would administer the horsewhipping he deserved for touching his precious daughter.

Although John had to wonder how precious she might be to Benbridge, if he allowed the family to call her Silly, gave her younger sister a come out and relegated Dru to the background. Dru did not seem to find it unusual. But John felt a growing outrage on her behalf, a need to rescue her, to take her away and prove to her that she was beautiful, cherished and desired.

And to be honest, he had his own reasons for offering. Although he had thought he understood love and the loss of it, the feelings he experienced when he thought of Drusilla Rudney were unfamiliar to him. There was the madness and rage that had taken him when he feared he might lose her, and the bliss of lying with her. And at all other times, there was… He searched his vocabulary and decided to call it a surety. It was as though they shared secrets that no one else had heard. When they looked at each other, there was knowledge. Trust. Communion. Quite simply, when she was beside him, things were right. And when she was not, they were wrong.

He had no idea if she felt something similar, for he had not spoken of it, or given her time to speak last night. What if it had left her frightened into silence by him and the possible consequences and the results that could be visited on her from his actions: disgrace, discomfort, pregnancy… She might be meaning to keep silent, as though it was something shameful and best forgotten.

His guts clenched at the thought of her, hiding her feelings behind a mask of stoicism, as she did everything else. Now that her sister travelled with them, it would be much more difficult to get her alone so that he might declare himself. And the fact that he had rushed into action, rather than wooing her properly, would make it harder for her to believe that what he did was not from obligation.

For a few blissful hours he had been only a man

and she had been a beautiful and impossibly high-born woman. Even now, while alone, he could barely find the words to explain what he felt for her. But last night he had let his body talk to hers, knowing that if he did not do something sudden and irrevocable, common sense would win the day and he would do the right thing. He would stay silent, take her back to London and give her up. Lying with her had been selfish, irrational and unwise. But he had wanted to do it more than he'd ever wanted anything in his life.

And it had made her happy. Because of that, if nothing else, he had known that it was the right thing to do. Now it was simply a matter of finding the right thing to do next.

When he came down to the taproom to arrange for breakfast and ready the carriage, he saw no sign of his Dru. He smiled. Perhaps she was sleeping late, for they'd had an active night.

He did see Priscilla, sitting on the same bench in the parlour that she had shared with Gervaise, soaking in a patch of sunshine like a pampered kitten. He hoped the sun was doing her good. Her cheeks were wan and her eyes rimmed faintly with red. It had been a difficult night for her. But she had already been unhappy when he'd found her. He doubted that parting from Gervaise had done her any lasting harm.

Lady Priscilla was as pretty as Dru had said, in a fragile, flawless way that seemed to come naturally to the aristocracy. And while he had found the same sort of look quite attractive in his friend's wife, the eyes of the girl before him lacked the natural intelligence that he had found in Emily Folbroke.

Of late, John had decided that he much preferred a woman who could combine that intelligence with a sharp wit and a sharp tongue. And deep brown eyes. He tried to stifle his smile at the thought of Dru as he'd left her, lying in the tousled sheets, staring up at the ceiling as though she could not quite fathom how she'd come to be there.

But the younger Rudney sister had caught his mood and now, thinking it was for her, she smiled back at him. It was brilliant and captivating. It made him uneasy. 'Good morning, Mr Hendricks, it is a lovely day, is it not?'

He nodded in greeting to her, and said, 'Good morning, Lady Priscilla.' And then he fell silent, for he had nothing to say. Nor was it his place to make his feelings known about the day or anything else.

'Silly has told me so much about you,' she said, smiling even more.

For a moment, his mind stumbled over the nickname, wanting to rush to her defence and argue that there was nothing the least bit silly about his Dru. Then he caught himself and remained silent. There was something about the statement that sounded like a trap. When had Dru found the time to speak to her sister? He'd been with her most of last night. He suspected she would not have told Priss a single thing about the last few days, even had she had the chance. And now Lady Priss was angling for details.

'She spoke frequently of you as well,' he said.

'I am sure I gave her a fright, running off like that. But she needn't have worried.' She turned a little in her seat, to put herself in the best light, so that he might better admire her. 'As you can see, I am quite all right and well able to take care of myself.'

That was a patent untruth. He had never seen a woman more foolishly in need of rescuing. 'I am sure Lady Drusilla is gratified to find you so.'

Priss smiled all the brighter. 'But she would not have done so without your help, I am sure. The roads were most difficult on our way north, and we were delayed several times. It is a wonder that you were able to catch us so quickly.'

So that was it. She wished to know what her sister had been up to, perhaps wanting to hold an impropriety over her head to fend off the anger of their father.

'Lady Drusilla was most eager that you be found and scandal averted,' he said, still not sure if it was the sister or the man she had been trying to find.

'And you helped her.' Priscilla gave a moue of sympathy, rather as though, in looking at her sister's ability to appeal to a man for help in anything, she were staring at the runt of the litter.

'She engaged me to do so,' John said firmly.

'And it was nothing more than that?' she asked, quite candidly. And for a moment, he saw the firm look that Dru used so frequently on him. It was as though the younger girl were daring him to admit any impropriety so that she could punish him, had he caused harm.

'What else could it have been?' he said, lying through his teeth. 'I met your sister on the road, just three days ago. It was most fortuitous that I was in need of a position just at the time she needed help.'

The girl seemed to relax in relief. 'Oh, Mr Hendricks, you are so gallant that I am sure it was more than that.' Dru's sister fluttered her eyelashes at him, but the eyes under them were as sharp and discerning as her sister's.

'Not at all, Lady Priscilla.' There was something about the calculated way that she did not stare at him that put him on his guard.

'No, really. In helping her, you have saved me from a disastrous mistake, and I have much reason to thank you. If anything about this trip got out, my reputation would not survive it.'

He gave her a reassuring smile. 'No word of it will pass my lips, my lady.'

'And you have seen to it that Mr Gervaise will have no cause to speak either.' There was a slight tightening of her brow as she said it, as though that had not been what she'd intended at all. She stepped closer to him, until he could almost feel the warmth of her little body. 'How can I ever repay you?'

He gave a dismissive shake of his head and took a step back, bumping against the table, suddenly sure that the girl had meant to say, *How can I pay you back for this?* He had spoiled some plan or other, and it had nothing to do with thwarting her chances for true love.

'No thanks are necessary. Your sister engaged me to help in this matter. I was most eager to discharge the duty.' He moved clear of the furniture and took another half-step back. There. That should put things back on a professional standing.

'No, really. I was quite overcome by the excitement of it. Men, fighting. And over me.' She looked to be near swooning, until he stared into those very large, very blue, very cagey eyes.

'Well, it was, in a sense, a battle for you,' he admitted. 'But it was to defend your honour, my lady. And that is a cause that any gentleman would be happy to defend.'

'But surely the victor deserves a reward.'

'As I said before, Lady Drusilla will be amply compensate—'

The girl made a sudden lunge forwards, as quick and deft as a trained fencer. As she did so, she rose on to tiptoe and seemed to fall into his arms and, open-mouthed, onto his lips.

There was an awkward moment of surprise on his part, then a tangling of tongues—and the horrible realisation that there was too much experience on her part, far too much eagerness and the subtle shifting of her body against his that hinted he was likely far too late to save her honour by scaring off the dancing master. The best that could be hoped for at this point was to get her safely back to her family, so that the doors could be double locked to prevent another escape.

And then he would get Dru away from the girl. For if she was the one tasked with keeping Priss on the straight and narrow, she must see that it was a losing battle.

He slid her feet back to the floor as gently as possible, hearing her moan at the friction between them, and untwined her vine-like arms from his neck. 'As I said, my lady—' he did his best to sound properly sub-servient '—what I have done for you was all in a day's work.' He looked her squarely in the eye. 'No further thanks are needed.'

'So you say, now,' she suggested. 'But if your mind should change on the subject...'

'I will bear your offer in mind,' he responded.

The girl stepped away from him, at least temporar-ily satisfied that she had made a conquest of him. He would need to steer clear of her until he could speak to Dru. Once he had her heart secure, he could counter any further attacks on his person with the assurance that he held only brotherly affection for Priss, tempered with the need to keep on her good side lest she run to her father with tales.

He straightened his glasses, which had been knocked askew by the force of her attack. And when he looked up again, Dru stood in the doorway, a stricken look upon her face.

How much of that had she seen? he wondered. More than enough, no doubt. It would do no good to deny the occurrence. He could hardly claim to be an innocent victim of an attack by her sister, no matter how true that might be. Blood would tell then, he was sure. If Dru had brought them all this far for the girl and not the gentleman, then she would never forgive him if he said anything less than flattering about the foolish little trollop they had rescued.

He turned to her, giving a short formal bow. 'Lady Drusilla, I apologise for my behaviour. Your sister was overwrought. I offered comfort and the situation got quite out of hand. It will not happen again.'

'See that it does not, Mr Hendricks.' Her demeanour was as cool as it had been on the first day, but when he looked into her eyes he saw hurt. Tears. Damn it to hell, he had made her cry, when nothing else had. 'Priscilla, come away from Mr Hendricks this instant.'

Her sister gave a saucy smile and a half-shrug of apology to him. And then she winked, as though to say the only thing she was sorry for was the fact that they had been caught. 'Coming, Silly. Do not raise such a fuss.'

Dru's eyes narrowed and she pulled her body in tight, proud and studiously unaffected by what she had just seen. It was as though, in a heartbeat, she could some-how draw the tears back up her cheeks and inside of her again, so that no one would know her feelings. She gave John a withering glare, then turned her disdain on to her sister. 'I can see, Priscilla, that we will need to have another talk about the sort of people it is proper to associate with. First you run away with a dancing master. And now?' She gave a dismissive wave of her hand. 'This.'

He tried to cast his eyes in the direction of the open door and held out a hand in supplication, hoping that Dru would understand the awkwardness of the situation and his need to speak to her alone, to explain.

But either her almost preternatural perception failed her, or she chose to ignore it. And him as well. She was looking at him as though he was something less than a man, less even than a piece of furniture. Worse than that, after all that had happened between them, it was as if he did not even exist as a part of her world.

'My Lady Drusilla,' he said hurriedly, not wanting her to leave. 'I spoke hastily last night, when I tendered my resignation. If you still require my services...'

Dru glanced from him, to her sister, and he saw the slight slump of resignation in her shoulders. Did she seriously think he could change his heart so quickly?

Of course she did. She seemed to think Priscilla was irresistible and her superior in all things related to the male sex. And what reason would she have to trust him after all he had told her of Emily, and his undying love that had not lasted out a week of separation? If she thought him faithless, it was because he had given her ample reason.

When she spoke, her voice was cold and superior, and she sounded as one might when speaking to a servant that one did not much like. 'You still deserve compensation for what has gone before, and will receive it if you return to London with us. But neither of us will need or accept the kind of personal attention that you have provided these last few days. Is that clear, Mr Hendricks?'

'Of course, my lady.'

She gave another sharp gesture to her sister, demanding that she follow. Then she turned from him, retreating at an unhurried pace. But as she went, he saw her reach for the handkerchief tucked into her sleeve.

Chapter Sixteen

The Benbridge carriage rambled on at a sedate pace towards London, with the windows open to fight the oppressive summer heat that had followed the rains. Dru fanned at herself with the open book in her hand. For all that had occurred since she'd left London, it was perhaps the best use for sermons. Priss seemed to be unaffected by the temperature. She looked just as fresh as she had when they'd found her and fully recovered from her bout of tears.

Apparently, it had done her good to casually take the only thing of value from her older sister's drab life. The image sprang fresh in her mind of Priss in the arms of John Hendricks. And with it came the heat of rage, and the desire to clout Priss repeatedly with the book in her hand. The girl was unlikely to gain any sense from the disaster she'd made of the trip. But if Dru could raise a drop of sympathy in her heart for the feelings of others, and maybe a small bump on that pretty blond head…

She fanned herself all the faster, trying to cool her blood. She should have been prepared for the inevitable, when it happened. Men invariably turned from her, once they had met her sister. But it had never hurt so much as this.

Of course, no other man had held her in his arms, nor whispered of her beauty and his uncontrollable desire, nor acted upon those feelings so enthusiastically before. While she understood that what had happened did not always mean marriage was forthcoming, was it too much to expect a day would pass before she was betrayed by both lover and sister?

If Priss had been willing to think of anything other than her own feelings, then Dru could have requested that, of all the men in the world, with just this one she might make an effort to be less than her completely charming self. And to try to act as though she was a little shamed by the trouble she'd caused, and not on a week-long holiday.

Of course, there was little wonder that Priss looked happy and rested. She had not been forced to drag herself through the mud, skip meals and sleep in the hay. When Dru had managed to part her from the contents of her reticule, she had found more than enough money to take them home properly and in comfort, stopping wherever they liked and sleeping in proper beds.

Dru's eyes narrowed as she looked at her sister. It was just like Priss to create a disaster, yet suffer no discomfort from it. But she did not usually finish by reducing her older sister to broken-hearted tears in the public room of an inn.

'Do stop harumpfing at me, Silly; it is quite a waste of your time,' Priss said. 'It is not as if I mean to learn my lesson from the experience. Better you should learn not to follow me.'

'As if Papa would ever let me forget it, should I leave you get up to such foolishness,' Dru bit back, annoyed at her own shrewishness.

'Papa would not let you forget it, even if I had behaved,' Priss said in disgust. 'I swear, Silly, you think far too much of him, and what he approves or disapproves. His favour is hard to earn and seldom lasts.'

'That is no way to speak of our father,' Dru said, almost as a reflex.

'But it is the truth,' Priss said firmly. 'Read that book in your hand and I am sure you will find something favourable on the subject of speaking the truth. Especially when it is plain before your face.'

'It also demands that we honour our parents,' Dru snapped.

'And so we have,' Priss replied. 'For we have little choice in the matter but to do so.' And then, wilting a little under her sister's critical gaze, she amended, 'And you do enough of that for the both of us, I think. And you get far too little of the credit for it.'

The compliment was surprisingly welcome. And though it did not make up for even half of what had occurred, Dru managed a weak but sincere, 'Thank you.'

Priss sighed. 'I have inherited Father's temperament, I am afraid. Being just as headstrong as he is makes it difficult to obey without question. And you are too often forced to play peacemaker.'

'Someone must,' Dru said, wishing she could stay angry with a girl who so heartily deserved a scolding.

'For the moment, you could try to enjoy your time away from that abominable house,' Priss encouraged, in a way that seemed like sincere concern. 'And I promise that I shall give you no trouble at all.'

Making trouble came as naturally to Priss as breathing did. There was no point in commenting on it.

And then her sister said, with a sly smile. 'I suspect that you would have no real complaints about travelling with Mr Hendricks, if you would allow yourself to relax. He really is the most fascinating man.' She was staring out the window, to where Mr Hendricks rode beside the coach. 'Although, behind those ridiculous glasses, it is hard to see the colour of his eyes.'

'Golden brown,' said Dru, absently, looking down at her hands. 'His eyes are amber.' In the moonlight, one might even call them gold.

Her sister continued, as though she had not heard. 'I wonder, can he see without them? For I expect he would be much more handsome, were he to forgo them.'

'It would be quite foolish of him to do so,' Dru snapped. 'He is very sensible, not the sort of man at all who would sacrifice clear vision in the name of vanity.' Surprised at her own outburst, Dru bit her lip to prevent herself from mentioning some of the occasions that had caused him to forgo the spectacles.

Priss smiled. 'But I am sure that he is not unaware of the effect he has on women when he takes them off.

There is not a man alive who is as proper as you make him sound, Silly.'

Dru pulled her skirts more tightly around her legs. Last night should have proved to her that he was as prone to sins of the flesh as the worst of his kind, and willing to take advantage of a helpless female, without regard to her reputation or modesty. And to make no mention at all of it the next day, but instead, to begin a systematic wooing of the female's sister.

She could feel her knuckles going white as the nails cut little crescents in the palm of her hand. It was all the more foolish that she could not seem to manage the correct response to what had happened. She should have cried out last night, and to devil with the consequences. This morning, she should have been racked with guilt and shame and fearing for the safety of Priscilla while the villain stalked her under the guise of assisting them.

Instead? She felt…

Jealous. The sight of Priss in his arms had left her burning not with shame, but with anger. And not at him alone, but at her sister. It was Priss who had led them to this pass, and who now could not seem to understand the gravity of the situation for both their reputations, and the difficulties she faced in the future. After all the fuss over running off with Gervaise, she seemed not bothered in the least that the man was for ever gone from her life.

Instead, she had moved on to the next available man, using charms that had brought the males of the *ton* to their knees. Did she bother to think, even for a moment, that her quarry might have formed an attachment else-

where? Or that someone might have formed an attachment to him?

Not that Dru had any real evidence that what had
happened on the previous evening was any more than
a biological reaction to stress. It was wishful thinking
on her part that filled every corner of her head with
fancies about John Hendricks on one knee before her,
pleading for a chance to make things right. Or sweep-
ing into her bedroom tonight, as he had on the previous
one, overcome with desire and with no cares at all about
right or wrong.

Instead, this morning she had found him, warm and
soft with her sister, but stiff and formal to her, as though
she no longer mattered to him, now that she had been
bedded. It had given her the strangest feeling inside,
cold and sharp and painful, as though she was full of
broken glass. And so she had done what came naturally
to her. She had focused her mind on them until the
shards were on the outside, where they belonged. There,
they would hurt others and not herself, and she would
be protected, safe and untouched inside the barrier they
created.

However, she was conscious of the emptiness at their
absence and the way that John Hendricks had retreated
to a safe distance. It was just as she had commanded
him to do this morning. He was not bothering her, or
her sister. He rode just outside the carriage, where she
could catch only the occasional glimpse of him.

Now Priss was craning her head out the window,
waving to catch his eye. She glanced back at her sister.
'It is a shame that he does not ride with us, is it not?

I asked him to. But he told me that he does not enjoy being closed up in the body of the carriage.'

That was little more than a polite and unconvincing lie. He had not seemed to mind it much as he'd ridden with her. 'The way he was carrying on with you this morning, I think it is just as well that he remains outside, as I requested. It will save him from the stern lecture I would give, to remind him of his place. For the duration of this trip he will aid us in the task at hand. Just as Mr Gervaise was brought into the house to teach you to dance. Such men should know better than to get above themselves, and you should learn not to stoop.'

Perhaps if she could persuade Priss, she could learn the same thing herself. But after so long in his presence, just the sound of his voice as she scolded him would be a welcome thing. She missed the feel of his body close beside her, his leg pressed against her skirt and his arm at her waist to protect her.

Of course, the family carriage was exceptionally well sprung, and she hardly needed a sheltering body to guard her against the bumps and the jolts of the road. But luxury had never felt so empty and unwelcome.

Priss shook her from her reverie with a sharp tap upon the hand. 'Really, Silly, you mustn't brood so. One kiss is hardly a sign that I do not know a servant from a suitor.'

Nor, Dru supposed, did one night mean anything. No matter how much she might wish it did.

'The scenery is quite beautiful, and yet you are glaring out the window as though it were a dark day in

December. Can we not stop for a time and enjoy the countryside?'

'It is only three miles to the next inn,' Dru cautioned, pulling herself away from the window to stare at her sister. 'If we are continually stopping, it will take ages to get home.'

'But now that you have your way and I am returning to there, must we rush the trip? There is no one fashionable in London in the summer.'

'Father is there,' Dru said, firmly. 'And that is where we will attend him.'

'And I know you well enough to be sure that you have notified Papa of our return. You can tell him just as easily that we are delayed. It is nearly noon. I am stifling, and hungry as well. It would be delightful to have a picnic. Please tell the driver to stop and get down the hamper so that we might refresh ourselves.'

Dru sighed; now that her sister had the idea in her head, there would be no peace until she had her way. So she signalled the driver to stop at a wide spot in the road.

Mr Hendricks reined his horse and displayed no emotion save one barely raised eyebrow when he realised the purpose of the delay. He was likely eager to meet her father, receive his payment and be totally out of their lives.

The thought made her jaw clench; she ordered him sharply to lay out the blanket and help with the opening of the wine and the slicing of meat and bread. If he wished to act like a servant towards her, as though there was nothing more between them, so she would treat him.

Once he had seen to the comfort of her and her sister, he moved a respectful distance away, taking a small portion of the food for himself and leaning his back against a nearby tree.

'This is much better, is it not?' Priss insisted, then glanced at their companion. 'Mr Hendricks, would you not be more comfortable sharing the blanket with us?'

'I am quite fine here, my lady.'

'Oh, but I insist.' She patted the ground at her side.

'Oh, yes, Mr Hendricks. Do come and join us.' The sarcasm in her own voice was so thick that even Priss recognised it and stuck out her tongue in response, before sending another hopeful look in the direction of Mr Hendricks.

There was the barest hesitation before he pulled himself smoothly to his feet and joined them, dropping into the space between the two of them and allowing exactly the same distance so as not to show any partiality. Then he went back to the piece of bread he had been eating, as though nothing had changed.

'There. That is much better, I think.' Priscilla favoured him with another brilliant smile. 'It is a lovely day, is it not?'

'As you remarked earlier,' he responded.

She considered for a moment. 'When we were at the inn, the air was not quite so fresh. Here, we have the scent of the dog roses growing along the road.'

He noted the position of the flowers and nodded politely.

'Are they not lovely as well?' Priss coloured up in a way that looked almost sincere. Dru wondered how she could manage to control what should have been an autonomic response.

He turned his gaze on them again and answered. 'Indeed, my lady, they are most pretty, if one likes such things.'

'I doubt there is anyone in England that does not like a rose,' Priss said with a definitive nod of her head.

'But those are rather common flowers,' Dru answered, in some annoyance. 'And I expect they have thorns.' The cloying scent of the things, combined with Priss's annoying prattle, was giving her the most abominable pain in her head.

'A wise man learns to look past the thorns, at the beauty,' Mr Hendricks said, after a small pause. 'There is much reward to be had if one is willing to get past the prickly bits.'

Dru looked down at her hands, worrying that, if she looked up at him, she would find him staring at her in a most improper manner. Or, worse yet, that she would see him staring at Priss, with no idea of how his last statement might have sounded to her. When she finally gained the nerve to check, he was staring at nothing in particular, eating the sandwich he had made of cold meat and cheese.

Dru's eyes wandered to their surroundings, which were as annoyingly beautiful as Priss had said. Sunshine and roses—a lover at her side whom she dared not speak to, not even in anger, and a sister who was both chaperon and rival. Priss might find it pleasant and long to dawdle. But to Dru it felt unnatural, as though she were play-acting at being Priscilla. Everything was unbalanced. Someone had to keep their head, even when the roses were in bloom. And Lord knew there was not room in any family for two of them to behave like Priscilla.

'If I might be so bold as to ask a question?' John Hendricks's voice was polite and proper, carrying the subtle undercurrent that had led her into trouble in the past.

Dru put up her guard, but Priss responded, 'Oh, do. Ask anything at all, Mr Hendricks.'

'Lady Drusilla has mentioned that you are out, Lady Priscilla.'

'Indeed, sir. I expect I shall be married by the end of the year. Of course, I am quite without suitors at the moment.'

'Really, Priss,' Dru hissed. 'You are barely clear of Gervaise.'

Hendricks ignored the tension, and went on. 'But Lady Drusilla has said nothing of the results of her Season. And she is the older of the two of you, is she not?'

'At twenty-three, I am hardly an ancient,' she snapped, feeling as faded and rough as a dog rose in a hot house.

'She is bitter about it, because she did not receive a Season.' Priss put the truth bluntly, and yet there was sympathy in her voice. 'Mama died and Papa and I were distraught. Dru was brought home from school to take charge of me. And after a year of mourning, we were both old enough for the marriage mart. But she put me in her place.'

'At the expense of herself?' Hendricks asked, as though she was not even there.

'To have both of us out at the same time would only have divided the attention of the *ton*,' Dru informed him, to remind him of her part in the decision.

'Other families have managed to launch two marriageable daughters, even when they are not as wealthy as yours. Did you not wish for your chance to shine?'

It was an impertinent question, made all the more painful by the presence of her sister. 'We cannot always have what we want, Mr Hendricks. If there are two daughters in the family, one must needs be married first.'

'It is normally the elder daughter who experiences that honour.'

'But not always,' she said firmly. 'Sometimes, one child is more vivacious, more popular, more sought after. And when it is known that this is likely to be the case…' After four years, she could say it almost by rote.

'You sound almost as if the decision was made before you were brought home.'

'Priscilla was clearly the more eager of the two of us…'

'Because Mother filled my ears with talk of dancing and parties, Dru. You were sent off to school, to learn reason.' Priss looked directly at John, with none of her flirtatiousness and added, 'There is little mystery why we turned out as we have, sir. One of us was discouraged from being sensible. And the other was required to be.'

'Aptly put, Lady Priscilla. But you give yourself far less credit than you deserve. I suspect, in your own way, you are as astute as your sister.'

Now it felt as though the other two were passing messages between them that she was not privy to. Once again, she was on the outside, just as she had always been, looking hungrily at the green grass on the other side of the fence. But she was not hungry at all, really. She just wished that this horribly awkward conversation could be over. She nudged the food about on her plate and waited for Priss to declare herself ready to continue the journey.

Priss was still staring down the hill at the rosebush again. 'It is a rare man that pays me the honour of calling me astute, Mr Hendricks. Probably because I would much rather be thought pretty. And now, I think I would very much like a flower,' she said, scuffing the toe of her slipper in the dirt at the edge of the blanket. 'But I could never get it for myself, for I should certainly prick my finger upon it.'

Mr Hendricks gave a little sigh of amusement and put aside his meal. 'Then let me be of service.' His voice was as bland as if he were performing any other task put to him by a member of the family that employed him.

But he no longer worked for them. What he did now was merely a courtesy. And it angered Dru to see him scraping and bowing, especially to her sister, who was trying to get a rise out of him, to see some kind of reaction that would prove his true feelings for her.

'Oh, do leave off, Priss,' she said, her patience nearing an end. 'Let the poor man finish his meal, so that we might get back to our journey.'

But Hendricks was going for the flower, and Priss gave her a sharp nudge with her shoe. 'Nonsense. He didn't mind at all, did you, Mr Hendricks?'

'Of course not, Lady Priscilla.' And, as she had a hundred times when chaperoning her sister, she watched his manner for the eagerness or amusement, or a sign of hesitation that would make the flower a token of affection.

Mr Hendricks reached into his pocket for a penknife and cut through a stem, wrapping it carefully in his handkerchief to protect Priss's fingers from the thorns and offering it to her.

'It is so lovely. Thank you, Mr Hendricks.' The smile practically blazed from her sister's face in a way guaranteed to melt the reserve of even the most proper gentleman. Then she pulled a small mirror from her reticule and used the thorns to their best advantage to fix the blossom in her hair.

His name is John. Dru held the words in her heart, wanting to blurt it out to prove that, even for a moment, she'd had him all to herself. She felt her cheeks burning with something other than the coy charm that her little sister could manage. How did Priss make it all look so easy, wrapping a man around her finger just as she wrapped her curls around the rose? And leaving her, with a blank look on her face and straight dark hair that would not hold flowers, any more than she could hold the attention of a man.

She stood up too quickly, muttering something about needing a moment's privacy, and turned to step behind a nearby bush, praying that they would think she needed to relieve herself of anything but a foul mood.

'Dru.' He had caught up to her in a step or two, saying her name so low that no one but she could hear. But there was no blandness about it. It was a low growl of command that touched her, making her head snap back to look at him. He had cut another blossom from the rosebush and was examining it carefully to make sure there were no cankers. He turned his back so that Priss would see nothing, skinned the thorns from the stem with his knife, and held the bloom to his own nose, as though admiring the scent, brushing it gently against his lips as he did so.

Then he presented it to her with a flourish, touching it lightly to her cheek as though he could transfer the kiss he had given the flower.

She gasped in surprise; when she took the flower from him she held it so tightly that she feared she might break its stem.

'We must talk.' His voice was rough and urgent.

And do so much more than that. For she was sure she could feel the touch of his lips still. And then she remembered the much more earthy kiss he had given Priscilla, just that morning, when her bed was hardly cold. 'Go back to my sister. For I am sure that she is most eager to speak with you.'

He stifled an oath that was delivered so quietly that

even she could hardly hear it, though she stood close by. 'I come to pour my heart out to you, to offer apologies for my shameful behaviour. And I find you are jealous of your sister?'

Her cheeks were burning now. She gave her head a little shake, as though to deny the obvious.

He looked her in the eye, and his molten-gold eyes turned hard behind the lenses. 'It is unworthy of you. And unnecessary.' Then he spoke, even more quietly and more urgently, as though there were a great many things he wished to say, and no time or place to unburden himself. 'What you saw this morning was no fault of m—' As though he realised how it would sound to her, he stopped. 'It was of no importance; I will see that it does not happen again. But whatever your feelings towards me, we need to talk, and there is too little time for it. The things that must be said cannot be blurted in the open where anyone might hear them. When we have stopped for the night, if you can get away unobserved, come to my room.'

'I most certainly will not,' she whispered furiously. 'What must you think of me, that you believe I would even consider...?'

'Please.' He grabbed her hand, rose and all, and brought it up to touch his face, rubbing the back of it against his cheek, pressing his lips against it, breathing in as though her skin was some sort of rare perfume. 'Please. I will not risk coming to you again. Someone might see. But you will know when it is safe to get away.' He pushed her hand away and half-turned from her, as though he had been balancing precariously on the edge of a cliff, and had only just managed to step away. Then he looked up into her eyes. 'You must be the one to decide if I can be trusted. After what happened last night, I am not fit or able to make that decision. But if there is anything left to say between us, then come to me. I will wait.'

'Mr Hendricks?' Her sister's voice cut the thick air between them, and his head turned in the direction of the sound. Then he took a hurried step away from her, guilt plain on his face and searched the cover they stood behind for another exit. He went around the far side of a nearby tree, working his way through a small copse, to return to her as though to pretend that he had been nowhere near Dru.

She peered through the leaves of the hedge that hid her, to see Priss glancing over her shoulder in his direction, eyes alluring and the rose he had given her tucked into the curls at the side of her head.

'Yes, my lady.' He went to her. Attentive, obedient. Dru watched him closely. And nothing more than that. Though her sister tried with enthusiasm to evoke a stronger reaction, he stood politely to one side, well out of reach of her.

Dru's heart beat fast in her chest, and she put her hand against it, wishing that it would calm and let her think. What did he mean by that? What did he mean by any of it? Had he seriously kissed the rose in her hand or was it merely a wish on her part? And to ask her to his room was every bit as improper as coming to hers. How was she even to find it, without asking someone and revealing what she was searching for? And would she have the nerve? If he came to her, they both knew that she could pretend she had no part in the meeting. But if she went to him? Then it sent a clear meaning that she had gone where she had gone willingly and with intent.

Stuff and nonsense, she told herself. She had shared lodgings with the man for almost a week and had no such qualms. She had even slept in his arms.

And that experience had not been the least bit innocent, no matter what she might pretend. She could not speak of it, should not even think of it. Going to his room tonight was out of the question. It would be better that every moment of the last week be forgotten. Not that she could ever forget—but perhaps she could try.

She shuddered, for she could still feel his hands on her, his body in hers and his breath on her skin. Without thinking, she wrapped her arms around herself, trying to capture the feeling and still the trembling. Then she stepped out from behind the bush and back towards the place where the footman was gathering up the remains of the picnic.

From across the clearing, Mr Hendricks's head turned, as though he had sensed her response. His eyes were innocently blank. 'Lady Drusilla?'

'Nothing,' she assured him. 'A momentary chill.'

He nodded. 'They come on sometimes, even in the heat of the day. Do you wish me to get your shawl?' Ever the attentive servant, willing to see to her comfort and meet her every need.

The thought made her shudder even more. 'No.

Thank you, Mr Hendricks. I think once we are on the road again, I shall be fine.'

And hardly thinking, she turned to catch his attention and slipped the rose down the front of her dress, letting the petals crush against the skin of her breast and release their scent, turning everything about the day from innocent sunshine to something hot and lush and exciting.

And she smiled as the man before her watched, stumbled and caught himself again, taking a moment to remove his spectacles and wipe at them, as though eager to focus on anything but the place the rose had gone.

Chapter Seventeen

John Hendricks waited patiently behind the partially open door of his room, as still as a man waiting at a springe to catch a hare. He had dropped a few rose petals on the threshold. Should Dru come to look for him she would guess their meaning and enter.

Anyone else who stuck their head in could be sent off with a curse and the slam of the door. But after last night, and the way she had looked at him today, there was little more he could do for her than to wait patiently for her to come to him.

He silently damned her sister for the trouble she had caused, hanging about his neck like an albatross and creating no end of trouble. But what could he say to Dru about it that would show him in a good light? *I am sorry, darling, but your sister is no better than a grasping whore.*

But a shrewd one at that. It was possible that Priss had taken Gervaise away from her older sister. And if she suspected even a modicum of affection between Dru and himself, she might try the same trick. But today, as they had eaten she'd been most candid in her assessment of Dru's place in the family and the unfairness of it. This evening, she had taken herself off to bed at an early hour and insisted that she have her own room, so that her sister would not bother her.

At first, he feared it was meant as an invitation to him. But Priss had given her sister a pointed look, as if issuing a last warning before turning a blind eye. It gave him some small hope that he had an ally in the winning of Dru's hand.

But now, there was a hesitant scuffling on the threshold, and a whispered, 'Mr Hendricks?'

John, he thought fervently. *By now, you are entitled.* 'Yes.' He rose quickly, opened the door and pulled her inside, closing it behind her.

In the candlelight, she was as lovely as he remembered. And all his plans for a rational conversation evaporated. She had a woman's body, ripe and curved, to match those full red lips. It was a body a man could sink into, hot and rich, heady and intoxicating like a good wine. He tried not to think about it. Instead, he touched her face, cupping the softly rounded cheeks in his hands, pulling the lips to his for a kiss. He had meant it as a chaste greeting, as gentle as the kiss he had given to the rose. But her lips parted to accept him and he could not resist.

She had been innocent, he reminded himself. Still was. To presume less was to insult her character. But still, it was amazing that such a gem had gone undiscovered. And that he had been the one to touch her. Now, she was willing and here in his room. And he wanted her, just as much as he had the previous evening.

The circumstances of that bit into his conscience. She had not fought him, but she had hardly given him leave to do what he had done to her. And now he was ready to do it again without a word of consent.

He pulled away from the kiss with a groan, feeling her lean after him as though she did not want to give him up. But when he tried to read her mood, her head dipped so that he would not see her expression. Her heavy black hair was unbraided and hung down past her shoulders, covering her breasts. He touched her chin, lifting her face to look into his eyes. Big, brown, liquid.

And fearful. She did not shrink from him, for her arms still clung to his waist as though she was afraid to lose him. But she was not smiling. And as he watched, her lower lip trembled and the first tear coursed down her cheek.

He wrapped an arm about her shoulders and damned himself for his hasty actions of the previous night. 'Sweet?' he said, brushing the drop away with the back of a knuckle, only to see another take its place. She closed her eyes then, and the heavy lashes grew wet. And then her lips moved, as though murmuring a prayer.

'Drusilla?' he asked again, more clearly. 'Speak to me.'

She gave a little shake of her head and he felt the pain of hurting her, sharp inside him, and a hunger to take back the last hour, to a time when she was not crying. 'I am sorry. I did not mean to hurt you.'

'Last night, you were upset,' she whispered.

'Not at you, love.'

'But you will be.'

He smoothed a hand over her hair. 'And why would I have any right to anger? It is you who must hate me, for I have been a brute, with no sympathy to your feelings, no consideration for your innocence. I should never have touched you. I had no right.'

'It is not that,' she whispered. 'It is that you did what you did with no understanding of who I am.'

And for a moment, the strange idea leapt in him that she was about to make some dark confession about being a governess or a serving girl, masquerading as Lady Dru. He almost crossed his fingers in hope of it, for it would make life so much easier if they were in any way equal. He would offer, she would accept and nothing would stand between them, ever again. 'If I do not know who you are, then you must tell me. I want to know, Dru. I want to know you.'

'No, you do not,' she was shaking her head again. 'My sister...'

'Priscilla?' he asked, hoping for a different answer. But she nodded.

'It is she who loved Mr Gervaise, however unwise that might be. And I came after her and her alone. She did not understand the damage she might do to her reputation.'

Damn fate. And damn Priscilla as well. Dru was as great a lady as he feared and had lost her own reputation in the flight to save her sister. 'You have rescued her. And there is an end to it.'

'Last night, you seemed to think that I held some feeling for Gervaise. That there was a penchant, perhaps.'

'And there is not?' That was some small scrap of good news. 'But when we first met, you said that you and he had an understanding.'

'It was not that sort of understanding. When he first came to the house, I saw the way he looked at her. But he was a very good dancer and only in the house for a few hours each week. So I paid him twice what he was worth and told him that the money would continue as long as he caused no trouble, but that he would get nothing but trouble if he tried anything more adventurous than a waltz.'

The plan was so very like his Dru that he smiled. 'I do not think you were successful.'

'I did not count on Priss,' she said with a sad shake of her head. 'But there was never anything between Gervaise and me. He did not care much for me. Nor did it matter to me how he felt, for I liked him no better.'

'And the reason for your tears…' He stared up at the ceiling, trying to fathom it. For her outpouring of emotion made no sense at all.

'You were angry with him when you came to me. If you did what you did—' she took a deep breath '…to punish him in some way, or to punish me for liking him…'

'No, love. No.' He put a finger to her lips to stop her nonsense.

'Then it would not have worked. Perhaps, if you had gone to Priss instead. This morning, you seemed to prefer her. But I did not want that. And so I said nothing.'

Now he felt near frantic with the truth of her feelings, and pushed himself away from her body. 'Lady Drusilla, you misunderstand me as well. I would not have gone to your sister, in any case. That is not how it was at all. I had no wish to hurt her, to spite Gervaise. Nor to hurt you. And if, in what happened between us, I forced you to endure and not to enjoy…' Now he felt sick, nauseous at the idea that he had forced himself on her, and that, to keep her sister safe from his clutches, she had said nothing.

She gave a deep, gulping sob, clutching her hands to her mouth, her arms shielding her body from his gaze. 'It is worse than that. I…I…enjoyed it. I wanted you to do what you did. Had wanted it for so long. But if you had known the truth, then I was afraid you might have stopped. So I waited until it was too late.'

She was saying something else, but he could hardly hear her, what with the rushing blood in his ears at the relief. And so he seized her again and kissed her, stopping her prattle with his tongue and kissing her until sanity came back to him. Her mouth was salty from the taste of her tears. But given the least reason, she was kissing him eagerly back, thrusting her tongue into his mouth in unsure little forays, as though still afraid that he would reject her. When he pulled away from her, he said firmly, 'Did you like that as well?'

She gave a hesitant nod.

'Then it is all settled between us. I had no intention of visiting your sister, either before or after. In fact, having met her, I am sorry, but there is nothing that could induce me to it.'

'But this morning?'

'Was a mistake.' He searched delicately for a way to phrase it. 'Your sister seems to have drawn the same conclusion as you did for my reasons to fight Mr Gervaise. But it was not in an effort to defend her honour so much as extreme frustration that such a worthless clod could have designs on you.' He smoothed a hand down her side, feeling the rich promise of her hip through the fabric, wondering if he dared to do what he was thinking. 'I will fight him again, if he comes back.'

'That will not be necessary,' she said absently. 'But this morning...you said nothing to me. You could hardly bear to look at me.'

'I did not dare, more like. Better for your sister to think she had ensnared me, than that I had dishonoured you. And I mean to give her no further encouragement. I just didn't want her guessing what had gone on between us. Even a hint of what has happened would hurt you—and destroy what little chance I have to offer honourably for you.'

'Offer,' she said, in a surprised whisper.

His pride stung along with his conscience now. They both knew that he was not a worthy suitor. But she could at least pretend otherwise. 'Of course I will offer. After last night, you must understand how I feel about you. When I found a beautiful woman rushing to stop an elopement, I incorrectly assumed that it was to retrieve your own wayward fiancé. And I damned the inequality of our births and my misfortune at not being the one to tempt you away from the life you deserve. But I doubt your virtue would have survived the first night, had I but known that your heart was unengaged.'

'You wanted me?' She had that curious little frown again that he found so appealing.

'Most certainly. Almost from the first moment.'

'But people do not—male people, that is, men—do not normally…once they have met Priss…' She was still trying to puzzle it out, so he kissed her again until he could feel the lines in her brow begin to relax, bringing his hands from her shoulders down to her waist and back up, over her ribs until the swell of her breasts filled his hands.

'Let us think no more of what other men want, Drusilla. My only care is for my own satisfaction. And my only desire is to find it in your bed. Not your sister's. Nor any other lady of my acquaintance, or of yours.

'Hmm.' He kissed her again, and felt her whole body relaxing against his, her arms creeping back around his waist. Her hips were locked against his, and after last night, she must have a much better idea of what was likely to happen, should she stay.

'Dru,' he murmured in a sigh against her hair, willing himself not to tighten his hands upon those delightful breasts. 'Must you return immediately to your room?'

'Priss is most adamant that I not disturb her until morning. And there is not another person for miles that would care what becomes of me.'

'There is one, darling.' He kissed the side of her

throat and felt her laugh. 'I know it is a day too late to ask, but have you given any thought to your feelings towards me? If I were to offer, what might your answer be?'

She gave a frustrated sigh. 'Father would never permit it.' Then she bit his ear as though she did not want to bother her head with anything so unpleasant.

It was not the same as a no, he told himself. And she did seem to be kissing him eagerly, as though she wished him to forget any impediment. 'Your father is not the one I wish to marry. If it were only us, then what might your answer be?'

'If you wish to marry me, then it would be most foolish of me to refuse,' she said, rather primly for one separated from him by only a nightgown.

'That is a sensible "yes" and, therefore, little better than a "no".' It was certainly not the enthusiastic answer he required. 'How do you feel about me? While I would marry you for duty, should you wish me to, just to restore your reputation, I would much rather it be a union based on mutual affection.'

Then her expression turned strange. A cloudy, dreamy sort of smile was on her lips, and her eyes seemed to be gazing far away. 'I never expected to be asked that question. How do I feel?'

'Yes,' he said, more urgently. 'Could you love me, just a little? For I swear, though I could love enough for both of us, it would be a burden happily shared.'

'I feel wonderful, Mr Hendricks,' she said, with a sigh. 'And while I do not know the emotion well, I think I might be in love with you.'

'John, darling. Please, call me John.' And then, he buried his face in her throat, wanting nothing more than to mark it with the force of his kisses. Instead, he inhaled her scent and licked gently along the cords of it.

'John,' she said resolutely, as though growing used to the name. And then, more softly, 'Oh, John.'

He laughed against her throat, drawing her back towards the bed with him, praying that it was not too great a liberty to want the woman he loved in any way he could get her, for the brief time they had to share. He whispered, 'This, darling, is where you are supposed to tell me that you will not countenance such behaviour from me until there is a ring on your finger.'

She sighed and pushed him back until he sat on the mattress. 'Then I fear I shall be no good at all. I have no intention of stopping you, and missing this opportunity. If I did, and some misfortune would befall us, if you were to change your mind…'

'I would never.' He laughed again, into the hollow between her breasts.

'Or if my father should forbid us…'

Now that was a distinct possibility, and one he did not wish to think about just now. So he leaned his head to the side and caught one of her nipples through the fabric of her nightgown.

She gave a gasp of shock, then put her hands to the back of his head to push his face into her breast, all thought of disaster fleeing from her mind.

And his as well. She was the sweetest thing, and her heart beat wildly against his cheek as he suckled her and reached to ease the hem of her gown up higher over her hip. With his other hand, he teased the place between her legs until her knees began to give way. 'Take off your nightgown for me. Let me see you.'

She hesitated, as though this act was the one that would prove her intentions to herself. But she did as he asked. And he fell to his knees before her, burying his face against her body. 'Do you know how long I have wanted to do this? Since the first moment I saw you in breeches.'

'You told me that it was only to make the riding easier…'

'And it was,' he assured her, kissing her thigh.

'But all the while you were looking at my legs.'

'They are very nice legs,' he admitted, kissing them again, and pushing his hand between them, slowly lifting the palm up until it could go no farther. He raised his head to look at her. 'I admired your breasts as well. Without a corset to hold them, they swayed whenever you moved.

'You are horrid.'

'Very much so. Let me show you.' And he followed his hand with his tongue and lapped at her sex.

'Mr Hendricks!' In her surprise, she had fallen back to her old ways of barking prim orders at him.

And so he responded in kind, and said, 'Lady Drusilla,' then covered her with his mouth. And for a while, all she could manage was a few stifled moans, then gasping as her hips bucked in his hands, and finally settled, soft and open as a dew-soaked flower.

He lifted his head to kiss her belly, regretting that he

had not bothered to undress before her arrival. But her smooth white hands were tugging at his shirt, and he rose and let her fumble at the fastenings of his clothing, the timidity of her hands all the more erotic. When he could no longer stand to wait, he hurriedly undid the last of the buttons, stripped to his skin and then laid her down on the bed and himself down beside her. Then he placed his member on the palm of her outstretched hand, curling her fingers around it and teaching her to stroke.

Now it was his turn to moan, for she was a quick study, eager to please him, climbing on top of him and pleasuring herself by using his body to touch hers, rubbing him in the wetness between her legs until he was near to sliding inside her.

He cupped her bottom and pulled her forwards. 'Tonight I will remember to leave your body before I spill my seed.'

'You will not,' she said.

'But we dare not risk…'

'I do not care.'

There was much she did not understand about the risk of children and his inability to feed them should they arrive before he had secured another position.

And then the thought fled, for she was experimenting with movement, flexing the muscles inside her body to trap him, rising up and dropping back again in a slow rocking that felt incredibly good. He leaned away from her, wanting the feeling to last and watched her touching herself as she moved until she shuddered in the throes of orgasm, her hair damp with sweat, covering her beautiful face in a veil as she lost control.

She opened her eyes and looked down at him, smiling in wanton surprise as she realised that he was still hard, still in need.

And he felt the aching tightness growing inside him and tried to rein it in, remembering that one of them must keep their head. But she broke that control as easily as a twig, moving on him again, scratching his chest, pushing her ripe breasts into his palms and leaning forwards to bite and suck at his shoulders and throat, marking him as hers.

He could stand it no longer. He rolled with her until he was on top, driving into her over and over, his mouth on hers to stifle both their groans so that they came together in a rush of silent, shaking power. He collapsed on her body, skin to skin. 'A night is not enough,' he whispered. 'I need you. All of you. Naked beside me.'

'Me,' she whispered back, still surprised.

'Of course, you. My darling, my beautiful Dru.'

She nestled close to him, her smile growing soft and fond. 'Tell me again that you love me.'

'I love you,' he said simply, feeling the inadequacies of the words. 'I wish there was a way that I could prove it. I would shower you with diamonds, if I had them. Rubies and pearls. I'd dress you in silks—' and then he stopped. For the likelihood of any of that escaped him. If she came to his house and his bed, she would be leaving luxury behind.

'Just words, please. I like to hear you say it.' She thought for a moment. 'Words and actions.'

* * *

The night had passed quickly. And the dawn left John wondering how he would manage to sit a horse for another day's ride without falling asleep in the saddle. He stroked the hair of the woman in his arms, feeling thoroughly depleted by her and satisfied in all ways but one.

He prodded her arm. 'Dru, wake up and speak to me.'

She gave a groan and then ducked her head beneath the covers, kissing his chest.

'Enough.' He pulled her up his body, so that he might look her in the eyes again. 'Do not try to hide from me. For if you remember, when I invited you here, I said there were things to discuss.'

'And we have hardly talked at all,' she said, with a wicked smile, as though it were an achievement.

'We will be in London soon,' he said. 'A day or two at most.'

'I know,' she said with a sigh. 'And then it might all be over.'

'What the deuce? Of course it will not,' he said. 'You have not been thinking all this time that I meant to let you go, have you?'

'I fail to see any other way that this can end,' she responded.

There was a sudden and unexpected tightening in his throat at the fear that he had been mistaken in her feelings. 'I thought that, after what has happened, it would end in our marriage. You said you loved me. And that you would have me, if I wished.'

She looked at him with eyes full of both worry and pity. 'Do not feel that you have to do that, Mr Hendricks.'

And there was that 'Mister' again, as though she had not lain in his arms these past two nights, murmuring 'John'. 'You are still describing a possible union between us as though it were some sort of obligation.'

'Is it not?' she asked. 'You feel that, since you have dishonoured me, you must make the offer.'

'Of course I do,' he said, exasperated.

'And you have said you loved me,' she said, with a happy sigh. 'And I love you as well. And because of that, I do not wish you to feel bad for what shall happen.'

She was being puzzling again, as she was sometimes. 'You speak as though it would be a hardship to wed you.'

'It cannot be what you expected, when you set out from London,' she pointed out.

'Of course not. But just because a thing is unexpected does not make it unwelcome. And I know I am unworthy. But you must tell me plainly, right now—will you have me or no?'

'Of course I would have you. I would like nothing better. If…'

'There need be no ifs or buts, Drusilla.' He wrapped an arm around her body, hugging her close. 'I do not wish to hear them.'

She sat up, gathering the sheets around her body. 'But now you must. We cannot be for ever on the road, my love. We will be back in London, just as you have said. And while I will take you gladly, my father will most certainly refuse to let me go.' She hesitated. 'You do mean to ask him, don't you?'

It would be so much easier if he did not, for she was likely right. If they simply turned their backs on London and went back to where they had been, he could take her over the border, just as Gervaise had tried with her sister. And though there was nothing fragile about his Dru, their love was new and might not stand the shock of the duke's displeasure. 'Of course I will ask him.' He looked up at her, reassuring.

'And when he says no?'

John grinned at her. 'Do not be so sure of that. I mean to make a very persuasive case for myself.'

She smiled at him fondly. For a moment, he imagined seeing that smile, just as it was, each morning for the rest of his life. Then she said, 'It will not matter. He has plans of his own in regards to the marriage of his daughters. And for all we might want it to be otherwise, they do not include you.'

'Are you promised elsewhere?' Again, panic gripped him, low in his stomach. For though it had not been Gervaise, perhaps his assumptions had some small grain of truth in them.

She shook her head. 'I have been far too busy seeing to Priscilla to think of such a thing for myself. And my father has been satisfied to have it so. If I marry, then who shall watch over her?' It was clear that the obligation of her younger sister was such a solid and palpable thing that she could imagine life no other way.

'Your father has the means to hire a companion. He must have considered it at some time.'

And there, when he looked in her eyes, was a curious blankness and a growing puzzlement, as if it was hard for her to imagine a life where she was anything other than spinster companion to the vivacious Priss. 'But then, why hasn't he?'

The hurt was so plain that he felt it in his own breast. She was like an animal so accustomed to its cage that an open door did not signal escape. And in that moment, he hated the duke, and was sure that Dru's predictions were correct. The man would hate him in return for daring to ask for her hand, and his birth would have nothing to do with it. For whatever reason, Dru was not meant to marry and never had been.

So he took her in his arms, letting the anger and frustration leave him in a kiss that left her breathless with its force. 'I do not know, darling,' he said, when it was through. 'All I know is that I want you, and with all my heart. Despite what you may think, it is not a sign of desperation, or a weakness in my character to do so. If I have a fault, it is that I am prone to aspire far above my station. And now I have set myself the task of winning a woman of great wit and beauty. I will go to your father, whether it is wise or no, and I will ask for your hand. And we shall see what he has to say in the matter.'

'And when he refuses?'

He looked into her eyes, so that she would know he was serious. 'Then I suppose it will be up to you what happens next. I do not mean to be parted from you, until you send me away.'

Chapter Eighteen

I want you.

The words were still ringing in her ears as the carriage made its way the last miles of the road to London. The echo of them was almost loud enough to block the continual sighing of her sister, who had grown tired of the journey and was shifting restlessly in her seat and offering meaningless interjections that broke Dru's train of thought.

John had been very specific about that. And very insistent. She hid the smile on her face by turning to look out the window.

'I wish you had not come for me, Silly. It would have been better if it had been Father.'

Dru glared at her. 'And he would have raised such a fuss that the whole house would have known of your disgrace.'

Priss sighed. 'You will manage to hush it up and the whole trip will be for nought. Still, I suppose it is better that you found me when you did. I could not manage to drag my feet any longer. And if we'd have crossed the border, I might have ended up married.'

'I am glad that you are finally coming to your senses,' Dru said. 'But you need not worry. Mr Hendricks has got rid of Gervaise and he will never bother you again.'

'Nor I him,' Priss said emphatically.

'You must not take the blame for this upon yourself,' Dru said, trying for a change to be a comfort and not a scold. 'You could not have known, when he took you from the house, what he was planning.'

Priss laughed. 'You do not still have some ridiculous idea that he forced me into the carriage, do you? I worried at the poor man for ages to get him this far.'

Dru could feel the knot of nerves in her head tightening again, as they always did when she tried to reason with her sister. 'Did you not realise what such a decision could do to your reputation?'

'Destroy it utterly, I should think. Of course, if I had been forced to marry him, it would have been better in one sense. I would have been off the market and totally forgotten.' But she gave a little shudder as though there was nothing to like at all about the idea of wedded life with Gervaise. Then she brightened. 'Now I shall simply be thought loose.'

'You foolish girl,' Dru exploded. 'Marriage to Gervaise would have meant penury, isolation, hardship. You cannot think that Father would condone such a union, nor contribute in any way to your well-being if you made the match.'

Priss gave her a weary look. 'I suspected he would

first try to undo it. And if he was not able, he'd have cut me off. But that was the only way I was likely to escape.'

'Escape? Whatever do you mean? You have everything you need, Priscilla, and have not known a moment's strife since the day you were born.'

'Nor have I known a moment's freedom,' her sister pointed out, and there was the smallest of frowns on her pretty face as she did it. 'You are wrong to think I can destroy my reputation over something so small as this.'

'I know you will not,' Dru said, with some bitterness. 'Because when we are properly home and Father is finished shouting, we will find a way to make it disappear.'

Priss gave her a strange smile. 'I hope not. Perhaps I am beyond redemption. Then we shall be spinsters and grow old together. Will that not be nice?'

Dru thought of Mr Hendricks and blurted, 'It most certainly will not.'

And she was surprised to see Priss falter. For a moment, there was a sparkle in her eyes that looked almost like the beginning of tears. Then her little sister regained control and smiled again. 'Well, never mind. You needn't worry that I will be a burden on you much longer. Father will pave it over, as smooth as glass. And when he has selected a husband for me, I will marry, and that will be that.' She sighed again. 'In the meantime, I suppose there shall be parties and picnics full of men to flirt with. And that will be some consolation.'

'When Father hears of what you have done, you will

be lucky if he does not send you straight back to Scotland for an extended period of rustication.'

Priss looked at her speculatively. 'And you must come along with me. That might work well for one of us, now that I think of it.'

'I don't know what you mean.' But there had been that sudden, unavoidable image of making her own trip to Gretna Green.

'Of course you don't, Silly.' Priss rolled her eyes. 'But even if we are sent from town, within a year I shall be right back to London and married to the man of our father's choosing. It will be the sort of man who values the good opinion of Benbridge over mine, and is willing to overlook my unfortunate past. He will be more concerned with the advancement he might gain than the foolishness of his wife.'

'No matter who you marry, you will never know want,' Dru insisted. 'And it is not as if Father is likely to choose a cruel man to wed you.'

Priscilla laughed again. 'After three days with Gervaise?' She gave a little shudder of disgust. 'I think my only want is to remain unwed. And I shall be experiencing a permanent want of that shortly. As to whether or not my husband will be cruel? I doubt it matters one way or the other to Father. My husband will be rich and politically well placed.' She gave the coldest smile Dru had ever seen on that sweet face. 'But he is unlikely to be the heir to a dukedom, now that I have sullied myself. Father will have to settle for a second son, or perhaps an inferior.' She gave a short laugh. 'God forbid that he find nothing better than a baronet for me.'

Dru's already short temper snapped. 'And God forbid that you should settle for the man offered, when he will at least take the time to find you someone. There are others in the family that have even less freedom than you, and are just as unlikely to ever see a Season. Nor will we marry the man of our choosing.'

'Mr Hendricks,' Priss said with finality. 'Say the name, Silly. We are in the privacy of the carriage, with no one else to hear. You can admit to me that he is the one you want.'

'I…I have no idea what you are talking about,' Dru faltered.

Her sister gave her a sly smile. 'Mr Hendricks. Do not pretend that you have not thought of marriage with him. The man has been bedding you from London to Gretna and back. Oh, do not give me that look, Silly. I may be a sound sleeper, but not so sound as all that. I heard you creeping down the hall this morning, on your way back to your room. And I saw the look on your face when I kissed him. And his as well. He looked, for all the world, as though he had sucked a lemon.' She smiled. 'You need not worry. I have no intention of saying a word to anyone on the subject. And I applaud you for your good sense in this matter, taking advantage of my misbehaviour to have a little of your own for a change.'

'I did nothing of the kind,' Dru said, stomach roiling at the betrayal. It would be good, even for a moment, to tell someone the truth. To ask advice. Or to share the joy of it. But if she wished to defend her sister's honour, she could hardly admit to the cracks in her own.

Priss sighed again, sounding weary beyond her years.

'It would be easier between us if you trusted me, Silly. Just a little. Then we could talk as sisters, and it might not seem so...'

Priss was looking at her, as though waiting for some sign that she might lower her defences. It hurt to stay silent, almost as much as it had to lie about her feelings for John. But she had decided years ago that Priss needed a mother more than a sister. It was too late to retreat. And so she said nothing, giving her dear little sister the same stern look as she always did.

And Priss broke her gaze, staring in defeat at the floor of the carriage. 'Very well, then, Silly. Nothing has happened to either of us on this trip. We will remain in London, stifling in the heat. I will say nothing of the truth. Nor will you. Papa is likely to be very cross with you, for letting me run about so.'

And then Priss looked her in the eye, and her gaze was, for want of a better word, *knowing.* Now that Dru had experienced love herself, there was no missing the fact that Priss was as knowledgeable as she. 'And we both know he does not wish to know the answers to the questions he is most likely to ask. We will go home and live in silence and denial, just as we always have, until Father chooses an appropriate husband for me. Perhaps then I shall have you stay with me, to keep me company. You will have more freedom in my house than you will in his.' Priss thought for a moment. 'Considering the sort of man that Father is likely to pick, it would be quite useful to have someone to explain where I have got to, when I choose to be somewhere other than where I am expected.'

'You are planning alibis for your infidelities, even before you know the identity of your husband.'

Priss gave her a blank stare. 'It is better to be sensible and prepared, Silly. Have you not taught me that?'

'But that is not what I meant at all.'

Priss stared at her, as though she could not believe her sister's stupidity. 'Then you have been using your considerable organisational talents to no purpose. Our lives as I have described them are just as they are. Father means for me to be married. And for you? I doubt he thinks of it at all. I am his favourite. We both know it, although you will not admit it to yourself. With Mother gone, it has been your job to watch over me. Where I go, you will follow. Or you can stay in Father's house, play hostess and housekeeper, and grow old while he dangles the possibility of marriage until even you see how laughable it is.'

'No.' She was beyond speech now, beyond thought. With only that cold and very real future stretching before her.

Priss squeezed her hand, and said softly, 'It was not just my childish inability with Drusilla that lead me to call you Silly. You really are the most foolish girl. But it is all right, darling Dru. I will take care of you. If I can, I will force my husband to hire your Mr Hendricks. Then you shall visit me whenever you like.'

So that was to be the plan of the rest of her life: she was to be guardian of her sister's fragile reputation. And since Priss had no care for it herself, she was to be little better than an abbess, arranging liaisons, and making sure that the truth did not become too well known.

She looked back at Priss, disheartened. 'It was not until just now that I realised how aptly you have named me, Priss. I would need to be quite silly, to have such a life.'

She glanced out the window again, her fingers clasping the edge of the frame and praying for even a glimpse of John Hendricks.

And as though he could sense her desire, he rode even with the window and smiled in at her. Then he signalled to the driver to stop. It was not yet luncheon, and they hardly had need of it, for they had been on the road for only a few hours.

But Priss accepted it eagerly, and was out of the carriage as soon as the steps were down, as though she could not wait to be away from her sister. After the conversation they'd shared, Dru felt uneasy as well, and was glad for a respite.

And John came to her in the only way he could. He was polite, formal and distant, as though there was nothing more important between them than to discuss the condition of the roads. 'Lady Drusilla?'

'Yes, Mr Hendricks.' She waited until she was sure her sister was out of sight, and the grooms and coachmen were busy with the horses. Then, very deliberately, she smiled at him.

John returned her smile, looking more like a shy lover than a servant. He took a moment to fiddle with his spectacles, composing himself, until he was simply Mr Hendricks again. 'How is your sister faring, on the return?'

'She is resigned to it, I think.' Dru frowned. 'And

less than happy with her lot in life. But there is very little I can do for her, in that respect.'

'Now that I am sure you are safely on your way, I will leave you to find your own way home.'

'No!' There was nothing proper or composed about her response. The single word came, so sudden and anguished, that the servants looked up, ready to come to her aid. Even Priss turned back to see what the matter was.

'It is all right,' John said back in his composed servant's voice. 'We will not be parted for long. Only a day or two. And I have a reason for it. If I am to see your father, I do not wish to arrive along with you, half-shaved and covered with muck. I am going on ahead to prepare myself for the visit, and to prepare the way for you, as well. It might be easier for you if I explain what has happened before you arrive.'

'And what, precisely, do you mean to say, Mr Hendricks?' Priss had returned to them, and was standing a little way away, looking daggers at him.

He looked back, bland, innocent and, as always, helpful. 'That I am unsure of the reasons for your departure. But that I happened to meet Lady Drusilla while travelling, and she was most distressed. I found you in the company of a Mr Gervaise, who was a base and unworthy fellow. I gave him a sound thrashing and made sure that he would bother you no further. Then I aided you in returning home. You are both shaken by the experience, but in good health. Does this meet with your satisfaction?'

'Well enough,' said Priss. 'It will cause the least trouble for Silly, at any rate.'

'But you will visit, when we have returned?' If nothing else, he could say goodbye. If Father sent him away, she was entitled to one last kiss.

'Of course I will visit. As soon after your arrival as is decent.'

Priss laughed. 'It does me good, Silly, to see you in such a state. With me, you act as though you are made of granite. But at the brief loss of Mr Hendricks, you are very nearly wringing your hands.'

'I am not,' Dru said defensively, knowing that she was. A day without him would seem like for ever.

'You have done her good, Mr Hendricks. In a week, you have made her human. Now kiss her and go.'

'Priscilla.' Dru barely had time to begin her outraged harangue, before he'd responded,

'As you wish, Lady Priscilla.'

And he seized her, quite capably, and pulled her off balance and into his arms. The kiss was the best one he had given her, deep and slow to make his claim on her in front of sister and servants and anyone else who might see it.

Dru flapped her hands in protest for a moment, before deciding that to struggle would be to waste an opportunity. So she stretched out her arms around his neck and kissed him back until she heard her wayward sister say, 'Really, Mr Hendricks. That is quite enough to prove your point.'

Then she felt Priss tugging her away and upright again. 'And you, Drusilla. You are near to eating the man alive on a public highway and making us all nauseous. There will be time enough for that later, when you are alone.'

'She is right, Dru.' John was straightening his coat and looking at her with a polite smile. 'Let me go and talk to your father. I will see you again, after.'

'After,' she said, holding on to the word and managing a wave of farewell. No matter what happened with her father, she would see him again, even if it was only to say goodbye.

Chapter Nineteen

John removed his hat and waited in the entry of the Folbroke town house for the butler to announce him. It was strange, after little more than a week, to be actively seeking the company of the very people he had run from. But in those few days much had changed, and he needed the advice of a friend. Now that he was not in the service of the Earl of Folbroke, he could think of no one in his life that better fit the position.

This particular house had been shut for so much of his tenure with the family that he hardly remembered it. On the few occasions he'd had to visit it, the Holland covers had been on what furniture remained, and the rooms eerily silent. It was quite different from Adrian's old digs, which were barely large enough for a bachelor and a small staff. They had been sufficient for the earl's reclusion from his wife, but unsuitable for a happily married man.

John smiled at the thought of Adrian's sudden eagerness to indulge his wife and probed his own heart for any hint of jealousy. He was relieved to find none. The care of Emily had been his sole concern for years. The idea that she somehow belonged to him had come on him slowly. But the madness had left quickly enough, when it was clear that she'd returned to her husband.

The reconciliation between husband and wife appeared to be a permanent thing, if Emily was setting up the London house, just as it always should have been. From his position in the foyer, John could see a steady stream of furniture going in and out of attics and box rooms. And he was sure that when Emily was happy with it, the composition would be both fashionable and easy for her husband to navigate.

From a door on his left, there came the familiar tap of the cane, and the call, 'Mr Hendricks. Back already? Do not hang about in the doorway, waiting for an invitation. My study is just to one side of the stairs. It is the only peace you will find in this house, until my wife is done arranging the chairs.'

He smiled in spite of himself, for as it always had, the 'Mistuh' before his name had the sharp call of a commander, and a tone that could cut through the chaos of a battlefield. 'Yes, my lord.'

'Or, at least, I think it is orderly and peaceful,' Adrian Longesley added. 'I barely know myself.' He had made his way into the hallway, his cane held casually in front of him so that he might feel for obstacles.

John resisted the desire to set his former employer on the right path. He knew, despite the man's blindness, that he would prefer to make his own errors than to be led about his own house like a wayward child. 'It presents a challenge for you, does it not, when you move from familiar surroundings?'

'The rooms in Jermyn Street were simple enough, but I'd grown far too comfortable in my misery there. Emily has seen to it that my study here was the first to be finished so that I might have sanctuary. The problems have been minimal.' He grinned at the thought of his wife. 'But she is always thinking of such things. I swear, Hendricks, it is quite miraculous the way she has adjusted to my quirks.'

'I am not the least surprised,' John replied. His only real surprise was the lack of trepidation he felt in meeting with Lady Folbroke again.

Adrian led him back to the study and gestured him to a chair, almost as if he could see the thing, then took a seat behind his own desk. 'But what brings you back again so soon, John? Not seeking your old job, are you? It has been barely a fortnight since you left me, you know.' There was a small amount of reproof there, and John wondered, should he be forced to ask for it again, if he would be welcome. Then the earl smiled. 'I had high hopes for you, when you stormed out of here. It was kindness that kept you at my side, after the war. But you are capable of more than the duties you performed for me.'

He hoped Adrian was not expecting him to give a polite insistence that the duties had suited him well, as had the pay. Perhaps they had, at the time. Instead, he said, 'I am beginning to suspect that you are right, Lord Folbroke. It is not that they did not please me while I worked for you. I left, planning to seek an equally satisfactory position. But I've recently come to the conclusion that I must aim higher. I doubt that my old salary will be sufficient, now that I am to be married.'

'Marriage!' Adrian laughed, and slammed his palm down upon the desk. 'I will help you to make your fortune, John, in any way that I can. But there must be quite a story attached to this and I will not lift a finger until I have heard it. Who is the girl?'

'Her identity is part of the problem,' Hendricks admitted. 'She is the daughter of a duke.'

'Better than the wife of an earl,' said Adrian. The blank eyes looked at him intently, but without animosity.

'If a certain member of the peerage did not have such a damned appealing countess, it would never have been a problem.' He glanced towards the hall, and said quietly, 'How is she?'

'As long as you mean to give your heart elsewhere, you must tell me for yourself.' Adrian called into the hall, 'Emily, come to the study. We have a visitor with a most interesting tale to tell.'

John stood to greet the Countess of Folbroke, giving his spectacles a nervous polish before she entered. It was not necessary. For even without them he could see that she was as beautiful as she had been. After only a moment's hesitation, she reached out her hands to him and he clasped them in greeting. 'Mr Hendricks.'

He dipped his head in a half-bow and said, 'Lady Folbroke.' There was the raised chin and the clear discerning gaze that he had found so attractive. But strangely, she seemed smaller, after his two weeks away. Everything about her was less than he remembered.

Then it struck him. The features that he had most admired in her, the strength, the forthright nature and the tenacity, were as flowers in bud, compared to the rose he had discovered on the way to Scotland. And Dru had the colouring to suit her temperament. He thought for a moment of that thick black hair, falling through his hands.

He fiddled with his glasses to hide his distraction, and his relief at being able to see the woman before him as clearly as he did. And then he turned to the earl and lied through his teeth. 'If it is possible, she is even lovelier than when I last saw her.'

'Perhaps our reconciliation has done me good,' she said, smiling at her husband. Without another thought for John, she released his hands and went behind the desk to perch herself on the arm of her husband's chair. In an equally unconscious gesture, the earl's hand came to her waist to steady her. Hendricks had to admit that, seeing them together this way, all was right with the world.

Adrian looked up at his wife fondly. 'Mr Hendricks is in need of our help. He has got himself affianced to some young thing that is quite above him.'

'Not affianced,' Hendricks insisted. 'It has not come to that yet, although I have asked and she has said yes. It is her father that is likely to be the problem.'

'And who might he be?' Folbroke asked.

'His Grace, the Duke of Benbridge.'

Adrian's mouth puckered as though he had been

forced to taste something foul. And Emily nearly sprang from her chair. 'Do not say so, Mr Hendricks. I had thought that you had more sense than that. Why…the girl is quite unsuitable.'

'Now, Emily,' her husband cautioned. 'Mr Hendricks will think you have some unfair motive to reject his beloved out of hand in this way. The father is a pill, of course. But surely the girl—'

'Is someone you have not met,' Emily said firmly. 'And though she is pretty enough, Priscilla Rudney is a cloth-brained goose.'

Hendricks stifled a smile. 'Then I must assure you, it is not Priscilla at all that I mean to snare. It is the elder sister.'

'She has a sister?' For a moment, Emily seemed quite baffled. Then she said, 'A tall, dark girl, is she not? Or a woman, I should say. She must be almost four and twenty.'

'And still unmarried?' Adrian said in surprise.

'Her name is Drusilla,' Hendricks said, equally surprised at the protectiveness he felt for her.

'Her family calls her Silly,' Emily interjected.

'And I assure you, it is a most inappropriate nickname.'

Emily nodded in relief. 'That is some comfort to me then, for I would hate to think that the older daughter was any worse than the younger. Very well. You wish to marry above you, and it will be a challenge to present the suit to Benbridge. But, and you must forgive me for saying it, Mr Hendricks, at her age, the girl is on the shelf. He will not be so particular as he is for the younger one. If there is affection on both sides of this match—'

'There is,' John interposed. 'Very much so. And I have come to suspect that she is not on the shelf, so much as she has been placed there by her father. All his attention has been focused on Priscilla, at the expense of Dru.'

'And it has made her spoiled and wilful,' said Emily with conviction. 'But I will trust your judgement that Drusilla does not share those particular faults.'

All in the room grinned like fools at the thought of their own particular happinesses. Then John said, cautiously, 'It has all come on me rather suddenly. And as you can see, if I mean to have Dru, I have set myself a task. So I come to you, not so much seeking a position as seeking the advice…' he gave his spectacles another polish '…the advice of friends. I will go to meet Benbridge later in the day, to explain the circumstances in which I met his daughters, which are unusual. I am going with no family, no title, and not even a stable position. I have very little to offer but my love for his daughter, and her love for me.'

Adrian frowned. 'I am sorry, John, but while that might matter to another, that will mean less than nothing to Benbridge. The man is a miserable old sinner, with a heart like a flint. Still, tell us your story, and we will put our heads together so that you might present yourself in the most favourable light. I am sure that we will be throwing orange blossoms by spring.'

Chapter Twenty

'A Mr John Hendricks to see you, your Grace.' John had wondered, as he spoke to Adrian, whether it would be better to present himself as Captain Hendricks, and had been assured that a lowly captaincy would mean nothing, even if he were in command of a ship. But that it should not dissuade him, for it was nothing personal. Benbridge was so stiff that he was just as likely to wipe his feet upon a major as speak to him.

'It is in regards to their ladyships.' From the hall, John could hear the butler give a respectful pause.

'Bring him here, immediately.' *Sliced thin and served with mustard.* For all the warmth and concern in his voice, his Grace might as well have been ordering supper than expecting word of his daughters' safety.

John entered the study and stood in silence before the man, waiting his turn to speak.

'I left the city for barely a day,' the duke began, low and cold, 'and returned to find that all hell had broken loose, and there was nothing left of my family but a brief and inadequate note. My daughters had no plans to travel, nor did they have my permission to do so. What part did you play in their departure?'

He had not led with the question that John had expected. *Who are you?* But it seemed that the duke had reached a station in life where courtesy was neither required nor expected. He knew that John was a nobody, or he'd have known him already. Only his daughters mattered. 'I had no part at all in their departure, your Grace,' he answered with great relief. 'But I did my humble best to aid in their return.'

'From where, Mr Hendricks?' his Grace snapped.

'Kendal. A little south of the Scottish border.'

'I see. Which one was it, then, that caused the trouble? And how did you become involved in it?'

And please, sit. Though they would have been welcome, they were not words he was likely to hear, now that he had met Benbridge. Apparently, the length of the story or the comfort of the teller was of no concern to the audience. John took a well-measured breath to show that he was not the least bit ill at ease. 'These are the facts as I know them.' He proceeded to tell the most abbreviated version of them he could manage. He began with the carriage ride, omitting any mention of his drunkenness or the sleeping arrangements. He explained Dru's goal, while showing no particular interest in the scandal of it. He explained the problems with the carriage, while conveniently forgetting the trousers. And lastly, he explained the discovery of the runaways in the most deliberately vague way possible, eliding dates and ending with an assurance that the dancing master had decided it was in the best interest of his health to remain in Scotland.

When he finished, the Duke looked at him with a jaundiced eye. 'You say that before the journey, you were in the employ of Folbroke? He must be ruing the loss of you, for it is a rare talent you possess to spin a tale that is equally devoid of truth and untruth.'

'Thank you, my lord.' John was not completely sure that it was meant as a compliment, but he decided to accept it as one and let Benbridge make what he would of the irony.

'What is your opinion on the state of my daughters' reputations?'

'I cannot be positive that this will go unnoticed, my lord. I am more sure of Lady Drusilla, for I was with her from the first.' And knew exactly the risks that they had taken. 'Lady Priscilla was, perhaps, less careful.' And there was an understatement. 'But though the roads were beastly, the accommodations were crowded with people well below the level of the *ton*. It is quite possible that there will be no tales spread abroad at all.'

The Duke looked at him again, eyes sharp. 'No one will hear, unless you would choose to speak of it.'

'I find, even now, sir, that I have trouble remembering the particulars, or the name of the young women involved.'

The Duke gave a slight nod. 'I should have known as much. Silly would never have engaged you if she did not have total confidence in your discretion.'

There was the nickname again, delivered as offhandedly as breathing. And to a girl that was as unlike it as it was possible to be. He held his ground and remained emotionless.

'She promised you payment, did she not? It seems you have managed well. Knowing my girls, you will have worked to earn any reward. Many would not have taken the trouble with them, for they are high spirited, always getting up to some trouble or other.' He thought for a moment and then added, 'Priscilla, at least.'

John bit his tongue to keep from chiding the man that there was nothing of simple high spirits in the behaviour of the younger daughter, for he did not want to think that it was blackmail that brought him to thus.

The duke reached into his desk and produced a chequebook.

'About that, your Grace...'

The man stopped his hand on the way to the ink well, probably expecting John to haggle over the price.

'It is not that I am unappreciative of your offer. But I find that there is something I would value, more than reimbursement.'

'And what is that, then?' Benbridge seemed puzzled that there could be another reason for John to be still standing before the desk, other than the collection of a debt.

'In travelling with her for nearly a week, I found your daughter to be a most charming and agreeable young lady.'

'People often say that of Priss,' he said, as though another compliment meant nothing to him.

'Your elder daughter, my lord. Lady Drusilla.'

'Silly?' her father said, as though the idea had just occurred to him that there were two.

'Yes, my lord,' said Hendricks, trying not to wince. 'She is a lovely girl, with excellent manners, an even temperament and a quick wit. I have grown quite fond of her. And I have reason to suspect that she might return my feelings, given the chance.'

To this, the duke said nothing at all, as if he could not quite believe what he was hearing and was waiting for some word from Hendricks that would make it clear.

'I wish to pay my addresses to her, with your permission of course, your Grace. Considering the delicate nature of our acquaintance, I would seek a proper introduction, here in London, so that there could be no question of our meeting in such inappropriate circumstances.' He waited for a response, assuming that the duke would question him about his prospects.

Instead, the man said, 'Oh, no. That will never do. I am sorry, of course. And glad that you have come to me first. But. No.' He did not seem without sympathy, but neither did he show any desire to continue the conversation.

'May I ask why, your Grace? If you have doubts, the Earl of Folbroke will assure you of my good character. I have sufficient funds to support Drusilla comfortably.' The last was a lie. But a small one, he was sure. 'And secure plans for the future.'

'Perhaps that is true,' Benbridge said, with a sad shake of his head. 'But you cannot claim a title, can you? Do you have family connections that might mitigate the fact? Are you a second son, perhaps? If so, is your brother in good health?'

John pitied his imaginary brother, to see him wished to death. 'No, sir. I am the natural son of a gentleman who saw fit to educate me, and place me properly, though he did not wish to make a formal acknowledgement.'

Benbridge drew away from him, as though the very air around him was contaminated by his parentage. 'Surely, you can see, now that you have been forced to admit it aloud, that such would never do for Drusilla. If you are as fond of her as you claim, you must wish something better for her, just as I do.'

'Of course, your Grace. But my feelings are strong and they moved me to speak.'

The duke smiled at him, relieved that the matter could be settled without fuss, since it involved nothing stronger than emotion. 'Well, then, if there is nothing else?' And then he snapped his fingers. 'But you needed reimbursement, did you not?'

'It is hardly necessary.' He said it a little coldly, for if the man thought that he had come begging for the price of a carriage ride, he was sorely mistaken.

'No, sir. I insist. For the kindness you have done for our family, if nothing else.' And the duke opened the chequebook and with a flourish signed over an amount that was equal to three years' wages. Heedless of the insult he had paid, he looked directly into John's eyes so that there could be no question of the reason for the payment and said, 'I trust this will be sufficient?'

He stared down at the duke without speaking, trying

to see what Dru saw when she looked at the man that would make her care at all what he thought. Benbridge was every bit the image of his younger daughter, with blue eyes and hair that was almost ginger. But with the ruddy complexion and voice of a man who liked riding to the hounds in sun and wind, and following his exercise with a glass or two. Or perhaps three, judging by the thin veins that showed at the edge of his nose.

John had seen a portrait of the family in the front hall. If one measured the ages of the subjects, it had been painted some ten years past. From her mother, Priscilla had taken the delicate manner, the milky skin and the vivacious character.

And his Drusilla? It appeared that she had taken nothing from either parent, laid like a cuckoo's egg in the Benbridge nest. John suspected that, should he visit the house a quarter of a century past, he might meet another dancing master. Or perhaps an artist. Or a close family friend that could give him an easy explanation for how the duke could come to have a daughter so unlike himself.

And one for whom he seemed to care so little. In all his mentions of her so far, he had been respectful, pleasant and candid, but John could hardly call the man's actions loving. While he might dote on Priscilla, he looked at her sister rather as one might a distant cousin, who deserved better than she wanted, but should settle for what she was given.

You are like me, my darling. Even if you do not know it. We are natural children in an unnatural world. And we belong together. It gave John reason to hope.

Now, John stood there in front of the great dark wood desk, holding the bit of paper that the duke had given to him, feeling like a fool for ever having thought that the meeting would end in any other way.

'Of course, your Grace. You are most generous in your thanks.' The words were dry and bitter as ash. He forced his arm to bend and tucked the cheque into his pocket, swallowing bile until he could manage a tight smile of gratitude. And then, as if he was remembering the matter that had brought him here after all, he said, 'There is one other small thing. A nothing, really. Various personal items belonging to your daughters were left in my keeping, forgotten in the carriage when we parted. A ribbon. A book, a glove. A few small articles that slipped from a trunk when they were packing at an inn. I wish to return them, if it is not too much trouble.' And see his love again, to explain the difficulties and plot their next move.

The duke nodded. 'Very conscientious of you, sir. And careless of them for leaving the things. Bundle them up and have them sent to the house by mail, so that they can sort them out betwixt. You needn't trouble yourself with another call.' He looked at John in a flat, uninterested way, as though he had already forgotten why the man might want to visit, firm as a stone wall, and just as likely to be worn away by John's continued visits.

'Thank you.' John managed a nod, as though this suggestion had not just thwarted his plan. 'Tell Lady Drusilla to expect something in the afternoon post.'

Chapter Twenty-One

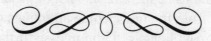

Dru entered the Benbridge house in London, pulled along in the wake of her sister. Now that Priss was resigned to the return, she took the lead, treating Dru as though she were nothing more than a servant, waiting to catch what scraps of affection remained after the tearful reunion with Father.

'Priscilla!' The duke had heard the commotion and came into the hall, hands outstretched, when they had barely crossed the threshold. 'I wondered at your absence. And all I had was your sister's cryptic notes.'

He glanced at Dru with a raised eyebrow. 'But your Mr Hendricks has been to explain already, and I am not quite so in the dark as I was before.'

'He was here already?' She hoped she did not sound as eager as she felt.

'You missed him by little more than an hour,' her father said.

Dru nodded, as though it were little more than a

sign of his efficiency, and not a missed opportunity for another look at him. 'I am sorry, Father, that I was not able to explain further, nor to give you warning of his visit. But the situation was quite complicated. And speed seemed to be required.'

'You were in a great hurry. Yet you had time to engage Mr Hendricks.'

She wondered what John had said, on his visit, for it did seem that Father was unusually suspicious. 'That was a fortuitous happening, and nothing more. He protected me from the unwelcome attentions of another passenger. And I engaged him in case further aid was needed.'

'Next time, Silly, have the sense not to leave without a maid.' After one last glare, he turned his attention to Priss. 'And I suspect that you did not leave for Scotland unaccompanied?'

'No, Papa.'

'But that you returned alone.'

'Yes, Papa.'

'And does anyone else know of this trip that I am unaware of?'

'No, Papa.'

'Then we will speak of it no more.'

Even Priss seemed surprised at how quickly it was to be dismissed. 'I was gone for quite some time with Mr Gervaise, Papa.'

'According to my estimation, almost four days.'

'And in that time—'

'I said,' their father's booming voice cut the sentence short, 'we will speak of it no more.'

'Yes, Papa.' Whatever declaration Priss had been preparing was discarded and forgotten.

'And you, Drusilla, will speak with me, in my study.'

'It is hardly fair, Papa. For if you mean to lecture her for something that I...'

'I said, Priscilla, we...will...speak...no...more. Drusilla!'

Priss seemed to recede from the scene almost without moving, and Dru did not even have the time to cast a backward glance of thanks. The effort to defend her had been kind, even though it was ineffectual. It had been more than she'd expected to receive from Priss.

But it had failed, and she had no choice except to follow her father into the study, to give her side of events and accept punishment for her part in them.

Once behind the closed oak door, her father appeared almost warm to her, holding a hand out to her and gathering her into his arms to offer a fond kiss upon the cheek. 'It is so good to have you home, my dear, and that you have brought Priss back to me unaccompanied. I meant what I said before, although perhaps I should not have been so harsh with you. You cannot traipse across the country without so much as a groom.'

She gave a respectful nod. 'I would not have done it, your Grace, if I had been able to think of another way.'

'See that it does not happen again.'

Dru swallowed the confusion, for it did not seem that her father understood the gravity of the situation. 'Let us hope not. For Priss's behaviour tarnishes my reputation as well as her own. If she is so foolish as to breathe a word of what she has done, her supposed friends in town will use it to their advantage against us.'

He nodded. For a moment, she thought that he cared what might have happened to her. But then he said, 'It is better, if she ran at all, that she went without you. It was far more likely that she would have been recognised had the two of you been seen together. Next time, do not chase her. If I learned anything in the years your mother was alive, it was that when a woman realises that no one is in pursuit she will find her own way home.'

'Oh,' she said. For what more could she say to that? For it seemed that however it might seem, her father did not care any more for Priss than he did for her. Then she added, 'But it was good that I had Mr Hendricks to help us on this trip. Once he realised my dilemma, he was most eager to assist me.'

'Ah, yes. Your stalwart companion,' her father said, making a small face. 'I am sure, once he realised that you were my daughter, he smelled the money on you and could not keep away.'

'Not at all, sir,' she replied. 'He came to my aid before he so much as knew my name. It was only later, when I offered to retain him, that we discussed my family.'

'Well, he knows it now, for I have just had a visit from him.' Her father was laughing. 'If you could have seen the poor man, Silly, you would have been most amused.'

'Really,' she said faintly, listening to the blood ringing in her ears.

'He stood before me, all pomp and ceremony, polishing his little spectacles, and asked to pay you court.'

'He did?'

'He was quite effusive in his praise of you. Complimented your easy temper and your wit.' Her father gave a derisive snort. And then, as though he had forgotten, he added, 'And your looks. He seemed to favour them.'

John had wanted her, then. It had not been a mistake. Her heart leapt like a doe. Then it came crashing back to earth and she said, cautiously, 'How kind of him.' And added casually, not wanting to ruin the moment by seeming too eager. 'What did you tell him?'

Her father laughed again. 'I told him to go away, of course. Although he is well mannered for one of his sort, he is far too common for you, my dear.'

'I found him to be most gently bred,' she said, a little hopefully. 'And most pleasant company.'

'That is all well and good. But nice manners do not make a husband.'

Then what does? she was tempted to ask. But there was little point, for she knew what the answer would be. The man she wanted had no title and no money. If those two faults could be remedied, all others would be overlooked.

Unless Priss had been right. And then, no fortune or rank would be sufficient.

'I do not think I would mind so very much, if my husband was not a lord,' she said. 'And would it not be better for me to marry first, so that it would be quite clear to any potential suitors, that there is no impediment to courting Priss? I would hate to stand in the way of her happiness.'

He looked her over carefully, as though searching for the things that this strange man had seen in her, and then nodded to himself as though he had confirmed his first assessment of her. 'Do not worry, Silly, my dear. The men who court your sister are not bothered by your presence in the least. You will make a match yet. Perhaps next Season, when your sister has had time to cool her blood, I will send the pair of you on the rounds of Almack's and you shall have your pick of the young bucks there.'

The odds on there being a young buck that would notice her if she travelled with Priss were near to non-existent. That her own hunting should be put off for a year, while her foolish sister rusticated after this last embarrassment, or that hunting was even necessary, now that she had freely given her heart...

And her body...

She swallowed, not wishing to give away the sinking feeling inside at the risk she had taken while pretending that she would not be parted from him. 'It is really not necessary to give me another Season, Father. I fear, after all this time, there is little hope of success. And Mr Hendricks did seem quite capable and devoted to my happiness, even if he was not what you expected for me.'

'Nonsense, my dear. He was nothing more than a fortune hunter.' He stared at her.

Suddenly she was sure of a thing she had only suspected before. This was why there had been no shouting or threats over her lapse in allowing Priss to escape. This was to be her punishment. Her father knew she wanted John. And that was why she could not have him. 'No,' she said softly, so that there could be no misunderstanding. 'I am quite sure of it. He wished the best for me.'

'But you will need to fix your affections on a man that is more constant than that, if you wish my consent.'

'Not constant?' For that was the last word in the world she would have chosen, had she wished to insult him. John Hendricks was as constant as the rising and setting of the sun.

'He gave up the idea with barely a fight, I assure you. Left here with my cheque in his hand and his tail between his legs.'

'Your cheque?'

'You did not think that I would send an employee off from my service without paying him, did you? Considering the audacity of his interest in you, I think a reference is quite out of the question. But the ten thousand pounds I gave him covered the matter of his help, and there was more than enough extra there to make him forget his penchant for you.'

'You bought him off.' She would have sworn that it was not possible. The things he had said to her, the way he had sworn. And the way he had made her feel. All had counted for nothing, when compared with such a sum.

'The money was well earned if he managed to scare the dancing master away from your sister as handily as he claimed. The man is not all bad. But when all is said and done, he is no better than a servant. But he assured me he will be returning whatever love tokens you have pressed upon him with this afternoon's post. Then he was gone. That should tell you all you need to know about the focus of his affection. It had very little to do with you, and much more to finding a way into our family, and our fortune. He chose you because you are the weaker and more vulnerable sister. After this recent escapade with Gervaise, Priss would have seen through him and sent him packing. Now dry your eyes and go upstairs to see to your sister. I am sure she is most cross to have her plans so easily thwarted, and your hands will be full with placating her.'

As she walked from the room, Dru wiped absently at her face with the back of her hand, surprised to feel no tears.

Chapter Twenty-Two

She walked slowly, numbly, back to her room, as silent and polite as she ever was when in her father's house. And with each step, her brain screamed.

How could I have been so wrong?

Wrong about her life, which had seemed full, but was proven empty. And wrong about John, who had said he loved her. After the return from Scotland, she had been sure that she would see him again. Not positive he would go through with his plan to visit her father, but fairly confident that he could be persuaded to attempt it, if he faltered once he had seen the formidable Duke of Benbridge.

She had been much more confident of her father's response, which had been the dismissal she had expected. Of course he would say no, for he would see no further than the Mr at the beginning of her love's name. But she had assumed, after the initial disappointment, that John would come to her. She could have told him not to be put off by the first inevitable refusal, and when best to approach for another interview. Perhaps, with time and strategy, some progress would have been made.

If her father could not be moved, then at the very least they could have prolonged the parting so that he would have been allowed a proper goodbye to her. She had not thought that, with all the pride he had shown, he would simply take the money and leave. By doing so, he had proven all that her father had ever believed about the common men of England. And about her as well.

If he left so easily, what reason could he have had to attach himself to her, other than as a way to increase his paycheque? John had thought her gullible. He had forced himself into her rooms, taken advantage of her inexperience and her feelings for him. He had reduced her to a state where her virtue had seemed more of a disadvantage than a precious gift. Now he was ten thousand pounds richer. And he was gone. Lost for ever, for she had no clue how to contact him.

Though if she had, she did not know what she would say. She did not think herself likely to weep and beg him to return, for if she had nothing else, she had her pride as well. If she were a man, she would have called him out, for the embarrassment of being tricked and acting the fool for him was still stinging in her heart.

He was no better than Gervaise.

She lay down upon the bed, wishing that she had the abilities of her sister to throw a proper sulk. Priss would begin with tears, follow with the kicking of slippers and pounding of pillows, and finish by shrieking loud enough to bring the above-stairs servants to whisper at the door, and raise her father's anger at having his peace so disturbed. She would have a new gown out of it to stop her crying, and perhaps some ribbons as well.

And Dru would have a megrim. She sighed. There was little room in the emotions of the house for another fuss. Even if she had attempted it, her tantrum would have been met with a simple, 'Do not be absurd, Silly. Now see to your sister, for she seems most unhappy.'

She lay still in the bright sunlight of the room, wishing that there were tears sliding slowly down her cheeks and into her ears and hair. What Priss had to cry about, she was not sure. Unless she had realised what Dru had: that they might both be in the very devil of a fix, in a month or so.

But was that anything to cry over? Father might be less particular of their choice of suitors, with less than nine months to make a decision.

She smiled a little in grim satisfaction at the thought, and felt the first angry tear burning her cheek. While it worried her that a child might be possible, it hurt far more to think that she had been so easily abandoned by its father. After all his high-and-mighty words about not caring for rank or wealth, he had taken her father's bribe and never looked back.

She wondered, as she always had, if it would have been different if he'd met Priss. Quite possibly Mr Hendricks would be howling outside the gates like a rabid wolf, eager to have the company of one who was not only rich and well born, but vivacious and pretty as well. For had she needed to protect her little sister from the likes of John, she doubted that she would have been so successful.

She blotted her tears with the edge of a pillowcase, surprised that they had not yet stopped, for she was rarely able to manage more than one or two of them, even with effort. But the thoughts of her sister and John—Mr Hendricks, she told herself firmly—had been so clear in her head, that for a time, it had consumed her. The sly smile he had given her when he had begun to take liberties, and the masterful way he had of touching just the right places on her body, were not things she wished him to share with any other woman in the world.

If her father was right, he had chosen her specifically because she was the weakest link in the family. While Priss was just as likely to have fallen from grace, she doubted that it would do the girl any permanent harm to be rid of Gervaise. While she might enjoy raising a fuss, Priss would not waste much time crying real tears over a man who was even tonight drowning his sorrows in expensive wine and a willing and experienced woman, laughing at the foolish heiress he had left behind.

Time had passed. Dru had a vague recollection of her maid poking a head into the room with offers of luncheon, and then tea. She had sent the girl away with a cross word, preferring the way the bitter emptiness of her stomach matched the sharp, empty feeling in her heart. This time, when the maid came again, she sat up and hitched up her skirts, grabbing a slipper and preparing to toss it at the head of the unsuspecting girl.

'My lady,' she said hurriedly, shielding her face against a blow. The poor thing had already been to see Priss and prepared herself for battle. 'There is a package for you, come with the afternoon's post. If you wish, I will take care of the contents.'

'No.' Dru took a deep breath, for even the one short word made her head sound stuffy and weak. Hadn't her father said something about John returning her possessions to her? Although what she had left with him, she'd no idea.

'Do not touch it. Bring it to me. I will open it here.' Perhaps it would be the letter of farewell that she hoped for. For if she was to be guilty of a horrible misalliance, she at least deserved a *billet doux* to hold against her quaking breast so that she could weep and swoon, cursing her father and the gods.

Priss had a box full of them, after all. And when she had nothing else to do, on a rainy day, she pored over them, reading choice lines and sighing. It was not too much to ask, was it, if Drusilla could have one such for herself?

But the package the maid brought to her looked more like forgotten laundry than it did anything else. Dear God, had she left some personal item in John's room that might indicate what they had been to each other? She was torn between the equally horrible ideas of him keeping a shift or a stocking as a trophy of her downfall, and the idea that it would mean so little to him that he would think she'd want it returned. The least he could have done was pined over the thing, whatever it was, to make her believe that he had trouble parting with it.

The girl was reaching for the strings to untie the bundle, and Dru said sharply, 'Leave it.' When the girl hesitated, hoping to get some glimpse of the contents, Dru dismissed her, then waited the few minutes it took until she was sure that she was alone.

Then she pulled on the string that held the brown paper in place.

There was but one item within. A pair of familiar leather breeches, and a single sheet of paper pinned to them.

Eight o'clock. Tonight. Hyde Park.

Chapter Twenty-Three

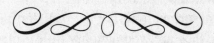

She waited at the gate, unsure of what it was that he'd meant her to do. It could not be safe for her to go, unescorted, into the darkness of the park. But it wasn't all that safe to wait alone on the street.

Suddenly, arms grabbed her from behind, pulling her into the shade before she could manage so much as a cry.

She was being kissed, and, Lord help her, handled. And before the fear could overtake the surprise of it, she realised that the taste of the mouth on hers was familiar, as was the way the hands gripped her. And so she relaxed, kissing back, and whispering, when he allowed her breath, 'Mr Hendricks?'

'Please, darling. After all we have been to each other, you must call me John.' And then he went back to kissing her, running his hands over her body, under her cloak. 'You disappoint me, love. You are not wearing the gift that I sent you.'

'Because there was no shirt or coat,' she said sensibly. 'I could not very well come to meet you in a public place wearing naught but the breeches under my cloak.'

The growl he made in response made her think that he would not have minded at all if she had.

'But I am wearing them, although they are hidden under my skirt. Mr Hendricks. Mr Hendricks! John.' For he had lifted the skirts, plunging his hands beneath to check for himself and was massaging her bottom in way that was most disconcerting.

'Just reassuring myself of the fact, darling,' he said. 'And there they are, you naughty little minx.'

There was certainly nothing little about her, nor did she think of herself as a temptress. 'If I am naughty,' she admitted, 'it is because I am most sorely tried by the company I have been keeping of late. I think you are a bad influence upon my character.'

'I only mean to care for you, my love,' he answered back. 'For if you stay in my company, you will be in for quite a bit of riding.' But the way he was touching her now, with the heel of his hand resting firmly between her legs, she wondered if he meant to be talking about horses, or something else entirely.

'Where might I be going?' she whispered back. And then gave a shudder, and thought, *I will be going over the moon, if you continue with what you are doing, John. And I wonder, do you know?*

'Scotland,' he answered back. 'The blacksmiths are most obliging, I hear, when met with thwarted lovers.' Then he proved that he knew exactly what he was doing to her. He was moving his hand over the leather, making firm tight circles with it, and she wrapped her arms about his neck to steady herself against the collapse that she was sure was coming.

'I thought that my father told you that your advances on my person were not welcome.'

'Not by him,' John agreed, and speeded the movement of his hand. 'But you have yet to tell me otherwise. And even if you do, I mean to ignore you. Do not think that I will let you choose the sensible course and lead me back to your father for another go round in the study. It is quite plain to me that he will never change his mind on the subject.' He was kissing her throat now, running his tongue along the place, just at the back of her ear, until she shuddered and clung to him, almost forgetting her objections.

'You took his money to stay away from me.'

'I did nothing of the kind,' he answered. 'He wished to pretend that it was a reward for returning you safely. It would have been churlish of me to call it the bribe it was. But neither would it make sense to refuse payment for my services. I am not a gentleman of leisure, you know. I am a simple working man.' But there was nothing simple about the things he was doing to her now. With a final touch, he brought her easily over the edge, to leave her weak and trembling in his arms. And she clung to him, vulnerable and needy, and felt the old fear of being helpless in the face of another's plans for her.

Then his arms came around her, supporting her, but not trapping her. As an experiment, she relaxed her muscles, as though ready to fall into a swoon and drop from his arms. Other than a slight tightening to keep her upright and close, there was no change in him.

And she knew, for all his forceful words about taking her against her will, that he would release her if she struggled, or carry her if she collapsed. They were in tune with each other, as two parts of the same instrument.

'Do you truly think ill of me for the money?' he asked. 'Although the sum was generous, I did feel that I deserved recompense for enduring the company of your sister. I am sorry, Dru, but I find the girl tiresome in the extreme.'

She sighed, leaning a little harder against him. Although she did not wish to think ill of her sister, she had never expected to hear words so sweet. 'She is not so bad, once you get used to her. And much smarter than she first appears.'

'She would have to be. For I doubt that it would be possible...'

'John!' She was surprised at how easy the name came to her, now that she felt free to speak it.

'Darling.' He kissed her, smiling. 'You may scold me all you like, so long as you call me by name.'

'Then I will insist that you admit the truth. You know why my father gave you as much money as he did, John. He wanted you to stay away from me.'

'If he meant to imply that the cheque was contingent on my avoiding your company?' She could see his wicked smile, and the glint of the moonlight on his glasses as he dipped his head to her throat again. 'Then I am afraid we are at cross purposes. There is no sum that would keep me from you, now that I have experienced the delight of your body.'

'You vile man. Is that all you want from me?' she whispered as sternly as she could manage. Although if the answer was affirmative, she doubted she would mind so very much.

'Not at all,' he snarled. 'There must be some strange weakness in me that makes me long to feel the lash of your tongue, or the cold razor edge of your intellect.' He kissed her on the mouth again with such force that when he had finished with her, she could hardly string two thoughts together, much less wield a razor of them. Then he pulled her pliable body close inside the shelter of his heavy topcoat. 'Or perhaps it just sweetens the moment when I have such a strong woman completely in my power.'

And it was true. She was in his power, quite deliciously helpless for the first time in ages. She did not have to see to the running of her father's household, or watch over her scapegrace sister. Or wait for the chance to live her own life and find her own happiness after the futures of all around her were secure. Judging by the path of his fingers on the inside of her thigh, John Hendricks was about to force her to face her happy future right now, in a public park in the middle of London.

'In any case, the money your father gave me is already gone. I have no intention of giving the cheque or his daughter back to him.'

'Spent?' she gasped, trying to gather those wits that he claimed to find so attractive and push herself away from him.

'Invested,' he corrected, kissing her again. 'With a friend. I told him I meant to take a wife. He had suggestions for a man with some capital. When we return from our honeymoon, I will introduce you. The Earl of Folbroke and his lovely wife, Emily. My once and future employer. My ambition has grown beyond the menial tasks he required of me when I was his secretary.

'And fortunately for me, his interests have changed as well. He is in need of a steward for his philanthropic efforts, and was seeking a forward-thinking man who can be trusted to work independently. In the future, I will be more of a partner than a servant. We will be quite welcome in their house, which will give me the opportunity to make contacts...'

'Of what sort?' she asked, somewhat surprised.

'Political ones, I should think.' He grinned at her. 'What with the changes underway in the country right now, there will be a need for men with vision and an interest in reform.'

'Reform?' Dru smiled wickedly. 'My father will be horrified.'

'I expect he will be. But you needn't fear the damage to your reputation that such a poor marriage will likely make. A public servant will be better than a tradesman for you.'

'I am not giving my status in society two thoughts, John Hendricks,' she snapped. 'I have had quite enough of being Lady Drusilla if it means I am never to be a wife. And I will live in a haystack with you, if you wish.'

He laughed. 'That will not be necessary. Although

I will instruct our driver to stop at one, if you wish. I have hired a coach for us, so that we may travel north in comfort.'

'You have thought of everything, haven't you?'

'I did not wish to marry you, until I was sure that I could provide for you,' he murmured between the kisses on her throat. 'I am not worthy of you, after all. And it will not be as you have lived. But if you come with me tonight, you need never doubt my loyalty to you. Or my love.' He groaned. 'Or my need. Oh God, Dru, do not deny me this. I swear, I will die without you. Come away with me. Marry me. Let me make you smile.'

She bit her lip, not wanting to seem too eager, or to admit aloud that the only thing that had really mattered in his last speech was the word marriage, and the thought that, wherever she would be, she would be spending her nights safe in the arms of John Hendricks. She moved against him, feeling her own arousal growing, again. 'Can we be in Scotland tonight?' she whispered.

He answered her in that calm and confident voice that made her believe he could dispense with any difficulties that stood between her and happiness, 'Gretna Green is over thirty hours away, even if we take the mail coach. But you should know by now, my Lady Drusilla, just how long it takes for me to get you to the border.'

And then he touched her.

* * * * *

*Paying the
Virgin's Price*

CHRISTINE MERRILL

Chapter One

February, 1814. London

The air of the Fourth Circle gaming hell was thick with the usual miasma of tobacco smoke and whisky, blended with the tang of sweat that Nathan Wardale had come to associate with failure. *Another's* failure, fortunately for him. Nate stared over the cards in his hand at the nervous man on the other side of the green baize table. He was hardly more than a boy. And he was about to learn the first of manhood's lessons.

The manchild cleared his throat. 'If you could see your way clear...'

'I could not,' Nate responded without emotion, shuffling the cards. 'If your purse is empty, then you had best leave the table.'

His opponent bristled. 'Are you implying that my word is not good?'

'I am implying nothing of the kind. Experience has taught me never to accept an IOU. If you have nothing of value upon your person, then play is done.'

'It is most unfair of you to stop when I am losing.' Though he had just come of age, the young man was also a marquis. He was used to getting his own way, especially from one so obviously common as Nate.

Nate shrugged in response. 'On the contrary. It is most unfair of you to expect me to treat a promise of payment as a stake in the game. While I do not doubt that you would make good, I have found that gentlemen behave rashly when their backs are to the wall. Later, they regret what they have promised in the heat of play.'

The boy sneered as though what other men might do meant nothing to him. 'And what do you expect of me, then? Bet my signet against the next hand?'

'If you wish.'

'It is entailed.'

'Then you are finished playing.'

The other's chin jutted out in defiance. 'I will say when I am finished.' He pulled the ring from his finger and tossed it onto the table. 'This is easily worth all that you have in front of you. One more hand.'

'Very well.' Nate yawned and dealt the cards. And a short time later, when the play had gone the way he knew it would, he scooped the ring forward and into his purse, along with the rest of his winnings.

'But, you cannot,' the young noble stammered. 'It is not mine.'

'Then why did you bet it?' Nate looked at him, un-blinking.

'I thought I could win.'

'And I have proven to you that you could not. It is a good thing for both of us that you were willing to trade such a small thing. It is only a symbol of your family's honour. Easily replaced, I am sure. I will add it to the collection of similar items that have come into my possession from people like you, who would not listen to reason.'

The boy watched the purse vanishing into Nate's pocket as though he were watching his future disappear. 'But what am I to tell my father?'

'That is none of my concern. If it were me, I'd tell him that he has a fool for a son.'

The boy slammed his fist against the table so hard that Nate feared something must break, then he sprang to his feet, doing his feeble best to loom threateningly. Nate could see that his opponent was wavering on the edge of issuing a challenge, so he prepared to signal the toughs that the owner, Dante Jones, kept ready to eject angry losers. But as Nate stared up into the young man's eyes, he watched the other's expression change as he weighed the possibility that Nate might be as successful at duelling as he was at playing cards.

Then the boy stood down and walked away from the table without another word.

Nate let out his breath slowly, so as not to call attention to it. He could feel the weight of the signet in his pocket, but it would not do to examine the thing while here. It would appear that he was gloating over the fallen. And though the infamous gambler Nate Dale had many faults, he did not gloat.

He was quite sure that he had taken a similar ring from the boy's father, not two years ago. The current ring was not a true part of the entail, but a duplicate, made to hide the loss of the original. The real ring was in a box on Nate's bed chamber dresser. It was just one small part of a collection of grisly trophies to remind him what men might do when the gambling fever was upon them and they were convinced that their luck was about to turn.

He wondered what that feeling was like, for he had never had it. It had been years since there had been a doubt in his mind on the subject of *table luck*. There had been bad hands, of course. And even bad days. But things always came right again before he felt the sting of loss. He had but to remain calm and wait for the tide to turn. To all and sundry, he was known as the luckiest man in England.

So it was with cards or dice. And as for the rest of his life? He had learned to content himself with the fact that it was unlikely to get any worse.

He stared around the room at the typical night's crowd assembled there. Winners and losers, noise and bustle. A few widows who enjoyed games more intimate than faro. One of them gave him a come-hither look, and he responded with a distant smile and a shake of his head. What must that say of his state of mind if he had become too jaded to value her considerable charms over an evening spent at home alone? But the energy in the room seemed to sap his strength rather than restore it, and it was wearying beyond words to think that tomorrow night would be just the same as tonight.

At least tonight was over. Nate started to push away from the table, then felt a shadow fall across it. When he glanced up, another player was moving into the chair that had been vacated by the previous owner of Nate's new ring. The stranger was dark of hair, eye, skin and mood. Though he was smiling, the expression on his face was every bit as foreboding as a storm cloud on the horizon. Perhaps it was from the pain of a recent injury, for he bore his left arm in a sling.

Nate barely bothered to look at the man's face, turning all his attention to the shuffling of the deck in his hands. 'Fancy a game?'

The stranger nodded, and sat.

Damn. Nate kissed goodbye to his plan for a warm drink by his own fireplace, and a chance to sketch a bit with pen and ink, thinking of nothing at all. Whenever he tried to limit his play, the hours grew even longer. It was as though fate knew his intentions and laughed at them. Certainly it was not the location that drew the pigeons to him. Suffolk Street was a long way from the comfort of White's. The clientele at the Fourth Circle was a curious mix of true lowlifes, habitual gamblers, members of the aristocracy who were fallen from honour because of their gaming, and the curiosity seekers of the Ton.

And Nate. He was the curiosity they sought, known

for his preternatural luck at games. They brought with them the idea that it was skill, and that his would prove inferior to theirs: the conviction that it was possible to beat the unbeatable. The naïve hope that their reputation would be made with their success. Others sought him out as a rite of passage. It seemed everyone in London had, at one time or other, lost his purse to the infamous Nathan Dale.

Nate wondered what category this man fell into, and decided either habitual gambler or local tough. Perhaps he was an actor. Although he carried himself with an air of nobility, his clothes were an odd mix of fashion and cast off, flamboyant enough to be laughable in a drawing room, though they suited him well. His blue velvet coat was well tailored, but unfashionably loose, and he wore a striped silk scarf in place of a cravat. There was a glint of silver peaking out from under the lace at his wrist. It was a bracelet or cuff of some kind: most unusual jewellery for a gentleman. He wore a thick gold hoop in his left ear.

Nate could feel the subtle shifting of attention in the room as the heads turned to follow him with interest. Depending on their natures, the men touched purses or weapons, as though to reassure themselves of their security. But from the females present, the man's striking good looks and exotic costume drew a murmur of approval. It was irritating to notice that the widow who, just moments before, had been overcome with disappointment from Nate's rejection, had more than recovered at the sight of the handsome stranger.

Nate looked across the table at him with the dispassionate eye of one who made his living by correctly judging his opponents. *Gypsy*, he decided. But a Gypsy with money, judging by the jewellery. And so the man was welcome at Nate's table. He dealt the cards.

His opponent took them in silence, speaking only when necessary, losing the contents of his fat purse quickly and without emotion over a few hands of *vingt et un*. Such disinterested play made the game even more boring than the continual whining of the last man. The Gypsy made no effort to remove his jewellery after the last hand. It was some comfort, for it proved that he was not too lost to know when to quit.

And it was with relief that Nate watched the man reach into his pocket, as though searching for one last bank note or perhaps a sovereign that had become lodged in the coat lining and left for emergencies. 'If you are without funds,' Nate drawled, 'then it is best we not continue. I should have warned you when we began that I will not accept a marker.'

'I have something better than that, I am sure.' The man's continual smile was most disquieting. In Nate's experience, losers were not supposed to be quite so jolly. 'One more hand. I have something you will accept from me, because you have no choice.' And then, the Gypsy reached into the pocket of his coat, and dropped the thing onto the table.

A scarlet silk rope lay there like a snake, coiled upon itself. The end was carefully tied in a hangman's noose.

For a moment, it looked no different from the one

Nate had seen so many years ago—on the day they'd hanged his father.

Nate pushed away from the table so quickly that it tipped, sending the rope, drinks and stakes into a heap on the floor. The man across from him took no notice of the mess, but continued to stare at him with the same fixed expression and knowing smile, as though satisfied with the reaction he had received.

Nate stared back into the dark face, noting the lines in it, the shape of the eyes, and even the cold quirk in the smile. *He knew that face*—although coldness had not been there when last they'd spoken, nor the sharpness of the features, nor the hard set of the man's shoulders.

But if he could imagine this man as the boy he'd once been? Nate said in a voice made hoarse by shock, 'Stephen?' He looked again into the cold face across the table. 'Stephen Hebden. It *is* you, isn't it?'

The man gave a nod and his smile disappeared, as though to remind Nate that any meeting between them would not be a happy one, no matter how close they had been as children. 'I am Stephano Beshaley, now. And you call yourself Nate Dale, even though we both know you are Nathan Wardale.'

'Nathan Wardale died in Boston, several years ago.'

'Just as Stephen Hebden died in a fire when he was a child.' The man across the table held out his hands in an expansive gesture. 'And yet, here we are.'

Dead in a fire? It shamed him that he had given so little thought to what had become of his best childhood friend, after their fathers both died. But circumstances between the families had made the break between them sudden and complete.

Nate pushed the past aside, as he had so many times before. 'Very well, then. Mr Beshaley. What brings you here, after all this time? It has been almost twenty years since we last saw each other.'

'At my father's funeral,' Stephen prompted. 'Do you remember Christopher Hebden, Lord Framlingham? He was the man your father murdered.'

Nate pretended to consider. 'The name is familiar. Of course, my family was so busy that year, what with the trial and the hanging. But I do remember the funeral. It is a pity you could not return the favour and come to my father's funeral as well.' He waited to see if there would be a response from the man opposite him. Perhaps a small acknowledgement that Nate had suffered a loss as well. But there was none.

So he continued. 'When the hanging was done, we had to wait until he was cut down, and pay to retrieve the body. With the title attainted, using the family plot was out of the question. He is in a small, unmarked grave in a country church where the vicar did not know of our disgrace. I rarely visit.' He locked eyes with the man across the table, willing him to show some sign of sympathy, or at least understanding. But still, there was nothing.

'That burial was an intimate gathering, for all our friends had abandoned us. Although there was crowd enough to see him kicking on the gibbet. I thought the whole town had turned out to see the peer swing. And then your mad Gypsy mother screamed curses out of the window and hanged herself in full view of everyone. It made for quite a show.'

And that had done it. For a moment, Stephen tensed as though ready to strike him, the rage blazing hot in his eyes. And Nate welcomed the chance to strike back at someone, anyone, and to finally release the child's fury he had felt that day.

But then, Stephen settled back in his seat and his face grew cold and hard again. Despite that brief flare of temper at the direct insult to his mother, there was nothing left in his dark face to prove that the words had any lasting effect. If they had still been playing cards, Nate might have found him a worthy opponent, for it was impossible to tell what he might do next.

At last, Nate mastered his own anger again and broke the silence. 'Why are you here, Stephen?'

'To remind you of the past.'

He let out a bitter laugh. 'Remind me?' He spread his arms wide. 'Look at my surroundings, old friend, as I do whenever I feel a need to remember. Are they not low enough? Was I born to this? The title is gone, the house, the lands. My family scattered to the four winds. At least you found a people again. Do you know how long it has been since I have seen my own mother? My sisters? Do you know what it is like to stand helpless as your father hangs?'

'No better than to have him murdered, I suppose. And to know that somewhere, the murderer's line continues.'

Nate laughed. 'After all this time, is that the problem? I am as good as dead, I assure you. I have nothing left, and yet you would take more.'

Stephen snorted. 'You have money.'

'And a nice house,' Nate added. 'Two houses, actually. And horses and carriages. Possessions enough for any man. I gained it all at the cost of my honour. We are not gaming at Boodle's, as our fathers did, Stephen. Because we are not welcome amongst gentlemen. A Gypsy bastard and a murderer's son. Society wants none of us. We are in the gutter, where we belong.'

His opponent tensed at the word—*bastard*— but it was no less than the truth.

'I am sorry that I am not suffering enough to satisfy you. If you wish, we can go out in the alley, and I will let you remedy the fact. If you mean to frighten me into losing with this?' He looked down at the rope at his feet, and kicked it until it lay in front of his former friend. 'I have the real rope that did the job. My family bought it to keep it out of the hands of the ghouls gathered round the gallows. There is nothing left for you to do that will frighten me. Since irony is not likely to prove fatal, I suggest that you cease playing games. We are no longer children. If you truly want me dead? Then be man enough to shoot me.'

For a moment, he thought that the taunting had finally hit home. For Stephano the Gypsy nodded and smiled, as though there were nothing he would like better than to kill Nate and put an end to the meeting.

But then, he said, 'I am afraid it is not that easy, Nathan Wardale.'

Nate cringed for a moment, and felt the old fear that someone might hear the name, and know him for the child of a murdering traitor. He might be cast out as unworthy, even from the Fourth Circle. And *then* where would he go? He recovered his poise and demanded, 'What is it to be, then?'

'That is not for me to decide. I am but an avatar in this. I bring you the rope. And now, fate will decide the method of your punishment.'

'My punishment?' Nate almost laughed. 'For what? When the murder happened, I was ten years old. Hardly a criminal mastermind, I assure you.'

'You are the son of the murderer.'

'Then your coming here serves no purpose, Stephen. My word is no good for anything but wagering. But if it were, I would swear to you on it that my family is not to blame for what happened.'

'Your father…'

'Was hung for something he did not do. He swore on the stand that Kit Hebden was dying when he found him. He did not strike the blow that killed him. He said the same to me, my mother and my sisters. By the end, there was no reason for him to lie to us. It would have gained him nothing, nor given us any comfort. He was sentenced to die, and we were quite beyond comforting.'

For a moment, he thought he saw a flicker of emotion on the other man's face that might indicate understanding, belief or some scrap of mercy. And then it was gone. 'If it is true that you are blameless, then circumstances will prove that fact soon enough. And I will break the curse and set you free.'

He laughed. 'It is a bit late to talk of freedom, Stephen. I have wealth, but no one to share it with. I have no friends. No one trusts me. No decent woman would want me. In the course of gaming, I have ruined many and caused men to do unspeakable things, convinced that one more hand will be all it takes to break me.

'And now, you will set me free? Can you wipe out the memory of the things I have done? Will you go to the House of Lords and insist that they clear my family's name? Can you get me my title? And my father, as well? Can you raise the dead, Gypsy? For I would like to see you try.'

Stephano the Gypsy spat upon the floor, and passed his hand before him as though warding off the suggestion. 'Your father was a murderer who deserved what he got. And I mean to see that you accept your share of his punishment.'

Nate had learned to see his past as a single dark shadow that threw his empty life into sharper relief. But now that the shadow had become the foreground, the picture created was so ridiculous, he let out with the first honest laugh he'd had in ages. 'My share of the punishment?' He leaned forward and grinned into the face of the man who had once been Stephen Hebden, daring him to see the joke and laugh along. 'Well I have news for you. You enriched me by a hundred pounds before you brought out the damned rope and began speaking nonsense. If this *is* a curse, then many would welcome it. But if you wish to see me punished? Then take my luck with you, and we will call it even.'

He pointed a finger at the rope on the floor. 'But do not come here, pretending to make my life worse with vague threats and portents of doom. There is nothing coming that will make things worse than they already are.'

And then the Gypsy smiled with true satisfaction. 'You think so, do you? We shall see, old friend. We shall see.' And he rose from the chair and exited the room, leaving the silk noose on the floor behind him.

In his dreams, Nate was at Newgate, again, surrounded by angry giants. They laughed and the sound was hollow and cruel, seeming to echo off the stone walls around him. He pushed through the crowd. But it was difficult, for he was so small and they did not wish to part for him. They had arrived early, to get a good view.

And he had come late, for he'd had to sneak from home. Mother had said it was no place for the family. That father had not wished it. But was Nathan not the man of the family, now? It was his responsibility to be there, at the end. So he had forced his way through the mob to the front, and had seen his father, head bowed, being led to the gallows.

He called out to him, and William Wardale raised his head, searching for the origin of the cry. His eyes were so bleak, and Nathan was sure he must be lonely. There was no friend left who would stand by him at the end. He looked down at Nathan with such love, and such relief, and reached out a hand to him, as though it could be possible to gather him close, one last time. And then, his hand dropped to his side, and a shudder went through him, for he knew what Nathan did not. While he was glad that his last sight on earth would be his son, he had known what it would mean to a child.

The hangman bound his father's hands, and the Ordinary led him through a farce of meaningless prayer. And all around Nathan, the people were shouting, jostling each other and swearing at those who would not remove their hats so that the men in the back could see. Vendors were hawking broadsides, but he did not have the penny to buy one. So he picked a wrinkled paper from the ground before him, to see the lurid cartoon of his father, and his supposed confession.

It was *lies*. Every word of it. Father would never have done the things he was accused of. And even if he had, he would not have told the rest of the world the truth on the final day, after lying to Nathan, over and over. But even if it was lies, there were tears of shame pricking behind his eyelids as he read.

The hangman was placing the hood now, and a woman began to scream. He hoped it was his mother, come to take him home before he saw any more. His coming had been a mistake: there was nothing he could do and he did not want to see what was about to happen.

But it was a strange, dark-skinned woman leaning

out of a window above the gallows. She was screaming in triumph, not fear, and her face had the beauty of
a vengeful goddess as she stared down at the bound man
and the laughing crowd.

And at him. She had found Nathan in the crowd, and
stared at him as though she knew him. And then, she
had shouted, in a voice so clear that the rabble had
hushed to catch her words.

*I call guilt to eat you alive and poison your hearts'
blood. The children will pay for the sins of their fathers,
till my justice destroys the wicked.*

She pointed at him as she spoke of children. And
smiled. The adult Nathan screamed to the child to look
away. The woman was mad. He should not mind her.
And he should run from this place. If he did not, it
would be too late.

And then, there was a thump, and his father's body
dropped as the floor under him disappeared. As he fell,
so did the woman in the window, dangling from the silk
scarf that was wrapped about her neck.

In his child's mind, Nathan thought that the worst
was over. But since then, the adult Nathan had seen
enough in the Navy to understand what happened to a
hanged man if there was no one to pull on his legs and
help him to an easier death.

The kicking had begun. His father, and the garish
puppet of a woman hanging from the window above him.

It had seemed like hours before the bodies stilled,
the crowds had begun to part, and his mother had
come for him.

* * *

When Nate woke, the bedclothes were wet with sweat and tears. And there was the Gypsy's silk rope on the dresser beside him. Why had he bothered to pick the thing up and bring it home with him? The gesture was macabre, and meant to upset him. He had been foolish to play along. And Stephen Hebden had managed to raise the old nightmare to plague him.

But Stephen was not Stephen any more. His old friend was long gone. The man who had visited him was an enemy. A stranger. A Gypsy who was as angry and full of tricks as his mother had been. He must never forget that fact, or Stephano Beshaley and his curse would taint his present, just as the man's mother had marked his childhood.

He might not be able to prevent the dreams, but during the day he would keep his mind clear of emotion, just as he did when he was at the gaming tables. His waking life would be no different, because of the Gypsy's visit. At one time or another, Nate had endured public disgrace, loss, starvation and physical hardship. There was little left that could move him to fear, anger or joy. He'd held a hangman's noose when he was still a child. The colourful rope on the night-stand—and its accompanying nightmare—did not compare to the horror of that day.

But his mind wandered to the people Stephen might search out when his plans for Nate failed. His sisters, perhaps?

Even a Gypsy could not stoop so low as to hurt

innocent girls. Beshaley's mother had stared directly at Nate as she'd said her curse. And he'd felt marked by the words, as if touched by a brand. Surely he was meant to pay the whole debt. Helena and Rosalind would be safe.

They had to be. How would the Gypsy even find them? When last Nate had seen them, they were tending their failing mother, waiting for him to come home. But he had lost them in the throng of strangers that was working-class London and had searched for them without success. Mother must have died, never knowing what had become of him, for she had been very sick, even before he'd disappeared. Helena and Rosalind were as lost to him as if they had never been born. It made him ache to think on it. But he could take some consolation in the fact that it would leave them safe from harassment.

Then who else would the Gypsy turn to, once he had failed with the Wardales? Did Nate owe Lord Narborough and his family a word of warning?

His own sense of injustice argued that he owed them nothing at all. They had heard about the curse as well. But they viewed it as little more than a joke. It had not scarred their lives as it had his. There was no sign that Marcus Carlow had been touched by fear. Nate should think of him as the Viscount Stanegate now that he had grown into his title. From the occasional mention of him in *The Times*, he had become just the man his father had hoped. Upright, respectable and honest. The sort of man that all their fathers had expected their sons to be.

If there was fault to be found, it did not lie with

Marc or his siblings. It was their father who should bear the blame. Lord Narborough had claimed to be a friend of his father, but shut his doors to the Wardale family when they had needed help.

And Narborough had been the one to pin the blame on Father, when the murder had occurred. He had wasted no time in seeing to his apprehension and imprisonment.

It had gone so quickly. Too quick, he suspected. It was almost as though Narborough had seen the need for a scapegoat, and chosen William Wardale. Nate was sure, with all his heart, that his father was not a murderer. But someone had done the crime. And if there was a man alive who knew the truth, then it was most likely to be George Carlow. The murder had been committed just outside his study, after all. And he had been the one who called the loudest for a hurried trial and a timely hanging. Suppose his father had blundered on to the scene just after George Carlow had struck the fatal blow?

Nathan tried to muster some glee that the Gypsy would visit them next. The Carlow family was due for a fall. But he could find no pleasure in it. While he was sure that the senior Carlow was a miserable old sinner, the Gypsy had called for the punishment of the next generation. Would it be fair to see the curse fall upon Marc or his good-natured brother Hal? And what of their sisters, Honoria and Verity?

Nate thought again of his own two sisters, hiding their identities from the shame of association with the Wardale name. Even if George Carlow had been the true murderer, did the Carlow girls deserve to be treated as his sisters had? If Stephano Beshaley removed the protection of the older brothers, then brought about the downfall of the family, what would become of them?

Even if justice for Lord Narborough was deserved and forthcoming, could it not be delayed awhile? The girls were infants when he'd seen them last. They must be near old enough to make matches for themselves. If it was possible to stall the Gypsy, even for a month or two, then they would be safely out of the house and with families of their own, when retribution came.

It went against his grain, but Marc Carlow deserved some warning of what was coming, so that he could watch out for his sisters. They had all played together as children, and been good friends—until after the trial, when their prig of a father had forbidden further association.

Stephen had been there as well, of course. Once, they had been as alike as brothers. He forced the thoughts out of his head. With nostalgia would come sympathy and regret. And after that: weakness and fear. He could not afford to feel for the man who wished his destruction. Stephen Hebden had died in a foundling-home fire. And Stephano Beshaley was a bastard Gypsy changeling, who had turned on them the minute he had a chance.

And the man who had once been Nathan Wardale would not let himself be ruled by curses and grudges and superstitious nonsense any more than he had already. The Carlows would be no more happy to see him than he would be to go to them. But he did not wish them a visit from the Gypsy, now that Stephano had taken it into his head to resurrect the past and deliver vengeance where none was deserved.

Nate dressed carefully, as anyone might when visiting the heir to an earldom, and tucked the length of silk rope and its accusing knot into the pocket of his coat.

Chapter Two

Diana Price resisted the urge to place her head in her hands and weep in frustration. The Carlow daughters were pleasant, and she viewed them more as friends than a responsibility. But some days her job as their companion was not an easy one. 'You will have to choose someone, Verity. The whole point of the Season is to find an appropriate match. It makes no sense to reject the entire field of suitors, before the rush is truly underway.'

She would have called the look on Verity's face a pout, had the girl been prone to such. 'I know what the point of coming to London was, Diana. But I had hoped that if Honoria would take care of the obligation and find herself a husband, then you would all leave off bothering me. Do you think Marc will force me to marry this year, even when I can see already that none of the available suitors are likely to suit?'

'Your brother will do nothing of the kind, Verity. But

if you claim that none of the gentlemen in London suit you, then you are far too selective.'

'Only yesterday, Diana, you were criticizing Honoria for not being selective enough.'

'Because she was not. It does not pay to encourage the advances of every man who shows an interest, Particularly not when you are as lovely as Honoria.'

Verity gave her an arch look. 'And since I am not, I will be forced to marry a man who I do not love, just because he has offered?'

Diana reached out to hug the girl, who was quite as lovely as her sister, even though she lacked the older girl's confidence. 'That is not what I mean at all, dear one. It is simply that I do not wish you to discount gentlemen without giving them a fair hearing. You are young, yet. Though you might think that infatuation is the most important thing, it is not.'

'And you, Diana, are not so old that you should confuse the words love and infatuation. They sound nothing alike.'

'In tone, perhaps not. But when they are felt in a young heart, they can be easily confused. I am sure if you are given time, you will discover that there are much more important factors to consider when accepting an offer.'

Verity sighed. 'Like money, I suppose.'

'While it is nice, I doubt you will need to concern yourself with the wealth of your suitors.' Any fortune hunters would have a hard time getting close, as long as Diana watched carefully. 'I am thinking more of kindness, stability, common sense…'

Verity rolled her eyes. 'All characteristics that can be gained with advanced age, I am sure.'

'It is not necessary, or even advisable, for a husband to be quite so young as his wife. In some cases, it might be better for a wiser man to—'

'Ugh.' Verity put her hands over her ears. 'Do not talk to me further about the need to find a sensible old man to offset my youth and inexperience.'

'Not old certainly, but—'

And now, Verity was shaking her head. 'If that is the sort of man you wish for, then you had best find him for yourself. But as for me, I will choose in my own good time. Even if he is rash or foolish, if he loves me, I will accept him. We will learn moderation together.'

Diana sighed. The conversation was ending as it had several times before, with Verity stubbornly convinced that when it came for her, love would conquer all. In Diana's experience, love was rarely a successful combatant against an uneven temper or an irregular income. 'In any case, it is not something we need worry about today. If you find someone this Season who interests you—'

'Which I shall not.'

'—we will discuss his qualities before you make a decision. For now, it will please your father to hear that you are dancing and laughing, even if he is too ill to watch you.'

Verity sighed. 'And there you have me, Diana. You know I will not refuse, if it is so important to the family. As long as I do not have to tie myself to that odious

Alexander Veryan, just to make you all content. I swear, he is the biggest bore alive. The last time we danced, he trod on my toes half the night, while making sheep's eyes.'

Diana smiled in sympathy, thinking of the rather awkward young man and his pitiful attempts to capture Verity's affection. 'Your father would welcome a connection to the Veryan family, but respectability is not the only quality to seek in a husband. I am sure, if we put our heads together, we will find you a more suitable beau than young Alex.'

There was a quiet knock upon the door of the dressing room, and a maid entered. 'Miss Verity, there is a gentleman here. He wishes to speak with your brothers. But neither is home, nor expected. And Miss Honoria is…' The servant paused respectfully.

'Indisposed.' Verity looked helplessly in Diana's direction. They both knew that Honoria, who had none of Verity's reticence on the subject of marriage, had been up most of the night at a rout, dancing until nearly dawn. It would be quite beyond her to greet a visitor until noon, if then. 'I am hardly dressed to entertain. But I will come as soon as I am able. In the meantime, Diana, could you?'

Stall, while the girl finished her morning chocolate? It was full on ten o'clock, and Diana Price had been up for hours. She could hardly blame the Carlow girls for sleeping late. But she still found it vaguely annoying when the girls' suitors chose to arrive before lunch. With the men from the house, it left Diana in the awkward position of disappointing them. Until the girls had shown an attachment to any of the young men they had met, it would do the gentlemen little good to appeal to their older brothers on the subject.

She straightened her rather severe dress and put on her best chaperone's frown. 'I will see what it is about, Verity. If it is urgent, I will call for you. But if I do not, you may come down in your own good time. It serves the man right for arriving at this hour.'

Her friend gave her a relieved smile. 'Thank you, Diana. I don't know what I would do without you.'

She turned and walked out of the room and down the stairs to the salon. But the man waiting there came as a surprise to her, for he was a stranger. Her first impression was that he was far too old to be the usual post-ball suitor. His hair had not a touch of youthful colour left; It was a striking silver-grey. But on closer inspection, she could see that his back was straight, his skin tanned but smooth, and his green eyes had the clarity, if not of youth, then of a reasonable adulthood.

Physically, he was not much beyond her own twenty-seven years. But there was a quality in those eyes that spoke to her. They had seen much, and not all of it had been pleasant. But whatever hardship he had seen did not seem to have broken him. There was a solidness about him, as though he were made of stronger stuff than most men. With his striking appearance, it seemed to her as though an ordinarily handsome man had been cast as a statue, with burnished metal for hair and skin, and glittering gems for eyes.

Here was the sort of man she had wished for Verity: someone who could inspire confidence and trust as well as make the heart flutter. And apparently, even she was not immune from him, for she could not help smiling a trifle too warmly in greeting. 'I am sorry to disappoint you. Lord Stanegate is from home. As is his brother. May I enquire as to the reason for your visit, Mister…?' She left the sentence open, to remind him that he had not bothered to introduce himself.

He tilted his head and stared closely into her face, as though searching his memory, 'Verity? Or is it Honoria? I cannot tell. It has been so long…' He used the same puzzled tone that she had used, and there was a pause as he looked at her, a faint smile forming at his mouth. It was as though he had not expected her, any more than she had expected him. But the surprise had been a pleasant one. He was taking her in, just as she had him, forming opinions, searching for her past in her eyes.

Without thinking, she reached up to touch her hair, ready to push a loose curl out of the way, even though there was none. And then stilled her hands, and kept them demurely at her sides. 'No, sir. I am companion and chaperone to the Carlow daughters. My name is Diana Price.'

She must have misjudged his stability after all. Her introduction seemed to stagger him, and for a moment, he tottered as though he were a feeble old man. He reached for the arm of the nearest chair, and unable to control the rudeness of his behaviour, dropped unsteadily into it, taking a deep gasp of air.

'Sir?' She stepped closer, ready to offer assistance. 'Are you ill?'

'No. Really. It is nothing.'

'A glass of wine perhaps? Or a brandy?' It was far too early. But the man needed a restorative.

He gave her the strangest smile she had ever seen. 'Water, only. Please. The heat…'

'Water, then. I will fetch it,' she said, pretending to ignore his condition. It was barely past winter. There was no heat to speak of, nor was it particularly cold. But if the man wished to make excuses for an odd spell, it would do no harm to allow it.

She went to the carafe on a nearby table, poured out a tumbler, and brought it to him. As he took the glass from her hand, she felt the faintest tremble in his, as though the touch of her fingers had shocked him. He drank eagerly. When he set the glass down on the table beside him, a little of the colour had returned to his tanned face.

She sat in a chair opposite him so as not to call attention to his breach of etiquette.

He looked over and gave a weak smile of gratitude. 'Thank you for your kindness. Forgive me…Miss Price.' He took a breath. 'My name is…Dale.' His voice steadied again. 'I am an old friend of the family, but it has been a long while since I have had reason to visit this house. When I was last here, Miss Verity was but an infant and Honoria not much older. And seeing you, knowing that they are out…I was overcome with how long it had been. Are the girls well?'

'Yes, sir. Both are well-mannered and accomplished young ladies.'

'And lovely, I am sure. Just as I am sure that their good behaviour is a testament to your steady influence.' He fidgeted in his seat as though the burden of polite conversation was one that he was unaccustomed to. Then he stilled, as though gathering himself to the task at hand. 'But my business today is with their brothers. You say they are from home. Will they be returning soon?'

'Lord Stanegate is travelling with his new bride in Northumberland.'

'Marc married, eh?' Mr Dale got a distant look and he muttered, 'Felicitations. And Hal?'

'Somewhere on the Peninsula, I believe. He is a lieutenant in the Dragoons.'

The man nodded. 'It would suit him, I am sure, the life and the uniform.' And then he muttered, more to himself than to her, 'Very well, then. They are both safely out of the way, and I will not worry about them.'

It was good to hear that he seemed concerned, although why he should feel the need to worry over Marc or Hal, or think that it was safer to face Napoleon than be in London, she was not sure.

And now, he was looking at her again, as though he had forgotten that she was in the room with him and could not think what to do next. Then he said, 'If you could provide me with paper and pen, I would write a message to Marcus.'

'If the matter is important, I can give you the address at which he can be reached,' she offered.

Mr Dale waved a dismissive hand. 'If he is happy and away from town, I would not dream of bothering him.'

'Perhaps Honoria…'

'No,' he said a little too quickly. 'Do not trouble the girls with this. I doubt it will involve them. This is a matter to be settled amongst gentlemen. And I would hate to think I'd been a source of worry to them. A brief note to Marcus will suffice. If you could relay it when he returns, I would be most grateful.' He favoured her with another bright smile. And this time, she was sure that he was deliberately attempting to charm her. Most likely, he wished to make her forget his strange behaviour.

And it annoyed her that he had succeeded. He had a nice smile, friendly and unthreatening, yet a little knowing. There was something about the way that he sat in the chair, now he had recovered himself, that made her think he was usually an adventurous man. Wherever he belonged, it was somewhere much more exciting than a drawing room. As she got up and went to prepare the desk in the corner for writing, she could feel herself colouring at the thought that he was behind her and might be watching her move.

Had it been necessary of him to give flattering attention to a paid companion, just to get writing materials? She would have given him what he asked, even if he'd frowned at her, Diana thought. But his charming behaviour only stood to remind her how hopeless her fantasies might be. In a short time, he would be gone and she would be here, delivering the note like the servant she was. He would have forgotten all about her.

And she would be left with the memory of that smile.

Mr Dale came and sat at the place she prepared for him, at the tiny desk by the window. He thought for a moment, then scrawled a few words on the paper, blotted it, and stared at the sealing wax for a moment. Here he would show how little he trusted her with the contents.

Then he put the wax away, and looked directly into her eyes—the green light in his sparkled like emeralds—and his smile changed to a thoughtful frown. 'Miss Price. I do not wish to trouble the girls with the reason for my visit. My fears for the Carlow family might be for naught. But you are their companion, are you not? A watchdog for their honour and reputation?'

Diana nodded.

'Then should they receive the attention of a dark gentleman who calls himself Stephano Beshaley, know that he is a danger to them. Watch him carefully. And watch the girls as well, for he is just the sort to try and turn their heads. Should he appear, you must find Marc or Hal immediately and tell them. Can you do that for me?'

She nodded again, more puzzled than she had been before.

'Very good.' He handed her the folded sheet of paper. 'You can give this note to either Stanegate or Lieu-

tenant Carlow, when next they are home. Marcus pre-
ferably, since he is eldest and most responsible. But
either will understand its meaning. Thank you for your
time, Miss Price.' He gave a short bow, and turned to
leave.

'Wait.' She held up a hand to stop him before realizing that she had no reason to call him back to her, other
than an irrational desire not to let him go.

He turned back, an expectant look on his face.

'If they wish to reply, where shall I direct the
message? Or will you be returning?'

He gave the barest shake of his head. 'Do not concern
yourself. They will not wish to reply to me, any more
than they wish a visit from Beshaley. But now, my conscience is as clear as I can make it. On this subject, at
least.' He gave her another strange look, as though he
were apologizing for something, even though he had
done her no wrong. 'Good day, Miss Price.' And he was
gone.

She walked slowly back up the stairs to Verity, with
the note in her hand, wondering what she was supposed
to do with the thing. She could forward it on to Marc
on his honeymoon, she supposed. But he and Nell were
not due back from Northumberland for weeks, and she
hated to bother them. The time before their marriage
had been stressful enough. Surely they deserved a few
weeks of peace.

The paper before her was not sealed. Mr Dale had
left it to her discretion. And although she would never
peruse Marc's mail under normal circumstances,

perhaps this one time it would be better to read the message to see if the matter was urgent.

There was only one line, scrawled hurriedly in the centre of the paper.

Marc,
The Gypsy has returned.
Nathan.

Her breath caught a little in her throat. The words were ominous: black and spidery against the white of the paper. But it was nothing that she did not already know. Nor would Marc be surprised. He had explained to her what happened, before he left, the harrowing fight, the single shot, and the evil Gypsy who had been calling himself Salterton falling to his death in the icy water. Marc had cautioned her to be on her guard and watch the girls closely, in case he had been wrong. If the man lived, he might return to bother them.

She bit her lip. If only there were some way to draw Mr Dale back and ask him if this information was recent or some time in coming. It was possible that he'd met the Gypsy before his demise on the ice some weeks ago. Marc had warned her before he'd left to be on guard against all strangers, particularly one with dark hair and skin. She was to summon him immediately if anything or anyone unusual appeared.

This morning's visit had certainly been unusual. But Nathan Dale was not dark, nor was he threatening. He had been trying to help, and had brought a scrap of information that was already known to the family. If a specific threat had been imminent, surely he would have said more, or seemed more worried. And he had been smiling just now. How serious could the situation be?

She would adopt a wait-and-see attitude, doing just as Marc had asked. She would watch the girls more closely than usual. And if Mr Dale returned, she would try to find a way to draw him out and gain more infor-mation—without revealing that she had opened his note.

On thinking of it, she very much hoped Mr Dale would return. She suspected he was a most interesting gentleman and it intrigued her to know more about him. It was as though hard weather had rubbed away at a softer, less substantial person, until the core of vitality could shine through to the surface. There was an air of confidence about him, as though he had already seen and survived hardship and knew better than to be rattled by anything less than the gravest circumstances.

Perhaps he had already dealt with the Gypsy's threat and was only tying up the loose ends of the contact, making sure that the man could do no damage else-where. If she needed his help during Marc's absence, there might be some way…

Of course not. She reminded herself firmly of her first suspicions regarding the man: that he might be a suitor of Honoria or Verity. If he was a friend of Marc's and sought the company of any of the women in the house, there was no reason to think that he would seek the friendship of their companion nor that he wished to be bothered with her concerns over the girls.

It was just that she had found the sight of him to be rather dashing, and now she was spinning fancies that they would have more time to talk.

She glanced down at the note, and *Nathan* written at the bottom. And she shivered. It was good that she had conversed with the man before seeing it, for past experience had taught her to dread that name, and all who carried it. If she had known he was a *Nathan*, she might have let an unreasonable prejudice colour her opinions of him. And then she would have been deprived of that marvellous smile. She smiled back, even though he was not there to see it.

Verity looked up as she entered the dressing room. 'Who was it?'

Diana tucked the note into the pocket of her dress. 'It was the most extraordinary man.' Without meaning to, she gave a little sigh of pleasure. She had nothing to fear from *this* Nathan. He looked nothing like the man her father had warned her of, ten years ago. Mr Dale was not cold, or emotionless or the least bit cruel. Her spontaneous attraction to him came from the openness of his countenance, his easy nature and his selfless concern for others. He had a robust physique and the healthy colouring of a man who enjoyed nature, not the stooped frame, pinched face and anaemic pallor of a habitual gambler.

In short, he was the diametric opposite of Nathan Wardale.

Chapter Three

Nate hurried out of the Carlow town house and down the street, feeling the cold sweat beading on his brow. Of all the people, in all the places, why had he been greeted by Diana Price? He had been nervous enough, going to the house at all. But once he had arrived on Albemarle Street, the feelings of his youth returned. As a boy, he had run across the chequered floor of the front hall, chasing and being chased, laughing and playing. It had been as a second home to him. And to feel that moment of pleasure, as the young woman had entered the room. The Carlow daughters grown to beauty? But no. A stranger. A very attractive stranger. Delight, curiosity, an awakening of old feelings in him, long suppressed.

She was a lovely thing, with shining dark hair, and a small pursed mouth, ready to be kissed. Her large brown eyes were intelligent, but full of an innocence he never saw in the female denizens of the Fourth Circle.

She had looked at him without judgment or expectation, and a hint of responding interest that proved she was not wife to Marcus or Hal. Nate had felt quite like the man he once hoped to be. For a few moments, he was an ordinary gentleman meeting a pretty girl in a nice parlour, with none of the stink of the gaming hell on his clothes or in his mind.

And then he had discovered her identity, and it had all come crashing down. Thank God he had not decided to use his true name, for if she'd realized...

He hailed a cab in Piccadilly to Covent Garden and Suffolk Street, to the low haunts inhabited by Nate Dale the gambler. If the man he sought was anywhere, he would be here, waiting in the spot that he'd last been seen.

Nate went from the dim street, into the dim tavern connected by a tunnel to the Fourth Circle. 'Mr Dale, returning so soon? And in daylight.' Dante Jones saw him less as a friend than as a way to bring more people to the tables. 'To what do we owe this honour?'

'Mr Jones,' he responded, with barely a nod, resenting the grimy way he felt when the man looked at him as though he was nothing more than a meal ticket. 'Where is the damned Gypsy?'

'The man who you beat last night? In the same spot as when you left him. And I am glad to have him, for his play draws quite a crowd. He is very nearly as lucky as you.'

'Not any more.' Nate stalked past Dante and into the gaming room to find Stephano Beshaley, or whoever he chose to be called today, seated in Nate's regular chair, as though he owned it. He seemed impervious to the action around him, nursing his drink, long slender legs outstretched, as though he had been waiting for Nate's return.

Nate pulled the silk rope from his pocket, and threw it down on the table in front of the Gypsy. 'Take it back.'

Stephano only smiled and sipped his drink. 'Once it is given, there is no returning it.'

'Take it back. You have had your fun.'

'Fun?' Nate's former friend greeted this with a bitter twist of his mouth and an arched eyebrow. 'Is *that* what you think this is for me?'

'I think you take pleasure in tormenting me. But you have done enough.'

And there was the ironic smile again. 'You have changed much, in a few short hours. Last night, you said that there was nothing left to hurt you.'

'And I was wrong. I freely admit it. You have found the one thing.'

Beshaley laughed. 'I? I found nothing. But apparently you have. And I wish you to get what you deserve from it.'

'You knew where I would go, when you returned. And you knew that Diana Price would be there, waiting for me.'

'Who?' The Gypsy seemed honestly puzzled.

Nate reached into his pocket, and removed the tattered piece of paper that he had carried with him for ten years, like Coleridge's albatross. He set it on the table before his old friend, who read aloud.

Should I lose the next hand, I pledge in payment my last thing of value. The maidenhead of my daughter, Diana.
Edgar Price
June 3rd 1804

Beshaley sneered back at him. 'Just for a moment yesterday, I almost believed you. If you are innocent of any crime, then to carry vengeance to the second generation is to damn myself. But a man who would take such a thing in trade for a gambling debt deserves to suffer all that fate wishes to bring him.'

Nate glanced around, afraid that the people nearby might hear what he had done in that moment of madness. 'I was young. And foolish. And in my cups. Edgar Price was my first big score, and I was too full of myself and my own success to think of what I might do to others. When I suggested this bet, it was intended as a cruel jest. I'd taken the man's money. And his house, as well. I live there still. He'd bankrupted himself at my table to the point where his only options were debtor's prison or a bullet. And yet, he would not stop playing. Like every gambler, he thought that his luck would change if he played just one more hand. I thought to shock him. To embarrass him. That if I pushed him far enough, he would slink from the table. Instead, he signed this to me.'

Nate took the paper back and stuffed it into his purse so he would not have to see it any more. It still pained him to read those words. 'He cried when he lost. He begged me for mercy. And I told him that if I ever saw him again, or heard of him frequenting the tables anywhere in London, I would find him and the girl and collect what was owed me. And to his credit, I never saw or heard from him, after that day. I keep the paper to remind me what can happen when a man is pushed too far at the tables. And I have not taken a single marker, since.'

'How noble of you.' The Gypsy looked ready to spit in disgust. 'You are lower than I thought you, Nathan. And after seeing this, I feel considerably less guilty about delivering the rope.' He pushed it back across the table toward Nate.

Nate stared down at the symbol of disgrace, and in his heart, he agreed. He deserved punishment. But his mouth continued to try to justify the unjustifiable. 'I thought the girl long married, by now. It has been years. She must know that I am no threat to her. But I went to warn the Carlows of you. And she was there. She is chaperone to Honoria and little Verity. You knew, you bastard. You knew it all along.'

The Gypsy smiled in satisfaction. 'I knew nothing, other than that I would bring the rope to you, and see what resulted from it. Normally fate is not so swift. By your actions, you have made your own hell. Do not blame me, if today is the day that the devil has come to claim you.'

'Whether or not you have staged this meeting with the girl, it will be the last one between us. I mean to leave Diana Price alone, just as I have always done. Now take this back.' He slapped the rope upon the table.

Stephen arched his eyebrows. 'And what will happen, if I do? Will she vanish in a cloud of smoke? You created the problem, Wardale. You must be the one to solve it.'

'I can hardly be held to blame for what happened to her father, Stephen. He came to me, and he would not leave. He wanted to gamble. I am a gambler. I never set out to be what I have become. It is all the fault of your mother and your people.'

'You won someone's daughter at faro, and it is all my mother's fault, is it?'

That sounded even more foolish than the rest of it. God knew how mad the rest of his defence would sound. 'Did you know me for a gamester, before the curse?'

The Gypsy snorted. 'You were ten years old.'

'Yet I'd ruined my first man before I could shave. And that is the way it has been, from the very first wager. I am lucky. And it is all because of the curse your mother placed upon me.'

The Gypsy laughed. 'You believe in luck?'

'What gambler does not? I cannot claim that skill has brought me all that I have gained. I win far too often to think that it is always by my own abilities.' He waved a hand in the direction of the faro tables. 'These tables? All gaffed. Dante cheats. Only a fool would play here.

But if you like, I will beat them for you. No matter how much Dante might cheat, he can never beat me.' He stared at the tables in remorse. 'No one has ever been this lucky. No one save me. It is not natural. And if I cannot lose? Then to play against others is little better than robbery.'

'Then stop playing. Or tell them to.'

'I cannot.' He gritted his teeth. 'Every night, I swear I am through. But the next night falls and I come back to the tables. I mean to play until I lose. Not just a hand or a single pass of the dice. When I lose all of it, every last thing I have won, then maybe I will understand how the others have felt. Only then can I stop.'

The Gypsy's snorts continued, combining into a gale of laughter. 'First you thought I conjured the Price girl. And now you wish to blame me for your excessive good luck. That is the maddest thing I have heard yet.'

'You do not believe in your own magic?'

'I do not have to. Not if you do. I come here with a reminder of your family's villainy. And you proceed to fill in the rest. In less than a day, you are near to prostrate with guilt. If you want freedom, Nathan, use this rope for the purpose it is intended.' He held the noose at eye level, until he was sure the meaning was clear, and then tossed it back on the table. 'Then my doings with your family will be over and you will no longer be able to concern yourself with the families of your victims.'

His self-control was a distant memory, as Nathan felt the long-buried rage burning in him again at the old accusation. 'My father was hanged for a crime he did not commit. My family has paid more than enough, with that. Take back the curse, Beshaley.'

'No.'

'You dirty Gypsy. Take back the curse.' In fury, he reached out and grabbed his former friend by his bad arm, squeezing the bicep.

He had found the injury. Stephano Beshaley went as white as his dark skin would allow, and the pain of the contact brought him out of his chair and to his knees.

Nate was overcome with a shameful glee to see his enemy humbled before him, and he remembered why it was so important to keep one's emotions out of the game. When one always had the upper hand, it was too easy to take pleasure from the suffering he inflicted. He pushed the anger from his mind, and squeezed again with clinical precision, watching the other's face contort with pain. 'Take back the rope. Let me go, and I will release your arm. You have my word.'

The Gypsy took a deep breath, as though he were trying to drive back the pain with the force of his will. Then he raised his shaking white face in defiance. 'Your father was a coward and a murderer. And you are the sort who would gamble for a girl's honour. Your word means nothing to me.'

Though the first statement angered him, the last was so true that his grip slackened on his old friend's arm, and he watched as the colour returned to the man's face. And in the place of the nothingness inside him, there was now a deep bone-aching remorse. 'Please. I am sorry. For all of it, Stephen. *Let me go.*'

And for a moment, the man on his knees before Nathan was plain Stephen Hebden, as hurt and bewildered as Nathan was. 'I cannot. I am as much a slave to the curse as you are, for I was the one left to administer it. If your father was innocent, then you are already free and what you think is a curse is all your own doing. But if not?' He shrugged with his one free arm. 'I can do nothing for you.'

Chapter Four

'Well, this was a most satisfying afternoon,' Honoria announced, as they neared the end of their shopping trip to Bond Street. 'And perhaps next time, we will persuade Diana to buy something for herself.'

'There is nothing I really need,' Diana said, as much to persuade herself as the girls. It was always tempting, on these forays, to make a purchase of some sort. But even a small one was an unnecessary indulgence.

'Then perhaps what you need is to sit down and have an ice. It would be very refreshing, after such a long walk.' Honoria was looking longingly in the direction of confectionary.

'The walk was not very long at all, Honoria, and should hardly exhaust you. Exercise, when taken in moderate amounts, is beneficial to health. And I am sure that tea at home will be refreshing enough.'

'Sometimes, Diana, you are far too sensible.'

Diana smiled at the accusation. 'I need to be. Or you

would indulge every whim, and grow too plump for your new gown.'

'Is that the gentleman who called yesterday, Diana?' Verity Carlow was staring in the opposite direction, and making an unladylike effort to point over the stack of parcels she was carrying, at a man on the end of the block. 'Oh, do say it is him. For he is every bit as striking as you described him.'

Diana prepared a reprimand, and then glanced in the direction her friend was looking, and saw the sun glinting off the silver hair of the man she had seen in the parlour. In the last twenty-four hours, she had spent so much time thinking of him that it felt almost as if she had conjured his image to appear on the street. It was hard to believe she was truly going to see him again after such a short time. But he must be real, for he looked very different than he had when she had seen him in the house. Today he seemed carefree. He was without a hat. And with the wind ruffling his hair, and his green eyes squinting into the sun, he looked almost as though he belonged on the deck of a ship, staring out at the sea.

She wondered if that was his true job. Sea captain. Or perhaps privateer. Surely something very romantic and commanding. He stood on the sidewalk as though he had conquered half of London. And here she was, spinning more romantic fancies around the poor man. But she had to admit, the effect that the sight of him had on her was sudden and difficult to control. It brought with it a faint breathlessness that increased as she realized that he was coming in their direction. 'Yes,' Diana said, trying to keep the excess of emotion from showing in her voice. 'That is Mr Dale. Whatever can he be doing here?'

'Shopping, I am sure,' Honoria said. 'Just as everyone else is doing. Perhaps he is visiting the tobacconist or the bank.' Apparently, the man's imposing nature was lost upon her. She was looking at Diana in a most searching way. 'While you made his behaviour yesterday sound very mysterious, you noticed nothing about him that would prevent him from mixing in society, did you?'

'Well, no.' It was just that she did not ever remember seeing him here before. And she was sure, had he shared the street with them in the past, she would have noticed.

Diana doubted Marc's apparent friendship with the man would require his sister's association with him. If it did, Marc would introduce them properly, in his own good time. For safety's sake, she prepared to steer Verity and Honoria to the other side of the street. 'You are probably right. He is shopping, or running errands of some sort. But I doubt he means to mix with us. He seemed most uncomfortable when visiting yesterday, and was in a hurry to leave.'

Verity gave her a round-eyed look. 'He did not seem to hold us any ill will, did he?'

'Of course not. But neither did I have any reason to think he might wish our company today.'

'Nonsense,' said Honoria. 'We do not mean him any

harm. We are only being friendly. It is not as if Verity and I are angling after him, no matter how flattering your description might have been.'

Verity shaded her eyes with her hand for a better look. 'Flattering as well as accurate. He is most handsome, is he not?' She grinned at Diana. 'And it would show an amazing lack of Christian charity to appear to shun our brother's old friend, if we meet him on the street.'

Although she was sure that Verity's heart was at least partly in the right place, Honoria must know that an act of Christian charity by a marriageable young lady towards an attractive, eligible man was liable to be mis-interpreted. But it was too late to explain this, for Honoria was waving her handkerchief at the gentleman in question. 'Here, Mr Dale! Over here!' She set out at a quick pace towards the man, who was momentarily curious as to the identity of the person greeting him. But then he recognized Diana, trailing in Honoria's wake. And his eyes took on a distinctly hunted expression.

'Honoria!' she said sharply, hurrying after the girl. 'You have not been properly introduced to the man.'

Honoria ignored the tone of warning. 'Nonsense. He told you he had seen us as children, did he not? Then surely we need not be so formal. But if it bothers you, then you must remedy the fact immediately, and present us to him.

'Mr Dale? I understand that you are an old friend of our family. I was most disappointed to be indisposed when you visited yesterday.' She favoured Mr Dale with her most brilliant smile and then cast a significant glance in Diana's direction.

Diana gave up, and said, with a resigned tone, 'Mr Dale, may I present Lady Honoria and Lady Verity Carlow.'

He gave a somewhat stiff bow, and answered, 'You are correct, ladies. We are already acquainted. Although you were both much too small to remember me, and I was but a boy when I last saw you.'

Verity said, 'Miss Price and I were speculating on your appearance in Bond Street. I do not remember seeing you here before.'

Diana coloured and gave a small shake of her head to indicate that they had been doing nothing of the kind, for the last thing she wanted was to reveal the true nature of her speculations. She was sure that her head-shake looked nothing like the saucy toss Verity was giving her golden curls, to make them catch the sunlight.

Nathan Dale was wearing the same poleaxed expression that men often got when the Carlow sisters turned their considerable charms upon them. He muttered, 'Tailor,' as though he could barely remember what had brought him out to shop.

'So you frequent the area?' Verity gave Diana a triumphant look. 'I suppose we have seen you in the past. But the renewed acquaintance of our families puts a fresh face on the experience. Now that we know you again, we shall be running into each other all the time.'

Diana was sure that this was not the case. She was convinced that she would have been drawn to the man's striking appearance, had she seen it before.

For his part, Mr Dale looked positively horrified at the notion that he would be seeing them again and again.

But Verity ignored this as well, and said, 'Now that we have found you, may I ask you to be of assistance? We are overburdened by packages. If you could help us regain our carriage?'

No gentleman could refuse, although this one looked like he wished to. He glanced around for a moment, almost as if he was embarrassed to be seen with them. But then he bowed again and took the packages anyway, then turned to help them find their transport. Once that was achieved, it seemed Verity would not be satisfied with the aid of servants, but required Mr Dale to escort them all the way back to the house.

Diana could see him struggling to come up with a polite refusal, his eyes finding hers and holding them with a mute appeal for aid. But then, Honoria linked her arm through his, and all but dragged him into the carriage to sit beside her. 'There,' she said, giving a sigh of satisfaction. 'This is much better, is it not?'

Mr Dale gave a nod of polite agreement. Although since she was seated opposite him, Diana could see from his miserable expression that this was the last place on earth he wished to be. He remained in strained silence as the normally quiet Verity prattled on in a most annoying way about the price of ribbons and the challenge of finding a sufficiently fluffy *coq* feather in exactly the right shade of blue.

Diana had no idea what had gotten into the girl, although she suspected it had something to do with silver hair and green eyes. But she was well on the way to giving her a megrim. Mr Dale seemed of a similar mind, squirming in his seat as though he wished to fling open the door and dart from the coach, willing to risk a fall beneath the horse's hooves, over slow death by millinery.

Honoria was no better, clinging to Mr Dale's arm as though she sensed his desire and was trying to prevent the escape. If the girl truly wished to gain the man's attentions, she would need to choose another approach entirely. And much to Diana's dismay, she could find no desire to help either of them. If the man took a sudden and violent distaste to the Carlow sisters, it would forestall the risk that she might have to chaperone any of them, enduring painful evenings of lingering glances, staring intently into her needlework while ignoring their whispered endearments.

Was it only yesterday that she had been eagerly awaiting the appearance of Verity's first real suitor? She loved the girl, and wished her well as she struggled in the shadow of her older sister. If Verity finally made a choice, then Diana should be relieved, not annoyed. Unless it was this particular man.

And while she was sure of Honoria's ability to captivate any man, she could not warm to the idea that the object of her affection was the enigmatic Mr Dale. No matter that she thought he was exactly the sort of man she could put forward as a steadying influence on either of them. To be forced to sit in the corner and watch as Nathan Dale grew increasingly besotted over either of the Carlow daughters would be the most difficult thing in the world.

Perhaps Mr Dale thought the same, for he was squirming again. He stretched his long legs out before him, and they brushed against Diana's skirts.

She gave a surprised jump as his calf touched hers.

He straightened suddenly, mumbling apologies.

Honoria nudged Verity with her toe from the opposite seat, and there were a few muffled giggles from the two girls until Diana gave a disapproving cough.

Mr Dale seemed to fold in upon himself, trying to take as little space as possible and cause no further incidents.

At last, the carriage arrived in front of the Carlow town house, and before it could come to a full stop, Nathan Dale had the door open and the step down. He offered a hand to Verity and then to Honoria. Once he had seen them both safely to the ground, he turned back for Diana. He wiped his palm upon his coat-tail and gave an embarrassed bob of his head, as though he did not wish to look into her eyes. But at the last moment, he looked up, his amazing green eyes catching hers and holding them. And then, his hand touched hers.

Her feet were on the ground, and he was turning away. But she had the strangest sensation that an important moment had passed, though she had no recollection of it. And it was a shame, for if the time had been spent with her hand in his, she thought that she would very much have liked to have a clear memory of it.

She came back to herself offering a silent prayer of relief that the trip was over, only to hear Verity insisting that Mr Dale simply must stay for tea, and her sister heartily agreeing. Honoria had reached out to catch the man by the arm again, before he could escape into the street. And now, she was reminding him that it was teatime, after all.

After dragging him so far out of his way, it was only logical that the girls offer him refreshment. Diana should commend them for their hospitality. But the events so far had left Diana's nerves frayed to the point where she was sure her cup would be rattling on the saucer loud enough to block out the sound of conversation.

And Mr Dale, damn him, could not seem to find voice enough to refuse the girls. If he did not wish to be with them, then why could he not say so—and end her torment? Instead, he allowed himself to be led as meek as a lamb into the sitting room for tea and cakes.

They were barely seated, before Verity sprang to her feet. 'I wonder what is taking so long? Cook is normally much more prompt than this. Perhaps someone should go and check.'

Diana was weighing in her mind the possibilities. It would not do to leave the girls alone in the room with a stranger, while she went to talk to the help. If that was what Verity was attempting to orchestrate, she underestimated her chaperone. She would tell the girl to ring for Wellow, the butler, and lecture them both later about the need to sit patiently when one had guests.

But before she could take action, Honoria announced, 'I will just go and see after things.' And she was up, out of her chair and out the door. She turned back. 'And Verity, you must come with me.'

Her sister rose. 'Can you not find your own way to the kitchen?'

'Of course. But I suspect I shall eat all the sandwiches before they are even brought here, for I am famished. If you do not come to watch over me, I swear, I will not leave a thing for Mr Dale.'

'Really, I…do not require anything,' he finished to the closed door.

And Diana found herself alone again, with Nathan Dale.

There was a moment of very awkward silence. And then, he spoke. 'Miss Verity did not talk nearly so much when last I saw her. Of course, she was an infant at the time.'

'She did not talk so much when last I saw her either, and it has been barely an hour. I do not know what has got into her.' Diana hoped it did not sound like an indictment of her friend.

Apparently, he feared the same. For he said, 'I mean no disrespect. For all her chatter, she is a pleasant girl, as is her sister. Have you known them long?'

'I came into the household when Verity was almost fifteen. She is still nineteen and barely out.'

'And Honoria twenty. The family must be very proud

of them.' For a moment, his gaze grew distant, as if remembering the past. And then he focused on her again. 'And before coming here, did you have another position?'

'As companion to an elderly lady in Kent.'

He leaned forward as though he found her rather uninteresting life to be riveting. 'And did you prefer that job to this one?'

She smiled, surprised at his questions. 'One position is much like another, I expect. But on the whole, I find it more enjoyable to watch the young. It was difficult to see the person in one's care wither and die, knowing there was nothing to be done. Much more pleasant to see them blossom, as young Verity has.' She gave a small sigh. 'Soon, they will have no need of a chaperone here. The girls shall be fine married ladies, with husbands and houses of their own.'

'And you will be out on the street.' He looked as though the prospect alarmed him.

She gave a little laugh of reassurance to soften the blunt way he had described her pending unemployment. 'Hardly, I am sure. Lord and Lady Narborough have been most kind to me. They will see to it that I am properly placed somewhere. I trust them to help me, when I am no longer needed here.'

'You might be surprised.' He muttered the words under his breath, and for a moment, she suspected that his fondness for the family was not as great as it had at first appeared.

'Well, in any case, I am not too worried,' she lied. 'When this job is finished, I will find another family who needs me. There are always openings for sensible women of a certain age.' Although they might not be as enjoyable as her current place.

'*A sensible woman of a certain age.* I see.' Perhaps he found her good sense to be a disappointment. Or perhaps it was her age that bothered him. He was frowning at her. 'But should you not find a place to your liking, do you have family to return to?' He was on the edge of his chair now, as though her answer were deeply important to him.

She shook her head. 'It has been just me for almost five years. But my situation is hardly unique. And in some ways it was easier for me than it has been for others. My mother died when I was young. And I was well-settled in employment before my father died. There was no period of sudden turmoil, as I found myself homeless and alone with no plan for the future.' In fact, the turmoil was several years past, and her anger with her father had cooled by the time she'd lost him for good.

'But you have no one else? I mean: no prospects, other than employment?'

She looked at him sharply. Was he enquiring if there was a gentleman in her life? 'Certainly not.'

And now he'd realized how that question had sounded, for he fell into pensive silence, before beginning again. 'I am sorry if my curiosity was inappropriate. But if you should find yourself in constrained circumstances and there is anything I can do to help...'

And now it sounded as though he were about to offer

a *carte blanche*. 'No, Mr Dale,' she said firmly, so there could be no question of her meaning. 'I can assure you, that whatever my circumstances might be, I will not be needing help with them.'

A short time later, Verity and Honoria returned followed by a footman with tea things. Apparently, the time away had calmed Verity's nerves, although Honoria had the same enigmatic smile on her face as before. They set about arranging the table for Mr Dale, like consummate hostesses. They were solicitous of his needs without clinging, and they conversed without the annoying chatter that had bothered her in the carriage.

It gave Diana the chance to retreat to a corner with her cup and stay well out of the flow of talk, allowing the girls to get to know the gentleman better. If he could be called a gentleman, for his behaviour to her had been most forward and more than a little strange. She wondered if she had given him too much credit the first time they had met, swayed by his charm and his physical appearance.

And if her silence now permitted time to observe the fine features of Mr Dale? Then she doubted he would notice, and she could hardly be blamed for it. She did find him to be a very handsome man. And she sincerely hoped she had misunderstood his intent toward her. He spoke easily enough with the girls, now that she was out of the way. There was nothing improper about his speech or manner. And he'd lost that curious sense of agitation he had brought to even the most mundane of his questions to her. When he rose to go, he thanked

Verity and Honoria in turn, then paused as he looked in her direction, seeming to swallow his nerves before giving her the same polite words of thanks and a short stiff bow. And then, he was gone.

There was a moment of silence, as though Verity wished to be sure that the man was totally out of earshot, before she spoke, as though he could hear their opinions of him through the brick walls and on the street. Then she turned and smiled at Honoria. 'Well?'

Honoria smiled and nodded. 'Oh, yes. I think most definitely.'

And then she turned to Diana. 'And what do you think of the gentleman, Miss Price?'

Apparently, she was to render the final verdict, and she did not wish to, for her own opinion was most decidedly mixed. She took care to discount her own strong reactions, and did her best to view him as she would any other prospective suitor. 'I am glad that you are both so definite on the subject of Mr Dale. He seems a fine person, and was most courteous in his behaviour. Your inviting him into the house was not inappropriate, although it was somewhat unplanned. If there is a past history between your families it cannot be too terribly improper. But despite what you might think, we do not know him very well at all. I doubt your father or brothers would approve, should things progress to the point where he might make either of you an offer before they can be consulted.'

'Us?' Verity sat down, laughing heartily. 'Oh, Diana. If you do not see the truth of what has been happening, you must be blind. However are we to trust you with advising us on our futures, if you cannot manage your own?'

'What has my future to do with it?'

Honoria grinned. 'We heard the way you spoke of him, after his visit here yesterday. The vividness of your physical description was enough for Verity to pick him out of the crowd on Bond Street. And apparently, you did not see the way he looked at you when we met him. His eyes followed you as though you were the only woman present. So we waylaid the poor fellow and made ourselves as tiresome as possible. Then we left you alone together, as soon as we were able. You did not expect us to play chaperone, did you? For that would be more than a little ironic.'

'Me?' Her voice cracked on the word.

'Yes, you, you goose,' said Verity. 'I wondered what would become of you, once I was wed. It would be so much better for me, were you to be a proper married lady as well, and not a companion to another. For then we could all remain friends and see each other as often as we liked.'

'Me? Married?'

'To Mr Dale,' Honoria completed the thought. 'You are right, Verity. It is the most perfect idea in the world.'

'Me.' And now that they had placed it there, the thought was stuck in her head and would not be dislodged. 'Married.' It had been so long since she had even thought of the word as it pertained to herself, that she could not manage to form a sentence around it. 'To

Mr Dale.' If it had been one of the girls displaying an interest in the man, she would have given a lecture at this point about the importance of knowing a gentleman better before using such a word in connection with him. Horses should be put before carts. There should be frequent meetings between the interested parties. Affection and love were things that should be nurtured before a more permanent arrangement could be considered.

But suddenly, she felt as foolish as either young girl. Her head was flooded with visions of a home of her own, a husband of her own, and her own children, all with the sparkling green eyes of Nathan Dale.

If she were thinking clearly, then she would have told the girls that, if a gentlemen were as rushed into making an offer as they wished for Mr Dale to be, the offer he might make would be one that no proper woman could accept. What must he think of her? He must suspect that she had arranged their private conversation by manipulating the girls, all in an attempt to court him for herself. How would she be able to speak to the man, when next they met, if her head was full of romantic nonsense and his ideas were much more worldly?

She forced her fears into the background and looked at the girls with her most prim and sensible gaze. 'No. I am sorry. The idea does not appeal to me in the least. If this visit with him was arranged for my benefit, then while I thank you for the concern, I can assure you that no further such plans are necessary.' She swallowed hard, and lied. 'I am quite content to remain as I am.'

Chapter Five

Nate went back to his house in Hans Place, with the Carlows' tea sitting uneasily in his stomach. The feelings of disquiet grew with each step towards his home. By the time he had stepped through the front door, it felt as though ants crawled upon his skin.

That was a near one. It had been a misfortune to meet the girl once. But to find her again so soon, after years of avoidance? It was another part of the Gypsy's damn curse, he was sure. As little Verity had been quick to point out to him, now that he had found Diana Price, he was unlikely to get free of her.

The thought flitted across his mind that he had no desire to be free of her. Under better circumstances, he'd have been enjoying the association immensely. And she seemed to enjoy it as well, if there was any meaning to the pretty blush upon her cheek when they'd been left alone.

But then, he had proceeded to make an ass of himself

by prying into her personal life and asking questions
that no stranger should care about. He had left her with
the impression that he was the sort who would make
advances towards a vulnerable woman within moments
of being alone with her. Damn it to hell, he had only
wanted to make up for what he had already done to her.
Instead it had sounded like he wished to set her up in
an apartment as his ladybird.

Although, once the idea had entered his head, he had
to admit that there were advantages to it. If she were so
inclined, it would be pure pleasure to watch those eyes
widen in pretended shock at his suggestions, only to be
lulled into catlike satisfaction when he acted on them.
She must realize that the way she pursed those full lips
in disapproval at him only made them more tempting.
He suspected that, should she fold her arms beneath her
high breasts, or place her hands upon those softly
rounded hips in a gesture of disapproval, she could
easily bring a strong man to his knees.

It was all quite hopeless. Even if she was less than
the proper lady he suspected, she was Edgar Price's
daughter and therefore the last woman in London he
should be wishing to bed. He might pretend to be Nate
Dale for a while with her, he supposed. But knowing
his luck when away from the gaming tables, it was
only a matter of time before Hal or Marc arrived and
recognized the man who was courting their sisters'
chaperone. Or perhaps he would be the one to let some
word slip that would make it clear to Diana Price his
true identity.

Until a few days ago, it had been easy enough to think of himself as well and truly Nate Dale, and to think of Nathan Wardale as a distant memory. But now, he could not help but see his current life as a thinly drawn fraud. When the truth came out, he doubted that there were enough words in his vocabulary to talk himself out of the situation.

He looked around, at the entry hall to his house. Although the place had been home to him for almost four years, and he had long ago come to think of it as truly his, suddenly, he felt like an interloper in the home of Diana Price. As he glanced around, he was qualifying everything in his life into two enormous piles: things that he had bought and things that had been in the house when he had won it. Even the servants were Price's, although it had been many years since he had felt any disloyalty. Those who had not wished him as master had quit on the day he'd accepted the deed. But most were content enough, when they realized that the new master could easily meet the back payments on their salaries and manage a raise as well.

He had followed his sudden arrival with an unexpected six-year absence. And in that time, the servants might as well have been sole possessors of the house. The man of business he had retained to pay the bills knew better than to meddle in the mundane details of running it. They had relaxed in the knowledge that the chaos the house had undergone from the previous owner's gambling was at an end. If the new master was also a gambler? Then at least he was a winner. Their positions were secure.

And if any one of them had ever wondered what had become of Diana Price or her father, then they had never spoken the words aloud in his presence.

But now, everywhere he looked, he saw reminders that he had taken this house right out from under the woman who sat so patiently at the side of the Carlow sisters. He walked up the stairs and hurried down the hall to his room. It was the only place in the house guaranteed not to remind him of the previous owner, for he had bought everything in it, brand new, even stripping the silk from the walls and taking up the rugs to prevent the ghost of Edgar Price from intruding on his dreams. Once he was shut inside, he would have peace.

But to arrive there, he needed to pass the locked door at the head of the stairs. He almost made it by without looking. In truth, he had trained himself never to look in that direction. To not see the door. To imagine it as a blank square of wall. But once remembered, he could not seem to put it from his mind.

When he reached his room, he rang for the butler.

'Sir?'

'Benton, do you have a key for the room at the head of the stairs?'

'Miss Diana's room, sir?' The man had been butler of this house since long before Nate had come to it. And although he appeared loyal, now that he was pressed on the subject, he made no effort to hide the fact that there was still one area of the house that did not belong to the new owner. When Nate had returned from America, the single room had been left untouched, as though no one could bring themselves to store the contents. And now, Benton's tone was worried, as if the idea disturbed him that it might finally be time to pack the contents away.

Nathan nodded. 'Miss Diana's room.'

The butler did not say another word, but removed a single key from the ring in his pocket, handing it to Nathan as though he wanted no part in what was to happen nor in whatever cosmic repercussions might fall on his master's head as a result of his actions.

Nate sighed. 'Thank you, Benton. That is all.'

The man removed himself, and Nate made his way back down the hall to the locked door. He turned the key quickly and jerked open the door before stepping inside, leaving it open behind him, so that he could see by the light from the hall. The room was dustier than he'd remembered, but other than that, unchanged. The wardrobe doors were thrown open, as though the occupant had been forced to pack and leave in a hurry. She must have taken her day dresses; a large section of the wardrobe stood empty.

But the ball gowns had been pushed to the side, and left behind. She'd known, even then, that her days as a debutante were over. If one was about to seek a position, then one did not need finery. He glanced around the room, taking note of the things missing and the things left behind. The hair brushes were gone but the ornaments remained. The jewellery box was open, and the contents scattered, as though she'd thought to take it all, then come to the conclusion that it had been lost to her along with everything else and settled on taking a few small pieces as remembrance of her old life.

There was a book on the table by the bed, the reader's place still marked by a scrap of ribbon. Did she ever finish it, he wondered, or had the little book been forgotten in her rush to go?

He thought back to his own departure from Leybourne House. The way his mother had told him to pack only what was needed. He had just turned ten, and still thought toy soldiers and wooden swords to be among life's necessities. After seeing the enormous pile of his possessions, she had sat down with him, and explained that, from now on, life would be different.

It was the first time, in all the harrowing weeks, that he had seen his mother cry.

He looked again at the contents of the room around him. He remembered how it had felt to be so totally displaced. And yet, he had done it to others. To the sweet-faced girl who had absented herself from his conversation with the Carlow sisters with the talent of one whose sole job was to fade into the background. She should be dancing at balls beside Verity and Honoria, not sitting in the corner with her book.

He had done that to her. He had ruined her chances, and her life. She should be married by now, with children of her own and servants to care for her needs.

He could feel the marker, heavy in his purse, as though it sought to burn through the leather and scar his skin. He had been telling himself for years that he had done the best he could by Diana Price. That it was enough: not following through on the damn thing. As bad as he had been to take it in the first place, he could have been worse. He had never demanded payment. He held himself forever in check, trying to prove his good character by the one thing he did not take.

Small comfort to Diana Price. He had not made her his whore for a night. He had left her with her virtue while denying her a lifetime's comforts.

He sat on the edge of the bed and looked around the room. She had been happy here, he was sure. It was smaller than his room, of course, but well-appointed and cheerful. It suited her. Without thinking too much about it, he stretched out on the bed and he picked up the book.

He woke nearly an hour later. He could remember reading. It was a volume of Shakespeare's sonnets. He had read and enjoyed them many times before. But the surprising warmth of the room and the peace of it had overcome him. Was it the quality of the light through the windows? Perhaps, when he had chosen his own room, he should have taken this, rather than the master suite. He had rested better during the little nap than he had in his own bed. And now, he was shaking off the vision of a pretty young girl with wide dark eyes, sitting in the window seat of this very room, legs tucked under her skirts, a half smile on her sunlit face and the book in her lap.

In his dream, she had looked up at him, where he lay on the bed, and put down the book to come towards him. The glint in her eyes was as welcoming as he might wish, and she had smiled. And then, thank God, he had awakened. If the dream had gone as he expected—with her lying in his arms—he was sure that it would have ended in a nightmare, once he'd realized who she was.

He got up quickly, trying to clear the fog from his brain, then left the room, locking the door behind him and dropping the key into his pocket. Then he bypassed his own room and went down the stairs to his study. Or was it Edgar Price's study? He was no longer sure. He had been so proud, when he'd first won this house, although much less so of the rest of that evening. There would have been room for Helena and Rosalind, and Mother as well. They would have lived happily enough, he was sure, once he had found some way to persuade them that he had come by it properly.

He had meant to break the news to them gently, making sure that everything was legal and the way prepared. His mother had never approved of his gambling to make the rent. She had wanted him to find an honest trade to help contribute to the family. And if she had realized how high the stakes had risen, and how quickly? If it upset her that he was winning coins off navvies or a few quid off of drunken clarks to help pay the bills, then she would have been appalled to see what he had won from Price.

It would not do to drop his family into a house full of unwilling servants, with the previous owners' possessions strewn about and Price's pipe still burning on the mantle. So he had toured the premises, released any servants that did not feel they could make peace with a change of masters and arranged things so that his mother need never again be troubled with the butcher's bill. He topped up the household accounts with several more fine scores at the tables. When he was through, the place would run like clockwork. His mother need never think about the time he'd spent gaming for the money she lived on, or waste her fading energy in sympathy for the source of their wealth.

But it seemed that fate was working against him, yet again. For no sooner had he finished his plans, than he was set upon by a press gang. He did not wake from their tender ministrations until he was onboard ship and well on the way to France as a member of His Majesty's Navy.

When he had managed to make his way home, he found the house little different than it had been when he'd left it. He had returned to a life that was quite comfortable, and further gambling had made it even more so. But it meant nothing if there was no one to share it with.

And now he could not shake the feeling that it was not his life that he was living, but one that rightly belonged to another. He gathered paper and pen, and addressed a hurried letter to Miss Price, care of the Carlow family.

And what did he mean to say to her? 'I am sorry,' hardly seemed enough, nor would it do any good to explain himself. It might appear that he thought he had suffered more than she, and he doubted it was possible to compare burdens. At last, he decided to leave the contents blank. Then he turned out his purse and piled the folded bank notes neatly inside the paper, reaching for the wax to seal it all up tight before sending. He almost marked it, but thought better of it. She did not need to know the sender, nor the reason. After this afternoon, she would not wish to take a penny from Mr Dale for fear of encouraging his attentions. And if she should discover the real reason he had done it, he dreaded her response.

But if he could reimburse her, in some small part, for the damage he had done.

It was not enough. It could never be enough. But perhaps he could find other ways to help her, without giving the wrong impression, when her position with the Carlows was at an end. It was better than nothing.

But *nothing* was what he had done in the past, and he found it would no longer content him.

Chapter Six

As she sat enjoying morning tea in the small dining room with Verity, Diana tried not to think of the day before. So the girls were convinced that Mr Dale was considering marriage. The idea was as ridiculous as it was appealing. His interest could not be too strong, for she was sure he would not have returned to the Carlow home had Verity and Honoria not forced the issue.

But once there, he had been more than willing to speak to her. And it was more than that. It was far more telling that he listened. Anyone might speak when trapped alone in a room with a stranger, just to fill the embarrassing silence. He had said very little about himself, but made every effort to draw her out.

And he had made the curious offer of aid. Perhaps she had misunderstood him, putting too ominous a spin on the words. After years of watching out for the virtue of others, even the most innocent of unguarded comments might be seen as an improper advance. She replayed the exchange endlessly in her mind, trying to see it from all sides. But it became even more confusing with repetition.

And now, whether she saw him again or not, Verity and Honoria would tease her endlessly on the subject of Mr Dale, just to see her turn pink at the mention of the man's name.

But if she did see him?

It was all she could do not to moan aloud at the thought. Her curiosity about him had grown to fascination, and then obsession. If she saw him, she would make a complete cake of herself. Any interest he might have felt would turn immediately to distaste, once he saw her behaviour.

It was disaster.

She gave Verity a weak smile over her cup of tea, and wished Honoria a good morning as the girl appeared in the doorway, yawning and sorting through the morning's mail. 'Here, Diana. A letter addressed to you.' Honoria held it out to her, and then snatched it back, holding it to her temple, as though trying to divine the contents. 'Too thick for a *billet doux*. I wonder what it might be?' She passed the letter to her friend.

'What utter nonsense, Honoria. You really are being most unfair to me. If you are not careful, I shall remember this behaviour. And when you receive a letter, I shall return the torment.' She tried not to appear as excited as she was, but she rarely received mail. It was even more rare to receive it unexpectedly, and she had no idea what this might be. She ran a finger along the edge of the folded paper to pop the sealing wax.

Bank notes fluttered to the table in front of her. It was as startling as if she had opened the letter to a flight of moths. She leaned back in her chair, as though afraid to let the things touch her dress.

'Ohhh my.' Verity had no such fear and came to her side to scoop the notes off the floor and into an organized pile on the table, counting as she went. 'There is all of thirty-four pounds here. Who sent it?'

Diana's mind was too numb to scold her charge for the impudence of the question. In truth, she was curious to know the answer. She picked up the letter, searching both sides for information. 'I do not know. There is my address, right enough. But there is no return.' She turned the paper. 'And no message, either.'

'Why would anyone send such an odd number?' Honoria asked. Was there a debt that needed paying?'

Diana stared at the money on the desk. 'None owed to me.' There might have been, to her father. But it was far more likely a debt was owed by her, than to her. And why would the money have come to her now, so many years after it might have helped?

'Well it is nowhere near your birthday. Or Christmas, for that matter,' Verity said.

Honoria riffled through the stack. 'And it does not look as if the person went to the bank for the money. The bills are all odd. Creased. Old.'

'But legal tender, all the same,' she told them. The Carlow girls were used to their money, clean and neatly folded, going straight from their brother's hand into their reticules. They had never been forced to search their father's pockets after a night of gambling, hoping that there would be a little left to pay the grocer.

The memory shocked Diana, for it had been so long, she'd thought it forgotten. But at the sight of the somewhat ragged bills before her, the past came flooding back and brought bitterness with it. Pound notes hurriedly gathered and stuffed into a pocket or purse. Not stacked neatly, but front to back, and upside down. This was enough to be very near a year's salary to a paid companion. But someone had thrust it into an envelope as though it were nothing, and addressed it to her. She stared at the writing on the letter, trying to divine masculine from feminine. The letters were roughly formed, as though the writer had wished to conceal his or her identity.

'Well, whoever it was seemed to think it most important that you receive this,' Verity said. 'You are sure that you have no idea?'

'None.'

'No belated gifts from estranged godparents?'

'I have none, estranged or otherwise.'

'No family that has gone to the continent or the colonies to make their fortune?' suggested Honoria with a smile.

Diana held it up to her. 'It is a London postmark, Honoria. There is nothing exotic about it.'

'No pending bequests from rich uncles?'

Diana laughed. 'Of course not. You know I have no family. And even if I did, they would not be so secretive.'

Verity smiled in triumph. 'Then it must be from an admirer. Someone is pained to see you forced into the shadows, toiling to maintain our good name. That someone wishes you a chance to better yourself. And I know just such a one. It is from Mr Dale.'

'Verity!' Diana was sure that her cheeks could not get any more pink at the thought of the man, for she could feel them burning already. 'It can be no such thing, and I forbid you to say that again. Mr Dale would have no reason to send me a large sum of money, on a whim. And even if he did, the gesture would not be kindly in the least. It would…' She struggled to think of a way to explain, one that did not confirm her worst fears about the man. 'It would be most improper. Only one sort of gentleman would offer money to a female. And only one sort of female would accept it.'

'Do you think that he means to make you his mistress?' Honoria's eyes grew wide with curiosity.

'Honoria! It is most unladylike of you to entertain that idea. But if a gentleman well outside of his dotage gave me a substantial amount like this, I would not think that it was out of concern for my future or well-being. I would return it immediately, for I would assume that he expected something in exchange for it that I did not wish to give him.'

Honoria stared at the pile of bills on the table. 'Then he would be the most cold-blooded and foolish paramour imaginable. Surely he must know that jewellery would be a better temptation, when persuading a woman to part with her honour. And to not enclose an address?' She waved her hand over the money. 'It is very difficult to demand thanks for the gift if one does not identify oneself when sending. Is he likely to make an appearance, regretfully inform you that he forgot to enclose his card when offering a *carte blanche*, and then expect you to fall at his feet? I seriously doubt it, Diana. More likely, he was moved by your situation and feared you were in need of help. But the natural shyness and reservation he displayed towards you, when talking with us, left him awkward and unsure of how best to aid you. So he posted you the contents of his purse. But he feared that you would take it just as you have suggested, and throw the money back in his face. So he gave no return address to prevent you.'

Diana dearly wished that this was the case. For it would allay her suspicions about their last meeting. But if he had truly meant to offer help, why could he not have forgone the money and renewed the offer with a note of apology and explanation?

Unless he did not wish to see her again, or lead her to believe that there was anything at all romantic about his interest in her. Her heart fell a little at the most probable truth. And then she looked back to the money and sighed. 'Well, whoever sent it, I certainly cannot keep it. They are mistaken if they think I need financial help. I am secure in my position here.'

'Until we are both married,' Verity pointed out. 'And I suppose that will happen soon. Honoria, you must make a choice from amongst your many admirers, for it is cruel to make them wait. And for me?' She sighed as well, as though the idea were a burden to her. 'There is the matter of finding an appropriate gentleman. But once I apply myself to the task…'

Diana cut short the girl's fears, for sometimes it did not sound as if Verity wished to marry at all. '*When* you settle is beside the point. You will do it when the time is right. You need not give a thought to what will happen to me after. But when you no longer need me, I have set aside a small savings that will keep me until another position can be found.'

Verity looked at the money again. 'We will not worry, for we know that you have at least thirty-four pounds. Enough for a year's worth of rainy days, right there on the table.'

It nearly doubled what she had set aside for herself. 'But I cannot keep it,' Diana said again, firmly so as to assure herself. 'It is far too much to be proper. Perhaps a deserving charity—'

'How utterly ridiculous.' Honoria's autocratic nature was showing again. 'You are worthy enough for this, Diana. And we will not allow you to get up on your high horse and give this away. Is there nothing you want? No unfulfilled dreams that might be achieved with the help of this money?'

'Dreams?' Diana resisted the urge to flinch at the word. She had worked very hard in the last ten years to rid herself of dreams. But now that the money was before her… 'No,' she said firmly. 'There is nothing.'

'There is,' Honoria said in triumph. 'I saw it in your eyes, just now.'

'It is not enough money. It hardly matters, really.'

Verity tugged her arm. 'Speak, Diana. Tell us. You know you want to.'

'A house.' Diana blurted the word. 'Just a cottage. It needn't be much. But all my own. And enough money to live in it, and know that it would be mine forever.' With a door to lock, should her father's biggest mistake ever catch up with her.

Honoria was looking at her with the eyes of one who had never known loss. 'Well. That is certainly not what I expected you to say. Not very exciting at all.'

Diana thought back to the day when they had been forced to leave her home, just minutes ahead of the arrival of the new owner, fleeing in terror of a man that she had never met. 'Excitement is not always what we expect, Honoria. It might not be pleasurable at all.'

Verity was blinking at her in confusion, with the blank look of one that had been coddled and protected her entire life. But good-hearted soul that she was, her expression quickly changed to one of sympathy and encouragement. 'How foolish of us. It is quite possible for your dreams and ours to be very different, and yet very important, is it not?' She held out her hands to her friend. 'Forgive us. If it is a cottage of your own that you wish, then there would be no harm in keeping the money, would there? Perhaps it is not enough. But surely, it could be a nest egg. You will have it on that day that you have no more silly young girls to care for.'

She looked down at the money again, letting Verity's words tempt her. Perhaps it would not be such a bad thing to hold the money for a while. At least until she could figure out who sent it. There might be a perfectly logical explanation that she had not thought of. And she would feel most foolish if she gave away a windfall that she was truly entitled to. 'You are right, I think. It does no harm to keep the money, as long as I do not mean to fritter it away on nonsense.'

'Like another trip to Bond Street?' Honoria suggested.

Which was tempting, Diana had to admit. It would be too easy to convert some of the money in front of her into a new bonnet, which was a thing she wanted, but certainly did not need. She shook her head. 'That is exactly the sort of foolishness I mean to avoid. It will be far better for us to go to the park for a time, and take some fresh air.'

Chapter Seven

Nate lifted his face to the sky, looking at the light dappling through the leaves in the trees of Hyde Park. The sun was shining bright today, and it was good to be out in it. After all the long months onboard the *Endeavor*, being burned and blinded, Nate had thought he'd had enough of the damned sunlight, and that the windowless gloom of a gaming hell was most preferable. But this morning had been different. When he'd sent the money off to Diana yesterday, he had felt the change. Even after gambling until almost dawn, he'd felt an unaccustomed lightness of spirit that had been buoyed as he'd tossed a portion of his winnings to the children begging on the street. He could not make all things right for the girl by putting a few pounds in an envelope, but at least he had done something. Perhaps, with time, he could come up with a better solution.

On the cab ride back to Hans Place, he'd signalled

the driver to let him out before the park so that he might walk the rest of the way. He needed a fresh breeze and spring sunlight on his face. He needed a change. He took a deep breath and smiled. This was what he needed: to walk in daylight like a normal man, instead of creeping home with the dawn and sleeping through the day. Even if it was just for the morning, he needed some proof that his life could be changeable, like the weather. A sign that he was on the cusp of a new season.

'Mr Dale!' The voice of Verity Carlow cut through him like a sugar-coated knife and reality came crashing back. It had been foolhardiness itself to attempt a walk through Hyde Park at this hour, when anyone might be taking the morning air. And if Miss Carlow was present, then that must mean…

He turned towards the voice with a pained smile. 'Lady Verity. And Lady Honoria. And Miss Price as well. How good to see you all.'

The ladies made their curtseys, and Verity addressed him again. 'And you as well, Mr Dale. It is just as I suspected. We are destined to meet.'

'Yes. I suspect it is our fate.' Damn that Gypsy. 'You are all well, I trust?'

'Very much so, sir.'

He glanced over at Diana Price, who seemed to be going pink in the early morning sun. 'And you, Miss Price, are better, I trust?'

'Better?' She looked at him curiously, with a slight smile. 'I do not recall being ill.'

Damn again. He had been thinking of the money, and

the difference it would make to her future. He should
know nothing of it, or what was the point of anonymity?
'Well, I mean. Well, as well. As well, as Lady Verity.
That is to say. Also well.' And now the words were
hopelessly tangled. He allowed them to trail into
silence.

The younger of the sisters gave a small giggle and
Lady Honoria said, 'We are going, after our walk, to
Bond Street so that Miss Price might buy a new gown.'

'Or perhaps not.' Miss Price seemed to be of two
minds on the subject, no matter how Honoria felt about
it. And then, she turned back to him. 'And in answer to
your question: Yes, thank you. I am most well. And you,
sir?'

He was in hell. Suffering the torment of giggling
debutantes and their dark-eyed companions. 'Fine also,
thank you.'

And that should have been all that was required of
him. But Lady Verity chose that moment to spy
someone over her shoulder. 'Penelope and Charlotte
Veryan are just down the path. I have been meaning to
speak with them for ages. And Honoria, you have as
well.'

'I have?' Lady Honoria seemed surprised by the fact.

Her sister seized her by the sleeve. 'Of course you
have. Now come along immediately, or we will miss
them. You do not mind walking a ways with Miss Price,
do you sir?'

Nate's head ducked beneath his collar, and without
thinking, he turned away, to make sure that the Veryan

sisters did not spot him, even in profile. He could not remember if they'd even existed at the time of the scandal, but it seemed unwise to give them a reason to take a description of him back to their father, Lord Keddinton of the Home Office.

The man was the number one spy catcher in the country, and had made a good part of his reputation on the disgrace and hanging of the Earl of Leybourne. God knew what he would do if he realized that Nathan Wardale had resurfaced and was sniffing about the Carlow family. He smiled at Verity and then at Diana, and lied through his teeth. 'Do I mind the company of Miss Price? Not at all.' In truth, it was almost as awkward as a meeting with the Veryans.

Almost, but not quite. And since the Carlow girls were gone as soon as the words were out of his mouth, he could not very well run off like a rabbit and leave Diana alone. He turned to look at her.

She must have seen the helpless confusion on his face, for she gave a short laugh. 'Really, Mr Dale. It cannot be as bad as all that to be forced into my company. You are free to go, if you wish.'

He hung his head, embarrassed to have been caught in the thought. 'Forgive me, Miss Price. It is not your company that concerns me. Well, not precisely. It is just that—' He broke off, before he told her any more of the truth and ruined everything. 'I must apologize for yesterday's conversation. I am sure that my excessive curiosity was most inappropriate. But I meant nothing by it.'

'Then I shall take nothing from it.' She smiled at him with obvious charity. But was there a touch of disappointment in her eyes. Why would that be? Unless she had enjoyed his interest in her and wished it to be more than polite small talk.

Then he realized that he had allowed a gap in the conversation, as he'd stood dumbstruck, trying to fathom what she might be thinking. So he cleared his throat, and said with a smile, 'And now, I am behaving strangely again, I think.'

She nodded. 'That is the way, sometimes. If one is by nature reticent, or unaccustomed to speaking with those of the opposite gender, then conversation can be difficult.'

She thought him shy did she? And awkward around women? The idea was so ludicrous that he almost laughed in response. It would not do for one so pretty as Diana Price to think him unable to talk to women. There were any number of ladies who could assure her that he was most charming. He was certain he had heard the word irresistible used on several occasions. 'That is not the…' And then he realized that the sort of women he normally conversed with could hardly be called ladies. And that there was a perfectly obvious reason that he found it so difficult to talk to Diana Price. But that he could not very well explain it to her. And so he allowed the untruth to stand, gave a shrug and added, 'It is far too difficult to explain.'

She smiled in encouragement. 'If you wish to attempt it, you will find me a most receptive listener.'

And there it was again. A sparkle in her eye and a hint that she would welcome his interest. He cast her a sidelong glance. 'I imagine you are skilled in that as well, since you are a professional companion.'

She nodded, making no effort to speak. Even in her silence, she was teasing him, and he relaxed enough to smile back. Without thinking about it, he turned and gestured to the path, away from Verity and Honoria. They began to walk, falling easily into step with each other. 'Perhaps I could persuade you to speak. It would be much easier for me to ask about you than to explain myself. Tell me more about yourself, Miss Price.'

She seemed just as surprised as he had been to have the conversation turned back to her. 'There is not much to tell that you have not already heard. I have been tending to the needs of others since I was seventeen. I believe we discussed it, when last we met.'

'And before that?' he asked gently.

She paused, and he wondered if it might stir some rancour or sadness in her. But her pace stayed as placid as it had been. 'I had an unremarkable childhood. My mother died when I was seven. There were no other children.' She gave a small frown. 'My father was very loving, but not particularly wise. He lost his fortune and our home, and I was forced to seek employment.' She glanced at him, quickly. 'That is not to say I did not love him very much. Or that he was not good to me, except in that one thing.'

'Of course.' He rushed to say it. 'But sometimes,

when a man is a gambler, he does not realize what he has done until after.'

She looked up sharply. 'I did not say he was a gambler.'

'You did not?' Of course she hadn't. And how was he to explain that bit of knowledge? 'I am so sorry if I assumed incorrectly. But that is frequently the cause of sudden reversals of fortune amongst gentlemen.'

She sighed. 'You guessed correctly, Mr Dale. But the problem was long ago, and hardly concerns me, truly. It has not been a bad life, not really. After the night he lost the house…my father ceased gambling.'

There was an odd pause in the middle of the sentence that made Nate wonder how much she knew about what had truly happened.

'After he saw me safely employed, he went North for a time. But he visited me frequently. Our lives were harder than they had been, of course.' She smiled at him, the lines on her face smoothing to tranquillity. 'But better. Everything was so much better, once he put down the cards for the last time.'

Did she know the reason for her father's sudden abstinence? If she did not know the full truth, then perhaps she felt Nathan Wardale had done her a service by ruining her father. But he knew exactly what had happened, and would never feel right on the matter. 'So it ended well, then. That is good to know.'

She turned her head and smiled fondly back at Verity and Honoria. 'I have been quite happy with the Carlows. And I shall be most glad to see them make matches. Their brother, Lord Stanegate, has recently found a wife. Perhaps it will inspire them.'

He smiled. 'Marc is the first of us to marry, then. But he is at that time in life when a man must consider his future.'

'You knew him as a child, you said?'

'Yes. He was a bit younger than me. Still is, younger of course.'

'And already married.'

And it was obvious the direction the conversation had taken. Without meaning to, he was half way to offering for the girl. Which could have been a fine thing, since she was delightful. She would have been perfect for him, if she had been any other woman in the world. And if perhaps, he was a different man.

He reached into his pocket for a handkerchief to mop at the sweat he could feel springing out on his forehead, and heard a small thump as something fell from his coat and onto the ground at their feet.

And there, before them, was the little volume of poetry from Diana Price's bedroom, her ribbon still marking the place. Without thinking, he must have put it in his pocket on leaving the room.

Being the helpful sort of person that she was, Diana looked down at the thing, then stooped to pick it up. 'You seem to have dropped something, Mr Dale.' And then, she saw the title. 'Shakespeare?' she exclaimed. 'Is he a favourite of yours?'

'Yes. I like him very much.'

'I do as well. I used to have my own copy of the

sonnets, and read it many times. But it has been so long.'

Of course she had. And here was her own hair ribbon in the same place she had left it, waiting to be recognized. He held his breath, expecting the moment of revelation. But it passed. For she opened the book, paging through it and removing the ribbon, tucking it to the back. It was a plain thing of blue satin, much like many others, he assumed. She was examining the book as though the marker held no special meaning. 'This is even the same edition I remember.'

'You must take it then.'

'That is not necessary,' she rushed to assure him. 'If I wished, the library…'

'It is hardly anything.' To give back something that had given her pleasure? That was less than nothing, for it only brought them closer to being even. But when he searched his heart, he knew that it was right, for it made him feel better to do it, even knowing that she might recognize the thing. 'Please. I insist. It is not new. But I would be honoured to part with it, if you enjoy it.' He reached out without thinking, and clasped Diana's hands to press the book into them. They were well shaped, tiny in his, smooth and warm in their kid leather gloves. He looked into her eyes which were shining bright with happiness.

And her gaze dropped demurely to the open book in front of her and the place where their hands were joined. 'The age of the book is not important. The words in it are just as true as they ever were. Thank you.'

So much joy from something so small. And the smile on her face made him feel like a Galahad. As long as the moment was taken out of context. Because otherwise… He looked up, desperate for a distraction. 'Ahh. I see the ladies are returning from their visit.' And not a moment too soon. He stepped hurriedly away from Diana and raised a hand to hail them.

The girls came back to them, in an obvious state of excitement. 'Diana,' Verity said breathlessly, 'the most wonderful news.'

Honoria continued, 'We have been invited to a party at Lord Davering's. Everyone of consequence will be there, I am sure. And we are to accompany Lord Keddinton and his daughters.'

And Nate watched as, without thinking, Diana forgot the book in her hand and the man in front of her, and dropped easily back into her role as chaperone. 'Would this by any chance be a card party?' She must know very well that it was, for the Davering parties were well on their way to being notorious.

'Small stakes only,' Verity insisted. 'A few hands of casino in the lady's room would do us no harm, surely.'

'A few hands?' Diana raised an eyebrow. 'It seldom stops at that.'

'It is nothing,' Honoria argued. 'Lord Keddinton is Verity's godfather. He does not think it improper, or he would not allow his daughters to go. And all the other girls—'

'Can do just as they please,' said Diana, closing the book in her hand with a snap. 'But they will do it without your help. You are not going to a card party, and that is my final word on the subject.'

And now, the girls turned to Nate, who took an involuntary step back as the combined weight of their charm was turned upon him. 'Mr Dale?' Honoria all but batted her lashes. 'Surely you can help us persuade Miss Price that it is nothing to be afraid of. She is tremendously silly on the subject of cards. She will not even let us play for buttons, when we are at home.'

'And if you accompanied us, as well?' Verity smiled. 'Then I am sure no harm would come to us.'

'No!' His denial shocked everyone with its suddenness, himself included. But the old swine, Davering, had learned of his reputation, and kept inviting him to those damned parties, hoping he would be the centrepiece of a night's play. What kind of a man would find amusement in watching his friends lose at cards? He gave the girls a stern look. 'Under no circumstances would you see me at such an event.'

The girls' faces crumpled in disappointment.

He took a breath, collected himself and said, 'I am sorry for the sharpness of my tone. But I am afraid I must agree with Miss Price on this matter. I do not attend such parties because I abhor gambling, and I would never encourage the activity for young ladies that I value as friends. You would do well to listen to your companion on the subject and shun anyone that encourages you to do otherwise.' He glanced up at the sky to read the time by the sun. It was late, and he had grown tired to the point of speaking nonsense. 'And now, if you will excuse me, I fear I must be going. Good day to you.' And he turned and walked away.

'How unspeakably odd,' Verity said, watching his sudden retreat.

'That you should try to coerce the man into escorting you to a party, instead of waiting for an offer? Your behaviour was shameful, both of you.' And utterly mortifying. Had their forwardness shocked him? Or worse yet, suppose he had seen through the obvious ruse of getting round the chaperone by tempting her with the diversion of his company? Either possibility was quite embarrassing. And it had all been going so well.

'But it does nothing to convince me that he doesn't fancy our Diana,' Verity added. 'See how quickly he came to her defence against us.'

'And more proof of how well they might suit,' Honoria agreed. 'His reaction towards a little card game was every bit as adamant as yours, Diana.'

And he had been so vehement that Diana wondered if there was more to it than just an interest in her approval. Was his past as scarred as hers, that he was so violently opposed to cards? A father, or perhaps a brother, lost to the game?

She felt a little fluttering in her heart at the thought. For although she did not wish him ill, if there was a greater proof that they would suit, she did not know what it could be. Today's visit had shown both a shared dislike and a shared pleasure. She held tightly to the book in her hands, and could not help smiling.

'And see how it has affected her.' Verity was positively grinning. 'It appears we shall not be able to orchestrate a meeting over the card table. But surely there will be another opportunity for us to make this match, Honoria.'

And should the opportunity occur, Diana doubted that she would resist their efforts.

'Well if she means to be courted, then she had best have a new gown,' Honoria said. 'Now that we have had our exercise, Diana, may we please go to Bond Street?'

Diana stared off in the direction that Mr Dale had disappeared, giving the book in her hands an affectionate squeeze. 'And perhaps after, we shall go to Gunter's for ices. Just this once.'

Nathan hurried down the path, out of sight of the ladies, the sweat on his brow turning cold with the early March air. And as he walked, there was the sound of masculine laughter, just behind him.

He turned to see the Gypsy leaning against a nearby tree. 'So you abhor gambling, do you?' Beshaley's grin was positively evil. 'It amazes me that you were able to say that aloud and with a straight face.'

The same thought had occurred to him, even as the words had left his mouth. He could not very well have let them go to Davering's. A misstep in such company would be the ruin of those poor girls. But neither would he offer explanation where none was deserved, lest it give the Gypsy something to use later against the Carlow girls.

Instead, he kept the focus upon himself. 'I did not choose my profession out of any great love for cards. I am sure you must know that many terrible things become palatable, once one's need is great enough.'

There was the slightest twitch at the corner of Stephano's mouth, as though he might know the truth of that even better than Nate. Nate filed the information away, hoping it could be ammunition of his own.

And then he smiled. 'If your object in troubling me was to see me make a fool of myself, then I hope you are satisfied. Not only did I tell a boldfaced lie, I gave her that damned book.'

And now the Gypsy grinned at him, and he cursed himself for saying too much. 'Do you think you can gain forgiveness for what you have done to her with such a paltry gift?'

'I think nothing of the kind. The book was an accident. I was reading it, and must have put it in my pocket. When she said that it was a personal favourite, what else could I do?'

He could have claimed it as his own and then put it away. Instead, he had stood there like a love-struck fool, and pressed the thing into her hands. But it would serve nothing to announce the fact to his opponent. So he gave Stephano a disinterested smile, as though what Diana Price might know or think meant very little to him. 'I doubt it shall be a problem. She was grateful, of course. But I do not plan to see her again to discuss the contents.'

The Gypsy gave him an enigmatic smile. 'I am glad

you have such confidence in plans, Nathan. It is probably because yours have been so successful in the past.' And with that, he turned and walked away.

Chapter Eight

'Diana, another letter has arrived for you.' Honoria brought the morning's post into the small dining room, with even more glee than she had shown two days ago.

'Is this one full of bank notes?' Verity asked hopefully.

Honoria gave the letter a practiced squeeze. 'Too thin. I would guess that it is single sheet.'

'Too bad. Then we shan't persuade her to go shopping.'

'Much more likely, it is a love note from Mr Dale.'

'Give it here.' Diana said more sharply than she had intended, for she did not want to show unseemly interest.

'Not until you promise to tell us of the contents.' Honoria held the thing just out of reach.

'If I feel that the contents are likely to be of interest to you, then of course I will share them.'

This seemed to satisfy Honoria, for she handed the

letter over, still crowding so close that Diana had to step back if she wished any privacy.

Miss Price,
Meet me again today at ten o'clock, in the place
where we last met. I have a matter of importance
I wish to discuss with you. Please come alone.

Another cryptic note. It was not signed. But she smiled, for she could easily imagine that the word Nathan had been omitted from the bottom of the page.

He wanted to meet her. Alone. This time there would be no pretence that he was interested in the Carlow sisters. It would be just the two of them, walking down the path in the park. She clutched the paper to her breast so that no one could see the words.

'Well?' Honoria still stood expectantly before her.

'It is nothing.' And that was an enormous lie. For in a few words, it was everything. 'Of no concern to you, anyway.' Much closer to the truth. For she did not want to share the message any more than she wished to share Nathan Dale. Even if it was just for one meeting, he would be hers alone, and so would the secret be.

Honoria smiled knowingly. 'I do not think you have to tell us, for the look in your eyes says enough. It is from Mr Dale, and the words are sweet. When you are ready, perhaps when we are all old and have children of our own, you must show us.' She reached out and enveloped Diana in a hug. 'But for now, all we need to know is that you are happy.'

Diana dressed carefully to prepare for the meeting and wished for a moment that she still had the fancy day dresses she had owned in her youth. It was a curse to be as sensible as she had become, for it showed in her wardrobe. And when she had finally allowed herself an extravagance on their last outing, what had she been thinking, to let Honoria persuade her to buy a dinner gown? It would have been far better to purchase one or two simple dresses, and some ribbons to refresh her tired bonnet. The green silk dress she had chosen instead would make it appear that she was trying to outshine the Carlows, should she wear it in public.

Although sometimes, it was nice to be noticed. She glanced in the mirror, smoothing her hair, and tying the sad bonnet ribbons into a creditable bow. Perhaps her plain appearance did not matter to him. He had taken the time to discover that today was her day free of duties, without bothering to ask her. He must be more than a little interested in the woman under the bonnet to take the trouble.

She walked to the park, doing her best to maintain an even pace, to arrive neither too early, nor late. It might not be that unusual for a young woman to walk alone in the park, but it would be too far outside normal decorum to appear to be loitering there.

But it was not necessary to be concerned. For at exactly ten o'clock, she saw him striding down the path in her direction in a purposeful way, as though he were no more interested in being caught lingering than she was.

'Mr Dale.'

She could tell he'd recognized her voice, for his head snapped up at the sound of it, looking for the source. But his face did not hold the welcoming smile. Instead he wore a look of alarm. His bright green eyes had a trapped quality, as though she were the last person he expected to be meeting.

And now, he was smiling as though he thought it possible to disguise his initial reaction. 'Miss Price. What a coincidence to see you again, so soon.'

'Coincidence?' Something was very wrong. Perhaps she had misread the date on the note. But more likely, she had jumped to a conclusion as to the sender. She could feel the blush rising on her cheek and ducked her head hoping it was not too late to hide it from him. 'You are clearly in a hurry. Please, give me no mind, for I would not detain you. Good day.' And she made to pass, hoping that he would think she also had somewhere to go.

'Wait.' He reached out and caught her arm before she could get away, and the warmth of his fingers seemed to sink through the cloth of her gown. He was smiling sympathetically at her, as though he could sense her confusion and wished to put her at ease. 'This is not a chance encounter, is it? You do not seem at all surprised to see me.'

'I thought that you wished… But obviously not…' And now she was sure she must be crimson, gone past embarrassment and into mortification. 'I am sorry. I should go.' She turned from him again, looking desperately back up the path that would take her towards the Carlows' town house.

He renewed his grip on her arm. 'Please, wait. There is something wrong, isn't there? Explain it to me.'

She reached into her reticule for the note, and closed her eyes as she handed it to him. 'What must you think of me? I swear, I am not normally given to meeting alone with gentlemen. But I thought if it was you it would not be so wrong.'

'It is not signed.' He said it very reasonably, as though it surprised him that she could not see something so obvious.

'I know.' Without opening her eyes, she said, 'It was not from you, was it?'

'No, it was not,' he admitted.

She opened her eyes again, and gave a little shrug to hide her embarrassment. 'And now, I look a fool for jumping to such conclusions, based on an unsigned note that is obviously some sort of prank.'

He sighed, but then smiled back at her. 'I think it was a perfectly honest mistake. We had a lovely conversation when we were here before, did we not? And it was interrupted when I hurried off.'

'Yes.' She pursed her lips and tapped the letter with her fingers. 'But I am very angry with the girls, for I suspect that they are in some way involved with this.'

'You do?' He seemed a little surprised by the idea. But it was probably just that he did not wish to think ill of ladies. 'I suppose that is the most logical explanation.'

He was allowing her the benefit of the doubt,

although he did not seem convinced. So she added, 'Of course, it does appear to be in a man's writing.'

He nodded. 'I do not blame you for your mistake, for it is rather like my hand. It appears Lady Honoria had an accomplice. A footman, perhaps?'

She thought for a moment to correct him on the likelihood of a footman having such a fine hand or for that matter, being able to write at all. 'Although it is just the sort of trick Honoria might play, if she meant to try to get around me. She must have got Peters or Richards to help her. Or maybe it was John the coachman.' She gave the paper a little rattle, hoping that rough handling of it now might make it less obvious that she had pored over the thing, reading and rereading, searching for a happy meaning to a few short words.

And then, his hand covered hers to still their movement. 'No matter. If I had a pen, I would solve it all by putting my name at the bottom of it and pretending that it came from me.'

And his smile was so warm and his touch so comforting that she felt her hand begin to relax. 'But you did not mean to see me.'

'That does not imply that I do not take pleasure at the meeting.'

'Thank you, sir.' And then, she added impulsively, 'And I enjoyed talking with you, as well.'

'Then it is settled. We are both glad to be out in the park on a lovely spring day. Especially after such a hard winter. Let us walk a ways together.'

When she looked up his eyes seemed very green, and

staring down at her with an intensity that made her heart jump. And she remembered that their meeting was not really proper. She should have separated from him after the briefest of greetings. 'I am afraid it is not wise for us to be seen together. It might appear to some that we are having an assignation.'

He smiled, for he must have realized that that was exactly what she had been expecting. 'I have always thought it more a proof of the small minds around us, that they can be so eager to think ill of a lady of good character, such as yourself. But if it puts your mind at ease, we will keep to the less-travelled paths, away from prying eyes.'

And that was exactly what she should have feared. A man who was less than a gentleman would take advantage of such privacy. But surely, Mr Dale was not such a one. So she said, 'Thank you for your understanding. Perhaps I am overly sensitive. Since it is my job to guard the reputations of others, I work very hard to set an example to them by my own behaviour.'

'Then I will take care to do nothing that is beneath reproach,' he said, offering her his arm.

She tucked the note back into her reticule, then reached out gingerly to put her hand upon the crook of his elbow. He turned and guided her off the main path. And then he said, 'What shall we talk of today? Poetry, perhaps? For if it is a shared interest…'

'No,' she said firmly. 'Today, I wish you to tell me something of yourself. For you have managed to ferret information from me that I would not usually tell a stranger. It is hardly fair. You must give me something in return.'

He thought on it for a moment, and a strange expression crossed his face. 'I suppose that is true. I must tell you about myself. Although, I am afraid that the story will not be pleasant.' And his arm tightened against hers, tucking her hand close to his side. 'I hardly know where to begin.'

She gave an encouraging squeeze to his arm. 'Begin with your family, then. Are they living? Or are you alone?' *Like me.* She had almost added the words, but did not wish it to seem that she was searching for more similarities.

'My father is…dead. He died when I was just a boy.' That seemed a difficult admission, and she wondered: had they been so close that it still grieved him?

'And what of your mother?'

'I have not seen her for many years, nor my sisters.'

'You are estranged from them?'

'Not by my doing, I assure you. I pray daily for their welfare.' It touched her heart that he looked so distressed that she might think him capable of abandoning them. It was just another example of his tender heart.

His eyes fell. 'After Father's death, there were difficulties. Our finances were strained. We children took employment, and each contributed to the family's welfare as best we could. But one night, when I was returning from…work. I was set upon by a press gang.'

'You were in the Navy, then?' It explained the commanding way he stood, as though the earth could move under him and he would not stagger.

He gave a sad smile. 'You make it sound very heroic. I was there against my will. Off the coast of France, and then the Americas. I spent the first months—sick as a dog from the motion of the water—trying desperately to contact my family, to explain why I could not come home to them. But I do not think the letters found them, for there was no response.'

'It must have been horrible, not knowing.'

His mouth made a bitter line. 'Six years of my life, wasted.' And then he looked at her, his eyes sombre. 'And this is where you will see me for the sort of man I truly am. For when I finally got the opportunity, I jumped ship.'

'You are a deserter?' She almost released his arm. For it was most shocking, and not at all in keeping with the man she was convinced that he was.

'Do you blame me? The law that took me was for trained seamen. It was never meant to drag inexperienced men to sea against their will so that they could lose the King's ration of bread and grog over the side whenever the ship crested a wave. I was a terrible sailor, from the day they took me to the day I ran.' He opened his hands, staring into the palms. 'Look here. See the scars? This is where I lost my grip on the sheets, and the rope near skinned my hands. I could show you the marks of the flogging I got for that, as well. And the places where the sun burned my skin to blisters. It was a hard life, and I was glad to be rid of it.'

'But to run away…' It was so different from what

she expected from him that she hardly knew what to think.

'They had no right to take me, and their callous stupidity jeopardized the safety of my family. God only knows what happened to them, without my protection.' He frowned. 'I tell myself that my sisters are most likely married, with families of their own by now. But I know that is probably a lie. And it is a shame. For over the years my fortunes have changed much. If I could but find them, I could support them in luxury and quite make up for the hardship I left them in.'

And knowing the sort of things that might happen to a woman alone, or even through the carelessness of one such as her father, she had to agree. 'You were right to worry, and I can understand your actions in trying to get back to them. But to live under the stigma of desertion cannot be easy. Perhaps if you appealed to the Admiralty, they would give you a proper discharge.'

'Perhaps. My claim is legitimate. But I have, shall we say, a certain lack of faith in the English courts. They have never been a friend to my family. And while the law clearly states that I am in the right, it would be scant comfort to have that as an epitaph, should they decide to execute me for desertion. Once I earned enough money in Boston to pay for a passage home, it seemed easier just to start anew. And mask my identity.'

The pause now was a long one, until he was sure that she understood. 'I am not at all the sort of man you might think me, Miss Price. Not in behaviour. Not even in name.'

Perhaps she did not know him as well as she thought.

Yet, when she looked into his eyes, and felt his hand on hers, she was sure she did. 'It does not matter.' She reached out with her other hand, and laid it upon his sleeve, giving his arm a reassuring squeeze that seemed to startle him.

He put his other hand on her shoulder. 'I did not wish for my story to sound like a morbid attempt to garner your sympathy.'

'I did not think you did. But it is a tragic story, all the same. It is all right. Your life has been difficult. You have done the best you could with it. I understand.'

He pulled free of her grasp and slipped his arm around her waist. 'You do not know how much your words mean to me, Miss Price. They are like a balm upon the old wounds. And I had never thought to hear them from your lips.' And with that, he pulled her close and kissed her.

The moment seemed to go on forever. But perhaps it was because she closed her eyes and held her breath, as if she could keep very still and hold time in place. She had spent much of the recent years interrupting such attempts by Honoria's suitors and thwarting their few successes. But at some point, years ago, she had quite given up the dream that a moment like this would ever come to her. And now that it had, she felt quite remorseful for depriving Honoria of the joy of it. For to feel the rough of his cheek brushing against hers, and the firm warmth of his hand, his breath upon her face, the softness of his mouth and the barest touch of his tongue against her lips was pure heaven.

And then he pulled his head away from hers, and

looked hurriedly around to make sure that they were alone on the path and that none had seen what they had done. He took his hand from her waist, laid a finger under her chin, and said, with a nervous smile, 'I am sorry. I did not intend to take that liberty. But your absolution moved me more than I could resist. Thank you.' He squeezed her hand again, and then released it and stepped back.

She was quite at a loss. For what was she to say in a moment like this? Pretending outrage was quite impossible, but asking him to repeat the action was very wrong as well. And she was sure that her cheeks must be flaming scarlet.

He smiled down at her. 'Miss Price?'

'Mr Dale.' She touched her hand to her bosom, as though she were trying to catch her breath after strenuous exercise.

He tipped his head, waiting for her to clarify her feelings. 'Are you all right, then? Can you forgive me that as well?'

And she struggled again, taking in a huge breath and letting it out in a sigh. Then she smiled at him. 'That was the most miraculous thing, was it not?'

He grinned back at her. 'For you as well?'

'Perhaps it was only because I have no knowledge of such things. I did not know what to expect. It was my first kiss, you see.'

He was still smiling quite broadly at her. 'I would be lying if I said any such thing about myself. But if it gives you comfort to know, that was quite different from an ordinary kiss. I wonder, have I gained skill since the last time, or do you have undeveloped talents? Or was that an unusual occurrence?' He looked around again, making absolutely sure they were alone. 'Let us try an experiment.' And without further warning, he pulled her off the path, behind a nearby oak. Then he leaned in and kissed her again.

This time, his lips were still as gentle but he placed his hands on her shoulders in such a businesslike way that it felt rather like a scientific study of the kiss. He took the time to adjust his position to an angle that was most pleasurable. Then he pulled away, looked speculatively at her, as though he meant to catalogue her response, and held the pose until it made her laugh.

Then he laughed as well, and kissed her again, more quickly and less expertly, and she sighed and wrapped her arms about his neck, hugging him to herself.

When they parted this time, his piercing green eyes were less focused, and the smile on his lips was of a man well satisfied. He gave a sensible straightening of his coat and smoothed a few loose hairs from around her face, making sure that her bonnet sat squarely upon her head and showed no signs of disturbance. Then he tucked her arm tightly into the crook of his, peeked around the corner of the tree to make sure that they were still unobserved, and led her back out onto the path, so that they might walk together, side by side, as though nothing had happened.

He looked out over the park, as though making small talk, and said, 'This has been a most interesting morning, Miss Price. And most unexpected. I think that further experimentation will be necessary.'

'And I think, with things as they are between us, Nathan, that you should call me Diana.'

He stopped dead in the path, and pulled his arm from hers, the smug smile disappearing from his face. 'How did you know my name?'

'Your name?'

'My given name. Because I am sure that I never used it in your presence.'

She took a step back, even more confused by this than she had been from the kisses. If his behaviour toward her this morning did not render them close enough for first names, then she truly did not know him as well as she ought. 'It was written upon the note you left for Lord Stanegate. You did not seal it. I suppose it is horrible of me to admit the fact, but I read the contents. I was only trying to assure myself that the matter was not serious.' She coloured in embarrassment. For she had all but forgotten the note and her indiscretion in reading it.

Instead of aggravated, he looked strangely relieved. 'That is all, then? But of course. It makes perfect sense.'

'Then you forgive me for prying?' For his anger was gone as quickly as it had come. 'If it is any assurance to you, Marc already knows the fact you wished to relay.'

'Marc, is it? You call him by his first name as well?'

She had expected him to question her further about the note. But she could see by the blazing look in his eyes that he was much more concerned with the reason for such familiarity with another man.

Who had ever noticed or cared about such a thing in regards to her? She could not think of a time when she had been the sole focus of a man's attention, and the thought sent a small thrill through her. 'I call him by name because I have known him for years. He is deeply concerned for the welfare of his sisters. And since his father is unwell, he has taken it upon himself to act as their guardian.'

He seemed to relax a little. 'Then you two are not—'

'Certainly not. He is my employer. And a happily married man. He would never…nor would I,' she added quickly, straightening her dress as though there were some way to retrace the last few minutes to prove to him that she was of better character.

'I am a jealous fool.' He said it softly as though it were some great personal revelation. Then he looked up at her again. 'Please forgive me. I am not usually prone to strange suspicions, baseless jealousy nor sudden rudeness.' He paused. 'Of course, until today, I was not prone to kissing young ladies in the park.'

'If you did not wish…'

He held up a hand. 'Let us start again. Or at least go back to the moment where you meant to call me Nathan and I was to call you Diana. Things were really going quite well, before that moment.' And then he smiled at her, full of mischief and shared secrets.

He held out his arm to her again, and they walked together, side by side down the path. And it occurred to her that their companionable silence was almost as

good as the kissing had been, for it made her feel close
to him, as though they were so much alike that words
were no longer necessary. The little fillip of jealousy at
the end of their encounter and his speedy apology for
it stood as a proof that he was engaged deeply enough
to want her all for himself. As did the lingering way he
released her hand when they reached the end of the path
and it was time for her to return to the Carlows—as
though he had no wish to let her go.

And she realized that she had no idea what to say
upon parting. Was it rude to seem eager for another
meeting? And where could it be? She certainly could
not go to his rooms, nor could she give him leave to call
upon her, since she had no place of her own.

But he understood. For he said, 'I suppose I must
leave you now, Miss Price. *Au revoir?*'

She gave him an embarrassed smile, and nodded.

'Perhaps we can meet again in the park. Next week
at this time?'

'I would like that. Very much.'

'Very good. I shall write to you on the day, to remind
you of our appointment.'

As if it would be possible for her to forget.

'And this time, I shall sign my name, so you shall know
that it is really me.' His smile was teasing. He reached for
her hand, bowed and brought the fingers to his lips, kissing
the air above them in the most proper way imaginable.

As she turned to cross the street towards home, she
could feel him behind her, watching her progress.

Chapter Nine

When Nate returned to his house, the rooms seemed brighter than he remembered. Perhaps it was because he usually slept so late that he did not often see them in full daylight. Or perhaps the sun was higher in the sky, now that winter was passing.

Or perhaps it was because he could not seem to stop smiling.

As he had watched Diana go back toward the Carlow house, he felt his lungs tighten. He had the most foolish desire that she should remove her bonnet as she walked, so that he might see the sunlight shine on her dark hair, or catch one more glimpse of her departing face as she went around the corner. Even the thought of that made him smile all the more. What a miracle she was. And what an impossible idea that she would walk bare-headed down the street, with her hair blowing in the wind.

Of course, all his thoughts involving Diana Price

were impossible ones, and his position had just become more difficult than he could possibly imagine. He had avoided her for so long, thinking a meeting to be somewhere between ill advised and disastrous. And now?

He had discovered his soulmate. Her sympathy towards him, the gentle touch of her hands, was like nothing he'd known. And he'd never suspected that she would be so beautiful, so graceful and so easy to converse with. After his confession to her, he'd limited his talk to the most innocent of topics, and she had hung on every word, as though he were profoundly interesting. He had meant to tell her the rest and make a clean breast of it. But with such a woman at his side the past was easily forgotten. And soon, it would become impossible to imagine a future without her. There was only one small thing standing between them and happiness.

Nathan Wardale.

What good had that man ever done for either of them? Diana most assuredly would not want to see the fellow. And he'd been more trouble to Nate than he was worth. It was Wardale that had explaining to do, should the Navy ever come calling. And Wardale was the one living with the taint of his father's disgrace.

Wardale had lost his sisters and mother as well, damn him. If there was some way to find the women in his family, then it might be time to reclaim the name. If he thought that his sisters would see the news and come to him? Then it might be worth having Nathan Wardale risk arrest and appear in public.

But he was not even sure that they lived, or that they would wish a meeting with him, after the way he had abandoned them. When he'd returned, his inquiries after them had gotten no response. A louder, more obvious appearance, after all this time, was just as likely to upset the lives of his sisters than to benefit them.

And it would upset Diana as well. If she thought of him at all, she must wish Wardale were dead. If they lived, his sisters must think him dead as well. They had probably finished grieving for him long ago. It would hardly be a fresh loss to them, should Nate Dale put a permanent end to him.

There was the problem of his profession, of course. Diana had no tolerance for gambling, and he could hardly blame her. But he need not continue in it, if he did not wish. He had lived with the nagging feeling at the back of his mind that his gambling was somehow the fault of the Gypsy woman and that he could not stop. But he had never really tried, had he?

Beshaley had said the success of the curse was a result of his faith in it, and nothing more. So from this moment on, Nate would choose not to believe. He would put aside the gaming. He glanced around him. He would have to give up the house as well. He would put the town house up for sale and remove to his home in the country, where no one knew the source of his income. Everything about his life would be new and different.

With the last trace of his old life erased, he would be free to marry.

It would be difficult for the current servants, of course. Perhaps he could arrange for the new owner to take them on. Many of them had known this place as their home for much longer than he had. He would make it easy on them if he could. But it could not be helped. He could not bring Diana back to her own home, with the butler knowing its master's full history, and expect the facts to remain concealed from her.

And that same butler appeared before him now, in a state of agitation. 'Sir. The drawing room,' he said breathlessly. 'A gentleman. I could not prevent him…'

The tone of the last made it clear that in the opinion of the butler, the *gentleman* was no gentleman at all. Perhaps it was an acquaintance from the Fourth Circle. Dante Jones had never visited him, and few others would have the gall to follow him and learn his residence. But if someone had, it was all the more reason for him to leave this place behind and start a fresh life with Diana somewhere else. 'Do not concern yourself. I will deal with him,' he said, putting the poor man at ease. It was not the first time he had needed to clear the riff-raff from his doorstep, but he was certain it would be the last. He strode with confidence down the hall towards the drawing room door, flexing the muscles under his coat.

And when he entered, there was Stephano Beshaley, drinking by the fire as though he owned the house himself. He was arrayed in a tatty green coat with tarnished brass buttons, striped trousers, and had a bright scarf tied about his dark hair, and a huge gold ring gleaming from his left ear. Quite out of character for the neighbourhood. And for Beshaley as well, he suspected. It seemed that he had gone out of his way to dress as a comic-opera Gypsy before forcing his way in through the front door.

Beshaley smiled at him as he entered, but did not bother to rise. 'Nathan. Old friend.' The bastard had the nerve to salute him with a glass of his own brandy.

'What are you doing here? You should know you are not welcome in my house.'

'Your house?' The Gypsy seemed to find this amusing.

'My house,' Nathan affirmed, giving him the same blank expression he used when at the gaming tables.

'Considering how long we have known each other, I did not think that your door would ever be closed to me.'

'Since you come here to threaten, you can assume that the door is closed. What do you want with me now?'

'Merely to congratulate you. I observed you in the park with Miss Price. Young love. Touching, Nathan. Truly touching.' The Gypsy gave a mocking sigh and put his hand over his heart. 'It did my soul good to see it.'

'You saw?' Nate's composure faltered. He had seen no one on the path after his spectacular lapse in judgment. It had given him the false sense of security that had caused him to kiss her again.

'Did I see? Every moment of your time together. And heard your sad story as well.'

He had been a fool to promise her safety, while opening the door to public disgrace. Especially as he remembered the reason for the meeting. 'You arranged it all, didn't you?' Nate pointed an accusing finger at the man sitting before him.

'And how would I have done that?' Beshaley gave an innocent shrug that in no way matched his evil grin.

'You saw to it that I was delayed at the tables, gaming until past sunrise so that I would be late coming home. And then you sent Diana the note. You brought her to the park under false pretences. You led her to believe that I was interested in her.'

'If you are not, you have a strange way of demonstrating the fact. What gives her reason to hope has nothing to do with some silly note I sent her. You kissed an innocent chaperone in broad daylight, in a public park where anyone might see. The poor girl would lose her position if someone told that old prig Narborough about it.' There was the barest hint of threat in his tone, although his expression had become benign.

'Do not dare.' Nate made no effort to hide the returned threat. 'If any harm comes to her because of your desire to meddle in my life, I swear by all that is holy, I will send you to the devil to answer for it.'

Stephano laughed. 'Do not think you can frighten me with the devil, Nathan. You are the one who needs to fear him. I mean no harm to the girl at all. I am only trying to protect her from you.'

'From me?'

'It is you who seem intent on harming her. You were

the one who ruined her father. You were the one who kissed her today. And you are the one who is hiding your identity from her, lying about your proclivities, pretending to be more innocent than you are in all things.'

'I will tell her everything, when the time is right.' He said it without flinching, for it was almost the truth. Since there could never be a right time, the facts would die with him.

The Gypsy shook his head. 'Do not try to fool me with lies, Nathan. You have told her nothing. You mean to tell her nothing. I saw the smile on your face when she parted from you. You think you can escape what you did in the past by courting her like a gentleman now and lifting her from her circumstances. And that there will be no penance to be paid for any of it.'

'I have paid enough.' He said it softly, hoping that he could move his old friend and that there would be some way to avoid what he expected was coming.

'I will tell you when enough is enough. Perhaps it will be when Diana Price knows the whole truth.'

He would not allow it. For a moment, Nate's mind clouded with violent fantasies, the satisfaction of feeling Beshaley's words stopped by his own hands on the man's throat. He took a slow breath and fought for control. It would take icy calm to outmanoeuvre a man so adept at using the emotions of others to get his way. When he had convinced himself that this conversation mattered no more to him than any other game, Nate knew it was safe to speak. 'I will not beg for mercy, if that is what you seek. My own father went to the gallows without breaking. I can withstand a few idle threats. If you want reparation for old wrongs? I will give you anything you wish.'

'Give me?'

'How much do you want?'

'You think you can buy me off, do you? Because I am a Gypsy. Cross my palm with silver, and I will leave you in peace? I have money, Nathan. More than you. All I want is justice. For my family. For myself.'

'Then we want the same thing. My family was treated as unjustly as yours.'

'If your father was innocent.'

'It is always harder to find the guilty than it is to persecute the innocent, as you do.'

The faintest shadow of doubt passed over Beshaley's face. Then he smirked, and the moment was lost. 'If I treat everyone involved equally, than I am reasonably sure that the guilty parties are punished.'

'It is not fair.'

'But very efficient. First, I will finish with you. Miss Price as well, if you claim her for yourself. And then, I will find the rest of your clan. You are not the only living Wardale, you know.'

At the thought of his sisters, alive but in danger, Nate's calm evaporated. 'I do not know if you are mad or merely cold-blooded. But it does not matter. As you value your life, stay away from the women.' He reached for the letter opener on a nearby desk. 'Just now, I was thinking of using this on you, you bastard. But murder is messy and you are not worth the cost of a new carpet. If you are so eager to avenge your father, then do it. But let my blood be enough.' He pushed the knife into the Gypsy's hand. 'Cut out my heart and be done with it, you coward.'

The sudden change in him must have caught Stephano off guard. For he lost control as well, lunging forward, weapon in hand. But before he could strike, his body tightened and he jerked back as suddenly as a dog might when it reached the end of its leash. His arm went wide in a convulsive movement, flinging the letter opener aside. And then he reached up with both hands to cradle his own head. He dropped back into the chair, gasping for breath, and looked up at Nate, through pain-clouded eyes. 'I would if I could, Nathan Wardale. Long ago, I'd have finished you all. But it is not allowed.'

Nathan stood over him, arms folded in satisfaction. The attempt at violence had left his opponent helpless. 'Allowed?' He smiled, for the man in front of him was in such agony that he had not been able to hide the truth. 'I take it, it is not an English law that binds you?'

The Gypsy shook his head gently, as though to move it hurt him. 'You have heard the expression, *This hurts me more than it hurts you?* Not more, perhaps. While I might laugh as you ruin yourself, to kill you would hurt my poor head more than I can bear.' He lifted his face to stare into the eyes of his old friend. 'Here is your chance to strike, Nathan. I cannot stop you. If you wish, I will move to the flagstones in the hall, to spare your carpet.' Then he laughed. Nate had heard that laugh often. It was the ghastly, hollow sound a man made when he knew he was beaten.

And it made him feel as he did at the game table, when another poor sod had overplayed his hand and left himself open to ruin. He could not manage sympathy, or even mercy. But it filled him with regret at having to play a part in the downfall of another, no matter how deserved that end might be. Nate stared at the suffering man before him, and shook his head. 'I cannot kill you either. I am no more a murderer than my father was. If I can prove that to you, will you leave me and my family in peace?'

'After so many years, what can you prove?'

He did not know. But what harm could it do to try? He had always suspected that Narborough had lied about the crime. But he'd convinced himself that the man was untouchable. If a confrontation now was the only way he might have Diana? Then what choice did he have but to hope? 'I do not know if I will find anything. But I intend to try. After so much time, you can wait a little longer for justice. I request a truce. You may leave here unhindered today, if you promise me two weeks without interference. If I can find evidence to clear my father, then you must go.'

The Gypsy considered. 'In exchange for my life today, you may have fourteen days.'

'And in that time, you will avoid Diana Price?'

Beshaley was still pale, and his brows drew together as though speaking was an effort. 'For two weeks only.

But even if I lift the curse and leave you, you must tell her the truth. If you are innocent of blame and as worthy of love as you claim, it will not matter to her.

'If you are guilty, then you will suffer as a guilty man should suffer, knowing the thing you desire most is forever out of reach. And I will have found satisfaction. But whatever you mean to do, Nathan, you must decide in this fortnight. Or at the end of it, I will make the decision for you.' And with that, he rose unsteadily from the chair and left a stunned Nathan alone before the fire.

Diana returned to the house with a smile on her face, glad that neither of the girls was to spoil the joy of it. Just for a moment, what had happened was still her secret. And what a sweet thing it was. But once she saw the girls, it would be over. If they sent the note, then they must know what had happened and she would need to upbraid them for tricking her into committing an indiscretion, even if it was a pleasant one.

She was sure she had guessed correctly. For the moment Verity looked up from her needlework, her face changed from a mildly inquisitive smile to a knowing grin. 'And how was Mr Dale today, Diana?'

She did her best to look stern. 'What would make you think that I saw him, I wonder?'

'The look on your face, of course.'

'There is nothing singular about my expression, I am sure.' She gave a hurried glance into the mirror above the mantel, checking to see if the time spent behind the tree had disarranged her hair in some obvious way.

Verity was almost bouncing in her chair with excitement. 'Why Miss Price, I do believe you are blushing.'

'I am not. I would never…' But denying it would do no good. It was there in her reflection.

Verity stifled a giggle. 'Turning crimson. Honoria, come see,' she called to her sister, who was passing in the hall. 'Diana is back from her walk in the park. And the air must be particularly fine today. She is positively glowing with good health and high spirits.'

Honoria came into the room and glanced in her direction, and then looked again as though seeing her clearly for the first time. 'Who is he, Diana?'

'There is no one…'

Honoria let out a snort of disgust. 'An assignation. With Mr Dale, no doubt. And I do believe he kissed you. See the look in her eye, Verity? She has been kissed. I am sure of it.'

'Honoria!' Diana's best warning tone fell on deaf ears, for she doubted it could be heard over the sound of Verity's giggles.

Honoria was laughing as well. 'Really Diana. It is not so big a thing. We are happy for you, truly. For it pains us to think that we shall both be married and you will have no one for companionship. Now, tell us. What is it like?'

She looked sternly at the Carlow sisters. 'I have no intention of telling you such things. You will discover all you need to know about them when you are properly affianced.'

'But it was wonderful,' Honoria pressed. 'Was it not?'

And she had to admit, it had been. It was hard not

to smile when thinking of it. Although now was the worst time in the world to smile, for it would give the girls the idea that such behaviour was acceptable. So she put on an even more stern expression and changed the subject. 'Never mind that. I wish to know what you know about this.' And she removed the note from her reticule and laid it on the table in front of them.

'It is the letter you received this morning, is it not? The one you would not show us.' Honoria examined it closely. 'And it was from Mr Dale, just as we suspected.'

Diana gave Honoria the disappointed look that normally broke through the girl's defences when she was concealing something. 'When I arrived at the park, Mr Dale knew nothing of the note. And I suspect you might have had a hand in this, since you are so eager to see the two of us matched.'

'He had nothing to do with it?' Honoria gave a rather unladylike snort. 'What utter rubbish. Perhaps he is too shy to admit it.'

'He was most insistent about it.' She folded her arms across her chest and waited for the confession.

But Honoria's face showed nothing but a thoughtful frown. 'You have no way of proving that he is not lying, do you? You have never seen his writing.'

'Perhaps I have. When Mr Dale was first here, he left a note for your brother.' It was vexing to remember that now, when it was too late. She could have compared the handwriting before leaving. But she had blocked the note from her mind, not wanting to see what was right under her nose.

'Let us see, then,' Verity said.

'You may not see the contents of the note. It is not addressed to you.'

'And yet you have read it,' Honoria challenged.

The truth stung. For when had she become so nosey as to do such a low thing? 'Only to know if I should bother Marc with it, now that he and Nell are finally alone.'

'Or perhaps you wanted to know the contents,' Honoria waved a hand. 'But never mind. We will not look, if it makes you feel better. But get the thing and look for yourself. Then tell us if both are written by the same person.'

She went to her room to get the letter, realizing as she did so, that it should never have been there. Why had she thought it acceptable to put the thing anywhere other than on the desk in Marc's study? But she had taken the paper out of Nathan's hand and walked directly to her bedroom to read it, as though it were a personal missive to herself and not business for Lord Stanegate. She was overstepping herself in so many ways lately that it would take all her self-discipline to return to the straight-and-narrow path.

After examination of the purloined note, she had to admit that the two hands were nothing alike, and she felt even more foolish for jumping to conclusions. She placed the thing in Marc's study where it belonged and returned to the girls.

They were believing none of it, even with the evidence of the note. 'Mr Dale was there when you arrived,' said Verity. 'So the person who sent the letter knew his schedule. And since we have no idea how he keeps himself—'

'When he is not dangling after you,' added Honoria.

'Then it should be proof of our innocence. And this note appears to have been written by a man.'

'Although it would have been a marvellous trick, had we have thought of it.' Honoria grinned. 'It is a great relief to me that you are affected by the same romantic notions as the rest of the world, Diana. While you are an excellent example to us, sometimes I wonder whether I am as weak as my mother claims or if you are the one who is unusual. But never mind that. Let us examine this letter and see if we can guess the sender.' She snatched the letter away from Verity and held it up to the light, but there was nothing extraordinary about the paper. Then she examined the writing. 'Did you save the paper that the bank notes came in?'

It was an interesting thought, and Diana tried not to rush as, this time, the girls followed her to her room. She went to her wardrobe and withdrew the pile of money. But she had discarded the note around it as worthless, for it had had only her own address upon it.

'That must be it,' Verity said. 'If you had kept the thing and could compare it to this, you would see that the hands are the same. It appears that you have a secret benefactor, Diana. If it is not Mr Dale, then it must be someone else who cares enough to see you both provided for and well settled in a home of your own. You are most fortunate indeed.'

And while it was a wonderful thought, that after all this time, there was someone who cared for her well-being, Diana had no idea who that person might be.

Chapter Ten

Diana waited in trepidation on the pathway, the following Tuesday. Nathan Dale had sent her a note, reminding her of the meeting, just as he had promised he would. But it had contained none of the romantic foolishness she had been hoping for. Just a few words requesting an interview at ten o'clock. The brevity of it made the tone seem almost curt. Perhaps the walks were not as important to him as they were to her. Suppose he forgot? Or changed his mind and remained at home? If that was the case, she could console herself that there were no witnesses to her disappointment. She recognized no one in the park this early.

But promptly at ten, she saw him striding down the path towards her, with a slightly nervous smile upon his face. If he had been coming to meet one of the Carlow sisters, she would turn her practiced chaperone's eye to him, and decide that he wished to gain the favour of a lady. But he was acting as though he did not expect to succeed.

She tried to hide her eagerness. For it was good to imagine, if only for a moment, that she could afford to be capricious in her affections. Or that his winning her favour could ever be in doubt.

'Miss Price?'

She curtsyed to him, and he reached out and took her hand again, as he had the previous week. The gesture was both warm and familiar, as though he found nothing unusual about her hand in his.

But for her, it was strange and wonderful. Other than a few stray moments on the dance floor when she was seventeen, she could not remember a man bothering to get this close. And then he slipped her hand protectively into the crook of his arm, as though it were nothing, and not everything in the world. He walked with her, down a quiet footpath, to a bench where they could sit close, side by side. 'I was afraid you would forget me.'

How strange to hear her own thoughts, coming from his mouth. 'And I feared you would not come,' she said in response, and with a bit of a smile.

'I promised I would.' He smiled a little as well, but with sadness. 'I should not have, I think. There are difficulties.'

'You had another engagement?' He looked so serious that for a moment she was convinced that there must be another woman who commanded his attention. But she could not have read him so wrong.

'No,' he confirmed. 'My time is my own. It is just

that you should spend yours in the company of one more worthy.'

'You? Unworthy?' She laughed. 'Certainly not, sir. I am humble enough, am I not? I know better than to set my sights higher than my chances of success.' And now it did sound like she was trying to ensnare him. She blushed. 'That must sound like a slight to your character, or that I assume anything will come of our meeting. I assure you, neither is true.'

He gave her a strange glance. 'I certainly expected you might think something would result in our meeting. If you remember, when we last saw each other, I kissed you.'

She felt her cheeks burning to show just how well she had remembered it. She had been able to think of little else for most of the week.

'I would not have done it, had my intentions not grown serious. And so very quickly.' He frowned. 'It was not what I planned to do, certainly.'

This must be the set-down she had expected from the first. She readied herself for the inevitable disappointment.

He was staring at the ground in front of them, refusing to meet her gaze. 'I meant to tell you this earlier, to make a clean breast at our last meeting. To explain my interest in you, and to make it clear why there can be no further meetings.'

No further meetings? It felt like she were falling from a great height. A rush of air and a frisson of nerves before the inevitable crash. She gave a shaky laugh. 'If that is to be the result, then I would prefer you not explain at all, thank you very much.'

He went silent on the bench beside her, as though he would be only too happy to stop talking. And now, she was the one afraid to look in his eyes, unsure of what she would see there. At last, he said, 'I am more than a little tempted to give in to your request, Miss Price.'

'It was to be Diana,' she reminded him. 'Last week I was Diana. And I wished to call you Nathan.'

She heard him give a little sigh at the sound of his own name. But he responded, 'I am not fit company for you, Miss Price. There are incidents in my past that are—' he struggled with his words again '—dark. They are dark deeds. I hesitated to tell you, for I knew how you would react. And I did not wish to spoil what was happening between us.'

She tried to keep her tone light. 'Best not tell me all, then. If it means that I will not see you again, just as I wish to. You have changed for the better, haven't you, since the dark time? The events are well behind you?'

'I have tried, God help me. My worst mistakes are years in the past. And for you? For you I would cast off what vices remain. I would be yours to command, truly completely and forever, just as I wish you to be mine. But I cannot hide the truth from you any longer. For should you discover it later…'

And she reached out and put her hand over his mouth before he could speak.

He was still for only a moment, and she thought that he would push her away and blurt the truth. Instead, he reached up and took her gloved hand in his, holding it to his lips, and kissing it with such fervour that she could feel the strength of his emotions through the leather, and through her other clothing as well. She could imagine his lips pressing against her bare skin, and her body tingled with answering desire. And she knew, no matter what he might think she deserved, that she deserved this. To have a man, who she loved and respected, who loved her with such passion in return.

She thought of her own secret. Would she be able to tell the man who loved her about the bet her father had made? She had thought it no business of another, and intended to keep the secret to her grave. Though she'd told herself that it was no fault of hers, she felt stained by it. It was as though she had been married against her will. Whether she liked it or not, a bond existed, and she was not free to give herself elsewhere. Deep down, she still worried that someday Nathan Wardale would appear on her doorstep and demand a reckoning. But Nell had said he could well be dead. She need have nothing to fear.

'I have a secret as well,' she finally admitted. 'One that I do not wish anyone to know. Not even you. At one time, I walked away from my past as surely as you wish to turn from yours. And if each party wishes to keep a secret from the other, and knows that there is ground that they must not tread, for fear that it would break the heart of the other? But that we swear to each other, with our whole hearts, that what is behind us does not matter? Then perhaps it is almost the same as telling the whole truth when we do not speak of it.'

His eyes were still averted as he clutched her hand tightly in his. 'It would not matter? It would be as though you were promising yourself to half a man.'

She smiled. 'If it is to be the good half of you? Then yes, I would be more than willing.'

He looked at her, then. And she could see the emotion in the green depths of his eyes, like a storm at sea. 'My darling, Diana, I want to believe you. If we were the last two people in the world…or if I could take you far away, so that we might never see another soul that knew us. But it is not as easy as that. There is someone who wishes to expose me for what I am. I swear I have done him no harm. But he thinks that I deserve punishment for a matter that did not involve me. I fear he will try to discredit me with you. I am trying to find a way to prevent it,' he said hurriedly. 'But if you do not wish to hear the truth from another, then there is something I must do, soon, that will keep you safe from this man. You may think my actions now are just as distasteful as my past. But I swear to you, what I will do may seem terrible, but I am convinced it is just.'

'If there is anything you need, I will help you.'

He smiled so very softly then, and shook his head. 'You do not know what you are saying.'

'That is for me to decide.' She wanted to be a part of his life, in any way that she could. 'How can I help you?'

He looked at her, speculatively. 'It will concern the Earl of Narborough.'

'And what does that have to do with you or me?'

'He is your employer,' he said. 'And you count the girls as friends, do you not?'

'Of course.'

'Suppose it were possible for me to bury my past, but it resulted in the downfall of the Carlows. What might you say then?'

This did not sound at all like the actions of a man she could love. 'You would ruin the family for your own gain?'

He shook his head. 'If what I suspect is true, Narborough dishonoured himself years ago. I would only be uncovering *his* secret to keep my own secrets safe.'

'After all that we have agreed about not looking back for unpleasantness, you would do to another, what you do not wish for yourself?' It was both mysterious and disappointing.

'This is quite different, I assure you. While I will admit that my past is shameful, I have not caused the death of any person, directly or indirectly, as a result of my actions. But George Carlow is responsible for at least two deaths, one by his own hand and one through the betrayal of a friendship.'

'Lord Narborough?' She almost laughed. 'He is a feeble old man.'

'And likely to go to his grave with the truth, if I do not act soon.'

She shook her head. 'He has never been anything but kind to me, nor have I seen him mistreat another.'

'Not recently, perhaps. But people can change for the

better, with time. Twenty years ago, he might have been quite different, and you would not have known.'

'Twenty years is a long time,' she agreed. 'But surely, something so long ago could have no importance.'

'For some, it is as fresh as the day it happened,' he said. 'You would do well not to belittle another's pain.'

She gasped, surprised by the vehemence of his reaction. 'Perhaps it would help me to know just what it is that you are talking about.'

'The murder of Christopher Hebden, Lord Framlingham, and the hanging of William Wardale, Earl of Leybourne.'

'You think that Lord Narborough was in some way involved?'

'I am sure of it. Hebden died at his house. And it was he who made the accusation against Leybourne.'

'But the earl was guilty.'

'How can you be sure?'

'If he was innocent, then why was he found with the dying man? Could he have done nothing to stop the crime? Knowing the Wardales as I do, I would believe them capable of anything.' The words flowed easily out of her. It surprised her, for she had not meant to come so close to revealing her own past.

He stared at her in disapproval. 'You can know nothing of that family. They were turned out of their home in disgrace and no doubt underwent hardships that were not in proportion to the crime. Think of it, Diana. A mother and three children. Two of them girls.

Lord knows what happened to them. And if the father was innocent, all along…'

And for a moment, she put aside her own story, and thought of Marc's bride, Nell, *Helena Wardale*, and the past that she was so careful not to speak of. 'Perhaps you are right. Some members of the family have suffered unjustly.'

'How gracious of you to admit it.' Again, she was surprised by his passion on the subject, and his harsh tone stung her. Then he seemed to realize how he sounded, for he calmed. 'Please forgive my outburst. It was uncalled for. Even if the matter was important, you are right that it is the distant past. It hardly concerns us.' And for a moment, his face took on a funny cast. 'But the events of twenty years ago are about to return to haunt the families involved. I came to speak to Marc Carlow to offer a word of warning that the truth was likely to come out in the near future, and to be on his guard. But it would be better for all concerned, if Narborough had any part in what happened, that he admits the fact so that his family might prepare themselves for it.'

'But what makes you think this is the case, and what does it have to do with you?'

'I can explain very little, I am afraid. Other than that I am sure of my facts. And I mean to gather the evidence necessary to prove them.' He squeezed her hand, as though wanting to assure himself that she was still his. 'Is that so very wrong?'

'If Lord Narborough is truly a murderer? Then I

suppose it is not. But Nathan?' She squeezed his hand in return. 'He is not guilty. I am as sure of that fact, as you are of his guilt.'

And suddenly, there was a strange light in his eyes. 'Then you would have to prove it to me. If he is as innocent as Leybourne was, I would be making a horrible mistake in accusing him. If there is some way that I can be sure... You are an intimate of the family. If you have a way to assure me, other than conjecture...'

She pulled her hand away. 'Are you asking me to spy on my friends?'

He looked alarmed. 'Certainly not. And I never intended to suggest such a thing. It was an idle thought, nothing more. I meant what I said at first, when I refused your help. It would be too difficult for you. And possibly dangerous, should it turn out that I was right. I would be asking you to face a murderer in my stead. It makes me uncomfortable enough to know that you live with them. For all your confidence, I am not sure of their intentions.'

'You think they are a threat to me? Surely not. Lord and Lady Narborough have been nothing but good to me, as has the rest of the family.'

He touched her shoulder to reassure her. 'My problem is not with the rest of his family. They are no more to blame than the Wardales were. Those girls were no different from Honoria and Verity. Little more than babes when it all occurred, and God knows what happened to them.'

She thought again of the haunted look in Nell's eyes when she had first come to them. 'If their father was innocent, they deserved better than they received.'

His face clouded. 'You deserve better as well. A life of ease and not labour. But you are content, because your work is honourable. Perhaps it is true of them as well.'

'Or perhaps not,' she said, and watched as his expression became even more glum. And suddenly, it occurred to her why he might be so interested in the Wardales. He must have some knowledge of Nell's sister, Rosalind. A *tendre*, perhaps? If she was part of the secret he did not wish to share, it must have ended tragically. Did he blame himself? Perhaps the mysterious stranger he mentioned was their brother, Mr Wardale.

'I think I can see why you are obsessed with the crime and its aftermath.' Though she had vowed to him that she would not be suspicious or question him about his past, she wondered all the same. If her surmise was correct, she feared a visit from the mysterious stranger, almost as much as Nathan did. 'And now that you have put the idea in my head, I doubt I will be satisfied until I know the truth about the Earl of Leybourne. Although I am sure that Lord Narborough did them no harm. And I think there is a way I can assure you, that will do very little harm to anyone.'

He hesitated, and then said, 'No harm? Because I would not put you at risk.'

'What risk could there possibly be to me? I will be

taking the girls to the Narborough's country house shortly, to visit their parents. Today, I meant to tell you that I would be gone for some days. In case you had been considering another meeting.' She gave a little dip of her bonnet to hide her face from him, for it embarrassed her to have him know how she had looked forward to their walk this week and that she was already planning for the next one. 'We will be leaving tomorrow. But once I am at Stanegate Court, I will have a chance to disprove your claim.'

His hand tightened on her shoulders. 'I would not have you snooping through drawers and searching the attics like some common thief.'

She smiled. 'That will hardly be necessary. Lord Narborough has kept a journal for most of his adult life. The full books are clearly labelled in a small library. Lord Narborough uses the space as his study, but I would hardly consider it private. No one will think twice if I go there in the afternoon to read. And once there, I am sure it would not be difficult for me to borrow the journal that corresponds to the year that Christopher Hebden died. If I find evidence that supports your claim, I will tell you.'

'You would do that for me?' He touched her face. 'I am not trying to turn you against your employer. Nor do I expect you to follow me blindly. I have not known you long enough to have earned your trust. I only wish you to exercise your judgment and objectivity over anything you might discover about the events in question. Look at it as a stranger might. If you find that

I am wrong, then you have every right to correct my assumptions. But if there is any shred of evidence at Stanegate that proves me right? You would not be disloyal to your employer, if he did not deserve loyalty.'

There would be nothing to find, for she was sure that if the journal contained anything but the most mundane information, it would not be sitting out in a common room. If she looked at it, she could assure Nathan that she had done her best. But what if he did not believe her? Supposing his insistence was some mad obsession on his part and that he insisted on more and more searches?

As if he read her mind, he said, 'I give you my word that I will trust your findings, if that is what worries you. No matter what you discover, I will ask no more of you. That you would even consider helping is more than I deserve. I trust you would not conceal the truth from me, for I believe, after our few conversations, that you are an honest and fair-minded individual. Nor will I bother you further, if you arrive at the house and change your mind about this. I will go my own way, and you will see me again when I have satisfied myself on the matter of Lord Narborough.'

And this, more than anything else, decided her. For she was enjoying his company too much to give it up so quickly. If she looked at the book, she would be guaranteed at least one more meeting with Nathan when she returned to London. 'It will do no harm just to look at a book. They are kept in plain sight and easy reach.'

'You are too good, Diana. And your help and friendship are more than I deserve.' He took a deep breath, and looked all around them, as though making sure that there was no one to observe them. Then he smiled at her, and there was a merry twinkle in his eyes. 'But enough of this talk of the past. We promised ourselves that we would look only forward, did we not?' And very carefully, he raised her gloved hands to his lips, and kissed the knuckles again. 'It is a beautiful day, and we will not see each other again for some while. Let us enjoy what time we have.'

Chapter Eleven

The trip next day to Stanegate Court was as it always was, an exhausting experience, even though it was not a long journey and the roads were good. The travel would have been quite pleasant, had the attitude of one of her companions been better. Verity was no trouble, as even-tempered and cooperative as ever. But Honoria approached the trip with the enthusiasm of a condemned prisoner. She overslept, dawdled over the packing—taking first too little and then too much for a week's stay. Once in the carriage, she spent the time in sullen silence while Diana attempted to cheer her by pointing out landmarks that they had all seen dozens of times.

She could not really blame the girl. Despite the frequent corrections she received from Marc and herself, London held nothing like the censure Honoria would receive in the company of her mother. Even when she was on her best behaviour, it was unlikely that she would find as much praise as her younger sister did. Lady Narborough's continual criticism would make her behaviour on their return to London worse rather than better.

Diana reached out a friendly hand and laid it upon the girl's, which were folded neatly in her lap. 'I know you do not wish the trip, Honoria. But think of the good it will do for your father.'

The girl sighed. 'I will do it for Father, of course, if it will cheer him to see us.'

'I am sure it will.'

'But we will not stay long, will we?'

'Not long.'

But once they had arrived, Diana worried that they would be lucky to manage even a short trip. The trouble began from the moment they entered the house. Lady Narborough greeted both girls warmly, commenting on their looks and demanding to know in detail about each dance at each party and every sign of interest from a gentleman of the Ton. But where Verity was congratulated on her good sense for her refusal to make a decision, Honoria was gently upbraided for being a flirt. Verity's dress was most flattering today. But Honoria's was a trifle too loose, was it not? And horror of horrors, her slippers were scuffed.

Diana felt a bit guilty for recommending the ensemble. For she had informed both girls that a trip to family hardly required their finest. And since Honoria exhibited a perfectly normal tendency to be active when in the country, it was better to add fresh scuffs to an old shoe than to ruin a new one. But Diana had long ago learned to hold her tongue in these situations. Lady Narborough meant nothing by her comments, and it was not Diana's place to explain to her how they hurt her eldest daughter.

After the grilling delivered by their mother, it was time to visit Lord Narborough. He was no longer confined to a sickbed, but according to the letters they had received in London, he rarely left his rooms. Diana had to admit that his colour was poor, and it appeared his appetite was as well. The contents of his lunch tray were nearly untouched.

Guilt, she wondered? And then checked herself. For the thought had never entered her mind that his failing health might be more than a normal weakening with age, until Nathan had placed it there.

'And how are my fine girls, Miss Price?' Narborough's eyes sparkled at the sight of them, and for a moment, he seemed more his old self. But she could see by the way Lady Narborough hovered at his side that she feared any shock might finish him.

'Well, sir.' She gestured the girls forward and they greeted their father warmly, assuring him that the time in London was happy, and regaling him with stories of the balls and dinners they had attended and the people they had met.

And Honoria's behaviour was exemplary, just as Diana knew it would be. The girl made her time in London sound innocuous and glossed over the more rambunctious adventures with such good humour that her father laughed out loud. Even her mother could not have complained for the positive change her visit wrought in the earl.

When she was sure that she was not needed, and that the family was as happy in their time together as they were ever likely to be, she excused herself. She walked quietly into the little room where the journals were kept. They were just as she remembered them, lined up neatly behind the glass doors of the bookcase, bound in leather with the dates stamped in gold upon the spines. They were the work of a man with pretensions of grandeur. Lord Narborough must think that his every thought was worthy of study by someone. Although who would wish to read them, she was not sure. She had never seen the books removed from the shelves in all the years that she had been in the household. Not even in reference by the man who had done the writing. His children, when faced with the things, silently rolled their eyes at the folly of an old man.

When she reached to open the cabinet, it became clear to her why the things never moved. The glass door was locked against casual reading. How strange. Did he fear discovery of something or merely wish to keep the things clean and organized?

She shook her head to clear it of suspicions. After her talk with Nathan, even the most common actions seemed fraught with guilt. Whatever the reason for locking the things up, she had no real wish to ask for the key and call attention to her interest, for she could think of no way to explain herself.

Fortunately, or unfortunately, such intervention would not be necessary. She carefully removed a pin from her hair, rearranging the curls to disguise its absence. Then she went to work on the lock with the bent bit of wire and a letter opener from the nearby desk. Now she would see if ten years of excessive virtue had dulled her skills as a lock pick. She had not had to behave thus since she was a girl and tried to get around her father and his gambling, searching for hidden money in locked desk drawers.

She felt the satisfying click of the lock's mechanism as the tumblers slid home, and then she pulled the door open and traced her finger back as though travelling back through the years to a point almost twenty year's distant, and removed the volume labelled 1794. This would have the information, if anything would. She set it aside for a moment, rearranging the remaining books so the gap in years would not be obvious. Then, she relocked the door and slipped the purloined volume into her pocket.

Before she left the room, she paused to listen for noises in the library, feeling less than comfortable with the relief she felt when she heard silence. If she was doing nothing wrong, then why did she feel so guilty?

The lock was the answer, of course. She had planned on simply removing a book from a shelf in a public room and sitting down to read. But the lock was a warning that the contents were not meant to be removed. So when she was sure that no one would see, she took the book to her room, closed and locked her own door behind her, and opened it to the first page.

What had been the day of the murder? Had Nathan even said? Best to begin at the beginning and work her way forward.

She flipped quickly through the first few months, surprised at how little the family had changed. There were stories of Marc, serious and quiet even as a boy, and the little scamp Hal. Honoria was not out of leading strings but had already gotten into a multitude of scrapes. Verity was still in the cradle, and there were detailed descriptions of the baby gifts that Lady Narborough still had on display in shadow boxes and glass cases around the house.

And then an entry in a shaking hand, as though the writer were consumed by emotion.

> *Don't know what's to be done with Will. His behaviour grows reckless. No better than Hebden. They are both detestable and I am sick to death of their company.*

He might have known a dozen Wills and Williams. It was not specific enough to connect with certainty to William Wardale, the Earl of Leybourne. Nor did it explain what might constitute reckless behaviour. She continued to read.

> *The situation grows worse with each day. Hebden's Gypsy brat now playing with my boys. Kit encourages the association. Seems to find it amusing to see the dark lad and treats him as though nothing is odd.*

I cannot believe that his wife, Amanda, turns a blind eye to it all. But she is raising the boy as her own.

She struggled to remember what she had heard of the scandal. Kit must mean Christopher Hebden. There was something about a lost child, after the father's death. A bastard son, who was sent away. And Amanda Hebden, prostrate with grief over the whole affair. Diana flipped through more pages.

A shocking discovery. No wonder Amanda does not clean her house of the Gypsy filth. She is too busy with Leybourne to care. How can Will dine with us at the club, and then go off to tup Hebden's wife? And Kit is too busy with his whores to care. They laugh and talk together, then go off to their sinful beds as though it means nothing.

They were the friends of my youth. But now I feel unclean by the association.

The book shook in her trembling hand, as she tried to imagine the frail man upstairs penning the angry words. Although he was most particular with his own reputation and that of his children, she had never seen him cross with anyone in all the time she had lived with the family. But perhaps he had been a different man twenty years ago. She paged eagerly on.

Another shouting match with Kit over the cipher business. Too much whisky on all sides and not enough sense. He called me a traitor. I called him out, told him to solve the damn cipher if he is so eager to find the spy in our midst. But he cannot. The thing is unbreakable.

Without Will there, we'd have come to blows. Very embarrassing. But nerves frayed all round. This cannot go on much longer.

Traitor? She had never thought of Lord Narborough as less than an honest man and proud defender of his country. But he did not deny the accusation. And then, another note, coming almost as a postscript to the last.

Hebden says he has cracked the cipher. Now the truth will out. There is no stopping it.

And all that was left of the next page was a ragged tatter. Someone had seized the thing and ripped it from the book. She ran her fingers along the place where the pages should be stitched, and counted the little bits of paper: one, two, three pages missing. And at the top of the next page, a single line, hanging as though forgotten.

Dear God, forgive me.

Her pulse quickened. It proved nothing. But whatever had happened was worse than she suspected. Accusations of infidelity and treason on both sides. The missing pages, as though someone did not wish the truth to be known.

And that last statement, which could mean anything,

but appeared damning when taken with all the rest. What was she to do with the information? It appeared that Nathan might be right. And it left her with a difficult choice to make. She'd lived in ignorance of any problems in this family and known Lord Narborough to be nothing more than a fond old man, caring deeply for his wife and children. But his health had worsened after the appearance of Nell and then the Gypsy. Was this because he feared the truth being revealed?

Had she found this information even a week ago, she'd have been tempted to turn her back on it. Better to let the matter rest and put the book back upon the shelf, instead of stirring up old troubles that could hurt more people than they helped. But now?

She took the book and set it in the bottom of her valise, and then covered it with a pile of folded stockings. She would pray that no one noticed its absence during the visit, and then she would take it back to London to show Nathan Dale. If he felt a pressing need to know the identity of the Hebden murderer, she would help him. It did not matter whether it was to avenge a lost love or free himself from the harassment of the same man that haunted her own past. She would do it, because in only a few weeks, she had grown to love and trust him beyond any loyalty she might feel to her old friends.

Because her objective opinion on past events, based on the contents of the little book, was that the truth could be every bit as bad as he assumed.

Chapter Twelve

During the week that Diana was away, Nathan could think of little else but her return. Although it was unlikely that he'd have seen her until the next Tuesday, even had she remained in London, he had not realized the comfort he felt in knowing that a chance meeting was possible. Now that she was gone, each mile between them was a hardship.

He went to the tables each night, just as he always had. But he played listlessly, paying little attention to the desires of men and women across the baize. Where once he would have watched without emotion as his opponents bankrupted themselves, now when games got out of hand he could no longer contain his disgust, with them or himself.

As yet another broken fool began rooting in his pockets for some treasured heirloom to cast away, Nate stood up from the table, hours earlier than normal, proclaiming loud enough for all to hear that he would rather play cards with the kitchen cat than to watch another soul publicly shame themselves at his expense.

As he pushed his way through the crowd, he heard the ladies muttering amongst themselves that, while they still found Mr Dale was quite attractive, of late he had not been nearly as diverting as they had hoped.

He smiled to himself at this. Her absence had convinced him that there was only one woman in London that he wished to entertain. But was it better to initiate contact, or to wait until she was returned and was ready to see him? Surely scrawling a line or two to welcome her back to London would not be seen as forward. But had she even returned from Stanegate? He did not know. When they had parted, she had been able to give him no firm date of return. As always, her schedule was at the mercy of the Carlow family.

He quietly damned them all for their hold over her life, and damned himself for placing her in the situation. A week without seeing her had seemed like an eternity. It had given him too much time to relive the previous meetings and imagine possibilities for the next. Assuming that there would be a next meeting. What if she had decided not to follow through on their plan, and realized that it would be better to remove herself from him? It was no less than he deserved. Perhaps she had found some other gentleman whose company she preferred. Or maybe the next meeting was assumed, and he would find her waiting in the park on Tuesday.

There were so many possibilities that he could not

choose and was driving himself mad with trying. At last, he decided there could be no harm in going to the park for a walk on the normal Tuesday, and went so far as to forgo his Monday evening at the tables so that he might be rested and waiting for her in Hyde Park on the following morning.

He arrived on the usual footpath by the Serpentine promptly at ten, to find Diana Price pacing the ground ahead of him in obvious agitation. Not only had she come, but it thrilled him to think she had arrived early, as though she were afraid she would miss him. He frowned. Unless there were some other reason for her anxiety.

When she saw him, she looked up with a relieved smile, and he hurried to her side. He clasped her hand, to assure himself that she was safely returned and not just a vision of what he wished to see. 'I was not sure you would come. Perhaps you were still travelling, or had decided that my last request was too forward? But I decided to wait here each Tuesday until you returned.'

'I hoped you would.' She gave a relieved sigh. 'But if you did not come, then at least you would not see me waiting for you.'

He grinned. 'I thought the same.' So she had been eager to see him. All of his previous concerns for her safety, and worse, her constancy, evaporated. 'Come, let us walk.' He offered her his arm.

'That would be delightful.' She took the offered arm, her fingers giving it a light squeeze that warmed his heart. 'And could it be somewhere secluded, if possible? For I have something to show you.'

He gave her a vague nod and set off with her, down the path and away from the other early walkers, laughing at his own foolishness. For a moment, he had quite forgotten the real reason for their meeting and had heard only what he longed to hear. It had sounded quite like she wished to be alone with him for no other reason than that they might share a moment of intimacy. But then he remembered the journal and the need to keep it a secret.

Devil take the thing. He still wanted to see it, of course. But he had not realized just how much he had wished to see its bearer, until he had spied her on the path before him. When he was sure they were out of sight of prying eyes, he pulled her into the shade of a nearby outbuilding and drew to a stop.

Then, she slipped the small leather volume from her pocket. 'I think this will be of interest to you. Read it, starting from where I have marked. And notice the missing pages? I fear that a lack of evidence may be as damning as an excess of truth. For what reason would he have had to remove the page, other than that he regretted what he had written about the night in question?'

Nathan was turning quickly through the book, scanning the pages eagerly, shocked at the vitriol of some of the posts. George Carlow had been no true friend of his father's, to be sure. The entries sounded as though any bond between them had been severed in the months before Hebden's death.

Then he came to the missing pages, fingering the

ripped paper scraps at the binding. The full story should reside here. Had it been torn out in anger? Shame? Guilt? It could be any reason. But it seemed plain that Carlow had not wanted the full truth known, so had disposed of the evidence.

He looked up at her, excitement on his face. 'There is a secret of some kind. It supports my suspicions, does it not?'

'I fear it does.'

'And now, I must decide what I will do with the information.' He frowned in distaste as a possibility occurred to him.

Lord Keddinton had risen far since the days when he was humble Robert Veryan and eager for a chance to dine with the Wardales. His help with the prosecution of the Earl of Leybourne had earned him his own title, just as it had taken Nate's away. 'There is a man who might help, if he had a mind to. He is an old acquaintance of my family.' He smiled bitterly. 'And I believe he owes me a favour. I will take it to him and see what he makes of it.'

But Lord Narborough would surely hear of an investigation and would punish anyone he thought disloyal. Nate gave Diana a worried look. 'But before I do anything, I must help you to get away.'

'Away?' She almost laughed. 'Away from what, sir?'

'From the Carlows, of course.'

'I am safe in London with Verity and Honoria. I have nothing to fear from them.'

'But I think you will, if the information in this book

becomes public and they understand how I came by it.' He reached out and took her by the hand. 'And I would not, for all the world, have anything happen to you, my darling Diana.' The endearment slipped easily from his lips, and he saw the sweet look of surprise as it registered on her.

And then, he was drawing her further into the shadows, and cupping her face in his hands. His hands strayed to the ribbon that held her bonnet, and she batted them away. 'What are you doing?'

'Being very impertinent, I think.' He returned to his task and untied the bow that held it in place, then reached up to lift it gently off her hair. He leaned closer to smell the soft scent of her, and whispered, 'I have been dreaming of seeing the sunlight on your hair. Would the lights in it be gold, I wondered? But I was wrong. They are the deep red of Spanish wine.'

'Oh.' Her voice was breathless, and her hands still rested lightly on his wrists as though unsure whether or not to stop him.

He traced the curves of her ear with his tongue, and his teeth caught the lobe, sucking it gently into his mouth. She was soft and sweet and wonderful. And she had no idea how the simplest mysteries of her body would affect a man. She had kept them all hidden, even such small treats as this. And the way she sighed in response to the slightest nip on her ear boded well for the future.

'We mustn't,' she managed, after a few more delicious moments. But the tone hinted that, while she was sure she mustn't, she wished for much more.

'Do not worry,' he whispered. 'We won't. Not yet, at any rate. But do not blame me too much for doing this.' He pulled her close to kiss the side of her throat, turning her so that he could reach the nape of her neck, and he felt her ribs moving under his fingers, for the kisses to her throat made her breath release in shallow gasps. 'And do not fault me for wanting to take down your hair, so that I might run my fingers through it. To see it free as it lies on the pillow, and tousled as it is when first you wake.' He touched her very gently, so as not to disturb her coiffure. The silken smoothness of it made his fingers itch for more. 'Maybe I could take a single pin. It could be a curl blown loose by the wind, or caught in a ribbon and disarranged. An accident. Nothing more. But no. Once I start, I will not be able to stop.'

For he was sure it would not be enough to take down her hair. Next he would be laying her down in the new grass, and begging to make love to her where they could smell the first scents of spring. It would be sweet disaster, but it would bind her to him in ways that would make her rejection impossible, should she learn the truth of his character.

He made to release her, for her good and the sake of his own sanity. But she reached up and took him by the chin, squirming against him until she could force his lips to meet hers. She rewarded him with the kiss he longed to give her: open mouthed and passionate, innocent and inexperienced. Utterly delightful.

And so, he gave himself up to the pleasure and did

not release her until he had marked every bit of her mouth as his. He heard the distant thump of her bonnet dropping to the ground and let his empty hands move over her, from shoulders to back to bottom, moulding her body to his, feeling the pressure building within him.

She should struggle, or argue or give some sign that she wished him to stop. If she did not, he did not know if he would be able to save them both from this madness. But instead, she wrapped her arms about his waist, clinging to him, letting him support her as he took all he wanted.

It was her total surrender to him that gave him the strength to break the kiss and push her gently away. He shook his head as he smiled to reassure her, then gave a quick look about them, to be sure that they were still alone. 'Oh, my sweet, I am foolish to risk you in this way. What will you think of me, when your head clears enough to realize how we have carried on?' He reached down and picked up her bonnet, which was looking rather scuffed after being crushed between them and then cast upon the ground.

She took it, and concentrated on straightening the flowers and fluffing the lone feather, and he wondered what had hurt her, his forwardness or the suddenness of his rejection? 'It is perfectly all right, Mr Dale. I was well aware of what I was doing.'

He scoffed. 'Throwing yourself away on a wastrel, without care for your reputation. And the only defence I can offer is that you have bewitched me with your beauty, Miss Price. One disapproving quirk of those very proper lips and I am lost to all propriety. I must have them. I must have you. I swear, the frown on your face right now is more delightful than a hundred smiles from another woman.'

There was the slightest smile on her lips as she finished with the bonnet, which he feared would never be quite the same, and placed it back on her head, tying it in a firm bow. 'Your praise would be more convincing, Nathan, if it were not so fulsome.'

He leaned back against the building, eyes closed and hands behind his head, and laughed, waiting for the beat of his heart to slow and his reason to return. 'Thank you, dear Lord, she is calling me Nathan again.' He opened an eye and peered at her. 'And smiling. The blush on that cheek is more perfect than any rose.' Then he said, softly and slowly, so that she might believe him, 'Forgive me my excessive praise. I have never been in love before, and I am rather at a loss as to how to go on.'

Love. He had said the word aloud to her, and now he would see what she made of it. Suddenly afraid, he went on talking, leaving her no time to respond. 'Give me time. I will grow into it, I am sure. And I will find a manner of praising you that suits your practical and modest nature. If you prefer, I will compliment you on your generous heart and your excellent manners, and remain silent with my suspicions that you are Venus herself, hiding behind a prim facade.' He patted the pocket that held the journal. 'When this is taken care of, we will have no need to sneak about in the woods, stealing kisses and tempting fate. I will take you away with me. And when I do, I mean to keep you safe and make you happy. I will make it right again, you shall see.'

She looked puzzled at his last words. And he realized that they made no sense. For why would Nathan Dale wish to make amends for her past, if he'd had no part in it? He waited to see if she understood. If she questioned him, he would tell her the truth and go where it led.

Instead, she said, 'I would like that very much.'

He was still free of the past, if there was freedom in hiding. But what did it matter, as long as she wanted him? And while she had not offered love in words, he had heard the truth in the response of her body to his. It would be all right between them, somehow. He smiled at her. 'I have much work to do. To secure our future.' He reached out for her, kissing her fingertips before linking her arm with his. 'Will you allow me to escort you home, Miss Price?'

'Gladly, sir.'

Chapter Thirteen

Nathan came back to the Fourth Circle that afternoon, flushed with the success of his walk with Diana. He had escorted her to the very door of the Carlow town house, and bid her a proper farewell. It had seemed the most natural thing in the world, and not an endeavour fraught with risk. He had pushed aside the hundred worries in his mind about his mending his tattered reputation and her preserving her spotless one, and enjoyed the little time they'd had as he should have done. Caution was all well and good, when kept in its place. But if he wished for a future that was a tenth as happy as this morning had been, it was time to act, even at the risk of failure.

Dante indicated with the barest nod of his head that he would find the Gypsy seated at their usual table. Nathan approached slowly, to assess the mood of the man. There was no sign of the headache of two weeks ago. And with a doxy on his knee and a drink in his hand, Stephano looked almost at ease. It seemed he had taken the two weeks as a holiday from his quest, as well. His usual dark mood was gone, and as Nathan watched, he leaned back his head and laughed at something the girl had whispered to him. It sounded nothing like the sour mirth Nathan had heard from him, when gloating over the misfortune of his victims. The girl responded with a kiss, and then tossed her head and laughed as well.

She was rewarded with jealous glares from the other women in the room, who were looking at the Gypsy as though they would gladly change places with his chosen *inamorata*, the moment he lost interest in her.

For a moment, it was as if Nate's old friend had grown to adulthood and sat before him, ready for a game of cards. Then Stephano looked up, and his good mood evaporated, as though it had not existed. The merriment disappeared and a cynically smiling mask covered his handsome features. He muttered something and pushed the girl from his lap, then raised his glass in a sarcastic salute. 'Nathan.'

Nate dropped into the chair opposite, noting the absence of a surname in the greeting. The Gypsy had not yet decided if he had earned the right to hide behind the name Dale. He said nothing in response and placed the journal on the table between them.

The Gypsy raised an eyebrow. 'What is this?'

'Proof enough for you to leave me alone. The entries in this book show Narborough to be no real friend of my father, nor of you. If you wish for justice, get out of my chair and go to bother him.'

Stephano opened the book at the marked page and began to read. When he came to the missing pages, he looked up. 'There is nothing at all here about the night of the murder.'

'Is that not strange? Was the event not significant enough to record in detail? Or perhaps George Carlow wrote the whole truth in an impetuous moment and then thought the better of it and tore out the pages.'

Stephen closed the book and offered it back to him. 'When you bring me the missing pages, I will tell you what I think.'

'Until recently, I would have been unable to get this much information. If you want the missing parts? Then find them yourself. I have given you more than enough reason to doubt.'

Beshaley gave him a sceptical look. 'Why would it matter to me what they say?'

Perhaps it would have mattered to the man who had been sitting here as he had arrived. So Nate appealed to him. 'For a moment, let us ignore the nonsense of your mother's curse. Stephen Hebden, if you care who killed your father, then this journal could make us more allies than antagonists.'

The man across the table from him did not respond, staring in response to his old name as though Nate had not spoken.

'All right then. Stephano Beshaley.' Then he continued. 'If my father died for a murder he did not commit, do I not have as great a reason as you to be angry? I lost a father, a title and my reputation, just as you did. And my family as well. You seem to have found a new one, when you returned to your people. But my sisters are lost to me.'

A shadow flitted across the face of his old friend, and then it was gone.

'I have no love for the Carlows. I've proved as much for you. Can you not lift the curse from the Wardales?'

'I tell you again, it is not for me to decide what happens. The curse is a test, Nathan. I have been called to administer it. You will pass or fail, according to your nature. If you are innocent, then nothing I do will truly harm you. There will be a period of hardship, and all will come right in the end. And perhaps it will bring me closer to my goal.'

Nathan laughed bitterly. 'I knew you once, Stephen Hebden. For that is who you were, though you wish to reject it. And I liked you. You were a kind boy, a good friend, and had things been different, you would have grown to be a good man. And now you are willing to destroy my life on a *perhaps*.'

The Gypsy shook his head. 'You give me too much power, Nathan. Only God can truly destroy a man, just as he created him. If I am not doing his work, then I cannot hurt you. It is up to him to decide your fate.'

'Small comfort. I will only meet my end if God thinks I deserve to. Any number of horrible things have happened to me when we were young. And I did not deserve a one of them. They made me into the man I am, a person I take no pride in being. Now, after life has driven all the goodness from me, you seek me out and hope that God will find me wanting, so that I may be punished further?'

The Gypsy gave him a wry smile. 'I'll take no joy in it, if that is the case. For once, I liked you as well. But take heart, Nathan. Whatever might occur, it will be over soon enough. For both of us.' He reached to pocket the book.

Nathan held a hand out for it. 'Here, then. If this will not end things between us, then give that back.'

The Gypsy shrugged, but returned the book. 'What do you mean to do with it? Confront Narborough?'

'That would make me no better than you. If you think my fate is in the hands of God, then I will take the thing to the authorities and see if they can make anything of the contents.'

Beshaley snorted. 'Because English justice has treated you fairly in the past?'

'Because it is the right thing to do. And what my father would have done, if he were alive.' Nate straightened his back. 'If I truly believe that he was innocent, then I had best start behaving so. If I think there is truth to be revealed, then I do not mean to skulk in the bushes like a common criminal. I will go to Lord Keddinton with it and let him use the information as he sees fit. He knew both our fathers and is well placed in the Home Office. He will have the power to follow through on this, if anyone does.' The idea had been but a stray thought when he'd mentioned it to Diana. But spoken, Nate knew the rightness of it. For suddenly, he felt more like the true Earl of Leybourne than he had since the day his father had died.

But Stephen was unimpressed. 'Good luck with it, old friend. I wish you success. I truly do. But if your father is innocent, you may find that the world is less interested in truth than you think.'

'I am Nathan Wardale. I wish to see Lord Keddinton, on a matter of business, please.' It had been so long since he'd used it, his own name sounded strange in his ears.

Perhaps the unfamiliarity showed in his tone. For the butler at Robert Veryan's country estate raised an eyebrow, as though doubting his word. Nate could offer no calling card to assure the man of his identity. So he stood his ground and gave the kind of cold stare that he might have given had he still been a peer, as though he was not accustomed to being kept waiting on the doorstep.

At least there was no sneering response to the name Wardale. The man was certainly old enough to remember the scandal, but too disciplined to show distaste for his employer's business. After a chilly pause, the servant stood aside to allow him entrance, taking him to a receiving room not far from the front door. A short time later, a footman came to escort Nate the rest of the way to Keddinton's office.

As he was presented, Nate resisted the urge to shift nervously on the carpet before the desk like an errant schoolboy called to the headmaster for punishment. Though Keddinton had been expecting him, now that

Nate stood before his desk, the man kept him waiting in silence as the footman retreated, and continued to read the papers in front of him. It was a move designed to demonstrate that whatever business Nate might have, it could not be of sufficient importance to hold his full attention for more than a moment.

Nate smiled to himself and relaxed, as he recognized the gambit for what it was. While some might take it for a masterstroke of manipulation, it was really no better than the bluff of an inexperienced card player. When did a man with a good hand need to work so hard? Lord Keddinton was wary of him. Perhaps even frightened. And knowing that made the waiting much easier.

But what had Keddinton to fear from him? The man had been a friend of his father's at one time—long ago, before their disgrace. There had never been any indication that he was less than fair in his dealings before the trial or since. Surely an appeal based on that friendship would be heard.

Robert Veryan need have no fear of vengeance from him, for he had done nothing to earn it. Let Beshaley harass everyone involved with his Gypsy nonsense, if he wished. If Nate wanted things settled, he had best start behaving as though he were a rational gentleman with nothing to fear. Vindication after all this time could mean a return of the title and his good name in a way so public that it would regain him his family.

And lose him his love. If he was revealed as Nathan Wardale, Diana would hear of it. Perhaps a public attempt to clear his old name would show her that he had changed and meant her no harm. But at least he would be honest with her. And he suspected that the truth would be easier to accept if she heard it from the new Earl of Leybourne. She would certainly like that better than if it came from Nate Dale. Or worse yet, from the Gypsy.

So Nate waited patiently in front of the desk, and at last, Keddinton looked up from his papers, showing little interest in the man before him. 'Mr Wardale.'

'Lord Keddinton. I have news of an old matter.'

'I assume it concerns the disgrace of your family.' Keddinton pursed his lips, as though the matter was distasteful to him.

Nathan nodded. 'Fresh information has come to me concerning the death of Christopher Hebden.'

'Concerning your father's part in the events?' Keddinton leaned forward.

'My father had no part in the events, other than to place his trust in the wrong people. I think the same as I always have. There was a miscarriage of justice. My father did not commit the crime he was charged with.'

Keddinton leaned back again. 'And you have waited twenty years to come forward with it?'

'There have been difficulties that prevented me.' Would the man check his background and find the desertion? It was probably within his power. And from the disapproving look on his face, it was no different than he would expect from a Wardale. 'Recently, something has come to light that might change your view of the situation.'

He pushed the book forward, onto the desk, so that Keddinton could see the title, in gold upon the spine.

The man stared at it without interest. 'And what might this mean to me?'

'Read it. Particularly the pages leading up to and following the day of Christopher Hebden's death.'

Keddinton opened the book and paged through it, stopping as he got to the marked page, then pausing to read. Then he looked up, his expression unchanged. 'And you think there is significance in this?'

'I should think it would be obvious. George Carlow's friends suspected him of being a traitor. And he says nothing to deny the claim.'

'An innocent man would not feel the need.'

'The missing pages imply guilt.'

'Or spilled ink. Or damage by mice. Or nothing at all. For all I know, you removed them yourself before bringing me this, in an attempt to shift your father's guilt on to Lord Narborough. Did you ask him to explain them?'

'Of course not.'

'He did not give you this book, then?'

'Why, no. I...'

'Then how did you come by this?'

Caught in the sudden barrage of questions, Nate understood how Lord Keddinton had gained a reputation as the most crafty of spymasters, for he was a difficult man to distract. 'That is not important.' And damn him if he hadn't tipped Keddinton to how important it must be by saying those words. But it had not occurred to him, when he had come here, how quickly blame might fall onto Diana.

As suddenly as the questions started, they stopped. The other man pushed the book aside and sighed, his sternness evaporating into sympathy. 'I understand, Nathan, that you are eager to clear your father in the murder. You lost much by it and must wish to escape the disgrace. You loved him, as a good son should, and do not wish to believe him capable of evil. But I have seen no evidence, in twenty long years, that there was anyone else at work against the crown. Although you do not wish to believe it, the activities of the spy stopped conveniently after the death of your father. You must also understand that I cannot act on guesses and assumptions. I will look into the matter, of course. For if we were wrong, and the traitor escaped?' He shook his head. 'That would be a most serious thing, indeed.'

He paused, watching Nathan for a bit, as though weighing out choices before speaking further. Then he leaned forward again and said, 'When you came to me, I had hoped…I should not even tell you this, for it is a fact that few know and a matter of state security. But you had no part in this crime. And I would like to believe you would help, if you could, whether your father was involved or not. You would put the good of the country before your own needs, would you not?'

'Of course, sir.' And again he wondered how much Keddinton might know of his time in the Navy, for would he have so easily trusted a deserter?

Keddinton paused again, still observing his reactions. Then he nodded, as though what he had seen satisfied him, and said, 'At the time of Kit Hebden's death, we were having a problem with confidential information being leaked regularly to our enemies abroad. The messages we intercepted were being transmitted in a code so difficult that only the most skilled cryptologist could have cracked the thing. Without knowing the key to the cipher, there was little way to even tell how to begin. We put Hebden to work on it, hoping that there would be progress. He had a keen mind and a fascination for such things.'

'Perhaps he was the spy,' Nathan suggested. 'If the problem stopped after my father's death, it could as easily have been because Hebden was gone as well.'

'True, I suppose,' Veryan conceded. 'But Hebden assured us all, when last we saw him at dinner the night before he died, that a solution was forthcoming. If he had been guilty, then why would he have bothered? He could have stalled indefinitely and told us the code was unbreakable. We'd have been none the wiser.'

Nate tried to contain his impatience. 'So there was a code, and Hebden had cracked it. What is that to me?'

'Possibly the key to it all, Nathan. I knew both men. I doubt that Hebden would have made a false boast that night. He did not speak the whole truth about the code because he felt the traitor was in the room with us. Perhaps he wished to give the man warning, expecting him to end his life with honour or flee the country. We were all friends, you know. I doubt he'd have wanted to see a friend hang.'

'Then he was softer than the rest of you,' Nate responded. 'You and Carlow had no problem watching my father die.'

The memory must have been a difficult one. For the implacable Keddinton almost seemed to flinch at it, before regaining composure. 'It was harder than you know, Nathan. But Kit Hebden was like a brother to us as well. What else could we do?'

'You could have believed my father, when he said he was innocent. And while I might believe that it pained you to watch him die, I do not see the brotherly feeling recorded in George Carlow's journal.'

Keddinton made a helpless gesture. 'These are the private rantings of a much younger man. And Carlow had a bit of a hot head, back in the day. He was a man given over to impulse.'

'All the more likely that he was the killer.'

Keddinton shook his head. 'Every man with a hot temper does not turn killer. I see nothing in the journal to persuade me otherwise.'

'Then what would convince you?'

'If you should turn up the code key, it would tell us much. I searched for it that night, expecting it to be on Hebden's person. But there was nothing in his pockets that might be a key. If your father stole it—' Keddinton held up a hand to forestall any argument from Nathan '—he would not have had time to destroy it. Carlow was there within moments of the blow being struck. And I searched the grate. The fire was still unlit and with no fresh ashes at all.' He looked seriously at Nathan. 'Surely your father had secret places, in his

study or somewhere else in the house. If he had concealed it upon his person, he might have had time to
hide it, before they took him to Newgate. Or maybe he
gave something to your mother. Perhaps he slipped it
between the pages of a book. I doubt it would be more
than a single sheet of paper. Perhaps only a half sheet.
Or even less, if the writing was small. Do you
remember anything in his effects that might have
seemed odd? An unintelligible thing, rows of numbers,
or a language you did not understand?'

'It has been so long.' And very little existed from that
time before it had all gone bad. 'I remember nothing
that was as you described. The contents of the house
were sold at auction, just after the hanging. How can
you expect me...'

And then he remembered the torn pages of the
journal. 'The only paper I bring to you is from
Narborough's library. Maybe if we could find the
missing pages, there would be some answer in them.
Perhaps Carlow had written it there.'

Veryan shook his head again. 'I will make inquiries
as to why the book is damaged, but I am sure they will
come to naught.'

'But if they do not?'

Keddinton stood to show that the interview was near
its end, and came around the desk to put a fatherly hand
upon Nate's shoulder. 'I am as interested in the truth as
you are, but for a better reason. The safety of England
is at stake. Leave your direction with my servant. I will
contact you, if anything is found, just as you must

contact me if you discover what your father did with the cipher key. But until that time, you must trust me to proceed in the way I see fit. And that will be with caution, and sensitivity. If there is any fresh truth to be gained, after all this time, it will not involve purloining journals, or making wild accusations. Do you understand?'

In truth, Nate did not. What good did it do to employ spies, if they stuck at spying on the people they suspected? But he did not wish to lose the trust of so powerful a man. So he said, 'Of course.'

'Good day then.' Keddinton stepped away from him and signalled the footman to show him out.

Chapter Fourteen

Diana woke with a start to find the sun already high in the sky. She had overslept again. This made the third time in two weeks that she'd had to hurry her toilet to beat Verity to the breakfast table. It was little consolation to insist that this was most unlike her normal behaviour, for she feared that an error made three times must signal a change in character.

Of course, so much had changed around her in the last weeks that she might have reason to fear its effects. The journal had shaken her faith in Lord Narborough, which made prompt attention to the needs of his daughters less appealing to her than it had been.

And after the kisses in the park and all Nathan's talk of secrets, she'd found her own secrets had come back to haunt her. Her normally peaceful sleep was disturbed by dreams. Nightmares might be a better way to describe them, although she was not sure. She awoke more troubled than frightened, and sometimes rose in the night to check the latch on her bedroom door. In her dreams, the past caught up to her with a knock upon that door, and the silhouette of a dark man, pushing his way into her bedroom and whispering, 'It is time to pay the debt.'

Nathan Wardale. If the man was anything more than a ghost, she'd have heard something before now. Or his sister would have known his whereabouts. If he had not already come, he would not be coming and the dreams were nonsense. It was only her closeness to another very different Nathan that was making the old fears reawaken. And the knowledge of his kisses, which were turning some shameful part of her brain to carnality.

For though in dreams of youth, she had woken struggling against the bedclothes, fighting to keep the shadow at bay, the new dreams were different. Now, the dark man came to find her bedroom door unlatched. And when he grabbed her, she did not struggle. When he kissed her, she opened her mouth. And when he pushed her back upon the bed…

What would she do if things went the way she suspected in her waking life? Would she find herself married to one man and submitting to another, in her sleep, night after night? And worse, that she might enjoy the dreams. For she awakened from them with only vague memories of what had occurred, but a licentious desire to close her eyes and escape back into them.

Thank God she had awakened before the end. Suppose he had stepped out of the shadows as the grasping little man that her father had described to her. In reality, he would be ugly and pale as the underbelly of a rat, and he would laugh as he took everything she had, with no thought to her happiness or her future, just as he had with her father.

To dissolve the terrible image from her mind, she rose quickly and splashed the cold water from the basin on her face. A good wash and a cup of tea would clear the foolishness from her head. And perhaps a brisk walk in the park, before breakfast.

It was not her usual day for a walk, of course. It was not Tuesday. She smiled at the secret, and put her fingers to her lips to hide the fact. In all her years of work, she had never longed for her free day, during the other six. In her time with the Carlows, the things she had done on it were rarely any different than the things she did while working. Perhaps it was because she enjoyed the company of the girls, and they did not mind her taking time to herself during the week, as she needed it. She doubted Verity would miss her overly, should she go out on her own this morning.

It was only since the arrival of Nathan Dale that she had felt a need for privacy or a desire to be secretive about any of her actions.

And perhaps that was why she felt a tingling sensation at the base of her neck as she walked along the path this morning. Was it the memory of the dream that still lingered, or of last week's kisses? Or perhaps it was guilt over the theft of the journal.

She did not like to think on that. It could not have been such a terrible thing to take a book that had been untouched in the library for years. If Lord Narborough had wished the secrets hidden, surely he would have burned the thing.

Or perhaps he had just destroyed the pages that contained the worst of it. That book had been one amongst many. If he had elected to destroy it, then its absence from the set might have been an even easier clue to find.

There was certainly something wrong at the heart of the Carlow house. Maybe her feelings of foreboding were not the result of her own actions, but the creeping suspicion that troubles that were likely to fall upon the family as a result of what was occurring.

Or perhaps… She darted a glance to her side. Had the man by those chestnut trees been looking in her direction, only to suddenly turn away?

Nonsense. But she quickened her step and took the less popular fork in the path, assuming he would continue straight down the way, and she would know that she was being foolish.

But instead, she saw him again a short time later. He was still behind her and closer to her than he had been. When the same thing happened at the next turning, she admitted the truth: The man was following her.

He was of average height, slender and dark, with a gold hoop in one ear, and determined smile upon his lips. It was the Gypsy that Marc had warned her about, making no effort to hide himself from her, stalking her like a fox might stalk a hare as she walked amongst the trees.

What had Marc expected from this man? She was not sure, but she hoped he was not a mortal threat. The turn had been a mistake, for the way she had chosen was not well travelled. Without thinking, she had wandered farther away from help, should she need to call for it. She glanced around her, looking for anyone who might offer assistance, should the man try to take her purse or physically accost her. But the path was empty.

The Gypsy must have guessed her thoughts. He smiled at her, teeth startlingly white, hands held at his sides, palms open and facing her as though to show he meant no harm. 'Miss Price?'

She turned to face him. 'How do you know me?'

'Suffice it to say, I do know you. And I mean you no harm.'

'I have been warned about you. By Lord Stanegate.'

'What I have to say to you has nothing to do with Marcus Carlow or his family. It concerns you alone.'

She felt a sinking feeling in her stomach. She could think of several reasons why a stranger might want to talk specifically to her, and she liked none of them. 'Why should I believe anything you might say to me?'

He laughed. 'It does not really matter to me, either way. If it makes you feel more at ease, I will not approach closer. If you do not gaze at me, no one need know that we are even speaking, should they view us from a distance. I have some information for you. Nothing more than that.'

'Then give it and be gone.'

'There is a man, come recently into your life. He is not as he appears. Do not trust him.'

'You are the man come most recently into my life, sir. At your own advice, I had best not remain here.' She made as if to go, but the route home would take her closer to the Gypsy, if only to pass him.

Realizing her dilemma, he stepped off the path to give her room. 'Very well, then. But I came to you because we have a common enemy. Did your father ever tell you of Mr Wardale?'

She swallowed her shock at hearing the name, and said nothing. But her steps slowed to hear what he might say.

'You are right that you have no reason to listen, even if I tell the truth. But if you pay an unexpected visit to your old home, everything will be clear to you.' He turned and walked away into the trees, leaving the path clear for her.

She went slowly, one foot in front of the other, knowing that when she left the park, she would hail a cab for Hans Place and do as the Gypsy suggested. She did not know what she would do if she found Nathan Wardale in residence there. But she had to know—one way or the other—if the man was alive.

And as to the Gypsy's warning about a man come recently into her life?

A possibility occurred to her that was too horrible to contemplate.

Nate sat at the desk in his study, chewing on his lip and absently rearranging the items listed on the paper before him. Although he should not tarry over the execution of the duties, there was no reason that he shouldn't tackle them in an efficient order. And much as he might like to go haring after Robert Veryan's mysterious cipher, it was ranked at the bottom.

The important thing was that he take action. Any kind of action at all. He would not spend another day sitting at this desk, drawing pictures, sketching on the blotter as his life passed away. After years of hiding and remorse, it would feel good to be doing something. He could almost feel his mind stretching for the possibilities, as though waking from a long sleep. He had lain down as Nate Dale. But he would arise as Nathan Wardale. And a glorious morning it would be.

Should he go to the Admiralty first? It would ease his mind considerably to know that he need not fear arrest, nor was he likely to find himself locked in some hold and on his way back to America.

Once he was safe from the Navy, he would place an advertisement in the *Times*, seeking information on Rosalind, Helena and their mother.

And on the very next Tuesday...

No. It would not wait so long. Although he feared the response, Diana Price must be the very first thing on his list. He would write to her immediately, and explain in detail who he was and what was about to happen. He would bare his soul to her before proceeding, so that nothing would come as a surprise. She would be angry, of course. And possibly frightened of him.

But Diana was not without a heart. He had looked into her eyes and seen nothing but love. She had said the past was not important. Now, he would see if she could overlook it, once the worst was known. He would tell her, let her judge. He would promise to wait each Tuesday morning, in Hyde Park, until she returned. Then he would wait. His entire life, if necessary. And one day, he was sure that she would come to him.

There was a commotion in the hall outside the study, growing closer as the people involved neared the door. The butler, Benton, had raised his normally placid voice in a greeting—and then in argument. And a woman was protesting.

And as the door opened, he realized his plans were useless, for he had made them a day too late to save his future.

'You.' She was framed in the doorway, bonnet askew and coat disarranged, as though she had hurried to confront him with little care to ladylike decorum. The composure that he so often saw in her features was collapsing into a mix of anger, tears, fright and disgust. '*You* are the gambler my father warned me about?'

'Diana.' His voice choked on the word. 'I can explain.' But of course, he could not. There was no explanation for what he had done. No defence.

'I think it is quite obvious what happened. You discovered my position in the Carlow household. You wanted to discredit Lord Narborough, just as you said. So you used my growing affection for you to manipulate me.'

'I did not. I had no idea I would meet you when I came to that house. And I could not anticipate how things would end.'

She sneered. 'I find that hard to believe, sir. You played me like a harp. You enquired after my past and my future. Then you used my own needs and desires against me.'

'I asked you about yourself, because I wanted to know. I did not intend…'

It was plain on her face that she did not believe him. 'Why did you need to be so cruel? Did it amuse you to arouse feelings in me? Why did you not simply use my father's note to gain my cooperation? You must have known I'd have done anything to retrieve it.'

'I hoped you had forgotten by now.'

'Forgotten?' She put her hand to her mouth as though she was about to be ill. 'My entire life has been routed around that night. What I am. Where I am. Who I am. You thought I would forget that a gambler holds my honour like it was cheap coin?'

'Because your father bartered it away.' He had not meant to say the words, for he was sure that the bluntness of them would hurt her. But why must he be the one to pay when fools came to play with him?

There were tears welling up in her eyes now, and he felt the pain of them in his own heart. 'He could not stop himself from playing. And you took advantage of his weakness, just as you have taken advantage of me. You tricked me into turning on a family that has shown me nothing but kindness for years.'

'I did not trick you into taking that journal. You volunteered. And when you read the thing, you agreed with me.'

'Only because you planted the seeds of doubt in my mind. You promised that we would be together, once it was settled. And I?' She laughed. 'I foolishly convinced myself that you meant something honest with those words. I had no idea that if you wished for *togetherness*—' she shuddered '—you had but to produce my father's note and demand to receive it.'

'But you understood me correctly. I intended to offer. What you suspect? It was not what I meant at all. Here.' He fumbled in his pocket. 'If it means so much to you, then take the damn letter from me, now.'

'You carry it on your person? You have had it with you, all along?'

And how could he explain that to her, when he could not explain, even to himself, why he had not thrown the thing in the fire on the first night. 'Yes.' He held it out to her again. 'Take it.'

She reached out a hand for the paper, and her fingers trembled as though she thought the contact would burn her. And then she stopped, her hand still inches away. 'You are toying with me, aren't you? What do you want in return?'

'Toying? Certainly not. Take the thing back.'

'Because I can give you money. Not much…'

And again, her words pushed him to the brink of anger. 'Think what you will of me, Diana, for I deserve your contempt. But do not tell me that your virtue can be measured in money. Even if it were, it would be worth more than thirty-four pounds.'

She fell silent, as the meaning of his words sunk in.

And as the silence wore on, he wished that he could call them back and start again. Perhaps then he could make something he'd intended as a noble act seem less common and thoughtless.

Then she said, in a voice barely above a whisper, 'That was you, as well. There has been no one but Nathan Wardale interested in me. All along.' And she said it like it was the worst thing in the world.

'I meant to help.'

'I thought I knew the extent of my debt to you. And now I find it is everything I am, *plus* thirty-four pounds? What a fool I was to spend some of it. I will have to dip into what little savings I have, to return the full amount to you.'

'You misunderstand me, Diana. I do not want money…'

'Then there is only one thing you could want from me.' Her gaze felt cold upon him. But there was nothing cold about her. Her eyes flashed, her skin was flushed a healthy pink, and the trembling of her lips made them all the more kissable.

He could feel his gambler's nerves trembling in answer beneath a facade of calm. Her disdain for him aroused him as much as it angered him. He could remember the feel of those lips, her hands on his face, her look of concern when he told her of his past. When he'd held her in his arms in Hyde Park, she'd been eager to forgive him anything and ignore his flaws. Was he so different today?

He threw his hands in the air. 'All right. I admit it.

All of it, Lord help me. I never wanted the letter in the first place. I begged your father to stop before it came to this. And when he would not, I thought to shock him to his senses with a bet no sane man would take. It was a mistake. It does no good to bluff a madman. And Diana Price, your father was too mad with cards to care about his own daughter's honour.'

She covered her ears as though the truth was something she did not wish to hear.

'So I did an unthinkable thing. But I did not seek you out. Not once in ten years. And when I found you, quite by accident, I had no intention of acting upon this letter. I gave you the money hoping to assuage my guilt, which has been acute.' He laughed at his own folly. 'And it seemed to help. I even thought, for a time, that all was forgiven. I'd convinced myself that it would be possible to offer for you honourably and hide what I had done. You would have been happy with your fantasy of Mr Dale. I would have made sure of the fact.

'But then, the Gypsy threatened to tell you the truth, and I was willing to do anything to prevent it. And he has gone and done it anyway, hasn't he? For how else would you have found me?' He silently cursed Stephano Beshaley, and his own folly for believing that there was any mercy left in the man who had once been his friend.

'You have come to this house, which once was yours, to demand the truth. I will no longer deny it. I am Nathan Wardale, the man who ruined your father and your life. And I want you. Totally and completely.

In ways that you cannot imagine, and that cannot be encompassed by this foolish bit of paper. The sight of you, the sound of you, the taste of you. Your sweet face, your soft skin, the way you tip your head to the side when you are thinking, and pretend to frown while smiling, so that you can appear to be the stern old chaperone, and not as young and lovely as the girls you watch. I can hardly breathe when I think of you. And the kisses we shared in the park?' He gave a slow shake of his head. 'The memory possesses me.'

'You villain.' She reached out a hand to strike him, but he caught it easily and pulled her body to his. The kiss, when it came, seemed both expected and unfamiliar. He opened her mouth and drank her in. She was as sweet and good as he'd remembered, her body warm and inviting. And he felt as she returned the kiss, her tongue moving in his mouth and her arms reaching out to circle his waist.

And then she pushed him away, wiping at her mouth as though her own actions disgusted her. 'I hate you.'

'You do not even know me.' He held out a hand to her, hoping that it would soften her mood. 'But I would like you to. We could forget the past. Start fresh, as we planned.'

'Not while that marker exists.' She swallowed.

'Here, then.' He put the paper into her hand, and curled her fingers about it. They were so cold, almost numb, that he feared she would drop the thing once he released it. And for a moment, he thought it was over. She had the note and he did not. That was what she had come for. Now they could start again.

But then, he saw the look in her eyes. She was still suspicious, waiting for the catch, the snare, the string that came attached to the paper. There was no good way to convince her that he did not expect a reckoning. If he left her alone, she would live waiting for it. And if he did not? Then it would be all she could think of, on their first night together.

'What do you want from me?' she said, her tone dry and empty.

And so he answered her. 'What do you think I deserve?' If she thought him such a demon, the least she could do was tell him so. Damn him to hell and call him unworthy.

She went to the sofa by the fire and lay down upon it, fumbling with her skirts, spreading her legs.

'Stop that immediately.' She had dropped the paper upon the floor. And without thinking, he picked it up again.

'I do not wish to live a moment longer with an unpaid debt upon my conscience. Knowing that you could come for me at any time? It has been unbearable.' Though she did not rise, she pulled away from him as he approached her, as though the thought that he might take advantage of what she was offering was almost unbearable. Her face showed such pain that he could hardly stand it.

'I asked you.' He pointed a finger at her, in accusation. 'I asked you if you were happy in your job as companion. You assured me you were all right. You were happy. And that it had all turned out for the best. Were you lying?'

'That was before I knew who you were.'

'And now that you do, it is all changed. I understand that you cannot be happy with me. But it appeared you were growing quite fond of Nathan Dale. Was that a lie as well?'

'It was a mistake.' She lay still upon the couch, her bosom heaving and skirts so disarrayed that he could see the slender ankles and shapely calves beneath them. Every movement, every breath, seemed an invitation. But she was looking at him with those wide, innocent eyes. And although the affection in them was gone, there was not a trace of guile. He had been sure that she wanted him, and yet she swore that she did not.

'Then it is a mistake that is easily corrected. Nathan Dale, who you loved, is gone, never to return. And between you and Nathan Wardale, there is nothing?'

She hesitated. It was less than a breath. Less than a fraction of a second. But it was there. And then she said, 'There is nothing between us but the writing on that piece of paper.' And when he looked into her eyes again, he saw it: the bluff that he had been hoping for.

He had broken her heart with his carelessness. She was disappointed and angry and afraid. But she was not afraid of him. She feared what she was likely to do, should he touch her again. And she hoped that a single, weak lie could make him throw down his cards and leave the table.

There was much more between them than she would admit. But if he allowed her to escape, she would never understand. He took a shallow breath, and read the paper, as though the words were new to him, but of little consequence. Then put it back into his pocket. 'Then I lied when I said I did not wish to redeem this. If that is all I am to you, if there is no love between us, then what reason do I have to yield it unpaid?' He patted his pocket. 'It is still on my person, as it has been for ten years. And during that time, I made no effort to hurt you, to hunt you down, to humiliate you with it. And so it will remain, if you wish to walk out of my life. But if it is so important to you, then you must retrieve it from the table beside my bed. Return here, at eight tonight. We will settle what is between us. If you wish to leave afterwards, the marker will go with you and you may do what you like with it. I hope you are happy together. But once you go from here, you will never see me again. Good day, Miss Price.'

He left her, striding out of the study and up the stairs to his room. She was still sprawled on the couch, and if he remained one more moment in her company, he would give in to his desires and fall upon her like the animal she thought him to be.

After what he had suggested, she would not dare to follow. His own words had shocked him. For what gentleman would ever say such to a lady? Especially the woman he loved. But if she did not see his self-disgust, then she could assume what she wished. And since she seemed to expect the evil seducer, that was what he would give to her. He would play her game—and beat her at it, for if he was nothing else, he was good at games.

And what was love, after all, but another game of

chance? He was sure she would come back to the house, prepared to make the ultimate sacrifice to conclude her business with Nathan Wardale. But when the door was closed and the lights were out, it would be a different matter entirely.

She had loved him before this morning. And if he had lured her to his rooms two days ago, and asked as Nathan Dale for what she was now willing to barter, she would have given it willingly. If she had the nerve to return to him, he would make her face the fact that she wanted him in the same way that he did her. He would give her the sort of night that any man would be proud to offer the woman he loved. And then, he would see if she was so willing to leave him.

Chapter Fifteen

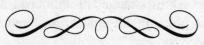

How could she have been so stupid?

The words echoed endlessly in her mind as Diana sat with Verity and Honoria in the white salon, mechanically jabbing the needle in and out of her embroidery. Had not her father warned her against just such a day as this? Had not she spent the whole of her adult life on guard, always suspecting that someday there would be a knock on the door and a man would come who would know far too much about her past?

Of course, Nathan Dale had not come as a seducer. He had come to speak to Marc and seemed surprised to meet her there. But his initial curiosity should have been a warning. Who would have reason to be interested in a paid companion? It was her own vanity that had led her to believe he fancied her. Nothing more than that.

Of course, her father's description had been totally different from the man who had come to her. He had described Wardale as little better than a boy. Pale of skin, thin of body, and with cold dead eyes. And having met Nell, she'd assumed a greater family resemblance between them than existed.

If Nathan Wardale's life had been as hard as the one that Nathan Dale had described to her, then the person her father had seen was but a shadow of the man to come. Whether he'd enjoyed it or not, life at sea had put muscle on him, changed his colouring and his gait. And hardship had made him serious, and sensitive to the feelings of others.

But those thoughts sounded almost like sympathy in her mind, so she pushed them away. His appearance did not matter, nor his reason for coming. He was still the person who was responsible for her current condition, and she had hated him for years.

Her inner turmoil must be reflected in her face. Verity had put down her work and was looking at her with concern. 'Are you sure you are all right, Diana?'

'I am fine.' Her voice sounded brittle in her own ears, and her smile must look as false as it felt. For now Honoria was staring at her with the same worried expression. 'Well you certainly do not look it. Perhaps this evening, it would be better if we attended the party without you.'

The party. She had forgotten, in her rash promise to Nathan Wardale, that she was already engaged to attend the Carlow girls at a musicale. And now, she must lie to free herself. 'I think you are right. It is probably just the beginnings of a megrim. I should make an early night of it. But that would leave you without a chaperone. And I would never…' She let the thought trail away, waiting for one of the girls to take the bait.

'We will be safe in the company of Lord Keddinton, I am sure,' said Honoria. 'And I promise there will be no ill reports of me tonight, for it would hardly be fair to worry you.'

Verity nodded. 'We will give you no trouble, and will be very quiet when we return, so as not to disturb your sleep.'

Or notice her absence, if she had not yet returned herself. 'Thank you,' Diana said with a smile, ignoring the pang of guilt she felt at how easy it was becoming to deceive her friends.

It was Nathan Wardale's doing. All of it. Until he had appeared in her life, she had worked so hard to resist temptation. But a few short weeks later, she was lying, stealing, and preparing to sneak away from the house, coldly contemplating the loss of her virtue to a man she detested. How many other sins would she commit before he was through with her? And did uncontrollable anger count against the total of them?

For she felt angry now. She had never been so angry in her life. Not even when father had lost their house, and sat her down with the tearful explanation of why they must go so quickly. And why she must, at all costs, avoid contact with a man named Wardale.

When that had happened, she'd felt shock. And fear. And for a time, she had been upset with her father. But it had been tempered with love and forgiveness. For what good did it do her to be angry with Father, when his behaviour never changed? She had learned to put anger aside as impractical.

But now? There was no sympathy in her heart for either of the men that had brought her to this. Had she meant so little to Father that he could not put down the cards? And that he would lose her to Nathan Wardale, of all the people in the world. He had become a man she could have loved and respected, had the past been different. Had it not been enough for him to know that he owned her body? Had it been necessary to win her heart as well?

Her response to him was infuriating. She had melted under his kisses and longed for the touch of his hand. Even this morning, when she was furious with him, he had managed to turn the heat in her brain to passion. It was like a red light, burning in her mind, obscuring rationality and smothering the calm and reasoned response she would have encouraged for anyone else. She wanted to hurt him. She wanted him to suffer as she was suffering.

And it was in her power to do so. The red light faded, and in its wake there was a horrible calm, as she saw the weapon of torture, plainly in her grasp.

She knew the location of Helena Wardale.

Had she mentioned the woman's name to him at all in their discussions? Obviously not, or he would have commented on it. If he had even suspected, he would have inquired in an offhand manner, about the birth name of Marc's bride. She had seen the hungry look in his eye as he had told her about his family. If he'd known how close he was to the solution, he'd have dropped his charade and begged her for the truth. He'd have done anything to know, just as he would make her debase herself for her freedom tonight.

But now? She would use his only weakness to her advantage.

She waited until the girls had gone away with Lord Keddinton, accepting their concern with a wan thank you, and a promise to rest well in their absence.

And as soon as the door latched behind them, she went swiftly to her room. She threw aside the dress she had worn as simple Diana Price, lady's companion, and pulled out the green silk gown she had bought with the money he had given her. Blood money, meant to salve his conscience.

She fastened herself into the dress and turned to admire it in the mirror. It was indecently low and the deep green of his eyes. Her breasts all but spilled out of the bodice, creamy white and beautiful. He would want to touch those breasts, she was sure, and felt a shiver run through her. She went to work on her hair, loosening the pins and freeing braids until the curls seemed ready to fall about her shoulders at the least urging. Another way to trap him, if his talk in the park was true.

She had always imagined herself, should she be forced, going to Nathan Wardale as a virgin sacrifice. But now? She would go as a conqueror. When he tried to take her, she would take from him as well. She would tempt him with her body. When he thought his moment of triumph was near, she would ask him what lengths he was willing to go to, to regain his sister.

And then they would see who was master. And who was slave.

Her preparations complete, she pulled on her cloak and crept down the backstairs and out onto the street to hail a cab. Once under way, she settled back into the squabs, revelling in the cruelty of it. How best to hurt him? If she attacked immediately, the shock might prevent the rest of his plans for her. If she offered to trade the information for the marker, she was sure that he would cave to the demand.

Or she could savour the moment, letting him think he was controlling her, all the while knowing that she held the true power. Perhaps she would never reveal the secret at all. She could tell him that she knew, but that he never would. Give hints of the truth, but no more.

She would let him suffer as she had, balanced on the knife's edge for years, never knowing when or if the revelation would occur. Withholding of good news would be as bad as the suspending of catastrophe.

The hired cab pulled up in front of the building that had once been her home. She wrapped the cloak tight about her body, pulling the hood up to obscure her face from the driver, signalled him to wait, stepped down into the street, then hurried up to the front door. Benton answered to her knock. He was the same as she remembered from childhood. He had been unable to contain his joyful, 'Miss Diana!' when he'd opened the door for her earlier in the day, as though her anger with him and Wardale could not extinguish his happiness at seeing her well.

Tonight, she said, 'I am expected.' And he answered with a dispassionate nod.

She gave him no other explanation, but he must have guessed what was about to happen. The shame of it took her in a wave, for it was as though her own father had survived to see her disgrace. He reached for her cloak, but she pulled away from him, as though even the slightest touch were an invasion.

Benton cringed at this, and his hands dropped to his sides. Then he muttered that he would get his master, and led her to the sitting room, closing the door against prying eyes.

The house seemed strangely quiet, for other than the butler, there was not a footman in sight, nor maids, nor any other sign of a servant. But it only took one set of eyes to see her enter the house. It would not be possible to keep the secret, once it got below stairs. How many people would know of her fall, by the end of this night? Could she ever go back to what she once was, after stepping across this particular threshold of her life?

Not possible. Less than a week ago, she had been a woman in love. That feeling seemed a distant memory, compared to the loathing she felt for the man now.

And the house gave her muddled emotions a nightmare quality. Everywhere she looked was familiarity. She knew the rooms as well as she knew her own hand. But it was all wrong. Here was the little marble-topped table she had played under as a girl. But that had been in the upper hall. How had it come here? Where was the chiming clock that had been upon the mantel? The bowl of fresh flowers that stood there now was quite attractive, but shouldn't it be in the foyer?

It was as though her childhood had been altered with time, as the tide might change the sand on the beach. It was wrong, all of it, and nothing like what she had pictured on the few times she had imagined returning here in triumph to oust the usurper.

It was not *her* parlour. But it was a lovely room, all the same. Under different circumstances, she might have found it comfortable, and the fire in the grate and the flowers above it would have seemed more welcoming than the cold ticking of a clock. She frowned. She had expected to feel more, somehow. Happy, or sad or more likely, filled with righteous anger at the man who had taken her home and worked to wipe the traces of her from it.

Instead, it was as though some portion of her anger was wiped away with the change. This was not her home any more. Even if she returned, a simple rearrangement of the furniture could not bring back the past. Nor could it change any of what had occurred.

The door opened, and Nathan Wardale entered, unannounced. He smiled at her, as though nothing had changed between them. 'Welcome, Diana.' He held out a hand. 'Benton did not help you with your cloak? Here, allow me. And then perhaps, a glass of wine?'

Rage simmered fresh within her. How dare he pretend that this was a normal visit, or that she wished his hospitality? 'Wine will not be necessary. Let us complete our business,' she said through gritted teeth. 'My cab is waiting, and I wish to return home before ten.'

'You told the driver to remain?' He gave her an odd look and then a pitying smile. 'I will go and send him away again. I would send a servant, but I have dismissed most of them for the evening. I assumed that you would prefer it.'

'The evening?' The insolence of the man was astounding. 'You misunderstand the amount of time I will devote to this enterprise.'

'And you misunderstand the amount of time it will take.' There was the smile, again. 'It is obvious that you have managed to retain the loan's collateral, for you are quite naïve. You must allow that I am more experienced in the events that will transpire tonight, and permit me to set the timetable.'

Before she could speak, he stepped out of the room, closing the door behind him. She drew back the curtain and glanced out of the front window to see him offering a bank note to the driver before waving the man off. The view of the street was just as she remembered. But the red silk that framed it was nothing like the green she had been expecting. She closed her eyes against the dissonance, and tried to decide whether his high-handed behaviour made her angrier or just nervous. It definitely added to the sense of disquiet she felt, as she waited for him to return to the sitting room.

It had been easy to plot against him, when not staring into those deep green eyes. And so easy to forget that the man was a master gamesman, adept at disguising his true feelings while parting others from their valuables. She needed to be on her guard. For if she began to think of him as legitimate master of this house, what right had she to be angry?

When he returned, he was smiling again, as though he found her impending downfall to be faintly amusing. 'On this night, of all nights, you wanted to hold the cab, as though you were running an errand. I am curious. Just how long do you expect this to take?'

She wondered if the question was an attempt to draw out the action, or did it have some logical purpose? But then, she'd wondered the same about all his other questions, since the day they'd met. 'The minimum amount of time necessary. It has taken ten years of my life already. I do not wish to spend a moment longer than I must.'

She had meant the words to sting, but if they did, it did not show on his face. Instead, he shrugged. 'It will take as long as it takes. Not so fast as you might like. Nor as long as I would wish. If I were ham-fisted, selfish or cruel, I could have had you back in your waiting cab before now. We could conclude our business here, on the rug or against a wall, without even bothering to undress.'

He looked at her again and his gaze grew as soft and warm as it had been on their walks together in the park. And for a moment she weakened, wishing the man in front of her could ever again be Nathan Dale. Then he said, 'I have heard tales of Sultans in seraglios, taking days, even weeks over this process. The slow baring of the flesh, the destruction of inhibition, the readying of the minds and bodies of both participants, the evoking and sharpening of each sense to appreciate the final consummation. It is not a thing to be rushed.'

The timbre of his voice dropped, and his pace slowed to linger on each word, each image forming in his mind. Was it her imagination, or could she smell incense, hear the exotic music and taste dates on her tongue? She could see herself lying back in silk cushions, the height of decadence as he bent over her, caressing and perfuming her skin.

She caught her breath, trying to find her anger again, for the image had been strangely pleasant.

She saw his half smile change again, as though he knew what she had imagined and it pleased him. 'I will have you home by dawn. Not too late to save your reputation, if you have managed to conceal your absence.' He paused again. And then said, 'If you still wish to go through with this, that is. I have no intention of forcing you to do something you find abhorrent.' He paused once more time. 'It is not too late to change your mind.'

'No. I am resolute.' But her voice did not sound that way in her own ears. He had given her the chance to get away. Why did she not take it and run? Or take it as her moment of victory. She had but to say the words, 'Touch me and you will never see Helena,' and the evening would be at an end.

But when she should have spoken, her traitorous mind had been wondering how the impending process could possibly take weeks. She had missed her opportunity.

Perhaps time was an illusion. Because he was progressing so methodically that each thought, each smile, each word from his mouth, seemed to take hours to reach her. Several more heartbeats passed before he said, 'Very well. Then let us begin.' He touched her shoulders with his hands, brushing the cloak out of the way, and draping it gently over a chair. When he turned and caught sight of her dress, he froze in place for a moment, and she could feel his eyes travelling over her body, lingering on the exposed flesh.

She waited for the pounce. The rough grasp and the shock of his ravenous mouth against her breast.

'So beautiful. But too much, too soon,' he whispered. 'You are like a feast, and I am a starving man. You come to me like this, knowing that, other than by accident, on the very first day, I have not felt the touch of your ungloved hand?' He reached for her again with tenderness, beginning at the shoulders and letting his fingers trail down until they barely touched her own, and then he took both her hands, and brought them to his lips in a gesture that was more reverence than kiss. Then, one at a time, he tugged gently at her fingers until he had pulled her long white gloves down, baring the flesh of her arms inch by sensitive inch. The gloves dropped to the floor and he brought her hands to his face again, rubbing them with his closed lips, binding them together with his fingers about her wrists as he kissed the palms, turning them so that they were cupped before him and he could taste each fingertip in turn before settling over her pulse point, his tongue flicking against the skin in time to the ebb and flow of her blood.

From somewhere deep within her, there came an unexpected shudder of delight.

He smiled. 'This is why it must not be too quick. We must not squander this night. Do you understand?' He held her by the fingertips, walking backward, leading her through the door and toward the stairs. 'I have so much to learn.' He never took his eyes from hers as he went, drawing her after him, up the stairs and down the hall, to the master suite.

She went with him, powerless to resist, as though the kisses on her hands had bound her to him more tightly than any shackles. She glanced about her as they walked, and saw that, in ten years, the decoration of the corridor had changed. Colours, furnishings, the hangings on the walls, all different or rearranged. It was a different house than the one she had left, just as she was a different person.

And Nathan Wardale was a different man from the one she expected to find here.

No. The same. He was the same man that had ruined her father, and she must not forget it. Nathan Dale's stories of hardship and loss meant nothing to her. They were not justification for what he had done to her. Other men had suffered, yet they did not buy and sell innocent girls over a gaming table.

And yet, he continued to stare at her in wonder, as though none of that had happened. He looked as she imagined a man in love might look, as though no past or future existed outside of his lover's arms.

They had crossed the threshold to his room, and he released her, closing the door to shut them away from the rest of the world. And for a moment, she wanted to reach out to him, to cling for support. Or run away. The world had gone mad and would take her with it if she thought too closely about what was happening to her. Then he came back to stand very near to her, and he kissed her on the back of the neck as he had in the park. It was sweet and soft, not like she had imagined the kisses of her despoiler to be. 'I wish to touch your hair.' There was a faintly wistful quality in his voice, as though he thought she could deny him.

She moved to the mirror above the tall dresser and pulled the remaining pins from her hair, ready to shake it free. And then she caught sight of him, watching as though mesmerized by the sight. She basked in the warmth of it, for his gaze was as gentle as the touch of his hands had been, when bringing her here. Though his words had been seductive, everything about his actions calculated to reassure and not threaten, to coax the responses from her gradually. Her anger faded as she watched him, and he felt it go. And then he paused to look into her eyes, and breathed, 'Let us undress.'

The anger came flooding back, and anxiety along with it. She did not see the note that she had come to retrieve. And how much longer did she wish to play this game, before bringing it to an end? Shedding a few hairpins and a pair of gloves did little damage to her honour. But she could not very well strip to her chemise before springing her trap. Or perhaps she could. For it was difficult to see the man standing so reverently in front of her as a true adversary. She took a moment to gather her courage, and reached to undo one of the tiny hooks at her back.

He shook his head. 'Let us undress each other.' And he caught one of her hands in his, rubbed the knuckles across his lips until he felt her fingers begin to relax, and then placed them on the end of his cravat.

She paused for a moment, unsure, still waiting for the move on his part that would give her reason to strike back. And then she took hold and gave a gentle tug, watching as the elegant knot dissolved into a wrinkled strip of linen and dropped to the floor.

His neck was bare. It had never occurred to her to look at a man's throat before. She was so used to seeing them covered. She reached up and touched him. He was soft and smooth, close shaven though it was late in the day. Perhaps he had done it for her. And without thinking, she undid the neck of his shirt and let her fingers linger in the hollow of his throat.

His eyes closed as though he were sleeping and lost in some very pleasant dream. And then, he leaned forward and kissed her again, one hand cupping the back of her neck. He was bolder this time, opening her mouth and letting her feel his hunger as he slowly licked into her and drew her tongue into his mouth. She should not enjoy this. And yet she did. Her hand still rested against his throat, and she could feel the way his pulse increased as he grew more passionate. He pulled away, to kiss the hollow of her throat, bending her back to lay his cheek against her exposed chest and press his lips to the upper slopes of her breasts. As a counterpoint to the dizzying feel of the contact, she felt the barest touch of fingertips at her back. And when he withdrew, her dress was open and loose against her body, the sleeves slipping off her shoulders.

He touched her face, then, placing his fingers under her chin and tipping her lips up to touch his. And he whispered, 'You are beautiful tonight. Even more beautiful under the silk you wear. And I swear by all that is holy that if you give yourself to me, you will not regret it.' He kissed her again, pressing his lips to her cheek, her hair and her neck, and wrapping his arms around her body.

He was warm, and it took away the chill on her back, so she nestled close to him, putting her arms around his waist under his coat. After a time, he whispered, 'Would you help me off with my coat, please?'

It was not such a hard thing to run her hands up his body until they reached his shoulders and to push the wool away from him. The coat fell to the floor. She glanced down at it, ready to bend and pick it up, for it would become wrinkled if they left it in a heap.

But he sighed, 'Unimportant,' against the shell of her ear.

And when he used that tone, it did seem so. He was making her feel as if she was the thing most important to him in the world. She laid her head on his shoulder, and felt how different it was. Now that the coat was gone, she could feel more of the man and less of the tailor. And she felt a strange stirring, as the outlines of his body were uncovered to her.

His hand was on her back, fingers spread to span it, and he rubbed gently, his other hand stroking her neck and her hair. And the buttons of his waistcoat were poking against her chest, so she undid them, one by one, and pushed it out of the way.

His breathing quickened and he kissed her again, running his tongue along the seam in her lips until she opened them again. The taste of him amazed her. It was wine and spice, and she could not seem to get enough of it. When she stopped for breath, she found that they had pushed her gown out of the way, until it hung from her body at the hip, and his waistcoat had followed his coat to the floor.

He looked down, and gave a shaky laugh. 'My valet will be appalled.'

'Oh, dear.' She looked in the direction of the changing room.

He gathered her to him again. 'I am teasing. Do not think of it. We are alone, remember? All alone.' He put his hands on her hips and pushed her dress the rest of the way off her body. 'No one will see. No one will hear. And not a word shall pass from my lips over this.' Then he reached around her and undid the knot of her stays.

She had a moment's fleeting longing for his first suggestion, that they do it quickly without bothering to remove their clothing. It was all getting out of hand, and her thoughts swirled into focus and away again. She would put an end to this. She would stop him, soon. Another minute. Perhaps two. But it felt so wonderful as he worked slowly to lay her bare. And to put her hand on his shoulder and feel muscle through the linen of his shirt was as exciting as feeling his fingers on the small of her back, with a bit of cotton lawn as the only protection. Without thinking, her hand moved on his body, and she could feel the softness of hair, the smoothness of skin and the hard flat nipples on his chest, resting just below her fingertips beneath the fabric.

He smiled at her, and then closed his eyes and sighed. 'Your touch is so gentle. I am not accustomed to gentleness.'

She wondered if he meant that he wished her to be more bold. She surprised herself, for even caring what he wished. There was nothing in their agreement that required her to act, only to submit.

He opened his eyes again. 'Touch me as you wish to be touched, so that I may know what gives you pleasure.' And he mirrored the position of her hands on his body, placing his fingertips against her nipples, but making no effort to do more.

It was maddening. The skin beneath his hands tingled in expectation of his movement, and her nipples peaked as though her body could imagine the brush of his fingers and the increasing roughness of his touch.

His face relaxed into a lazy, seductive smile, and he leaned forward to kiss her, catching her lower lip with his teeth and sucking gently upon it.

Her breast ached in answer to each tug upon her

lips, and she moved her hands experimentally over his chest, rubbing her thumbs against him.

In answer, he moved his hands on her, and kissed her again, his tongue tracing designs upon her lips.

Desire stirred within her. That was what she wanted. To feel him touching her, possessing her. She circled, rubbed, palmed and pinched. And he did the same. She pulled away from his kiss and buried her face in his shirt. She pressed her lips to him, licking softly against the linen until it grew wet and clung to his skin. She bit at him, sucking hard, doing her best to draw the little bud into her mouth.

He took a deep breath, and she could hear his heart, so near to her ear, beating faster. His hands on her breasts grew more forceful, tormenting her body as she did his. Then he took them away, and cupped her face, pulling it up to his mouth, and kissing her with the same demanding strength, pushing his tongue into her mouth, thrusting until she could feel the penetration deep within her body. He trailed down her throat, marking her flesh with the force of his kisses until he settled over her breast. He paused for a moment, letting his breath warm her, then took the cloth-covered nipple into his mouth. The sensations grew in her, and she dug her fingers into the muscles of his shoulders, as though she feared that the force of her feelings would rip her away from his body.

When it seemed all but unbearable, he released her and began again on her other breast. She gave a tiny laugh of relief, for she had forgotten that there was still more to feel. The same feeling of expectation was building, compounded with the excited nerves that he had left behind.

And the sudden knowledge that he could begin it all again, on naked skin, with no chemise as obstacle.

In response to her grip on his shoulders, his fingers dug into the flesh at the side of her waist, pushing her petticoat down and pulling her hips tight to his. And she remembered that what they were doing was nothing compared to what they would do.

Then the sensation broke over her, and she was gasping for control, her body shuddering, her muscles clenching as though they wished to hang on to the feeling, to take it inside and keep it forever. Nathan gave another pull upon her breast, as though he knew how to prolong her reaction, until she had experienced the last drop of the pleasure, before letting it slowly fade, leaving her weak and in his power. When she could manage to speak, she whispered, 'What is happening to me?'

He lifted his head and smiled up at her. 'Nothing that should not happen. And nothing that will not happen again. It is the reason that I did not think it necessary to retain the coachman. I had no wish for a few minutes alone with you, while I took without giving.' He dropped to his knees in front of her, letting his hands trail down her body until they touched her ankles. And then they progressed slowly back up her leg, touching her stockings until they reached the top. 'I recognize the sacrifice you make by doing this, and I mean to be worthy of it.'

His fingers were undoing her garters, and occasionally, some part of his hand would brush the bare flesh of her leg. Each time, she felt a fresh shudder go through her, as though her body remembered the release she had experienced as he'd kissed her breasts. But now, his face was settled between her legs, and she could feel the heat of his breath, pooling there, stroking her as gently as his hands were touching her legs. He drew each stocking down to her ankle, with long smooth caresses. And then he lifted each foot to remove slipper and stocking, and as she off-balanced, her body pressed close to his face for a fleeting kiss through the lawn of her shift.

The trembling within her was almost continual now, a strange fluttering that was a precursor to her body's surrender. Before he could kiss her again, she reached for the linen of his shirt and pulled it over his head, distracting him and leaving his chest bare for her admiration. He was still kneeling before her. And for a moment, she imagined him helpless before her, as though she were in the seraglio he had described and he existed only for her pleasure. Experimentally, she lifted her bare foot and ran it up the inner seam of his trousers, feeling the muscle of his thigh jump at her touch. He cupped her ankle and drew her leg higher, until her knee rested against his chest and her foot at the apex of his legs.

He stroked her instep, making her laugh, letting her foot struggle to escape the tickling. She nuzzled it against his body, stroking it against his member. Feeling him grow as she touched him, and watching his face contort with the strain of control. He positioned her against him, holding her there, showering her knee with kisses, his breath coming as a moan of desire against her skin.

Suddenly, he pushed her leg down and rose. He bent and caught her easily behind the knees, scooping her up into his arms and striding across the room to the bed, tossing her in a heap onto the pillows piled there. The skirt of her chemise rode high on her legs, and he stared down at her—thighs sprawled open, breasts straining against the damp fabric. In a scant hour with the man, she had become a wanton.

And she enjoyed it. He was staring at her body. She reached for the hem of her shift to pull it higher in invitation.

He held out a hand to stop her, then leaned against the bedpost, pulling off boots and stockings, and reaching for the buttons on his trousers. 'Do you understand what you are doing to me, Miss Price? A little more play, and I will spill my seed without ever touching you. And we shall have to begin, all over again.'

Her body gave an answering shudder, welcoming an idea that would have been abhorrent to her this morning.

He was naked before her now, fully aroused. He knelt upon the bed, between her legs as she pulled the last garment over her head, casting it aside and settling back into the pillows to await what she knew must come.

But instead, he covered her with his body, kissing her mouth, her eyes, her chin, and then slowly down, lingering over her breasts until she was nearly mad with desire, and then moving lower, to kiss between her legs, massaging her thighs with his palms, opening her with his tongue until she had no defences left and her body was wracked with wave upon wave of ecstasy, desperate to be filled.

And after he had claimed her with his mouth, he took her, when she was too lost with need to feel the pain, plunging over and over, while she shook with joy, tightening against him, welcoming him in. He shook as well and moaned her name. And then his body went still against hers.

He pulled her close, and rolled to the side, never leaving her, caressing her back and kissing her face as they lay nestled in the pillows on his bed. He reached to draw a counterpane over them, and whispered, 'My love.'

And from there, it was too easy, just to fall asleep in his arms.

Chapter Sixteen

Where were her gloves?

On the floor, where he had dropped them? She fumbled over the carpet of the darkened sitting room. The candles had burned away and the fire as well, leaving her cold in the predawn light.

'Are you all right, Miss Diana?'

She started, instinctively reaching to straighten her hair, her dress, anything…her hands fluttering over her body as uncontrolled as birds, desperate to assure herself that nothing on the exterior had changed and that the letter of debt was still secure in her pocket, where she had tucked it before creeping from the bedroom to find her cloak.

The voice had come from behind her, in the hall. The butler, again. If he did not guess the purpose of her visit when she arrived, he could have no doubt now.

She turned to him, trying to smile, pretending a composure that was not possible. 'All right? Of course, Benton. I am fine.'

He continued to stare at her, without judgment or disapproval, but with an unusual amount of concern. 'Are you sure, Miss Diana?' A cloud passed over the old man's face. 'He did not hurt you?'

And suddenly, she was sure that she had but to raise her voice in alarm and Nathan would be dragged from his bed and beaten bloody by his own servants.

She gave the man another false smile. 'Hurt me? Of course not, Benton. You have nothing to fear on my account. But if you wish, you may help me find a carriage. I would like to return to Lord Narborough's town house. Discreetly, if possible.'

'Very good, miss. Mr Wardale's carriage is at your disposal. I will see to it at once. And the other glove is under the side table. Allow me.'

He retrieved the thing for her, escorted her to the front door and stepped outside to arrange for her transport.

Once inside the carriage, she collapsed on the seat, her legs weak with relief. She was glad that her father had not lived to see this day: his only daughter turned whore to the man who ruined him. But there was some comfort in the remaining loyalty and discretion of the servants. She could see by the look in Benton's eye that he liked this no better than she did, and his sympathy did not lie with his new master.

Nathan Wardale was still asleep in his bed, with no idea that one of his sisters was alive and well. She had told him nothing, not even the evil hint meant to torment him. Just a few hours ago, she was taking great satisfaction in the fact that she controlled the degree of his suffering. But now, she had become equally to blame for anything that had happened between them. She could pretend that it had been forced upon her by a wicked man who deserved whatever misery she could provide. The first time, perhaps.

But what had happened, after…

She felt her legs go weak again. Without parting, they had dozed together for a short time. And she had awakened, restless, all thoughts of vengeance gone. She had pushed at his shoulder, playfully, and then rolled so that he was beneath her. She had kissed his lips, wrapped her legs around his body, and thrust her hips into his.

He'd returned her kiss. But he made no effort to hold her, although she could feel him growing hard inside her, again. So she'd sat up, straddling him. She'd rocked against him, and he'd bent his knees behind her, supporting her back, then lain back in the pillows and watched her give in to the needs of her own body. He'd guided her fingers, encouraging her to touch herself until she was a slave to the sensation. And then she had ridden him wildly, for her own pleasure. After wave upon wave of ecstasy, she'd clenched her thighs on his body until he'd responded with short, hard thrusts, smiling as he drove himself to exhaustion.

It had made her feel powerful, to watch him fall asleep beneath her, strong in a way that had nothing to do with vengeance. If this had been a battle, she had emerged victorious. He was conquered. And if she wished, she could celebrate the victory by having him again.

And then the doubts had begun to creep back in. When she was sure that he would not awaken, she had climbed carefully out of the bed, dressed as though nothing had changed, and taken the IOU. It was at the bedside, just as he had promised. She had closed the door as quietly as she could and started down the stairs.

And begun to fall apart. Benton was helpful. The carriage driver was polite and the trip short. She had crept back in the Carlow town house, successfully avoiding both servants and family. And now, she was on her way to her room. It was so late as to be almost dawn. She could lie down for a few moments. At least she would stay long enough to muss the bedclothes, so there would be no question of where she had spent the night. And then she would rise, wash, and go about her life as though nothing had happened.

But first, she would throw the accursed, life-changing piece of paper into the fireplace and watch it burn. She would poke it until there was nothing left but ashes, and then she would poke the ashes until they were dust.

And finally, she would be free.

She closed the door behind her, then took the paper out of her pocket, staring at the shaky writing of her desperate father. And she knew that she could no more throw it away than Nathan had. It held no power over her. Perhaps it never had. It was a nothing, a jot, a scrap. It was not a true debt of honour; there had been no honour in the giving of it, or the taking.

It was a strange, sad reminder of the night when everything had changed. That was why Nathan had kept it, she was sure. Not as a threat, nor a punishment. And never meaning to find her and call it in. He had kept it because he did not wish to forget what had happened, for he did not wish to repeat his mistake.

It was her own imagination that had turned the paper into a nightmare and turned the man that held it into a monster.

She turned it over in her hands, folding it along the old creases. Now, it was she who did not wish to forget. This paper had brought her to Nathan Wardale. To his life—and his bed. It would be eminently foolish to go back, now that she had left him, to devote herself to an unrepentant gambler who was no better than her father. But she did not wish to forget her time with him, nor to repeat the mistake of falling in love with a man so utterly inappropriate.

She took a deep breath, remembering the rush of panic followed by desire, and the deep satisfaction of the previous hours. And the cherished way she had felt when he'd held her afterwards, staring into her eyes. While it had been terrifying, it had been sweet as well. How nice it would be, to have a life full of moments like that.

But more likely, if she returned to Nathan Wardale, her life would be full of lonely nights, squalling children and an angry and distant husband who cared more for cards than he did for her. She remembered what it had been like for her mother when her father would not leave the tables, and how she had cried when she thought no one would hear. Nathan's luck was bound to change eventually. And then there would be debts, the men who collected them and eventual ruin. Unless she was prepared to see another paper such as this, to be sold when her husband treated her as chattel or to see a daughter similarly treated, she could not go back to him. She need only look at the paper to know why she could never return.

She would put it away somewhere. In the wardrobe with the bank notes. Or perhaps she could tuck it between the pages of a book and it could lie forgotten.

There, on the bedside table, was the little book of poetry. And she did not need to open it again to realize where it had come from or to know that the ribbon that marked it was her own. He had taken it from her old bedroom and given it back to her. Without thinking, she had taken the thing up and begun reading where she had left off, all those years ago.

He had been trying to tell her the truth. Before the note, before she had sought the journal for him. Even before the first kiss. He had been seeking a way to tell her, as gently as possible, who he was and that she need have no fear. And she had been so set on who she wished him to be that she did not see what was before her very eyes.

God help her, even if she could not forgive him for what had happened before, he deserved some small credit for trying to find a way to be kind. He had earned a measure of kindness from her in return. It was in her power to end some portion of his suffering, and Nell's as well. But she had kept it from him.

It made her ashamed. Whatever might happen in the future, no good could come of keeping grudges or offering punishments for ancient mistakes. When Marc brought Nell home from Northumberland, she would find a way to tell her enough of the truth so that she could find her brother again. Diana need never see the man again, of course. That would be too painful for so many reasons. But whatever he had become, he and his sister had suffered in ignorance of each other for long enough. She would not be the one to keep them apart. It was the very least she could do, if she wished to clear her slate with Nathan Wardale.

So she tucked the note into the book, along with what was left of the money, and tied the whole thing shut with the ribbon, as though it were possible to close off this chapter of her life, perhaps to open it again on a day when the whole story was not so fresh and painful.

Nate started awake, as though the awareness of a lack was sufficient to disturb him. He had meant to close his eyes for no more than a minute. But he had slept soundly, and now she was gone from his bed. He felt the sheets next to him, trying to decide if they were still warm from the body that had lain beside him. The letter was gone from the dressing table. Damn the thing to hell for all the trouble it had caused him.

There was a noise in the hall, and he jumped out of

bed and threw open the door, eager to catch her before she got to the front door. 'Diana, wait...'

The startled maid screamed at the sight of him standing naked in the hallway.

He stepped back and slammed the door again, muttering an apology to the girl through the oak panel. Then he requested, as calmly as possible, that Benton be sent to his rooms immediately. Embarrassed by his own behaviour, Nate returned to the bed, wrapped himself in a sheet and rang for his valet as well.

Did she not see, after what they had done together, that this was about more than a few words scrawled by her father years before they met? He had done everything in his power to show her, to love her with his body and prove that his words were not lies.

Yet, she had ignored it and left him. And he felt more desolate than he did after a night at the tables, as though there was nothing and no one in the world to erase the loneliness.

As the valet dressed him, Benton explained that Miss Price had left before dawn and in rather a hurry. She had requested that he bring the carriage around for her. She had insisted that she was fine and that there was nothing to be concerned about.

Of course she would. She was always insisting that she was fine, needed nothing, and was perfectly happy. She needed no one. And she did it so convincingly, so placidly, and with not a drop of excess emotion that it took a professional gambler to see she was bluffing.

The old butler said it all with a distinct air of disapproval. As though it were not clear enough that he found his master's actions towards the young lady near to reprehensible.

As did Nathan. Damn his own pride for thinking that his skill as a lover would have been enough to hold her. She had made it plain that she detested him and would never forgive what he had done. He must be as base as she thought, if he assumed that she would throw over her deeply held beliefs after a few hours in bed with him.

And damn again to his promise that he would not seek her out once she left. If he had the honour he claimed, he could not go back on his word. Better to have begged forgiveness at the start. He should have gotten down on his knees before her and pled for another chance. It would have been easy enough. For when he had seen her, resplendent in a pool of green silk, her mouth the same Cupid's bow, and her eyes wide and innocent, he had been a willing supplicant. And then, she had toyed with him…

Was she an angel or a tormenter? It did not matter. She was perfection. He never should have let her escape.

As if to reinforce the opinion, his valet tugged so tightly upon his cravat that he was near to choking before the tying was through. It was hardly fair, for the man had not even been a servant of the Price household. He had arrived here along with Nate. But it was clear that he'd chosen to add to the silent chorus of contempt that had been building in this house since the day he'd met Diana Price.

All the more galling that he deserved what he got

from them. Every arch look, every small shake of the head. Every indictment of his character. Every sniff of disapproval. They took his money easily enough, when it was time to collect their salaries. And he continued to play, telling himself that they depended on his gambling to pay their keep. It was his responsibility to continue.

But how much did he need, really? It had been almost honourable, when he'd had a mother and sisters to protect, however best he could. But once they were lost? He'd gathered enough winnings to support himself in luxury for the rest of his life. Gaming had become nothing more than a way to pass the time until the moment when some loser at the table decided to put a ball through him.

No more. Perhaps he could not stop going to the tables. For without Diana, what more was there left in his life? But he could stop keeping score. He glanced at the box on the dresser, full of signets, fobs, and bits and pieces of the lives of others. Each one a memory of a life he had changed.

And none of it all his fault. He had played and won, of course. But they had played as well, knowing that losing was all but inevitable. Did they not deserve some responsibility for their actions? If it was not his fault, then why did he keep the things? What earthly good did it do him to hang on to trinkets that meant nothing to him? *And the damned letter.* If he had refused it, or given it back? Then he would not be in the mess he was now.

He might never have met Diana.

But perhaps that was a good thing. For neither would he have lost her over nonsense. He was tired of being the sin eater for half of London. 'Benton, bring me paper. And string. Some small boxes, perhaps. I wish to post some packages.'

He gathered up the box and sat down at the writing desk in his room. It was not hard to remember the owners of the things. In many cases, the names were engraved on the items. But the loss of each was firmly engrained on his memory. Here were the diamond studs of a duke, who had sworn he would shoot himself over the loss. And the ruby necklace of the marchioness. She had thought to bargain her favours for another hand, and had stamped her feet and pouted when he'd demanded the necklace instead.

And now, she could have it back. They could all take the bloody things back. He cared little whether it might be blessing or curse to receive them, so long as he need never see any of it again. His heart felt lighter after each package. And when the box was empty, there was but one thing left.

He looked up at the butler and grinned. 'Benton. Go to the safe in my study. Bring me the deed to this house.'

The butler looked rather alarmed at the prospect, but did as he was told. When he had returned with the paper, Nate signed it over, with a flourish—to Miss Diana Price. Then he folded it carefully, sealed it, addressed it to the Carlow house, and put it in the stack with the rest, ready for the morning post.

Chapter Seventeen

The few hours of sleep that Diana managed to steal had done nothing to refresh her. The girls must have been out almost as late as she, for when she rose at nine she did not hear them stirring. It was a comfort, for it gave her some small time to prepare for the day, to wipe any traces of the night's activity from her mind. She looked into the mirror, smoothing her expression and her clothing, jabbing the pins into her hair until it was tight and smooth, with not a strand out of place. When she was through, she was sure that there was not a hint of awareness to give her away to the girls as anything less than the same proper, controlled woman who had watched over them for years.

As she pushed the last pin in place, there was a sharp rap upon her door. It was Peters the footman, coming to tell her that Lord Stanegate wished her presence in the study, immediately.

Marcus, here? Had he arrived while she slept, or

had he come in the night, before she had crept into the house? She should have recognized that returning to the house without incident was almost too fortunate. Her luck could not hold forever. It now appeared that she would face an interview with her employer's son, on this of all days, when she needed just a few more hours to understand the changes in her life.

When she came down to the ground floor, the house was abustle with the sudden arrival, as though the staff feared that their exemplary housekeeping was somehow at fault. They were behaving as if to placate a man in a temper.

She'd have understood it in another house. But here it was most unusual. And that the person who had frightened them into the boughs was Marc Carlow made the situation even more unusual. She hurried to the study to see the reason for it.

She walked through the open door and felt the change in him almost immediately. He was no longer the happy newlywed who had left London such a short time ago. Instead, he glared at her and snapped, 'Shut the door, Miss Price. We must speak in private.'

She did as she was told and went quickly to the desk where he sat. 'Is something wrong, Marc? There is nothing the matter with Nell, I trust.'

'I left her in Northumberland. This matter concerns you, Miss Price, and your behaviour in my absence.'

'I cannot think…' Which was a lie. She could think of several things she had done in the last few weeks that would upset him greatly.

But then he reached into his desk, and removed the journal that she had taken from Stanegate Court. 'Do you know what this is?'

'Y-yes.' And she was sure that the stammer was enough to give away the truth.

'And can you explain to me why it is not sitting with its mates on the shelf in the study off the library?'

Now that she knew him as a Wardale, Nathan's obsession with the thing made more sense. But it was horrible to think that he had taken the book and rushed back to confront Lord Narborough on his sickbed. 'Where did you get it?'

'That is no answer to my question, Miss Price.' And there was her surname again, used against her as though she was a stranger and not a trusted friend. 'I received this from a family friend who works in the Home Office. I suspect he received it from a man who is a sworn enemy of my family. The same man who caused my poor Nell so much grief. How did this book leave the house, Miss Price?'

But how had the Gypsy come by the book? Was Nathan a friend to him? Had he worked without knowing, to harm his own sister? Why had she not spoken when she'd had the chance? For it was too cruel...

'Miss Price, I await your answer.'

There was little point in dissembling. He knew she was the thief. He'd either guessed, or he could read it in her eyes. 'When I took it from the shelf, I had no idea...'

Marc shook his head. 'That statement says it all.

I could forgive you the theft, Diana. And the damage to the book—'

'But it was already—'

He went on, ignoring her interruption. 'It seems I have left my sisters in the protection of a woman who is easily gulled by just the sort of man I wish them to avoid. If you are working with the Gypsy? Even if it is without intention to harm?' He shook his head. 'Leave this house immediately, Miss Price. Your services are no longer required.'

'But I can explain.' She had so much to tell him. But it was even more important that she explain it all to Nell, who would be much less judgemental if she heard the details.

'I imagine you can.' The look in his eyes was sad, for it signalled the death of their friendship. 'But it will not move me from my decision.' He was staring at her now, as though reading a book himself. And she was convinced that the thing she most wanted to hide from him was written plain on her face. Then, he said, 'Your heart is involved, is it not?'

'Yes,' she whispered, letting him assume what he would. For now, it was better that he suspect the Gypsy than the man who was now his brother-in-law.

'Then you have made your choice in this matter. I have known you long enough to realize that you would not give your affections lightly. But through no fault of our own, Miss Price, my family is at war. You have chosen a side. And it is not ours. Please. Go to your rooms and pack your things. I will explain to my sisters. You are dismissed.'

Dismissed. She walked slowly towards her room. After all these years, that was all. She had done a better job of safeguarding the girls' honour than she had her own. She had thrown that away on a man who was unworthy. She was a thief and a liar. And worse.

What could she possibly say to Marc that would make things any better? It was bad enough that he suspected her of the theft. But if he believed she was unchaste? What kind of reference could she expect then? Why had she not realized that Nathan Wardale had been talking about the Gypsy, when he said an enemy would reveal his past? He was as trapped by the man as the Carlows had been.

She reached into her wardrobe, and removed a portmanteau. Then she set it upon the bed and began stacking her small clothes in it.

There was a shadow from the doorway, with the sound of Marc's shouted, 'No, Verity,' ringing in the background.

'How could you, Diana?' Verity gave a shuddering sigh and then burst into tears. 'I thoughtyou would never… And with father so ill…'

Honoria appeared at her side, reaching out to take her sister in her arms. 'We treated you as a member of the family. You were like a sister to us. And this is how you have repaid the family. Come, Verity.' She said the words loud enough for Marc to hear, and then turned back to her, and with an expression that conveyed the urgent need for secrecy, she held out a letter.

Diana snatched it from her hand, and gave a small grateful nod and a wave of farewell.

The girls nodded back, as though they understood as best as anyone could, that things were not as they appeared. Then Honoria pulled her sister from the room in a cloud of muttered remonstrations.

Diana returned to her packing. Even if the last scene had been a sham, Verity was right. Lord Narborough was too ill to face this latest problem, and it pained her to be the cause of it. Perhaps he was at fault for Hebden's death. Or perhaps only for a false accusation against Nathan's father. Whatever had happened, he was to blame for the fate of the Wardale family. Because of him, Nell had suffered, as had Nathan. And in his suffering, Nathan had struck out at her family, and she had struck back. And now, the misery was woven through their lives like a thread through a tapestry.

Marc had been right when he'd accused her of choosing a side. Without meaning to, she had given her heart and her loyalty to Nathan Wardale. However much she loved the Carlow family, she did not wish to stay with them until the truth was known.

She walked slowly to the wardrobe and looked down at the small pile of possessions that had accumulated during the course of the years she'd lived there. This was the sum total of her life, after all this time. It had felt very significant, and very permanent, just a day ago. And now it seemed as if she had no roots at all.

She began stuffing gowns into a carpet bag, thinking little of what the casual arrangement might do to the fabrics. She picked up the beautiful dress she had worn on the previous night and shuddered. It had been very foolish of her to squander a portion of the windfall on something she had no reason to wear. But at the time, she had been happy and in love, and giving no thought at all to what would happen after. And then, her hand fell upon the little book, at the bottom of the wardrobe.

All that he had given her could be tied neatly in a package. It was but a small part of her small life. But it was not quite all he had given, for there was still the letter that Honoria had just handed to her. She was sure it came from Nathan.

She reached out to where she had set it, on the bed next to the portmanteau. It felt thick enough to be an apology, but not so thick as to be the pile of bank notes that she would probably need, now that she had no position.

She wished that she had the strength to fling it into the fire, to show him and the world what she thought of the gifts of a man such as him: a gambler, a liar, a betrayer of women…

She closed her mind to the anger. For while some of the accusations might be true, they did not tell the whole of the story. And while she was not sure how angry she had a right to be, she could not afford to be a fool. If there was any chance that the letter contained more money, she would need to open it. His last gift had more than equalled what she had accumulated after ten years of work. He had seen that this day might come, and it was as if he had given her a gift of time. A year, perhaps, in which to plan what she might do next without worrying about her expenses. She cringed at the sight of the letter, because if there was money there, it would feel like a payment for the previous evening. But she needed all the help that she could get at the moment. With the options available to her in this crisis, it would not do to be too proud.

She steeled herself to read the actual words. They would hurt whether they were entreaties of love, apology, or the gloating comments of a rogue. They did not matter to her, for all were equally unimportant.

But the paper was blank, just as the first had been. And then, another paper fell out on the floor in front of her.

Her hands were shaking as she picked it up. The deed to her father's house. With her name written upon it, plain as day. After all this time, he had given it back to her.

There were at least a dozen reasons why she should return the thing immediately. He could not mean to give it without strings or obligations, for it was too large. It was too valuable. This was too much to grasp. Something would have to be exchanged for it. Although she suspected that he had been pleased with the activities of last night, her pragmatic mind would not flatter itself into thinking that anything she had done was worthy of an entire house.

He was trying to draw her back to him.

And it was working.

As though sleepwalking, she stood up, turned and exited the room, leaving her possessions behind her. She went down the stairs and out the front door of the

Carlow home, not bothering to tell anyone why she was leaving. It hardly mattered any more that she was going out. Marc had made it clear that he wanted her gone. How and where would not be so important as when.

It could not be wise to go back to Nathan Wardale. And so soon after leaving him. But she had to know the reason for this latest gift. Did he expect her to live publicly as his mistress?

Surely not. She hoped not, at least. She had almost convinced herself that such behaviour was beneath him. But why had he given her the deed? Whatever he wanted from her, she must return it to him, or she would be no better than the opportunist the Carlows thought she was.

Her feet carried her home, from Albemarle Street to Hans Place without even thinking of it, although she had long avoided the neighbourhood because of the painful memories it brought. And there was her old front door, no different than it had been ten years ago when she had left it, or this morning when she had left it again. She reached out with hesitation, and took the knocker in her hand, letting it fall once against the wood of the door with a satisfying clunk.

Benton opened for her, and in a move totally inappropriate to his station, reached out to her and pulled her into the house, encircling her in a fatherly hug before she could speak. 'Miss Diana. You are finally home. When he told me what he had done, I hardly dared hope. But you are here now.'

And then he released her. And straightened. And said, 'Ma'am,' with a respectful bow and a slight twinkle in his eye.

'I don't understand.' Which was perfectly true, although it was clear that she had at least one friend left, no matter what might happen. She straightened as well, so that she did not appear broken by her circumstances. 'I wish to speak to Mr Wardale, please.'

'That is not possible, I'm afraid.'

'If he is from home, than I shall wait.'

Benton shook his head again. 'It will do no good to wait, Miss Diana. He made it quite clear to us when he'd finished his business this morning, that he would not be returning. He said you were the mistress of the house and we were to obey you as we had him. Or better.'

The realization staggered her, and she would have fallen, had Benton not pulled her the rest of the way into the house and helped her to a chair. 'He has gone. And left me the house.'

'Yes, Miss Diana. He said to me, "It was hers all along." And he sent back all the things he had won from others as well. If he knew the owner of something, he bundled it up and shipped it off with the first post. And then, he left with the clothes on his back and a single bag.'

He thought the house was hers? She had wanted a house, of course. A cottage. A small place where she could live in security, answering to no one. But this house? It was nearly a mansion. Far too large for a single person. Even when she was small, she had heard her parents say it was far too much to keep for two people with a single daughter. With all the bedrooms, it was a better space for a much larger family.

A family she would never have. She looked helplessly at the butler. 'I cannot do this, Benton. It is too much. The size of the house. The servants. I cannot afford to keep you. I am little better than a servant myself.'

He patted her hand. 'Do not worry on that account. Mr Wardale set the place up, from the first, so that it very nearly runs itself. The household accounts are so well stocked that we have run for years at a time without the master present. I suspect we can go even longer for you. Your needs are likely to be simpler than his. In any case, do not worry. For now we are all safe and warm, and I have a better knowledge of what it takes to maintain the house and staff than you do. Even without cash in hand, there are things left, from your father's time, that are worth a pretty penny and would have been sold to keep the place afloat, had not the old master gambled them away to Wardale. But they are yours again, to do with as you please. You will find a way. And I will help you.'

She smiled sadly. 'But I cannot keep it, Benton. I simply cannot. It is too much, too soon, and I do not understand Nathan's gift, nor do I wish to take the house back from him. It would be like admitting…' She shook her head, and tried to rise, but it was as though all the stress of the week had hit her; she might as well have been asleep and dreaming, as sitting on a bench in a hall in the middle of the day. 'But for now, I need someone to go back to my old place of employment and fetch my things. I will stay here until it can all be sorted out. It has been a most trying day, and I simply do not have the strength.'

'Ma'am.' He gave a curt nod. 'I will send a footman to get them, and they shall be brought to your old room. You must have some tea, I think. And a light lunch and a nice dinner to celebrate your return. I am sure that Cook still has the menus from when you were a girl. If your tastes have not changed, she knows what you will enjoy.'

'Cook? Still here?' A wave of warmth and comfort swept over her, as her happier childhood memories returned.

'You will find many familiar faces, miss, once you have become used to the place. Mr Wardale was not with us much.' Benton cleared his throat, as though making a final effort to protect his master's secrets. 'Travelling, I think. And even when he was here, he was often away from the house. During that time, the running of the place was left to his man of business, who did not see fit to change the staff any more than was necessary. But now? I shall bring the tea. There is a fire laid in the sitting room.' He moved to open the door for her.

'Benton.' She called him back. 'What was he like?'

'Mr Wardale?' The butler seemed surprised that she would ask.

'Yes. I knew him for such a short time. It was all very confusing. What was he like?'

The older man gave her a thoughtful look as though trying to decide what he owed to a man who no longer employed him. 'He paid regularly. He was courteous to the staff. Although he kept irregular hours, he did not require that we do the same. In food and drink he was temperate, as he was in dress and decorum.'

'That is what he was like as a master. But what kind of man was he?'

'He was—' Benton frowned. 'Not what I expected. I have met men in his line of business before.' He cleared his throat softly. 'When working for your father.'

'My father had other enemies?' She did not remember any. But she had been young, and he had sheltered her from the worst of it.

'Yes, Miss Diana. For he lost more than he won. There were questionable gentlemen who gamed as a diversion, who would come to the house and take a note, or a ring, and then leave him in peace. But the men who took gambling as their sole occupation? They were the sort that would just as soon take a pound of flesh as let a debt go uncollected. Rum 'uns, to the last man. Coarse. Hard. Not fit to come in by the front door of a house such as this, much less to live here. They were men without honour. And I saw them too frequently at the end, for—you will forgive me for saying it, miss—your father was not one to let common sense stand between him and the gaming table.'

She had forgotten the truth, but truth it was. She had put the blame for her father's ruin squarely on Nathan

Wardale's shoulders for so long, it had never occurred to her that he was not the first to threaten her father with the poorhouse. Nor could she accuse him of using underhanded means to lure her father into the game that had finally ruined him. He had gone willingly at any opportunity.

Benton's frown deepened. 'But Mr Wardale was different. Perhaps it was because he was brought up as a gentleman before his family's troubles, which were no fault of his own. He knew life from both sides. He was deeply conscious of the effect his gaming had on others, and it troubled him. I doubt he spent an easy night in this house, knowing how he had gotten it. In a word Miss Diana? He was unhappy. He had no friends and many enemies. He did not seem to take satisfaction in his endeavours, but it was the only life he'd found that would suit him. It is only recently that I have seen a change in him. Of late, he seemed lighter of spirit.'

Because of me? She thought of the walks in the park and the way her heart had quickened from the first moment she'd seen him. And she wondered: had it been the same for him? Or had it been harder? For if there had been true feeling on his part, he had been forced to sit opposite her in the White Salon at the Carlow house and in the carriage, knowing who she was and what she would think of him should she learn his true identity. And now, she understood the awkwardness of their first meetings and the reason for the curious way he had behaved. He had treated her with the utmost care and concern for her welfare, without giving anything away. He'd opened himself to her gradually, knowing how it would most likely end.

She remembered him, as he came to her last night. When he had said, 'I have not known gentleness…' She had given him that, and he had been glad of it. And she had taken it away again.

Suddenly, she was overcome with need of him, and the desire to be gentle for him and gentled by him. To stay together in the bed upstairs, and to sit before the fire together in the drawing room for as long as life would allow.

When the butler went to find her refreshment, she moved listlessly through the house, haunted by memories of her past. Mostly happy memories: of mother and of youthful innocence. But there were touches of her father, here and there. The chair he used to love was still in the parlour. Although it appeared that Nathan had favoured a different one, for the seat closest to the fire was not one she knew.

And here was the study. She took a deep breath, and then pushed open the door. For whoever had left his mark on this room, there were likely to be memories of a man she wished to forget.

The walls were the same dusty gold colour, and the desk and shelves were just as she remembered from her youth. But the contents of the shelves were different. Her father had favoured atlases, poring over them as though he wished to escape. But it appeared that Nathan Wardale had had his fill of travel. The maps had been replaced with local histories and books on art and drawing.

She turned to the desk, where she had learned the importance of picking simple locks while trying to find enough money to pay the bills. The surface was clear of papers and more orderly than she remembered it. Her father's old glass inkwell had been replaced with a heavy silver desk set. And here was the little locked drawer where Father had kept his purse and his memories of Mother. There had been letters, a minia-ture in a silver frame, and a lock of her hair, bound up by silk thread.

Without thinking, she pulled a pin from her hair and set about bending it to the shape of the desk key. Then she inserted it into the lock, and gave a jiggle and twist, feeling the mechanism turn, just as it always had.

What had she meant to do, she wondered, other than to prove that she could? There was no need to go through Nathan Wardale's desk, if he'd left his money in the bank for her. Perhaps it was the same curiosity that had led her to keep his note to Marc. Though she might claim that she wished no more from him, she still wanted to know the state of his mind.

The drawer was empty, except for a deck of playing cards. In that, he was not so different from her father after all. In the place where her father had hidden his most precious possessions, Nathan kept nothing but cards. She picked up the deck and stroked it, feeling sad for the man that had owned this house. Then she sat, shuffled and went to lay out a game of patience.

And stopped as she turned up the first card. Apparently, Nathan was something of an artist. He had transformed the cards, drawing little pictures around the pips. The clubs grew in flower gardens, dogs and cats played amongst the diamonds, the spades had been turned into fish.

And the hearts. Her breath caught in her throat. The hearts were her. She was sure of it. The likeness was not expert. But there she was, in her old bedroom, reading a book, with hearts floating around her like memories. And here on the five was the bonnet she had worn on her visits to Hyde Park, with hearts hidden amongst its flowers. On the ten, her hand was outstretched, to hold one of the hearts in her palm.

And as she looked at it, the conviction grew in her that it was his heart she held. If he'd said it to her face, she'd never have believed the words. But when he was alone in his study, with nothing to prove to anyone, what reason would he have to lie?

She cradled the card in her hand for a moment, and then gathered up the deck and thrust it back into the drawer, so that no one would see. It was a precious secret, and deserved to be kept safe. Then she ran out into the hall and called for the butler.

The man came hurrying to her side, probably fearing an emergency, for the tone she was taking. 'Miss Diana?'

'Benton. Where did he go? If I meant to find him…'

'That would not be wise, miss.'

'So few things I have done recently are. But I mean

to do it, anyway. Please, tell me, Benton. Where is Nathan Wardale?'

'If he is not here, I expect he is where he always is, Miss Diana. He has returned to the gaming table.'

Chapter Eighteen

Nate stared down at the perfectly arranged cards in front of him, and the shocked expression on the man across the table. Then he gave his usual cold smile and said, 'Another hand?'

'One hand too many, I think.' His opponent gave a shaky laugh. 'I should know better, Nathan. You and your damned luck.' And then he smiled. 'Next week, perhaps?'

Nate smiled and nodded, gathering the stakes into a neat pile before him. 'Perhaps,' he said, relieved the game was over. The man in front of him knew when to push himself away from the table, and might return as a diversion. Or he might not. But he would not reappear with a driving need to avenge himself or with a score to settle. Would that there were more like him, for Nate could take tonight's winnings in good conscience.

As soon as the chair was empty, another man seated himself. Nate looked up to see the Gypsy, darkening the table again. He smirked. 'And who are we today, then? Hebden? Or Beshaley?'

'As you prefer.' The Gypsy gave a bare nod of acknowledgement.

'I prefer that you leave. Both of you. But if you must stay, then let us play for something that has value to you. I should like to see you suffer, when you lose it.'

'Taking vengeance, Nathan?'

'If I can.'

'And how did your meeting with Keddinton go?'

'Just as you suspected. He was not impressed with the evidence, and had no real desire to help me. He expected me to work for him, as a matter of fact, in further smearing my father's name. I mean to take matters into my own hands, to go after George Carlow, once Diana is forever safely out of that house.'

'Revenge is not an easy course. I speak from experience when I tell you it takes as much from the wronged as it does from the cause.'

'Fine words from you, Beshaley. And meaningless. You speak as if you care for my future, after all you have done to me.'

The Gypsy gave him almost a clinical examination, as though he could see the spirit as well as the body. 'Nothing has changed then? Your luck holds?'

'As it always does,' Nate said. 'No thanks to you and your kind.'

'So the curse did not break.' The Gypsy seemed surprised at this.

'Did you think it would?'

'As a matter of fact, I did.'

Nate frowned. 'Perhaps the luck was my own then, and this has all been nonsense. If so, I hope you are through with me, for I have no wish to part from it. I should think, taking the father, the family, the house and the girl would be enough to satisfy your mother. You have ruined the better part of my life and left me with no hope for the future. Leave me the cards at least.'

The Gypsy held out his hands in a gesture of finality. 'For my part, you have paid enough. You are released in any way I can release you. What is left, lucky or unlucky, is up to you.'

'Too little and too late. But it is something, I suppose.'

They played in silence for a while, and the stack of coins in front of Nate became larger. Then he said, 'And what of you? Are there others who will receive your *gift*?'

The Gypsy rubbed his temple, as though his head ached. 'Unfortunately, yes. While this business may be through for you, it is far from done for me. Until then?' He shrugged. 'The shadow moves where the sun commands. I will go where fate leads me. And it will be done when it is done.'

'And if you find proof that Narborough knew of my father's innocence?'

'Then he is my father's murderer. Despite what you may think, his debt to me is greater than to you. It will end in blood.'

'If you can prove George Carlow's hand in this, tell me of it. We will finish him together.'

The Gypsy's mouth quirked. 'Together, as friends?'

'To call you friend goes too far, after what you have done. Ally, perhaps. Let us say we have a common goal.'

Stephano raised his glass. 'To honour and justice for our families.'

It was impossible to tell by his expression which family he meant, the Hebdens or the Beshaleys. And so Nathan responded, 'For our families. Whoever they may be.'

The Gypsy let out a bark of laughter. 'Very well. If I have information to give, you shall have it.' And then, with a sidelong glance, 'If, when the time comes, you are still so eager to throw your life away on the past.' He tossed his cards on the table and stood up. He waved his hand in a strange gesture of blessing, and said, 'God keep you, Nathan. May I dance at your wedding.' He moved quickly away, so that he could not hear Nathan's responding curse to such a sarcastic parting.

Nate rubbed his temples, wondering if the Gypsy's headache was contagious. The air was oppressive, heavy with tobacco smoke and the smell of too much whisky and too many overheated bodies. He longed for the fresh scent of the park, the feel of the cool breeze on his face.

And if he were honest, the feel of a small hand in his. But he did not dare go back. For suppose he was to see her? She could have the park and Bond Street, along with the house. Half of all London would be hers, if it meant that he would not have to see her again.

There was nothing left he could offer her. He had given everything he had, and there had been no response. He must accept it. This was home. Hyde Park was a million miles away from the room he was in, and as dangerous a journey as a trip to the Indies. It would be too painful to risk another meeting.

He heard ribald laughter from the front of the room, and then the crowd parted, as a woman timidly approached his table.

'Diana.' The cards slipped from his hands. He gathered them quickly and shuffled in a skilled, nonchalant manner, so that she might not see how her arrival had unnerved him. Why had she come here, just as he was trying to reconcile himself to the loss of her? He had to fight with all his might against the urge to jump to his feet, hide the cards behind his back and stammer an apology for being caught in so low a place.

But it would do little good. If she knew to seek him here, there was no way to present this to her as an isolated occurrence. He could not pretend that he was any different than what he was, a habitual gambler, as at home here as she was sitting before the parlour fire in his old home. And so, he composed himself. 'I beg your pardon. Miss Price.' He rose to honour her properly, and offered a bow and a smile that was courteous, but would give no indication to those around him that she was anything more to him than an acquaintance.

'Mr Dale.' She looked nervous. Was it just the gaming hell that made her uncomfortable or was it his presence? He had longed to see her again. But the sight of her unhappiness was even more painful than her absence had been.

'Mr Wardale,' he corrected. 'If you please.'

'You have decided to use your real name, then?' Her lips formed what might almost have been a smile of approval.

He nodded. 'It is time, don't you think? In the end, the alias proved to be more bother than it was worth.'

'What of your troubles with the Navy?'

'I mean to see to it that they are the Navy's troubles with me. They took me unjustly. They must acknowledge the fact.'

She nodded. 'It pleases me to see you are ready to face your past.'

And what good did it do him, that she was pleased? 'I assure you, it is hardly a magical transformation of my character. No matter my opinions on the past, the present is likely to stay just as it is.' He gestured around the room to remind her of their surroundings. 'I did not expect to see you again, certainly not in such a place as this. I trust that you will not think it a breach of my promise to leave you in peace. I will quit the city, if my presence in it is a problem for you.'

'No. No, of course not. That will not be necessary. It is a very big city, is it not?' She sat down at the empty seat across from him, fussing with her skirts. She was wearing the green silk dress that she had worn to seduce him; he wondered if that had meaning or was merely her attempt to blend with the gaudiness of the surroundings.

She leaned forward, almost confidentially. And he doubted, from the innocent look in her eyes, that she realized what a fascinating thing it did to her décolleté. 'There is more than enough room in London for the two of us.'

The two of them. If for once his life had turned out the way he wished, they would have needed very little space at all. He stared fixedly back at her, reminding himself that a gaming table was no place to show emotion. He looked directly into her eyes, waiting for her to speak.

Then, without a word, she removed a wad of folded bills from her reticule and set them upon the table, pushing them to his side. 'I believe these are yours.'

'Not any more. At one time, they belonged to your father. I no longer wish to retain them.'

Her returning smile to him was surprisingly cynical. 'If you meant to repay what my father lost to you, then it is not enough.'

He shrugged. 'There were expenses.' Then he pushed his night's winnings towards her across the table. 'If you wish more, then take. Or I can write you a bank draft.'

'That is not why I am here. I come to return what you have given me, for it was fairly won.' She reached deeper into the purse and removed the deed. 'And this as well.'

'It is yours.'

'*Was* mine. My father's actually. In the distant past. But it has not been in the family for some time.'

'How fortunate that you have it again,' he said, pretending that the matter did not concern him.

'I no longer wish it. That is why I have been trying to return it to you.' She was staring back at him, her kissable mouth fixed in a resolute chaperone's smile.

'Nor do I. That is why I will not take it back.'

'I understand what you are trying to do by returning it to me. But you do not have to. It is kind of you to wish a different life for me than the one I had, but it is too late. While you might learn to live with it, you cannot change the past, Nathan.'

She had called him Nathan. The other words in the sentence paled to insignificance, leaving only the sweet tone of her voice and the sound of his name. For a moment, it gave him some small bit of hope. 'If there is some way to soften the memory of them, I wish to try. Or to make you forget altogether.' He frowned. 'Although there are some things, one night in particular, that I wish you to remember in every detail.'

There was not a trace of blush upon her cheek to reveal that she understood him. Perhaps she had lost the ability, after the previous evening's activities. Or maybe it was a sign of rare composure and her ability to maintain an even keel, though the waters were rough.

She ignored his hint and went on. 'Your life was more difficult than mine, and you have been less content. There is much I would not change. More than one night, certainly. It does not do to put too much emphasis on the actions of a single day, whether they be good or bad.'

Did she mean their night together? Or his night at the tables with her father? Or perhaps both. For then she said, 'Whatever the past between us, giving me the house and the money means nothing. They are not what matters. They do not indicate whether a person's character is changed or constant.' She pushed them back across the table.

He glanced at the papers and gave a shudder of revulsion at the sight of the deed lying in front of him on the baize where it had been so many years before. 'My character has changed for the better from what it once was. If the change is insufficient and you do not like it as it is, then I am sorry. And if you do not believe me to be constant, then tell me what I can do to prove it to you.'

'You certainly do not need to do—' she waved a hand over the deed '—this.'

'And yet, I have.' Her stubbornness over the thing made his head ache, and he wished that she would take it and leave him with what little peace he had, instead of coming to give him a fresh reminder of how unsuitable he was. 'I will not take it back. I wish I had given it to you on the first day, the moment I realized who you were. It and the damned letter, and anything else I could think to give. And then I could have walked away from you before speaking a word, with a clear conscience.'

And that had an effect on her, at last. Her eyes grew round with shock and hurt. He could not help himself and hurried to soften the blow. 'Do not misunderstand.

My acquaintance with you was pleasant. More than pleasant. But it was a mistake. For now it hurts me to think of even the most pleasant moments, knowing they are all in the past. And the association hurt you as well. I could have spared us both so much grief by tearing up your father's note on the night he gave it to me.' He gestured to the money and the deed. 'This is all I have left to give you. Please, remove them from the table. If they are not stakes in a game, they do not belong here.'

'Stakes.' Her eyes had a stubborn sparkle. 'That is all these are to you? Nothing more? Then I…I wish to wager them.'

He laughed. 'You have no idea what you are talking about. And you know nothing of cards or gambling.'

'On the contrary. I may know nothing of cards, but I know more than you think about gambling and gamblers. And I know exactly what I am doing. You will accept this challenge from me, because you cannot help yourself. It is like a madness, isn't it? You have no control over it.'

Too true, although he did not like to admit it. But he could master it if he tried, he was sure. It was just that there was seldom a reason to try.

'You did not stick at winning the house away from my family the first time it was offered. Are you afraid that you will not succeed a second time?' Her voice was no longer the prim and proper tone of a paid companion, but the low, sultry murmur of the cards and the dice, cutting through his resistance.

The men gathered around the table gave a laugh. She had just called him a coward. He would have called out any man who said the words. He could hear the beginnings of mutterings, as a crowd began to gather to see the spectacle of the strange woman come to challenge the infamous gambler. And he could not very well let the insult stand. But neither did he want to play against her. 'It is just that I do not wish to take from you unfairly.' What had sounded like surety in his head, sounded overconfident, arrogant and dismissive as he said it to her.

'Since when have you turned away a game?' She was sweet and cajoling now. Intoxicating. If she were calling him to bed, he'd have gone in an instant. 'It is hardly unfair to play me in a game of chance. Unless you mean to cheat, of course.'

The crowd gasped. She had insulted him again. Even if it came from a woman, he dare not let that pass. 'Very well.' He'd said it more sharply than he intended, his fever for the game momentarily overcoming his fever for the woman. He spoke again, more calmly, 'What do you wish to play?'

She bit her lip, considering. 'What would you suggest?'

He groaned. 'Miss Price, the first lesson you must learn is not to allow me to choose the method of your destruction.' He shuffled quickly, giving the cards an elegant flourish, hoping that his dexterity would frighten her away. Then he dealt out the cards for a hand of Macao. 'I assume you are at least slightly familiar with this game? Let us make this interesting. Your house and money, against the contents of my purse.'

'I think that will be satisfactory. Thank you.'

Damn. If he'd had any intention of winning, the bet would have been unfair beyond words. Why did she not cry off? It would serve her right for insulting him if he took the things back, for she was too ignorant of the ways of the table to have any idea what was happening to her. If he was able, he would throw the game to her. And if not? At least it would be over quickly. 'Shall we begin?'

He had prepared himself to play as inexpertly as possible. But it was hardly necessary. For a change, his incredible luck was not with him; the cards would not go his way. She was most fortunate in the hand he had dealt, and as the game progressed she beat him easily. He smiled, relieved that he would have no further guilt upon his soul. Now she could take the things he had given her, knowing that she had earned them. He emptied his purse onto the pile of bank notes already on the table. 'There. You have bested me. The house and the money are yours, fairly won to do with as you wish.'

She frowned at the money in front of her, and her expression was no different from the people he had beaten over the years, as dissatisfied with winning as they were when they lost. 'But you did not try.'

'It is not enough to play your own hand but you must play mine as well?' He responded a little tartly to her criticism, for in the end, he had not been able to persuade himself to lose. He had played the best game possible with the hand he'd dealt himself and had still not been able to beat her. 'I tried hard enough against a player as inexperienced as you are. Enough so that you might have a chance of winning, if luck was with you. Which it was. And that is the end of it.' He pushed the pile of notes back to her side of the table.

'You insult me, sir. If you do not bring your full skill to the table? It is little better than cheating.'

There was that word again. 'Cheating? I?'

'Since the object is to win and you were attempting to lose, yes. I demand that we play another round.'

'Hand,' he corrected. 'And I do not cheat at cards.'

'Another hand, then. And if you do not cheat, then you are not as good at this game as I expected. Deal again, Mr Wardale.'

'The deal passes to you, Miss Price. Which should help to convince you that I do not cheat at cards.' He said it loud enough so that all could hear. 'I swear, I have never had such trouble over losing a game.'

Everyone laughed as she went about the painfully slow process of shuffling the cards to her satisfaction and carefully counting out the hands. She glanced up at him. 'I mean to bet all I have.' She pushed her pile of winnings back toward him.

'Then I shall put up something of equal value, this time, to prove to you that I am trying.' He thought for a moment. 'I have a country house as well as the town house. I meant to retire there. But you shall have it, at the end of this hand.'

'If you lose,' she said. 'But I expect you to do your best to defeat me.'

'My best?' She still did not understand what she was asking of him.

She nodded. 'Do not insult me. Play the game, as you would against a stranger, and let fortune decide the winner.'

Let fortune decide? He might as well take the house back now and not bother with the game. The last hand had been a fluke and he did not expect another. 'If you will force me to bankrupt another Price at this table, then you do not understand what the last game cost me.'

She looked back at him, her eyes tranquil. 'You will not bankrupt me, because unlike my father, I have the sense to stop playing, once I am satisfied with the results. You will leave me as you found me, with a small savings. Which was not such a bad thing, really. I have been behaving most strangely of late, and I date the change to the moment I opened your first envelope.'

She thought that the money was what wrought the change in her? He had hoped that it was more than that. For it would have been most flattering to think that she had felt changed on the day that they first met, as he had. He sighed. There was no way to leave her as he found her, if she wished honesty from him. And in comparison to that, the money was a small thing. 'If losing the house again is truly what you wish, I am sure another hand will do the trick.' And he bent over his cards in concentration.

And he lost again.

It was not unheard of, to lose two hands in a row. Uncommon for him, of course. But not impossible. She had been right. It was a game of chance. Anything might happen. And he had barely tried, on the first hand, so it should not count against him.

The woman across the table was livid. 'How dare you, sir? You are trifling with my…my…my patience.'

He stared at the cards, which had picked a most unusual time to betray him. 'I am doing nothing of the sort. I was quite fond of that house. If I'd known that the hand would not go my way, I'd have bet something else. My stable. Matched bays, a phaeton and a curricle. All on the table, Miss Price. Please do me the honour of keeping your original stakes. But give me a chance to regain the country house.'

'All or nothing, sir.'

'Damn.'

She drew in a sharp breath at the oath.

'Your pardon, Miss Price.' He glared at her, which probably spoiled the apology for his rudeness in swearing. But the temptation to let her win had dissipated. It was one thing to give up the London house, but to have no home at all was not what he had intended for penance. After all the years he had played here, it galled him to lose it at cards to a green girl. And at Macao, which was hardly worthy of his skill. He had a reputation to consider, and their play had drawn quite a crowd of onlookers. They would not let him forget it, if he cried off now.

But his luck was sure to turn on the next deal, just as it always had. 'All right then. If you insist. My stable against your houses.' He dealt the cards.

As he stared down at the unplayable mess in his hand, he bid a silent goodbye to the horses, and the houses as well. She set down her cards without joy, and called out 'Macao' as though it pained her to say the word. If she must beat him so thoroughly, the least she could do was take joy in it.

He glared at her again. 'Do not dare say that I arranged that for your benefit, Miss Price. It would give me more credit than I deserve.'

She looked up at him, alarmed. 'If not for my benefit, then why is it happening?'

'I have no idea. Deal the cards.'

'Certainly not. This has gone on long enough, and is not working at all the way I planned.' She rose to go.

'Sit!' He said it far too sharply, and she dropped back into her chair as though he'd yanked her into place. He struggled to control his emotions, trying to remember a time when he had been flustered at a gaming table. Embarrassing displays of temper were for his opponents, not for him. He took a deep breath. 'I beg your pardon. Please. Sit. You must give me a chance to break even in the game, at least. Another hand, please.'

She shook her head. 'I suspect that that is what my father said, when he gambled with you. He assumed, until the very last hand, that his luck would turn.'

That was what all his opponents thought. But they did not know what Nate did: There was no hope for any of them to win against him, until the curse was lifted. And this game would not go on much longer. Another hand and things would change in his favour, just as they always had.

Unless…

'Please,' he said urgently. 'One more game, Miss Price. For the sake of my curiosity, if nothing else. The contents of my bank accounts, against all that you have.'

She gave him an amazed smile. 'And what would that leave you, should I win?'

'Very little, I expect.' He grinned at her. 'And it doesn't matter a jot to me.'

'But how shall you live?'

'I shall find someone to stake me, and gamble again with someone else. As long as I have anything left of value, I shall return to the tables and wager it, Miss Price.'

She stared back at him, horrified. 'You are mad, sir.'

'I would have to be, to make my living as a gambler. Once begun, it is almost impossible to stop. But I have not enjoyed it.' He looked at her very seriously. 'The only true happiness I have felt has been most recently. And that, I fear, was a transient thing. It seems the feelings I had for a young lady were not reciprocated. She disapproved of my profession.'

'It is a most disreputable profession.'

'I know that. And I wish, most heartily, to have a provocation to end my gaming, just as your father did. It was only when he had reached the point where he'd lost all and was bartering with precious things he had no business offering, that he realized what he had done and changed his life. And from what you tell me, he was repentant, even to the end.'

'He was.' She said it softly, as though it had never

occurred to her that she had been the cause of his change.

'I suspect it was his stalwart devotion to you that affected him. There is much about you, Miss Price, that might cause a man to change his ways. Now if you please, deal the cards.'

Her hands were trembling as she pushed the rectangles of pasteboard to his side of the table. And it was just as he'd hoped. There was not a useful card in the hand, nor any hope of bluffing her to think otherwise. He smiled, relaxed in his chair and prepared to lose the hand.

She became more and more agitated with each trick she took. 'Do not grin at me so. I find it upsetting.'

He smiled all the more. 'But it does not seem to be spoiling your play.'

'It is pure luck, and you know it.'

'Since I have never seen it on the other side of the table from me, I hardly recognize it.' He tossed his cards down on the table. 'That is it, gentlemen. The lady has ruined me.'

But the poor girl across the table looked to be near tears. 'I did not mean to. I only wanted to give you your money back. I thought this would be the easiest way.'

'I am afraid, darling, that things are never easy between us. I have made your life difficult, right from the beginning. And I am most sorry for it. What has happened here is divine justice, plain and simple.' He stacked the deck and began to shuffle again, glancing up at the proprietor. 'Bring me pen and ink. If the lady will play one more game, against my marker, we will see if my current luck holds.'

'No! I do not want this. We have played enough. Let me go.' She was drawing away again, and he would have to be gentleness itself to keep her.

He put down the cards and placed his hand on hers, before she could push away from the table. 'Diana. I beg you. Do not go. Not yet. There is one last thing I have to offer. Although, I dare say, you have it already. And if it is yours, no ill can come to me by gaming with it.' He took the pen and scratched at the edge of the paper for a moment, trying to remember the words.

'To Diana Price, I promise you, in the event of losing this game, that with my body I thee worship, and with all my worldly goods I thee endow.' He looked up. 'Although I seem to have done that last already. But no matter. You get the gist of it.'

'Nathan Wardale, do not mock me.'

'I do not, darling. My heart is yours whether you wish it or no, just as my possessions are. I will lay them all at your feet, if you let me. But if you doubt the sincerity of my gift, then pick up the cards I have dealt and win it from me.' He looked at the people crowded around the table. 'Anyone here can vouch for me. As long as I am gambling, my word is good. If you win again, you may walk away from this table and I will follow, abject to your every whim.'

She was staring at him in a most odd way, and he feared she did not want him or his heart. She did not even want his money. And now she would prove it to him in front of all these people. She would push aside the cards and walk away and everyone would know him for a fool. Her gaze was fixed on him, searching his face for a bluff, trying to break his concentration, as he had done to opponents for years, and he could feel himself start to perspire. He wanted to blink and turn away from her scrutiny, ready to cry out that she should have mercy and be done with him if she didn't want to play. She could take the pot and go, and he would pretend that he had never made her the offer, and never bother her again. That he was sorry to have bothered her in the first place. Or her father, for that matter. Or anyone else in the room.

And then she said, 'You would leave the table?'

He blinked. 'If you wish.'

'And never return?'

His mouth opened automatically, ready to protest. But the thought that he could stop had never occurred to him. There had never been anywhere else to go. And now…

She went on. 'Because I would have no use in my life for a gambler, Mr Wardale. And certainly no desire to attach myself to a man who would bring ruin upon us both.'

Suddenly, it was clear to him how hard it must be for her to come to him and how fearful she must be that her married life would be a repeat of her mother's.

And he knew he was standing at a crossroads. He could keep the life he had known and spend the rest of it financially safe at the tables he detested. And he would spend his nights alone. Or he could go with Diana today, into the unknown, with no guess as to how he would make a living for her, if the money he had was not enough for a family. Did he have skills, beyond cards and dice? He knew he was not a sailor. And he could not be an earl. But other than that, he had no idea who or what he might be. Until he found his way in the world again, every day would be a gamble.

But then, he had always been a gambler. He smiled. 'This building has been more church to me than any other, for many years. When I am at the table, though I might bluff, I do not lie, I do not cheat, and I never welsh on a bet. If you win, I will walk away from here and I swear there will be no returning.'

She shook her head ruefully. And then she smiled, and reached for the cards. 'Very well then. It is a game of chance, after all. There is no guarantee of the outcome. And you are said to be very lucky. Let us see how the play goes.'

He looked down at his hand and knew that he could make nothing of it, and felt the swelling sense of relief that ultimate failure would give to him. 'I think I am very lucky indeed.'

She looked down at her own cards, and did nothing to disguise the little moue of surprise on her face that he might have used to his advantage had he thought himself up to bluffing her. The play continued, and as she had with the previous hands, she beat him easily. She stared at the note on the table and blinked up at him in shock. 'I won.'

'You did.' He grinned at her, feeling a lightness of

spirit that had been missing since childhood, as though some great burden had been lifted from his back.

'But does that mean…do you still wish…' Poor, sweet, sensible Diana was at a loss.

'Very much so. Miss Price, would you do the honour of accepting my offer? You would make me a very happy man. And I will do everything in my power to be the husband you might wish.' He stood up from the table and came to her side, offering his hand to her.

'I…I…Yes. I accept.' She was still looking at the cards, and then at him, as though the suddenness of it was quite overcoming her.

So he pulled her out of her chair and close into his arms. And then he kissed her. Gently at first, and then slowly, ardently, passionately. And he felt her kiss him back, first with hesitance and then as she had on the night they'd been together, as though she did not wish the moment to end. When they parted, she looked up at him with a twinkle in her eye. 'Mr Wardale, really. We are in a public place. This is most improper.'

He laughed. 'The place is most improper as well, Miss Price. My actions suit my environment. But if you wish to remove me from it, then perhaps my behaviour will moderate. Come, let us re-enter polite society. If you wish, I shall become the sort of lacklustre, milksop who would never dare to take you in his arms and kiss you senseless.'

She reached down to the table and scooped her winnings into her reticule. And as an afterthought, took his marker, folded it carefully and tucked it down the bodice of her dress. 'I should certainly hope not, Mr Wardale. For both our sakes.' And then she smiled. 'We have much to talk of. There is the matter of Nell, for instance.'

He smiled back, puzzled. 'And who might that be?'

She seemed surprised at his reaction, and then said, 'Perhaps you know her as *Helena*, although she does not favour that name.

'Helena?' His mind clouded for a moment, with distant memories. 'How could you know her? Or what she favours? I swear, I have said nothing.'

She touched his arm, and leaned close to him, whispering in his ear. 'She is safe and well. Married to a dear friend of mine. Although a full reconciliation might be difficult, given recent events. But considering what has transpired between us, anything is possible, is it not?'

'My sister, found safe?' He took a breath, and steadied himself as a feeling of relief hit him that nearly knocked him from his feet.

'There is much I need to explain,' she rushed to tell him. 'And I am sorry to have kept it a secret. For I knew how important it is to you. But for a time, I wanted you to be hurt, and then… It is all so very complicated…'

He stopped the words with a kiss. 'Do not trouble yourself. I am the last person to berate you for withholding a difficult truth from me.' He kissed her again. 'If Helena is safe, that scrap of knowledge is a gift. You can tell me the rest in good time. But we will have all the time in the world, soon enough. Marry me, Diana Price, and I shall truly be the luckiest man in England.'

Nate glanced up at the shadowy figure standing near the door and put a protective arm around his bride-to-be.

The Gypsy stared back at him, dark eyes unreadable. And then, he gave the smallest nod of approval, a shrug and a gesture that might have been a salute of farewell. And he was gone.

Epilogue

Diana walked down the hall of her old house, to the study of her new husband. He spent much time here, poring over old papers, still searching for anything that might lead him to the true killer of Christopher Hebden. If not that, then he was sending discreet inquiries as to the whereabouts of his sister Rosalind, or penning hopeful notes to Nell, while trying not to upset her with suspicions about her new family.

She hoped for success in this. But what little news she had managed to glean on the subject did not bode well for the Carlows. Although the girls had been forbidden to communicate with her, Verity had ignored her brother's command and sent several brief notes, urging her to seek a speedy reconciliation. In Diana's absence, Honoria was growing increasingly reckless. While Diana could not return as chaperone, perhaps the steadying influence of an old friend would be all that was needed to set things right.

It was some comfort that it troubled Nathan as much as it did her, that another family would be thrown into chaos over what he might find. Were it not for his soft heart, he would be no better than the Gypsy. It would do him good to see what she had found, no matter how unpleasant it might be. 'Nathan,' she reached out for his hand from the doorway. 'Come with me. There is something I wish to show you.'

He smiled at her, as he always did, and followed her up the stairs. She felt the warming of her blood as he paused, and she had to tug him past their bedroom door. 'Later,' she whispered.

His eyebrow arched in surprise. 'Of course later. But now is nice as well.'

'Later.'

'If not there, then where are we going? For you are wearing a green dress and you know the effect that it has on me.'

'It is a day dress and not particularly special,' she cautioned. 'And I often wear green because you claim to prefer the colour. If it troubles you, I will change.'

'I'd hardly call it trouble. My feelings on seeing you are most easily remedied. But if you wish to change, I will make a suggestion. You are very fetching in a green dress. But you will be even more fetching out of it.' He grabbed at her, and she wondered how she could have ever feared that he would prefer gambling to a wife and family. His preference for her was obvious. And his enthusiastic attentions made family almost inevitable.

She let him catch her, for a while. Then, she put his

hands firmly to his sides and said, 'Definitely later. First, there is something you must see.'

He sighed. 'Your tone is rather dire, my dear. I suspect you have put on the green dress to soften some kind of a blow.'

She gave him a worried look. 'I fear you may be right. But I know it is something that will interest you, and now that I have found it, I must tell you. There are no secrets between us, after all.'

'None,' he assured her.

She led him to the end of the hall, to the stairs that led to the attics.

'And what reason do we have to go here?'

'I got the keys from Benton, and went searching. I thought that perhaps there were things that I remembered from my own youth that might be pleasant to see again.' She tried to sound casual at the suggestion, for she did not wish him to think she was dwelling in a past that she had promised she would forgive.

But he nodded in perfect understanding. 'If you wish to see them, I will not have you traipsing round the lumber room in melancholy. And if you are adamant that you do not wish to redecorate the house…'

'I do not. It is lovely the way it is. And very much in tune with your character.' Perhaps that was why she liked it so. While it was not the home she remembered, it was the haven of the man she loved above all in the world.

He smiled, and there was a glint in his eye that made her think of Christmas. 'Then I fear we shall have to move your heirlooms to a place where you might enjoy them more fully.'

'The country house?' They had honeymooned there. It was just as lovely as Hans Place. And while she enjoyed the novelty of riding or walking through the fields, without seeing a single soul, it seemed very far away from everything she was used to.

He gave a small shake of his head. 'I was thinking, perhaps we could find a cottage. There is a place I know of, in Hammersmith. A few rooms, only. But there is a lovely garden and the deed is already in your name. If you wished to house your treasures there, you might visit them whenever you liked.'

'A cottage,' she said, confused. 'For me?'

'And me as well, if you would allow me there. Or not, as you choose. In any case, it is secured as yours, legal and proper.'

'How did you know?' For hadn't this been exactly what she had dreamed of?

He smiled again. 'Along with my other quests, I have been searching for a worthy wedding gift. And since I know very little about what a proper young lady might appreciate, I might have inquired of my sister, who might have asked the Carlow girls, who seemed to think you would be in favour of the idea. And considering my history, it does make sense, does it not? While I have no intention of backsliding into the gambling rogue that I was, let this gift be proof to you and those that love you that you will never be left homeless because of me.' He reached into his pocket and removed a most ordinary-looking key, which he placed in her hand, closing her fingers to wrap them around it. 'Does it please you?'

She swallowed back tears of gratitude, and threw herself into his arms, kissing him most passionately. And then she whispered, 'As long as there is room enough for the two of us, it pleases me very well.' She dropped the key into her own pocket, and whispered, 'We shall visit it, soon, I think. And when we do, I shall wear green.' And she watched his eyes go dark in response.

'But first, there is something I must show you. And I fear it is not so pleasant as what you have done for me.'

She felt the slightest hesitation in his step, as he followed her. But considering what his life had been, he had no desire to seek more misery, though she was sure he would do it, if she asked him to.

She led him to the back room she'd found and the small trunk under the window with the initials NW carved into the leather at the top. 'In searching for my own past, I have found a part of yours.'

He stopped, staring at it. 'I had thought it lost, after all this time.' He looked at her, worried. 'Do you know what is there?'

She nodded, for curiosity had caused her to lift the lid. 'It is better to face it, is it not? And there are papers.'

'If I wish to prove my father's innocence, then they are all I have.' He smiled at her. 'But I am glad that I do not need to do this alone.' He leaned forward to kiss her, putting his warm arms about her and holding her close so that he could rest his chin against her temple. 'Together?'

'Yes.' And she sat upon the floor beside him, as he examined the little chest.

He stroked the wood, and let his fingers trail along the brass fittings. 'I have not seen this in years. It was all I had left, before I was forced into the Navy. I cannot even remember bringing it to the house. But obviously I did.'

'Benton put it away, when you did not return. It has been waiting for you.'

'I am glad I did not know. But if the thing Veryan wants still exists, then this is the only place I would know to look.

She watched him steel himself, and unlatch the chest.

And there, at the top, was the real silk rope. He put his hand on it again, after all these years. It looked no different to Diana than other ropes. It was black, not the gaudy colours of the Gypsy's imitation that he had shown her. She reached out a finger and prodded it carefully. It was soft to the touch, for it was silk.

Nathan gave her as sad smile. 'As though it would be any better to be hung gently. I wonder if the person that had come up with the plan to hang nobles in silk recognized the irony of it? Or did they seriously think it was a last sign of respect?'

She shuddered. 'It is disgusting, in any case.'

'But better to keep it, than to see it cut into bits and

sold to collectors. This is the only entail I was left to offer our children.' He picked it up and set it deliberately aside, so he could get to the things beneath.

There was a loose collar stud in silver, engraved with a small L. A penknife, and pipe. He picked them up, and brought the pipe to his nose to get a whiff of the stale tobacco. 'Father's.' He gave a sentimental smile, and she rested a hand on his shoulder in support.

'And mine.' There was a tiny lead soldier discarded beside them. He picked it up, and put it to the side with the other things.

And then, there was a sheaf of paper. 'And this is what we have come to see.' He quickly sorted them into two stacks, by the hand they were written in. '*These* are the things written by my father. I do not see anything written by Hebden amongst the rest. I fear our quest is in vain, just as I thought it would be.' He riffled quickly through them. 'I must have read them all at one time, seeking comfort. And I don't recall anything that made me think of a code.' He shrugged. 'Of course, I was very young. Most everything that adults wrote might well have been a code to me, for all that I could understand of it.' He folded his legs, tailor fashion, and piled his father's letters into his lap to read by the light of the attic window.

He was silent as he read, lost in his own past. And there was little for Diana to do, so she contented herself with reading the rest of the stack. It made her heart break to think of the poor little boy who had gathered everything he could find hoping to preserve the few remaining memories of his father. Here was a tailor's bill. And here a note of thanks from a long-ago friend, concerning a weekend of shooting at the Leybourne estate. And then, a note in a woman's hand.

She read. And then said, 'Nathan, this is from Amanda.'

She saw her husband flinch at the name. 'Kit Hebden's wife. You saw the journal. You must know what was said about them at the time. That note will do us no good, if I remember it for what it was. She wrote to him when he was in jail. I think she wanted him to confess. He passed me the letter, and bade me hide it from my own mother, because he said it would distress her. And so, I brought it back to hide amongst my things.'

She gave him an amazed smile. 'That is not what this is at all. But you were a little boy when you read it. You must have stopped after a line or two, then put it away. What did you know of such things? Tell me if you do not see it differently, now.' She held up the paper and began to read.

'"Tell them, William. My husband is dead, and I do not care who knows. There is no reason that you need keep secret what happened between us that night. Not if it means death for you. Kit would not hold it against you, for you know as well as I that he knew the truth and did nothing about it while he was alive. You might think there is honour in secrecy, but if it means that I retain my reputation only to watch you hang, then what good is my honour to either of us?"'

He looked at her, his expression puzzled. And she said, 'Can you not see it, even now? He was with her on the night of the murder. At least the first part of that night. That is why your father was so eager for you to hide this letter. He was trying to protect her, and your mother. And she says that Kit Hebden did not mind. So it was not a crime of passion. Whatever was on your father's mind that night, it had nothing to do with codes or keys or spying. He had no reason to kill his lover's husband. The arrangement suited them all.'

He read the letter again, and she watched the paper shake in his hand. 'You are right. My God, Diana. I think you are.' He looked at her in amazement. 'I don't know what Veryan will make of this, if anything. And I don't know if I dare show it to the Gypsy, for if he has any scrap of love left for his stepmother, then he will not welcome this news. But you are right. Nothing here makes my father out as traitor.'

She smiled. 'And you thought there would be nothing at all.'

He smiled back. 'It is but a scrap of information. But a scrap is more than I ever hoped to find. It is enough to build on, at any rate.' He rose and dusted off his pants. 'And it renews hope in me. My father was innocent, just as he said.'

'And if that is true…'

He squared his shoulders. 'Then whatever people may say of him, I am proud to be his son. I will clear my name, and his as well. And even if it takes me a lifetime, I shall make you the Countess of Leybourne, my dear.' He held out a hand to her, lifting her to her feet again, and led her down the stairs to their rooms.

* * * * *